BARBARA DELINSKY

Sanctuary

HQN™

ISBN-13: 978-0-373-77618-4

SANCTUARY

Copyright © 2011 by Harlequin Books S.A.

The publisher acknowledges the copyright holder of the individual works as follows:

THE STUD
Copyright © 1991 by Barbara Delinsky

T.L.C.
Copyright © 1988 by Barbara Delinsky

Recycling programs for this product may not exist in your area.

This edition published by arrangement with Harlequin Books S.A.

For questions and comments about the quality of this book please contact us at Customer_eCare@Harlequin.ca.

® and TM are trademarks of the publisher. Trademarks indicated with ® are registered in the United States Patent and Trademark Office, the Canadian Trade Marks Office and in other countries.

www.Harlequin.com

Printed in U.S.A.

CONTENTS

THE STUD

CHAPTER ONE

IT WAS THE SCAR that scraped along his jaw that was so compelling.

No, it was his hair. Dark and windblown, it lent him a look that held more than a hint of the rogue.

Then again, it had to be his eyes. They radiated from the photograph, silver-blue and electric, which was startling since the photograph was black and white. But Jenna McCue had seen those eyes in person, and once seen, they were never forgotten.

Feeling oddly as though they'd touched her even then, she flipped the book over to bury the back-cover photograph in the seat of the car, which left the front cover staring up at her. *Green Gold* was the title of the book. The story inside dealt with the search for emeralds in the mines of South Africa, and it was a true story. Spencer Smith had lived through the adventure and written about it just as he had written about his search for treasure in the shadow of the pyramids in Egypt, in the Peruvian Andes, in pirate coves of the South Seas. His books weren't bestsellers. They lacked the requisite elements for commercial success, namely melodrama and sex. Rather, they were well-written documentaries, sure to fascinate the adventurer-at-heart.

Jenna wasn't quite that, since her life was ruled by routine, but Spencer Smith was the brother of her oldest and dearest friend. She would have bought his books out of loyalty to Caroline and her family, even if she hadn't found them intriguing. But she loved each one. Over the years, she had become the unofficial, if biased, reviewer of his books on her visits with the Smiths.

This visit had a different purpose, though. True, she had read and loved *Green Gold,* and true, she wouldn't have missed the senior Smiths' fiftieth wedding anniversary party for the world, but she had more on her agenda than drinking champagne, eating lobster and waltzing across the dance floor with whoever chose to ask her to dance.

She had something to ask of Spencer Smith. A favor of sorts. A proposition of sorts. A personal, *very* personal request. An unusual one, for sure.

He might be incredulous or mocking, intrigued or repulsed. Caroline had suggested all those things by way of preparing Jenna for the worst, but she had agreed with Jenna's idea, and rightfully so. It was a good one. From the moment she'd thought of it, Jenna had known that it made perfect sense. It would satisfy a number of people on a number of different scores. All she had to do was to convince Spencer of that.

Turning onto the private lane that led to the Smiths' Newport home, she pulled up behind the last car in line, climbed out and set off toward the house. Her heels were pale yellow and high, not ideal for walking over a dirt road, but they went with her dress, which was silk with a short skirt and matching jacket, and the entire look went with her hair, which was loosely curled and feminine. Normally she dressed more sleekly and knotted her hair back, as befitted a top-level executive. But even aside from the occasion of the Smiths' party, she was feeling softer.

It had to do with where she was in life and what she wanted in her future, which was where Spencer came in.

Ignoring the gentle curling in the pit of her stomach, she walked on.

The closer she came to the house, the more people she saw. She recognized several and offered warm hellos, then was quickly introduced to others, and while those others might not have known her on sight, by reputation they did. McCue's was a venerable name in New England retailing. The McCue chain of department stores, falling somewhere in style between Bergdorf Goodman and Jordan Marsh, had survived good times and bad to become the stalwart outlet to which New Englanders went for everything from polo shirts and jeans to suede suits, sterling-silver picture frames and designer bed coverings. Jenna, as the last living McCue, was president and chairman of the board. At thirty-five, she was an effective and insightful leader. As her father and her grandfather before him had done, she kept the store apace with the times, which was why McCue's thrived while others felt the economy's pinch. She anticipated problems and dealt with them before they became debilitating in any way, shape or form.

She did the same with her personal life, which was why she had to talk with Spencer.

He wasn't in the foyer when she entered the house, or in the living room when she passed through on her way to the patio, where Joe and Abby Smith were accepting congratulations from their guests. Jenna gave them both affectionate hugs and chatted for several minutes before moving on to allow other guests access. She had barely taken a glass of wine from a passing tray, when Caroline materialized beside her.

"You look spectacular," she said, giving Jenna a prolonged once-over before adding a dubious, "did I see that dress at the store?"

Jenna glanced around casually to make sure no one

was within earshot. There were perks to her profession, but she wasn't one to broadcast them. Sotto voce she admitted, "We ordered a few at the Paris show, then decided they'd be too pricey to carry in quantity. I took one of the few. Like it?"

"You know I do, but whether I'm more envious of the dress or your figure, I'm not sure. You're so slim. Lord, what I'd give to be a size six."

Jenna sent her a meaningful look. "Lord, what I'd give to have three kids." Her eyes searched the crowd. "Where are they?"

"Somewhere out there. I told Annie to watch Wes and Wes to watch Nathan, so the three should be running after one another all afternoon. I'm assuming someone else will notice if one of them falls into the pool."

"They're super kids," Jenna said, and meant it, though her eyes weren't at kid level as they continued to roam the crowd.

"He's not here yet," Caroline told her. "He called a while ago to say he'd run into thunderstorms over D.C. and had to detour to Pittsburgh for fuel. He says he's flying into Newport State. I wouldn't put it past him to land on our beach."

"He wouldn't."

The look Caroline sent her said that he very well would, and, giving it a second thought, Jenna didn't argue. For anyone other than Spencer Smith, landing on the rocky beach rimming Rhode Island Sound would be suicidal. But Spencer had a way of courting danger and emerging alive. Jenna supposed he could successfully land his Cessna on that narrow strip of sand, taxi up to the dock and step out of the cabin totally unruffled.

He was a strong man. He was an able man. He was a man with a natural curiosity, who wasn't afraid to ask questions or tackle the unknown. There were some who, in moments of sheer envy, called him a fool for taking the chances he did. But Jenna had read his books and knew that the opposite was true. As hare-brained as some of his escapades might appear on the surface, he never did anything without weighing the odds and ensuring that they were tipped in his favor. In that sense, he was extraordinarily intelligent.

Intelligent. Competent. Strong. Curious. Courageous. All were fine qualities, ones that Jenna admired, ones that a child of hers would have, if she had any say in the matter.

"He'll get here," Caroline said with a reassuring squeeze.

"But will he stay long enough for us to talk? I need privacy for this. It isn't the kind of question one pops with a zillion people listening in."

"He says he's staying through the weekend."

"He's said that before and then taken off. He has trouble sitting still."

"Only with his family. Set him up on the shores of Loch Ness, and he'll sit motionless for days waiting for the monster to surface. Newport makes him nervous. *We* make him nervous. He's convinced that the one thing we want most in life is to break him to a saddle." Caroline laughed. "As if we could." A second laugh turned into a groan. "What was that?"

Jenna had seen it, too, the streaking of a three-year-old child through the gathering of guests. "Looked like Nathan."

"Looked like wedding cake," Caroline muttered. "I'll kill him." With a murderous look, she was off.

Jenna watched her go, feeling both affection and envy. Then she took a deep breath and released it. Spencer wasn't there. He wouldn't arrive for a while. She could relax.

For the next two hours, she did just that. She liked
the Smiths' friends, many of whom were her own, and
socializing was second nature to her. Like Caroline, she
had been raised in the lap of luxury. Her parents had had
money to spare, and though they had loved traveling and
eating out and donating hospital wings in their name,
more than anything they had loved parties. From the
earliest Jenna could remember, they were either throw-
ing one or attending one. Out of sheer survival, Jenna
had learned to mix, and though she had never developed
the love for loud festivities that her parents had, she had
come to be perfectly at ease. The key, she knew, was to
smile, to indulge in amiable small talk, to read other people's needs and listen or respond accordingly—without
taking any of it seriously. Gossip never touched her. One
part of her remained removed from it all and therefore
protected.

She munched on the food that was first passed on
silver trays, then offered in a lavish sit-down buffet. She
chatted and laughed. She raised her glass when Caroline's husband, a state representative with a golden
tongue, proposed a toast to his in-laws, and she couldn't
help but think that Spencer should have been the one to
do that. But he wouldn't have. Not even if he'd come on
time. As adventurous as the man was, he wasn't a show-
man. As compelling as he was, he shunned the limelight.
While another man in his shoes would have brought a
film crew along on his trips, Spencer refused. He was
determined to enjoy adventure for adventure's sake. If
a book came later, fine. If the book was spiced up and
made into a movie, that was fine, too. He would serve
as a technical consultant, but that was all.

Spencer's toast wasn't missed. There were plenty of
others, offered by various and sundry of the Smiths'
friends and relatives, to the extent that the guests ceased

to sit between toasts. Even then, when Spencer appeared on the outskirts of the crowd, Jenna saw him at once. He was that kind of man. Standing six foot four, he was taller than most others in the room, but that wasn't what did it, as much as his aura. Complemented by his roguishly dark good looks and the confidence of his stance, he exuded independence, self-containment and, while not quite disdain, a disinclination to play games by any rules other than his own.

Jenna hadn't seen Spencer for six years, yet she felt his force at once. It was far stronger than anything she'd encountered on the back of a book jacket and it gave her a moment's pause. She wasn't sure she could approach him. He was so...*much*. And she'd never been terribly good with men in anything but business.

But this *was* business, she reminded herself, and with that thought stilled her wildly beating heart. She couldn't take her eyes from him, though, but watched him take in the situation and back off. He would wait, she knew, until the toasts were done. In the flurry of movement when people returned to their seats, he would slip into his own at his parents' table.

That was what he did. Slowly word spread that he was there, and though no one dared raise a glass to the success of *Green Gold,* those closest to the family made a point of going over to greet the author. The rest kept their distance, and wisely so. Spencer had never been the kiss-kiss type. His silver-blue eyes were legendary in their ability to cut phonies down with a glance.

Jenna, too, kept her distance, though not from fear of being cut down. As Caroline's friend, she had immunity. Spencer had always been kind to her, even gentle, just as he was to his sister. For whatever differences he had with his parents, Caroline was special to him. He never failed to call her on her birthday or to send a gift to one of her children on theirs. Jenna respected him for that. She also took it as a clue to his character, a part of him few people saw. She was counting on the clue being apt.

No, it wasn't fear of Spencer that kept Jenna from rushing up to him, as much as a desire to carefully control her approach. Her mission was a delicate one. She wanted to maximize her chance of success. Or so she told herself. But long after the band started playing and people had moved onto the dance floor, she hung back. She immersed herself in conversation with people who stood at the greatest distance from Spencer. She walked Annie, Wes and Nathan down to the beach when she was sure Spencer was with followers in the gazebo. She finally agreed to Charleston with an old family friend, but quickly moved off into the crowd and oblivion the instant the dance was done. When coffee was served and a tiered wedding cake rolled onto the lawn, minus several frosting roses that small fingers had filched, she clung to the fringes.

Her time would come, she knew. When the guests had left and things had quieted, Spencer would be feeling mellow. A mellow Spencer would be more approachable than one whose defenses were in place. A mellow Spencer would be more disposed to consider her proposal. A mellow Spencer would be more likely to accept.

But a mellow Spencer wasn't what she got when, with the party still in full swing, she felt a commanding hand on her arm. She barely had time to look around when, in his deep, brooking-no-defiance voice, Spencer told those with whom she'd been talking, "Would you excuse Jenna? I need her help with something."

Neither expecting, wanting nor waiting for permission, he drew her free of the circle. His large hand circled hers as he led her off.

"Spencer?" she asked.

But his attention was on working his way through the crowd. "Excuse us," he said, and slid through one narrow opening, then wove through another. "Sorry. Excuse us. Thanks."

Jenna didn't bother to say his name again. The set of his jaw told her that he was tense. She didn't want to antagonize him, when she had such a delicate favor to ask. So she went where he led, knowing that he would explain himself in time.

Indeed, as soon as they had cleared the gathering of people on the lawn, he said, "Walk with me. I need air."

Glad to be of help, she walked. From time to time, she trotted to make up a step on his longer stride, and by the time they reached the end of the lawn, where the retaining wall was broken by steps to the beach, the huff of his pace had eased.

"Can you handle the sand?" he asked with a glance at her shoes.

Using his arm for balance, she slipped off one, then the other of the pale yellow heels. He pushed them into his blazer pockets before she could protest the abuse of the fine cloth, and in the next breath, he pulled the tie from his neck and crammed it in with one of the shoes in a way that said he didn't care.

"You do know that it's painful for me to watch that," she teased, holding her hair back from her face, where the shore breeze seemed intent on blowing it.

The look he sent her was dark, but indulgently so. "You're Caroline's friend. You'll forgive me." Taking her hand again, he led her down the steps to the beach, along the narrow boardwalk that had been laid years before as a concession to the sharp pebbles, to the far dock. He didn't stop until they were at its very edge. Stepping out of his shoes—Jenna wasn't at all surprised that he hadn't worn socks—he tugged her down to sit beside him.

She gave a brief thought to the silk skirt that was sure to be bruised on the weathered plants—but only a brief thought. One skirt, silk or otherwise, was nothing compared to Spencer's good favor. One skirt was nothing compared to her future.

She wasn't sure why, but he continued to hold her hand. Since the feeling wasn't unpleasant, she let it be.

The tide was out. Their legs dangled a good eight feet above the water, which lapped softly at the rocks on the shore behind them. From a distance came the muted tinkle of a bell buoy. Both sounds were gentle, far more so than Spencer's expression as he stared across the sound.

"Things like this try me," he said after a long, brooding minute.

"Parties?"

"They're so excessive."

"But they give your parents pleasure."

"Does that justify the waste?"

With a sigh, Jenna faced the water. She wasn't going to argue with him.

"You think it does?" he challenged.

Gently she said, "Not personally, no. I lean toward moderation. But what's right for me may not be right for someone else. Your parents are like mine were. They're social creatures, and they have the money. If they want to spend it on a party, that's their choice. As long as they don't tell me how to live my life, I can let them live theirs."

Spencer shifted her hand from the small space between them to his thigh. He studied her fingers, which were absurdly pale and slender between his long, tanned ones.

"I won't run away," she said quietly.

He shot her a solemn look that was binding, given

the silver of his eyes. "I wasn't sure of that. You've been doing your best to avoid me all afternoon."

"All afternoon?" She tugged a strand of hair away from her mouth. "You haven't been here but half of it."

"Thank the good Lord for that," he muttered. He released another button—the third—on his shirt, filled his lungs with the tangy salt air and blew it out along, it seemed to Jenna, with a bit of his tension. His voice was as deep as ever but less tight. "I have trouble enough with my parents alone. With two hundred of their friends, I'm in pain."

"This from a man who once stood bound to a stake waiting to be boiled for dinner by a bunch of cannibals?"

"You've been reading too much," he grumbled.

"I like your books."

"So does Hollywood. *Green Gold* has been optioned for another Indiana Jones type of thing."

"That's great!"

"I'm not so sure. It takes away from my credibility. Treasure hunting is serious stuff."

"Yes," Jenna said with due graveness. "I can tell that from your books."

He looked at her.

"I can," she insisted.

"Mmm." Neither taking a breath nor looking away, he said, "Caroline told me you wanted to talk."

Jenna's heart fell. She hadn't wanted Caroline to say anything. She had wanted to pick the time herself, and this wasn't it. If Spencer had felt strangled at the party, this *definitely* wasn't it. She wanted him to be feeling loose and open to suggestion when she hit him with her request.

"It can wait," she said lightly.

"Caroline said it was important. Twice she told me that."

"She shouldn't have."

"It's not important?"

"It is, but there's no urgency to it. We should probably be going back to the party, anyway."

"I don't want to go back to the party."

"But it's your parents' fiftieth anniversary. That's a precious milestone."

"Uh-huh, and I invited them to celebrate with me in the Keys, but they refused."

"Because they're party people. They wanted *everyone* with them." Her curiosity got the best of her. "What are you doing in the Keys?" With his hair blowing in the breeze, his shirt agape to mid-chest and the scar slashing his jaw, she imagined him a pirate.

"Waiting for a court to decide whether I have the exploration rights to a site where a Spanish galleon sank in the eighteenth century."

Her eyes widened. "You've found the galleon?"

He nodded. "One of my divers, the first one to spot the wreck, took off and formed his own salvage crew and is claiming that the rights to explore it are his. Neither of us can touch it until the court acts, and the court is pathetically slow. Another six weeks and we'll be into the hurricane season. No one will be doing any exploring then until late fall."

She gathered her windblown hair in her free hand. "Is there gold on the boat?"

"If the boat turns out to be the one I think and if my research is correct, there is. There should also be a wealth of artifacts aboard."

"Perfectly preserved?" she asked. She was always in awe of the fact that things could emerge from the ocean floor intact after hundreds of years. There seemed something incredibly peaceful about that, which was ironic given the tumult of a shipwreck.

"Some things will be preserved. Others may have to be restored."

"Is this your next book?"

"If the court rules in my favor. If not, I'm out one adventure."

"You'll find another. You always do. How do you manage it?"

"I have friends in strange places. They tip me off."

"You network," she said with a smile at the term, which she never would have thought to apply to treasure hunting before.

"I suppose." He flattened her hand on his thigh and imprisoned it there. "What did you want to ask me?"

"Later." She could feel the heat and hardness of muscle, and tried to extract her hand, but he refused to let go.

"I may not be here later."

"Oh, Spencer. You told Caroline you'd stay through tomorrow." Again she tried to pull her hand free of his touch, this time as a gesture matching her complaint, but he held it fast.

"That was before I came."

"You've only been here two hours."

"And already I'm choking."

"Oh, dear," Jenna said before she could help herself, because if he felt like he was choking, the *last* thing she could do was to jump into a discussion as sensitive as the one she had in mind.

"You'd better take the chance while you have it," he warned.

"Why not when the party's done? Things will be quieter then."

He looked around. "Things are quiet now."

She let her free hand fall to her lap. The wind promptly dove into her hair, creating a veil of haphazard waves to protect her from his gaze. The next thing she knew, Spencer was gathering the long curls behind one ear and securing them with what felt suspiciously like his necktie. Left with nothing to hide behind, she looked up at him. His eyes were compellingly blue and heart-stoppingly direct. "Go ahead," he said, and captured her hand again. "I'm waiting."

Jenna's heart skipped a beat. *The time isn't right. The setting isn't right. He'll think I'm crazy. He'll say no.*

But his eyes wouldn't let up. They held her in a grip so firm that try as she might, she couldn't look away. His voice didn't help. It was deep and rich, part command, part dare. "Tell me now, Jenna. What is it you want?"

"A baby!" she cried. "I want a baby!"

CHAPTER TWO

JENNA HADN'T INTENDED to blurt it out that way, but once she'd heard the words, she knew there was no turning back. She couldn't hem and haw. She couldn't show doubt. If she was to win Spencer's cooperation, she had to make her case well.

To that end, she straightened her back, leveled her voice and said with calmness and just a touch of pride, "I want a baby. I've been wanting one for a while, but suddenly I'm thirty-five, and time's running out. The problem, obviously, is that I don't have a husband—and I don't want one," she hastened to add, lest Spencer think she wanted him for that. "I'm single by choice. I wouldn't dream of marrying just for the sake of having a baby. That could be disastrous all the way around."

Spencer was looking puzzled, something she'd never seen before. She would have laughed at the incongruity of the expression on his face if the situation wasn't so serious. Slipping her hand from beneath his, she tucked it into her lap, cleared her throat and went on.

"I've been thinking about this for a long time. I've looked at it from every angle. I've gone through all the possibilities—"

Spencer broke in, sounding as confused as he looked and oddly helpless. "You want me to help you find a baby? I know that adopting foreign kids is in, but Lord,

Jenna, that's not my thing. Sure, I'm abroad all the time, but there aren't many babies in the places I hang out."

"That's not what I want."

He frowned. "Then what is?"

She had practiced the speech so many times that she knew it by heart. Granted, Spencer's interruptions might shift around the order of things, but she was determined to get it all out. "Adoption is terrific for people who can't have children of their own, but I can. I'm perfectly healthy. I've been seeing a doctor who says I shouldn't have trouble conceiving."

"Is he volunteering to help you?"

"Yes," she said, thinking in medical terms until Spencer's faint leer stopped her short. "Not in *that* sense. He's willing to help me with artificial insemination, which, as I see it, is a viable solution to the problem."

"Artificial insemination?"

"You know, where—"

"I know what it is. I just can't believe you want to go in for it. In fact, I can't believe you have this problem at all. There must be scads of men out there who'd marry you in a minute."

"Yes," she acknowledged, holding her chin firm.

"But?"

"I said it before. To marry just to have a baby is absurd. I'd marry for love, but since love hasn't hit me in the face—"

"Don't you date?"

"Some."

"And you've never felt compatible enough with any of those guys to talk about having a child together?"

"None of them fitted the bill for what I want in the father of my child."

"Are we talking stellar genes here?"

"Stellar?" She averted her eyes from his. "I suppose.

I'd be a fool not to be talking that. What woman wouldn't want the father of her child to be brilliant and handsome and healthy and tall and athletic—"

"I get the point," Spencer cut in dryly.

"Mmm." She took a breath and regrouped. Looking over the sound, which was more soothing than meeting Spencer's probing eyes, she said, "I want the best for my baby. Kids nowadays have enough to face without having to worry about inborn deficiencies. I've looked into using a sperm bank."

"A sperm bank."

She kept her gaze on the water. "In theory, I could find a donor with all or most of the traits I want for my child."

"A sperm bank," Spencer repeated in a drone that brought her head around.

"I know you think the idea is ludicrous. Caroline said you might, but the fact is that it's done all the time. There's an increasing number of women in my position, wanting babies but for one reason or another not having a father for the child. That's one of the purposes of sperm banks. That's why artificial insemination has evolved into a science from an art."

He looked as though he wanted to laugh but was controlling the urge. "Artificial insemination is fine. So are sperm banks, but I still can't imagine why you'd want to use either. Come to think of it, I can't imagine why you weren't married years ago. You're pretty and smart and rich."

"Right," she drawled, "I'm rich, which means that some men would marry me just for that. I've had men tell me they loved me, when what they really meant was that they loved what I owned."

"They don't all mean that. Some of them must be sincere. You're a nice person, Jenna. You're easy on the eyes and on the mind. If I stayed put long enough, I could fall in love with you myself."

She took his comment lightly, as it had been offered. "But you won't stay put long enough, which is why you're just right."

His face went blank. For an instant, the only sounds were the water on the rocks, the bell buoy's jingle and the cry of a gull. Then he said, "Back up. You lost me."

Embarrassed that she had let the punch line slip before she should have, Jenna complained, "That's because you keep interrupting me. Will you let me take this step by step, Spencer? Let me say my *thing?*"

"Okay." He straightened. "Say your thing."

He seemed suddenly so much taller sitting beside her, that she felt foolish and insecure and presumptuous. She was *sure* Spencer wouldn't do what she wanted. He had his own life. If he wanted to father a child, he would have already found a way to do it. He was resourceful.

Resourcefulness. Another trait she admired. Another trait she would wish for in a child of hers.

Taking courage from that thought, she went on. "I'm perfectly comfortable with the idea of artificial insemination. Some woman inseminate themselves—"

"How?"

"With a syringe. Please let me go on?"

"Go on."

"I've decided to work with a doctor because the chances of success are greater. The problem is that I'm not comfortable with the idea of going to a sperm bank. I don't trust numbers on lists, and I don't care how many safeguards there are, I'd still worry that I'd get the wrong donor. Either that, or that the donor would have lied and wouldn't have half the qualities he claimed."

"Are you looking for an Einstein?"

"Spencer, please."

"Sorry. Go on."

"I'm looking for the best I can get, but there are some things a sperm bank won't tell you. They'll screen for sexually transmitted diseases, but they have no way of knowing whether one is contracted between the time of screening and the donation. They'll screen for physical traits and genetic abnormalities, but not personality traits. They won't tell you what the donor's parents or grandparents or siblings are like, and I think that's important information. Besides, sperm is usually frozen for storage in a bank, but a certain percentage of it is lost in the process. For that reason, fresh sperm is better."

Spencer was studying her in a way that would have made her squirm if she hadn't been determined to look confident. She had a feeling he sensed where she was leading. He was quick—another thing she liked about him. So she hurried on.

"I want artificial insemination, but I don't want to go to a sperm bank. The only option that's left is to find someone I know to donate his sperm, but most of the men I know are totally unsuited to the cause. Some of them would want to get married, and I don't want to do that. Some of them would want to take part in the raising of the child, and I don't want that, either. Some of them would sue for visitation rights, but when I think of my child going off with strange grandparents, I shudder. I can't think of any man around here whose family I respect enough to feel comfortable with that. Except you."

Spencer stared at her. After a minute, he said, "Go on."

"I want your sperm."

He stared harder. "You're kidding."

She shook her head. "I'm dead serious," she said with a fragment of breath. She was holding the rest, waiting for his full reaction.

"You want my sperm." It was more an echo than a question. She was sure she heard disbelief, which was better than dismay or revulsion. "How, uh, did you plan on obtaining my sperm?"

More than any other part of her speech, she had thought this part out the most carefully. She didn't want to offend a man who was as blatantly virile as Spencer Smith. Sounding as clinical as possible, she said, "My doctor has a standard procedure for this. I'd be tracking my basal body temperature to determine the exact time of ovulation. When that time comes, you'd go to his office, be given a clean container and the privacy of your own room. When you were done, you'd give him the sample and leave."

"I'd—" He made a gesture with his hand that was simultaneously obscene and accurate.

She refused to blush. "That's right."

His expression darkened. "I'd go into my own little room, lock my own little door, dream my own little dream and—"

"It wouldn't be so bad, Spencer."

"It'd be awful!"

"Men give sperm samples all the time. Remember *The Right Stuff?*"

"This isn't the movies. It's real life."

"And it's done all the time in real life. Sperm donors do it. So do men who are having fertility tests."

"So do perverts and gays and guys who can't find a woman, but I don't fit into any of those slots." He paused. When he turned his blue eyes on her this time, she felt the current down to her toes. "Why me, Jenna?"

She took a steadying breath. This was the easy part, and not only because he had to like what she said. But she believed every word, which meant that she could put her heart and soul into the argument. Turning sideways on the dock to face him more fully, she said, "Because you're right physically. You're tall and good-looking. You're intelligent and coordinated and healthy. You have all the traits I'd look for in a donor from a sperm bank, only with you I'd know the unknowns, too. I know your parents and love them. I know your sister and love her. I know that there aren't any genetic defects running through your family. I know that you have a temper but that you're perfectly sane and reasonable, and even if I don't agree with the way you deal with your parents, I admire your determination and consistency, and when it comes to a sense of adventure, you have it over everyone else hands down—" She stopped only because she'd run out of breath. As soon as she filled her lungs again, she rushed on.

"Don't you see, Spencer? Everything else is right, too. I don't want a husband—you don't want to get married. I don't want a man around—and you're never here. You don't want to play father—and I don't want to share my child. We're *both* rich, so neither of us would take advantage of the other. Think about it. This could solve your problem, too."

"What problem?"

"Your parents. They're dying for another grandchild, a child of yours this time." She knew the elder Smiths well. "Don't tell me they didn't mention it in the short time you've spent with them today." The look on his face was as good as a confession. She pressed her advantage. "They drive you *nuts* pushing for marriage and kids, but you don't want either. You don't want to be tied down. This way you could have your cake and eat it, too. You could have the child, which would please your parents and get them off your back, and you wouldn't have to give up a drop of your freedom."

Spencer stared at her for another minute before pushing a hand through his hair. A moment later, the wind mussed it again. A moment after that, he got to his feet.

"Where are you going?" she cried. There was more she wanted to say. She scrambled to her feet.

"I have to move."

Determinedly she moved right along with him. "You haven't said no. Are you considering it?"

"I'm trying to decide whether I should." He strode back along the dock with a loafer in each hand. "It's bizarre, what you're asking."

"Not bizarre. Just unusual."

"There's many a man who'd think you were crazy."

"But you don't, because you know me—" she launched into the next part or her argument "—and that's a plus for you. Yes, I know that you don't want to have a child, and yes, I know that if you did, you'd be perfectly capable of choosing its mother yourself, but I'd be a better mother than most, Spencer. You wouldn't go wrong from the physical standpoint. I have good hair, good skin, a good build."

"You're too short."

"Five-four isn't too short."

"It's nearly a full foot shorter than me."

"But a nice height for a woman. Would it bother you to have a daughter who's petite?"

"What about a son who's petite?" he tossed off as he left the dock for the beach.

"A son would inherit your height." She trotted a little to keep up, but she was hampered by the sharpness of the pebbles. "The only reason my height would be a problem was if we were actually lovers, but we're not. Everything would be done in the doctor's office." She hobbled over a particularly prickly stretch, then hurried to catch up. "I have no physical deformities, nor do my ancestors for three generations back. If my parents' plane hadn't crashed, they would have lived into their eighties as their parents did before them." He was lengthening the distance between them. She raised her voice to be heard. "I have perfect eyesight, perfect hearing, I can carry a tune and I played volleyball and tennis in high school."

"I saw you Charleston," Spencer called back.

She trotted two steps and limped on the third. "That's what I'm trying to tell you! I'm athletic!"

"So why can't you keep up with me now?"

Stopping dead in her tracks, she shouted, "Because I may be athletic, but the soles of my feet aren't made of leather! I haven't trained walking over beds of nails like you have! You have my *shoes,* Spencer!"

With little more than the toss of his dark head, he yelled, "Good! Then you won't go far until I get back!"

Jenna looked after him in exasperation, but that gave way to admiration as she watched him stride on. He was a striking figure. His limbs were long, lean but strong, and he moved with masculine grace and fluidity. She saw him stop and face the water. He lowered his head in thought. He glanced back at her.

For the longest time, she held his gaze, feeling its force even across dozens of yards of shoreline. Then, needing a respite, she retreated to the boardwalk to wait. He joined her there several minutes later, but before he could say a word, she resumed her argument. Though her voice was quieter, it held no less conviction.

"There are other reasons why, if you had to have a child, I'd be a perfect mother for it. I'm smart—between you and me, the child wouldn't lack for brains. I'm patient, compassionate and even-tempered."

"You're also the head of a demanding corporation. How in the hell are you going to mother a child with all that work? Are you going to leave the poor kid with a nanny all day?"

Jenna was offended and let it show. "Not on your life. I'm not having a baby just to add it to my résumé. I'm having it because I want to mother it, and I can afford to do that precisely because I *am* the head of a demanding corporation. I have a support staff that's capable of handling the day-to-day running of things, and I already have an office set up at home with phones and a fax. If I want to work, I can do it while the baby naps, and if I don't want to work, I don't have to. For that matter, if I feel like setting up a crib at McCue's, I will. I'm the boss—I can do what I want. I don't plan to hire a nanny at all, because I won't be needing one. I'll hire sitters sometimes, because there may be important meetings I'll want to attend and also because I think it's healthy for me *and* the baby. But I'll be its primary caretaker. Me, and no one else."

Fixing her eyes on his, she offered what she felt was her most powerful point. "I'll make a great mother because I want this baby so much. I'm not a teenager riding on a whim. I'm a mature woman who has thought out every angle. I can afford to have this baby. I can afford to give it every advantage in the world. And I can handle single parenthood. It may not be easy, but nothing worthwhile ever is. The important thing is that I *want this baby*."

He nudged her shoulder to get her moving back in the direction of the steps to the lawn, but the pace he set was a comfortable one. Jenna dared to hope that he was beginning to see the merits of the plan.

"I take it you discussed this with Caroline."

"I have no family, and she's my closest friend," Jenna said. "She's known for years that I wanted a baby. When I first started considering artificial insemination, I discussed it with her. Then, when it occurred to me that you would be an ideal donor, I bounced the idea off her. She agrees that it's good."

"She would. Do my parents know anything about it?"

"Oh, no. I won't say anything to them. It's not their decision to make. It's yours and mine." She looked up at him. His profile was strong, made more so by his brooding expression. "My arguments are good, Spencer. You know they are."

"They only go so far. They totally ignore several pertinent matters."

"Like what?" Jenna asked in surprise. She was sure she'd covered everything. For the past few months, she had thought of nothing but this.

"The moral considerations on my part. I'm not looking to have a child, but if I were to agree to help you out, there would be a child of mine, flesh of my flesh, alive in the world. It's fine and dandy for you to say that you don't want me around, but don't you think I'd wonder about the child? Don't you think I'd feel some kind of responsibility toward it?"

"I'm absolving you of responsibility. I'll have papers drawn up to that effect, if you'd like."

"You're missing the point. The point is *me*—" he jabbed his chest with the side of one loafer "—inside me. I'm not a block of wood. One of the reasons I don't want to have children is that I'm not a good candidate for fatherhood. My work takes me all over the world. I'm never in one place longer than several months at a stretch. I go where I want, when I want, and I like it that way. If I had kids, I'd feel guilty doing that."

"There'd be no need for guilt. The ground rules here would be different. You could do your part and then forget about it."

"Come off it, Jenna," he snapped, and quickened his pace. "What about illness? What if the child developed something? Don't you think I'd feel anything? What if, God forbid, it needed a transplant of some sort? Do you think I could ignore that? And then there's the practical matter of getting you pregnant in the first place! Your doctor may have a standard procedure for this, but, according to what you say, that standard procedure requires that I be here at the time you're ovulating. Correct?"

"Yes," she said, working to keep up with him.

"Well, what if I'm not? You want fresh sperm, but what if I'm halfway around the world."

"Florida isn't halfway around the world. You said you'd be in the Keys for a while."

He stopped and scowled at her. "Did you set me up for that? Did you deliberately get me to tell you that to strengthen your argument?"

"No, I—"

"Your argument isn't strengthened at all." He set off again. "I'd have to be here to donate *fresh* sperm at the very time you're ovulating, which means dropping everything I'm doing to sit in a little room and whistle a happy tune. And what happens if it doesn't take? What happens if you don't get pregnant the first time? Does your doctor's standard procedure guarantee results?"

"Of course not," Jenna said, climbing the steps to the lawn only slightly behind him. "It may take a while."

"A while? Two months, three, four?"

"Maybe."

"And I'm supposed to fly up here each time and do my little thing?"

"I'm asking you a favor, Spencer. A *favor*."

"Hey, you guys!" Caroline called, coming at them across the lawn at the same time that they cleared the steps. "We were beginning to think you drowned."

Spencer sputtered out a mocking sound, but he didn't push his sister away when she slipped an arm around his waist. That didn't mean she was fully escaping his wrath. Gruffly he said, "Did you honestly think I'd go for this, Caroline?"

Caroline shot a worried look at Jenna, who had come to a halt on her other side. "He's mad?"

"Not mad," Jenna murmured. "He just needs more convincing."

Rising instantly to the cause, Caroline told Spencer, "I think it's a wonderful idea. Mom and Dad aren't the only ones who want you to have a child. I do, too. I miss you when you're gone, and you're gone all the time. If I had a little Spencer to be an aunt to, I'd be in heaven. If my best friend was my niece or nephew's mother, I'd be in *seventh* heaven."

"Yeah, and you think our parents would leave it at that? They'd be *demanding* that I marry Jenna and give the baby our name."

"That's out of the question," Jenna said with such force that both pairs of Smith eyes flew to hers. She looked straight at Spencer. "From the start, I told you I didn't want to get married, and I mean it. I'm not looking for a husband—I'm not looking for in-laws—I'm not looking for an aunt or grandparents for my child. I'm not looking for money, and I'm not looking for a name. My baby will be a McCue. So, much as I love them, if your parents start pushing for marriage, I'll fight them even harder than you will."

"You will?" Caroline asked with blatant disappointment.

"I *told* you I would, Caroline. From the very beginning, from the very first time I mentioned this to you, that was one of the ground rules. I don't—want—to get—married. *All* I *want* is a *baby.*"

"Which brings us back to the point I was trying to make," Spencer said. "What if you don't conceive right away? I can't be running back here month after month to fill little jars with—"

Caroline interrupted. "Uh, I think I hear Annie calling." Dropping away from Spencer, she leaned close to Jenna. "Love your hair ribbon. It looks slightly Milan. An Armani derivative, maybe?" With a wink, she was off.

Jenna gently released the necktie and handed it back to Spencer. "The wind isn't bad up here. Thanks."

"You should have left it on. It looked risqué. But then—" his eyes touched hers "—you're not the risqué type. You're straight-laced and conservative and proper. I can't believe you're thinking of having a child out of wedlock."

"What an outdated expression."

"It describes what you're doing."

"Lots of women are doing it."

"Women in prominent positions like yours?"

"Some."

"It's very daring."

She didn't blink. "Okay, so I'm daring."

"I wouldn't have thought that of you."

"Most people wouldn't, but I really don't care. I want a child. I'm willing to be daring to get it. Will you help?"

He grimaced. "Hell, Jenna, you don't know what you're asking."

"I do. I—"

She was interrupted by Spencer's father, who hailed them as he crossed the lawn toward his son. "Come see the Watsons, Spence. They've been asking for you all afternoon, and they have to leave soon." He threw an arm around Spencer's shoulder, which was level with his. Spencer had clearly inherited his blue eyes from his father, but Joe's blue, like his hair, had paled with age.

"They weren't here the last time you were home, and they may not be here the next. How 'bout it?"

"Sure," Spencer said.

Jenna shot him a look that said "Coward."

He regarded her with deliberate poise. "Want to come see the Watsons with me?"

Jenna had seen the Watsons earlier, which was more than enough for her. They were well advanced in age and profoundly hard of hearing. Conversations with them were exercises in futility. The most one could do was to smile, nod or laugh in response to whatever they chose to say, and since most of what they chose to say was based on their warped perception of what the rest of the world had to say, the encounter was often painful. Jenna could just imagine their seeing her with Spencer and drawing the kind of conclusion that she didn't want. Worse, she could imagine them airing that conclusion in the loud voices for which they were known.

"Thanks," she said with a sweet smile, "but I think I'll go comb my hair. It's a mess."

"Join us when you're done," the elder Smith invited. "You look good beside Spence."

Dying a little inside, Jenna turned away, but not fast enough to miss the scowl Spencer sent her. She hadn't taken more than two steps before she realized he still had her shoes. When she turned back, he was taking them from his pockets. He separated himself from his father long enough to return them.

"He smells something," he muttered.

"Not from me."

"Did Caroline talk?"

"She promised she wouldn't."

"If he starts pushing, I'm outta here."

"If he starts pushing, tell him to mind his own business."

Spencer snorted, shoved the shoes into her hands and turned back to his father. Without further ado, Jenna went on toward the house, but it wasn't until she was upstairs, leaning back against the door in the privacy of the bathroom adjoining Caroline's childhood bedroom, that she put a hand to her heart, closed her eyes and wondered where she stood.

He hadn't said yes.

He hadn't said no.

She slipped the hand to her belly, where it rested ever so lightly. Oh, how she wanted a baby. The longing was an ache deep inside, a tingle of anticipation, a shimmer of excitement. She pictured her womb, pictured an embryo forming in the vaguest of human shapes, pictured that embryo evolving into a fetus. Her breasts seemed to swell at the thought, then her heart when she imagined that fetus becoming a ready-to-be-born child.

If she had to, she would use the sperm bank. But the warmth inside her took on a special glow when she thought of her child being Spencer's.

CHAPTER THREE

AT TWO IN THE MORNING, Jenna's phone rang. Though she hadn't been sleeping, the sound was jarring in the stillness of night. Her heart pounded as she reached across the magazines that lay beside her in bed and picked up the receiver.

"Hello?"

"Did I wake you?"

The low voice was male and distinctive, and did nothing to calm her pulse. She pressed a hand to her breast. "No. I was reading." After the briefest of hesitations, she asked, "Where are you?"

"In Newport. At the house."

Jenna was in her own house, across the Seekonk River from him in Little Compton. "We all assumed you'd flown back to Florida." That would have been a typically Spencer thing to do. "I waited in Newport on the slim chance that you hadn't and would come back and talk with me. When everyone else went to bed, I ran out of an excuse to stay." She hadn't wanted to give the elder Smiths the slightest cause for speculation about something going on between Spencer and her.

"I was visiting a friend," he said. "I hadn't seen him for years. Someone at the party told me he'd been sick. We've been talking all this time."

"You don't have to explain."

"No, but I want to. I'm not heartless. I could see that

what you asked me this afternoon means a lot to you. I wouldn't have left without giving you some kind of answer."

Jenna held her breath.

"The problem," he went on, "is that I don't have enough information to give you any kind of answer."

Her hopes rose. "Then you're considering it?"

"Not seriously. I still think the whole thing's absurd."

She thought back over the years to some of the stories that had filtered back to Rhode Island from wherever Spencer was. "You do absurd things all the time."

"I do *daring* things all the time," he corrected, "and I only do them after I've researched them inside and out."

He hadn't said no. *He hadn't said no.* "I've researched this inside and out," she told him. "Ask me anything. Go ahead. I'll tell you whatever you want to know."

"I want to know more about you and why you want to do this."

"I want a baby. It's as simple as that."

"But *why* do you want a baby?"

Jenna didn't know what to say. She thought the answer was obvious.

Spencer must have taken her silence as criticism of the question, because he said, "I have a right to know. After all, you're suggesting that you be the mother of my child, and you're saying you'd be its primary caretaker. So whereas donating my sperm would be the beginning and end of my role in this endeavor, yours would be more far-reaching. If being a mother has become an obsession with you, the child will suffer. I wouldn't want to be party to the creation of a child that would be raised by an obsessive woman."

"I'm not obsessive. I've never been obsessive." Strong-willed, perhaps. Stubborn or determined or dedicated. But never obsessive.

"Then tell me why you want this baby."

She pushed up against the headboard, shifting to get the pillows more comfortably arranged. She pulled the white comforter to her waist, grasped the white sheet a bit higher. She settled the phone more securely against her ear.

"Well?" he prodded.

"I'm organizing my thoughts. I've wanted a baby for so long, and there are so many reasons why. Are you comfortable? This could take a while."

"The organizing?"

"The telling."

"I'm comfortable."

"Are you in the den?" She pictured the room. It was on the ground floor of the Smiths' house and was paneled in mahogany. Large, heavy-handed oils hung on the walls between books and electronic gadgets. It was a dark room, a man's room. She could see Spencer there.

"I'm in my bedroom."

That was a different story. She had more trouble picturing him there. The room was exactly as it had been when he had graduated from college, with banners on the walls and trophies on the shelves. It was a boy's room, but Spencer had left boyhood far behind. He was forty-one, with a harsh scar to attest to the dangers he'd met and a mature and imposing body to match.

"No comment?" he asked.

"No."

"Want to know what I'm wearing?"

"No."

"That's good, because I'd be hard put to come up with a respectable answer."

He was testing her, she knew. He was trying to see if she was squeamish, which would matter if she had a son. "You're not wearing anything?" she asked nonchalantly. "Aren't you cold?" Her cheeks weren't. Thought of Spencer sprawled naked on his bed heated them, and the thought wouldn't seem to fade.

"Are *you* cold?" he asked in a low, silky voice.

"I'm wearing clothes."

"At two in the morning?"

"A nightgown. I'm always cold."

"You need a man to warm you."

The statement was a sexist one. She might have taken offense if she hadn't been so sure of her feelings. "I have a goose-down comforter. I pull it up when I'm cold and throw it aside when I'm not. I drop my dry cleaning on it and pile my books on it, and I've been known to stamp around on it when I'm cleaning the dust off the ceiling fan. It takes whatever abuse I heap on it, and it doesn't complain. It's more indulgent and less demanding than any man would be."

Spencer was quiet for a minute. When he spoke again, his tone was serious. "A baby might throw up all over your comforter. It might keep you up all night if it had a fever, make you sit in the doctor's office for hours the next day. It might cry every time you tried to put it back in its crib. How would you feel then?"

"Badly, if the baby was sick. Helpless, if there was nothing to do but wait out the bug. Certainly more than willing to hold the poor thing if that was the only relief it could get."

"But why do you want that?" he asked, returning to his original question. "You have a perfectly orderly life. A baby will destroy orderly in a few short days, and it won't be restored for eighteen long years. Have you thought of that?"

"I have."

"And you're still game?"

"I am."

"Why?"

He sounded as though he was without a clue, legitimately puzzled about why she would willingly and knowingly wreak havoc with her life. He was challenging her, demanding that she make her case in a way that he could understand. She sensed that he was also looking for reasons why he should father a child.

After only the shortest pause this time, she said, "I guess the best way to explain it is to go chronologically." Her gaze touched the scrolled picture frame on the dresser. The faces smiling from it made her heart catch. "It's been eight years since my parents' plane went down. I was twenty-seven when that happened, and over the next three years, I was too busy dealing with the immediate future to think of the distant one. Then I turned thirty. McCue's was healthy. I was relaxed at its helm. I had time to think about my parents' deaths and my own mortality, and it hit me that the McCue name would die with me." As fate had it, she came from generations of single-child families. "I'm the last one left. If I die, McCue's will be sold. There's no one to pass it to. That's sad."

"You could have a child who doesn't want a thing to do with McCue's."

"True, but at least that child would have the proceeds from it to hopefully do something worthwhile with his or her life, and the thought of that gives me comfort. I don't want my family line to end with me."

After a moment, he said, "Okay. I can buy that. For starters."

"And that's all it was. Once I had the bug in my ear, I couldn't get it out. At first, it was just that idea of keeping the family line going, but then the physical part began."

Her hair was in a ponytail high enough on her head to be out of the way when she slept. She wrapped her fin-

gers around the band and drew them the length of dark
waves to the ponytail's end. It was a gesture she had
made hundreds of times in her life, usually when she
was either deep in thought or nervous. She was a little
of each just then.

"I'm listening," Spencer said.

Her voice was softer. "I know. It's harder to explain
this part."

"Take your time."

What she took was a deep breath. Time wouldn't help,
not when she had always been self-conscious about intimate things, and certainly not when she kept thinking of him lying buck naked in bed. So she spit out the
words with begrudging resignation. "I became aware of
my body. I was made a certain way for certain reasons,
and I wasn't fulfilling those reasons."

"What do you mean?" he asked.

He was a virile man with a knowledge of sex that she
couldn't begin to match. She assumed he was being pur-
posely dense. "You know what I mean."

"I want you to explain."

She closed her eyes. When she opened them, she focused on the driftwood sculpture she had bought in the
Bahamas several years before. It reminded her of sun
and sand, and was totally asexual. It took her mind off
Spencer. "I have ovaries to create a child with, a uterus
to carry a child in and breasts to put a child to. I haven't
done any of those things. It's a waste, wouldn't you say?"

"That depends on what else you do with those things.
Children aren't the only beneficiaries of breasts and ovaries. Men can be, too."

She forgot about the driftwood sculpture as a tingle
ran up her spine. She shifted her hip against the sheet and
laid her hand lightly between her breasts. "Ovaries?" she
asked weakly. "How do men benefit from ovaries?"

"Ovaries produce the hormones that make you different from me. They affect the way you look, the way you smell, the way you respond to me."

She wasn't touching any of that. Thin ice wasn't something she skated on for long. She took a shaky breath. "Okay. Well. I was talking about my body in relation to having children, and when it comes to that, I'm feeling very unfulfilled."

"Clearly you're unfulfilled when it comes to men, too."

"Why do you say that?" she asked in a huff.

"Because you're all but dragging men off the street in a bid for sperm."

She sat up straight. "I am *not* dragging men off the street. You are the only man I've asked, and I did that for specific reasons. Just because I don't know any other men whose genes I'd want doesn't mean I'm not *involved* with any men."

"Are you?"

"That's none of your business!"

"Oh, but it is," he said smoothly. "There are health issues involved, for one thing. You've told me you don't want a man around the house, but if you're hopping from one bachelor pad to another when you get the urge for sex, you could have picked up a disease. Me, I was using condoms long before it became the rage, because I didn't want to risk any unplanned pregnancies, but other guys may not be so careful."

"I don't have any diseases. I'm healthy. I told you that."

"Okay, then there's the issue of having men around this child you're proposing to have. I wouldn't like the idea of a child of mine having a stream of 'uncles' coming in and out of its life, any more than I'd like the idea of your leaving the kid with a sitter and running out for sex four or five nights a week. So are you sexually involved with any men at this time or not?"

"Not," she said, because the issue of pride was nothing compared to the issue of having a child. If letting Spencer Smith know that her social life was lousy was a condition of his donating his sperm, she'd do it.

"When was the last time you were sexually involved with someone?"

She swallowed. "Three years ago."

"Who was he?"

"A journalist from New York. I met him at a show in Paris. We were together there, then briefly when we got back."

"And before him?"

She plucked at the sheet. "There was an accountant a few years before that."

"A few?" he prodded.

"Four. We were together a month." She pushed herself on, but angrily and feeling suddenly close to tears. Remembering past relationships made her feel empty. "Before him, there was a guy I met in business school, and that's it. Not exactly a history of wildness. Nothing resembling nymphomania. Nothing to corrupt a child with. If I picked up a disease, it would have already shown up. You can call my doctor, if you'd like. He'll testify that I'm clean." She pressed a hand to her upper lip and held it there until the lip had stopped quivering. The effort preoccupied her, so much so that she didn't realize how quiet Spencer was until he finally spoke.

"That won't be necessary. I trust you."

"Well, thank goodness for that."

"But I had a right to ask."

It had hurt to list failed relationships that way, but he did have a point. She had put some of the very same questions to Caroline, who knew as much about

Spencer's love life as anyone did. Spencer's comment about condoms confirmed what Caroline had already told her.

"So—" his voice came over the line more gently "—you want a baby, first, to carry on the McCue name, and second, to fulfill the maternal functions of your body. Is that it?"

"No, that's not *it*. I haven't mentioned the most important part." But she didn't immediately go on. She needed a minute to gather herself, to put the past aside and focus on the future, to ease the gruffness from her voice and be her well-balanced self.

When she remained silent, he asked softly, "Are you falling asleep on me?"

Fat chance, she thought. "No. I'm organizing again. The next part has to do with emotions. It's the most important part. But I'm not sure where to begin."

"Begin anywhere. I'll sort things out when you're done."

She took a breath and, letting the rigidity out of her spine, slid her hand palm up into her lap. Taking him at his word, she began to toss out her thoughts. "I want to hold a baby and not have to give it back at the end of the day. I want to take care of a baby, to know what it likes to eat and how it likes to eat and what each little cry means. I want to love a baby and be loved back. I've watched Caroline raise her children—" she warmed at the image that came to mind "—and there's something heart-stopping when they're small and they throw their little arms around your neck and hold on for dear life. I want that."

"They don't stay small for long," Spencer pointed out.

"I know, and I know the saying that the bigger they get, the bigger their problems, but I can handle the problems. It's the love that's important. The outward demonstration of that love changes as they grow—it certainly did with my parents and me—but the love is always there. I want that." She rushed on. "I want noise in this house and toys on these floors. I want a direction to my life beyond business. I want someone to buy clothes for and take to the movies and go to Disneyland with. I want someone to think about besides myself. I want someone to worry about." She caught her breath and deliberately slowed. "That may sound obsessive to you, but, believe me, it isn't. Through it all, I'll still be a businesswoman. I love my work. I can make it take more or less of my time, but I won't ever let it go completely, and that means I won't be hung up when my child goes off to first grade or, even more, to college. I'll always have the business to keep things in balance."

She was silent a moment before continuing. "But the business alone isn't enough. It was when my parents first died, when I was overwhelmed trying to take things over and keep things growing. Then things settled down, and little by little I saw the hole in my life. I want a child to help fill it, a child of my own, someone with a blood bond. I want that *connection*. I don't have it with anyone else in the world." She curled her hand into a fist. Her voice was suddenly smaller, diminished by the overwhelming yearning she was trying to describe. "There are times…" She paused.

"Times what?"

"Times when I feel so *lonely* for family. Times when…" She struggled with the emotion, and he didn't rush her. "Times when I feel like I have so much feeling inside me with no place to put it. Times when I feel like I'll *burst.*" She paused again, then sighed. "Does this mean anything to you?"

He didn't answer.

"It probably doesn't. You have a family. You have

grandparents, parents, aunts, uncles and cousins, a sister, two nephews and a niece. Whenever you want you can come home to people you love and who love you. Do you know how precious that is, Spencer?"

He remained silent.

"Oh, look," she went on apologetically, "I'm not saying you don't, and I'm certainly not criticizing you. You've chosen to be footloose and fancy-free, and that's your right. You like your life. It's exciting and busy and full. You don't suffer from attacks of the lonelies. I'm not sure many men do. They're more self-contained than we are. They don't crave the soft, warm, silly family things women do." She leaned back against the pillows. "If I'd been born a man, my life would be perfect."

"I'm glad you weren't born a man" came the deep voice from the other end of the line just as Jenna was beginning to think *he'd* fallen asleep. "You're too pretty for that."

She didn't know what to say. Spencer had never given her a compliment before. She had always been his younger sister's best friend, and not even with Caroline was he a compliment giver. His affection for her came out in his interest in the things she was doing and in her children. Jenna had been simply one of the things Caroline was doing.

The compliment was kind, though Jenna didn't delude herself into thinking that he meant anything deep by it. No doubt, since she had just painted a picture of how alone she was in the world, he was feeling sorry for her.

Feeling strangely awkward and doubly grateful that they were talking on the phone rather than in person, she said in a quiet voice, "Well, that's neither here nor there. Have you decided whether I'd be a good mother for your child?"

"If I wanted a child, you'd be fine."

She sat straight again. "Then you'll do it?"

"I don't know if I want a child. I told you that this afternoon. I need time to decide."

"But I wanted to start on this soon."

"How soon?"

"I'll be ovulating in two weeks. You said you'd give me an answer before you leave."

"I will. That gives me another twelve hours to make a decision."

"Is it so difficult, Spencer?" she pleaded. "A few minutes of your time this month, maybe next. I won't ask a thing of you after that. Not a thing, and you'll have that in writing."

"I wasn't planning to have a child."

"But this will be like *not* having one, only your parents will be pleased."

He snorted. "Yeah, and they'll start in on me about coming home for the kid's birthday and Christmas, and they'll nag—"

"They won't," Jenna interrupted. She had strong feelings about that. "If you agree to this, and if I do get pregnant, I'll tell them the truth. They'll know that you were doing a favor to me, that I've insisted that your role be limited to the child's conception, and that I have sole custody. I've talked this part out with Caroline. She agrees that given the choice between accepting my rules or alienating themselves from my child, they'll let you be."

"But I don't *need* a child."

"I *do*."

Seconds stretched into minutes. When Jenna couldn't bear the thudding of her heart any longer, she said, "Spencer? Will you?"

"You have guts," he declared in a way that said he thought she was either very brave or very crazy. "I don't think there's another woman on this earth who'd ask me to do what you have."

"I'm desperate. I want my baby to be the absolute very best. For that, I need the absolute very best man, and you're the absolute very best man."

"Oh, please."

"It's the truth. Will you do it?"

"I don't want to."

"I know, but you're considering it." She held her breath.

He swore under his. She could picture him plowing a hand through his hair much as he'd done on the dock that afternoon. "Look," he said with a long-suffering sigh, "the best I can offer to do is to give it more thought. Can we meet later?"

"Name the time and place, and I'll be there."

After a minute, he grumbled, "Hell, I don't know when or where. I'll call you tomorrow. Will you be around?"

"All day. I won't go anywhere. I'll wait for your call. Spencer, thanks. I really appreciate your doing this."

"I haven't said I'd do anything."

"But you haven't said no. You're thinking about it, and that's all I can ask. If you decide you can't, I'll be really disappointed, but I'll understand. It wouldn't be right for you to feel forced into doing something that you're against either for moral reasons or for reasons that—"

"Go to bed, Jenna," he cut in. "I can't think when you babble. I'll call you later. 'Bye."

CHAPTER FOUR

SPENCER COULD HAVE easily killed Caroline. Lying in bed, feeling distinctly disgruntled at three in the morning, he swore he would have, if he didn't love her so much. But she had always held a special place in his heart. From infancy, she had adored him. Sure, his parents had loved him, but not in the unconditional way Caroline had, and in turn, he had used his six-year edge to protect her whenever he could. Time had put physical distance between them, as had the needs of their individual personalities. As she'd grown older, Caroline had even had a thing or two to say about his nomadic lifestyle. Still, she indulged him more than his parents did. She made Newport a less confining place for him.

Usually.

But she'd done it this time. She had actually told Jenna that he might go along with the idea of donating sperm for Jenna's cause, and though no one had told him he had to do it, though no one was holding a gun to his head or binding his arms and legs and milking his seed from him, he felt trapped in an invisible—and infuriating—kind of way.

Jenna was sweet and sincere. She was pretty in a dark-eyed, dark-haired, creamy skinned, well-bred kind of way. In the same well-bred kind of way, she was a successful businesswoman. He was sure she would make a good mother. He was also sure that despite any protestation she might make, she had her heart set on his helping her, which meant she would be crushed if he refused.

But he didn't want to have a child. He didn't want the responsibility—and he meant what he'd told Jenna: he would be aware of that responsibility no matter how fervently she absolved him of it. He didn't want to know that a child of his was alive in the world while he was running around having fun. True, it wasn't an irresponsible kind of fun. It was self-supporting, even profitable when he tallied in the proceeds from sales of his books and movie rights. Still, it was fun.

If only Caroline had nixed the idea from the start. If only she had told Jenna that he wouldn't go for it or that he would be furious if she asked, he wouldn't be in such a mess. But Jenna had asked him, and she'd done it in a way that had made it very, very difficult for him to turn her down—because some of her points were valid. He didn't want them to be. He wanted the idea of single motherhood to be totally off the wall, but it wasn't, at least not as Jenna proposed it. She had thought everything out. She had the means, the desire and, he was sure, the natural aptitude for motherhood. She was also right about his parents being thrilled and, therefore, appeased where his leaving an heir was concerned—which raised another point that she had made that kept sticking in his mind. His estate was as sizable as Jenna's, but he didn't have a direct heir for it, either. Not to mention the fact that they *would* make a good baby together, he and Jenna. She was right there, too.

So. What was he supposed to do? She was offering him something that he hadn't considered before but that had some merits. If he turned her down, he might never get another offer like it. If he turned her down, he might be sorry in ten or twenty years. If, God forbid, something happened to one or both of his parents the way it had happened to Jenna's, would he be sorry he hadn't given them the gift of a grandchild? If something happened to *him,* would he lie on his deathbed wishing he was leaving behind something more of his body than a golden urn filled with ashes?

He swore loudly and turned away from the light of the moon. Sweet, innocent Jenna had opened a can of worms. He kept trying to close it, kept trying to simply make the decision to see her in the morning and tell her no, then fly back to Florida and immerse himself in his work, but he couldn't make that decision. Something was holding him back. Some gut instinct.

Spencer had been in many a precarious position in the course of his travels, and if there was one thing he knew, it was that his gut instinct was sound, damn it.

JENNA HAD TROUBLE falling asleep. She didn't know whether to be hopeful or discouraged by Spencer's call. She hadn't realized how much she'd set her heart on using his sperm, until she realized that within hours she might know that she couldn't. Then again, if he said yes, she'd be on her way to having the most incredible child in the world. The excitement of that thought alone kept her up for a while.

She fell asleep shortly before dawn, which was probably why she didn't hear the doorbell when it first rang. She didn't rouse until the tone was coming in imperious bursts of threes, and then it was a minute before she could correctly identify the sound. She stumbled from bed and was at the bedroom door before she thought of covering herself. Ducking back in to snatch the decorative throw from the back of the wicker chair, she wrapped it around her and ran barefoot down the stairs.

Squinting out the sidelight, she felt a moment's panic. Spencer was standing there, looking freshly showered and awake enough to make her acutely aware of how awful she appeared. Her hair was a mess; her eyes were still only half opened; she was sure there were pillowcase creases on her face.

But he had seen her peering out, so she couldn't pretend she wasn't home. And anyway, she wouldn't do that. If he had made a decision, she wanted to know what it was.

Clutching the throw around her with one hand, she opened the door with the other. The sun hit her full face. She swayed sideways to use his large frame as a shade.

"What time is it?" she asked in a sleep-gritty voice.

"Eight-forty," he answered, sounding remorseless as he took in her disheveled appearance.

Wondering how he could look so good with so little sleep, Jenna swallowed and pushed loose wisps of hair back from her face. "Want to come in? It'll take me just a minute to put something on."

"Don't dress on my behalf," he said.

She took that to mean he wouldn't be staying long enough to make it worth her bother, and felt an immediate stab of disappointment. "You won't do it?" Tears sprang to her eyes. "Oh, Spencer—"

"I didn't say I wouldn't." He scowled at the tears. "There are a few more things I need to know."

"Oh. Okay." She glanced around, not sure whether to lead him into the living room or the kitchen. She wished she could think clearly, but his appearance had caught her off guard at a time of day when she was at her worst. "Uh, let me make coffee." The making would buy her time; the drinking would help clear her head.

Maintaining a grip on the throw, she went into the kitchen. Though she sensed Spencer behind her, she didn't look around. Rather, she did the best she could putting on a pot of coffee to brew. Working one-handed slowed her, but she didn't dare let go of the throw for fear it would fall to the floor. Her nightgown was of fine, soft, translucent cotton. She had nothing on underneath.

The instant she had the coffee machine gurgling, she said, "I'm running upstairs. I'll be back down in a second."

"Sit," Spencer ordered.

"But I'm not dressed," she protested, daring to look at him. It was a mistake. His scar was like an exclamation mark after his order, and above that, his eyes were compellingly blue. Though they didn't move from her face, she felt their touch all over.

"What we're discussing is pretty intimate," he said. "You're dressed just fine."

She wanted to argue but was loath to anger him. So she slipped into a chair at the small glass table and sat looking as poised as possible with the throw protecting her virtue, her legs pressed together and her ankles crossed and tucked under the chair.

Spencer leaned against the counter. He was wearing slim-fitting black pants and a loose black shirt. His hair had been parted and combed to the side, but spikes were already falling over his brow. In keeping with the scar, they gave him a commanding look, which he accentuated by folding his arms across his chest.

He regarded her steadily. "You mentioned basal body temperature. Explain that term."

She refused to squirm. "That's what my temperature is when my body is at total rest. I take my temperature every morning when I first wake up, even before I sit up in bed. Then I record it on a chart."

"You've already been doing that?"

"For three months, every morning. Except this one," she added, since it was obvious that she hadn't taken time for anything when the doorbell had rung. "But that's okay. I can miss a day or two. I know what my temperature would have been if I'd taken it."

"How?"

"There's a distinct pattern." More quietly she added, "And I'm very regular."

As though mocking her shyness, he said in a bold voice, "This relates to your period, I take it."

"Yes."

He waited, then gestured for her to continue. "Come on. Tell me. I want to know how it works."

The fact that he was listening and considering her request lifted her spirits above the self-consciousness she felt. "My temperature is below normal on the days leading up to ovulation. It usually drops even more when I actually ovulate, then starts to rise after that. It keeps going up until I get my period."

"So the exact day of ovulation is the critical one?"

"Kind of."

"What do you mean, kind of?"

"According to my doctor, it's best if sperm is already in the fallopian tube when I ovulate, which means doing his procedure just prior to that time. Actually," she mustered the courage to say, "if you were willing to hang around for a few days, he'd do the procedure twice."

"Twice, huh?" Spencer said.

"Only if you were willing," she rushed on. "I've done so much reading on this, and the books seem to agree that when a couple is trying to conceive, they should have intercourse, ideally, every other day around the time of ovulation. That gives the sperm count time to fully recover, and since sperm will stay alive for forty-eight to seventy-two hours, every other day makes sense—but that's for *couples,* and we're not a couple in *that* sense. I know you have other things to do, and that you don't like being around here with your parents and all, so if you could do it once, that'd be great. I mean, it could be that I'll conceive—" she snapped her fingers "—like that."

"It could be," he drawled, "that we'd need to do it a whole *lot* of times before you conceive." The look in his eye grew speculative. He dropped his gaze to her neck, which was encased in lace, then her breasts, which were bound by the throw, then her belly, which rested somewhere under multiple folds of fabric.

Jenna wanted to hide. She felt naked and exposed, and decidedly inferior to every other woman Spencer had been involved with. True, what she was proposing didn't mean *that* kind of involvement, but he was right. It would be a pretty intimate thing if she carried his child.

"I'll do it," he said.

Her heart tripped. "You will?"

He nodded.

She came to her feet with a huge smile. "You will?" She brought her hands together in front of that smile and looked at him through tears of happiness this time.

He made a sound that told her what he thought of the tears. Then he said, "On one condition."

"I'll do whatever you want." She beamed, feeling lighter and brighter than she had in weeks. "I'm so grateful, Spencer, *so* grateful, and relieved! I thought for sure you'd say no and then I'd have to use the sperm bank, and this way my baby will be perfect, absolutely perfect!"

"No artificial insemination."

Her breath caught. The smile faded. "No what?"

"Artificial insemination," he repeated. "It's the real thing or nothing."

"The real thing?" she asked.

He looked as if he wanted to grin but was holding it back. "Sexual intercourse, between you and me."

Jenna felt suddenly weak in the knees. Dropping back into the chair, she clutched the throw to her chest. "We can't do that," she said in dismay. "We're not like that with each other."

"We can be if you want my baby."

"I do, I do." She made a helpless face. "But you don't know what you're saying!"

"I know exactly what I'm saying. I've been thinking about it all night. I'm saying that if you're going to have my baby, I want it conceived the normal way. I'm also saying that I won't stand in a little room and pleasure myself when you could do that for me."

"But you're Caroline's brother!"

"So?"

"So, I'm like a sister to you."

Very slowly he shook his head.

"But I'm not good at sex!" she protested. As mortifying as it was, she had to tell him the truth. "I've been with three men, and none of them raved about my skill. I don't think I could *begin* to pleasure you."

"You could begin," he assured her, and his voice was suddenly thicker, "and I'd show you what to do from there."

"But you've been with so many women! You're so experienced! You're so *big*!" She grasped on to that. "You said it yourself—I'm too short. You're nearly a foot taller than me."

"You liked that when you were thinking of having a boy."

"I *do* like it, but that was when I thought we'd be doing this in a doctor's office. Honestly, Spencer, it would be so much better that way."

"Maybe for you. Not for me. And since I'm the one this thing hangs on…" Unfolding his arms, he straightened away from the counter. "Need time to think, Jenna? I'll give you time." He strolled toward the door. "Take as much time as you want. I'll be in Florida for the next six months, but after that I could be God knows where. Caroline has the number of my place in the Keys. You could leave a message, then when I get back—"

"Wait," she cried just as his foot cleared the threshold. She couldn't let him walk away, not when she was so close to getting what she wanted. "Okay." She rose from the chair, determined to commit herself before she could be paralyzed by shyness. "Okay, we'll do it that way if you want." She could handle it; she knew she could. "We'll do it that way."

A small smile lifted one side of his mouth. "Good."

"But will you promise me one thing in return?" she begged. "If it doesn't work that way—I mean, if you can't—if I can't help you—" She sucked in a breath and pushed it out with the words "If the actual act is a total disaster, will you do it my way?" Her cheeks burned, but she held steady.

"The act won't be a disaster."

"Don't be so sure. I'm *really* not good at this."

He frowned. "You think you won't turn me on?" He started toward her.

"It's been known to happen."

"I find that hard to believe."

"It happened."

He stood directly before her. "With all three of your lovers?"

"With the last."

"Then that was his problem. It won't be mine."

"How do you know? Here we stand, fully dressed— at least, you are, and I'm covered up. How do you know what will happen when we're in bed? This is like a business arrangement, for goodness' sake. Is it realistic to expect that you'll be turned on enough to—" she swallowed "—enough to..."

"Come?"

She nodded.

"Yes, it's realistic to expect that," he said. Lifting a hand, he ran the backs of his fingers along the side of her breast.

Jenna gasped in surprise. Her first instinct was to move away, but the lightness of his touch and the fact of who he was and what she had asked of him, held her to him. Within seconds, she'd begun to tremble inside. Eyes riveted to his dark face, she saw the small, seeming involuntary rise of his head and the faint flare of his nostrils. There was nothing more by way of touching, just the backs of his fingers shaping her breast through two layers of fabric for what couldn't have been more than another ten seconds, before he dropped his hand to her waist, then away. In the next instant he looked down at himself. Jenna followed his gaze to the swell of arousal at his fly.

"I don't think I'll have a problem," he remarked dryly.

Ridiculous, given the circumstances, but she felt guilty, as though she had walked in on him when he'd been performing a private act that had nothing to do with her. Unable to meet his eyes, she backed down into the chair.

"Anything else you want to test now?" he asked.

She studied her hands. "No."

"Want to change your mind about me fathering your child?"

She looked up at him. "No!"

He chuckled, then shot a glance at the coffeemaker. "That smells good. I could use a cup. Want one?"

"Uh, sure," she said, but she didn't move. She let Spencer do the pouring, while she struggled to regain her poise. One part of her was near to bursting with excitement about the baby she was going to have. The other part was totally unsettled by the thought of what she was going to have to do to get it.

She took the cup and saucer he handed her and quickly put them down on the table so that the shaking of her hands wouldn't show, then she waited while he set down his own cup and took a seat across from her.

"Okay," he said, stretching out his legs, "let's talk specifics. Yesterday you said you'd be ovulating in two weeks. Do you have your period now?"

She focused on the coffee. "I'll be getting it tomorrow."

"How can you be sure?"

"I have a twenty-eight-day cycle. Always. Besides, I can feel it."

"You're crampy?"

"Bloated."

"You don't look bloated," he said, then tacked on, "not that I can see much more than your face, but that looks fine."

Jenna didn't believe him for a minute. She had barely had four hours' sleep, and she hadn't washed, hadn't combed her hair, hadn't put on a bit of makeup. As if that wasn't bad enough, she felt totally unprepared for the conversation they were having. She knew everything there was to know on the topic of artificial insemination, but Spencer had shifted topics on her. It wasn't fair.

She looked down at her coffee again. "Spencer?"

"Yes, Jenna?"

She heard his amusement and felt worse. "I'm very nervous about this."

"I can see that," he said gently. "But I thought I put your worries to rest."

"There's something else. It's the awkwardness. You're Caroline's brother. I never intended we'd actually have sex."

"Neither did I, but I spent all last night thinking about it, and I was hard then, too."

"You're just saying that."

"I'm not."

"You never would have thought of it if I hadn't drafted you."

"Maybe not," he admitted, "but only because I'm not around here enough to get ideas like that. Which raises another point. Where should we do it? The doctor's office is out."

She eyed him beseechingly. "You could reconsider. It'd be so much more controlled if we did it my way." She watched him take a drink of his coffee and set down his cup, and noticed that his hand didn't shake in the least. He looked as though he was enjoying the discussion. No self-consciousness on *his* part.

"I don't like things controlled," he said, "not things to do with sex. So. Where'll it be? My place or yours? We could use a hotel, but that'd be kind of sterile, don't you think?"

"Sterile is fine. After all, this is a business arrangement. It's not like it has to be romantic or anything. We'll only be doing it once."

"I thought you said the ideal thing was to do it every other day around the time you ovulate."

"We don't have to."

"If we're going to do this, we'll do it right. So. We should get together twelve days from now?"

Her stomach was jumping. *The baby. Think of the baby,* she told herself. "Twelve days. That sounds right."

"Unless you want to take a few months to get used to the idea."

Jenna didn't think *any* amount of time would get her used to the idea of having sex with Spencer. Figuring that she was best to get it over with, she gave a quick headshake. "I want to get pregnant as soon as possible. I'll be ovulating around the eighth of July, which means that if I conceive right away, the baby will be born next April."

"Boy, you've got that down pat."

"I've had plenty of time to count."

He finished off his coffee. "Then I should fly back here on the sixth?"

"If you could." She thought ahead to that time. "I had everything figured out when I assumed we'd be using artificial insemination. We would have been able to see the doctor separately during the day and go our own ways at night without even bumping into each other. I thought it would be less awkward that way." She grimaced. "This way will be more complicated."

"How so?" Spencer asked. He sank down in the chair, stretching his legs out even farther. "I don't see any complications. I'll stay here. You have plenty of room."

"Here?"

"My parents and I don't do well under the same roof. I doubt I'll even tell them I'm in town."

"But they'll want to see you."

"They won't miss me if they don't know I'm here."

"What if they see you around town?"

"They won't. I'll stay here the whole time."

Jenna had visions of trying to entertain him and proving as inept at that as she would be at sex. He was a man of action. He was used to exciting things happening, which they certainly wouldn't do in her stately old house. "Good Lord, Spencer, you'll be bored. Besides, I was planning to work."

"No sweat. You can work. You won't even have to break up your day to keep a doctor's appointment, since we'll be doing our thing at night."

At night. Of course. She supposed it would be easier

in the dark. Then again, she doubted it would. Thought of being naked with Spencer—with Spencer Smith of the dashing scar, author, adventurer and expert on women—was daunting.

But she wanted that baby.

"We can't sleep together," she informed him in an attempt to set some rules that would make her less shaky. "I mean, we can't spend the whole night together."

He frowned. "Why not?"

"Because this is a business arrangement. It wouldn't be right."

He looked displeased. "But I was looking forward to having a warm body next to me. And what if we want to do it more than once? Am I supposed to run back and forth down the hall?"

"We can't do it more than once in one night. The books say that would be counterproductive. You'd be continually depleted."

Spencer arched a brow. "*Some* men might be depleted, but when I get going—"

She interrupted. "Please, Spencer? I'm trying to get comfortable with the idea of this, but you're not making it easy."

"It'd be plenty easy," he groused, "if you'd swing with it a little. This doesn't have to be all work, y'know."

"But it does. The only reason we're doing it is so I can have a baby. It's not like we *feel* anything for each other."

"We don't have to *feel* anything to be able to enjoy each other's bodies. I liked touching your breast. I might just like touching the rest of you, and the feeling may be mutual. I'm told I'm a decent lover."

"I'm sure you're a wonderful lover, but I can't play games." Feeling vulnerable, she whispered, "Please, Spencer? I've agreed to do things your way because I want this baby more than anything, but I can't pretend this is something it's not. I want everything we do to be honest. Please?"

Spencer stared at her for a long time. Finally, looking rebellious but determined, he got to his feet. "I'll be here on the sixth. If there's any change in the plan, you know how to reach me." Without another word, he left.

CHAPTER FIVE

THE SIXTH OF JULY FELL on a Saturday. Given a choice, Jenna would have had it fall on a weekday, when she could busy herself at McCue's from morning to night and thereby keep her nervousness about being with Spencer in check. But her ovaries knew nothing about apprehension. They operated the same as always. Her temperature followed its established pattern, staying well below normal in prelude to a dip on the eighth.

Spencer called on Friday morning before she left for work. "Just wanted to confirm our date," he said.

"It's not a date," Jenna chided. "It's an appointment." She was determined to keep things on the up-and-up regarding the exact nature of their liaison. Spencer hadn't chosen her as a lover. She couldn't pretend that he had—and she couldn't let *him* think she was pretending it. That would be humiliating. Things were awkward enough without it.

"Appointment, then," he conceded in a deep but agreeable voice. "Are we on?"

"Yes."

"Good." Nonchalantly, he said, "I made an appointment to have some work done on the plane. The best mechanic around is at Norwood Airport, which is about an hour's drive from your place. Feel like taking a ride and picking me up there tomorrow afternoon?"

"Uh, sure."

"That way we can talk a little before we—well, we can talk."

For a split second Jenna imagined that he was feeling awkward himself. Then she ruled out the possibility. Spencer wouldn't feel awkward about sex. He was too experienced for that.

"Sounds fine," she said, managing to sound fully composed. "What time should I be there?"

"I won't be able to leave here until afternoon. Allowing for air traffic, then time to make sure my guy knows what I want done—is six-thirty too late?"

She felt instant relief. "Six-thirty's fine." That meant she *could* keep herself busy all day, and it meant that she'd only have to worry about entertaining Spencer on Sunday. On Monday morning, she'd be back at work.

"Drive right around to Hangar C," he instructed, "and give a honk to let me know you're there. See you then."

"Okay. 'Bye."

HE LOOKED UNFAIRLY dashing. He was wearing a navy shirt with the cuffs rolled and the tails out, and khaki shorts that left his long legs bare to his deck shoes. He had a worn-looking duffel thrown over his shoulder and a bulging briefcase under his arm, and might have been mistaken for a weekending yuppie if it hadn't been for the carved lines of his face. They were bold and lent him an untamed look, upheld by his scar, his dark tan and his even darker, windblown hair. And then there were his eyes, always his eyes.

With a helpless sigh and more than a flutter inside, Jenna waved and waited while he crossed the tarmac to where the Jaguar was parked. She half expected him to come to the driver's side and shoo her over. Instead he opened the passenger door, tossed his gear into the back and slid in.

"Sorry," he muttered, and stared out the front. "The goddamn mechanic forgot I'd called, and he took off for the weekend. His partner was there, but he doesn't know his ass from his elbow. He's not touching *my* plane."

"So what will you do?"

"Mac'll be back on Monday. He'll have to do the work then." He looked at her. "Have you been waiting long?"

"Five minutes. It was nothing." She couldn't take her eyes from his. They were as intense as ever, yet distracted. "You look tired. Was it a difficult flight?"

"The flight was okay. It was everything I had to do beforehand. My editor doesn't like my latest manuscript and wants major revisions. That news came in the mail yesterday—the bastard couldn't tell me in person. I spent most of the afternoon on the phone with him. We were able to compromise on some of the stuff, but there's still a hell of a lot to be done. I'll have to work on it here."

Jenna couldn't believe her luck. She'd been granted a reprieve in the entertainment department. "That's fine. You can work in my office at home. There's a huge desk and good light." She would bend over backward to be accommodating. "Do you need a computer?"

He made a disparaging sound. "I can barely type, let alone use a computer."

She was amazed. Spencer always had such a capable air about him that she had assumed he was proficient in just about everything.

"Don't look at me that way," he told her. "I've been on the go since I was twenty-two, and computers only came in big after that. When would I have the time to learn to use one? I've always done just fine paying a typist." He scowled. "But let me tell you, revisions are a pain in the butt."

"When do they have to be done?"

"Last week."

"Oops."

His scowl faded. "Yeah. Oops." His mouth curved into a lopsided smile, and his eyes did focus on her then. They seemed suddenly warmer, then warmer still and filled with sexual innuendo.

Jenna tore her gaze away, only to have it land on his legs, which were nearly as compelling.

"Problem with the shorts?" he asked. "I'll have you know that in the middle of all that garbage with my editor, I kept thinking about what to wear today. Totally aside from the fact that it's summer and the plane can get warm, I thought it'd be good for you to see my legs so they won't be such a shock later on."

She forced herself to look more casually at the appendages in question. They were well formed, firm and long, as tanned as his face but hairy. "I've seen men's legs before. In fact, I've seen yours before."

He frowned. "When?"

"The summer between college and business school. Don't you remember? Caroline and I were traveling through the Greek islands. You met us on Crete."

"Oh, yeah," he said with a smile that spread over his face as memory returned. "I made you call home first thing, because neither of you had bothered to call the parents and they were frantic—which *I* knew because I'd had the misfortune to call home about something else entirely, and they let *me* have it like I was the one who was lost!"

"We weren't lost. We just couldn't get to a phone."

He snickered. "I've used that excuse too many times myself to buy it. You didn't *want* to call home. But, hey—" he raised a forgiving hand "—I can understand that. It was the first time you'd been away alone. The freedom you felt was heady."

Jenna smiled at the memory. "It was that." She took

a breath. "Anyway, you spent a couple of days with us, mostly at the beach. So I've seen your legs."

"You've seen a lot more if you were at the beach with me."

"You were wearing a bathing suit."

"Not much of one, if I correctly remember those days."

He did. His bathing suit had been small and sleek. Jenna remembered admiring him in it, but that was all she'd done. He was Caroline's elder brother, twenty-eight to her twenty-two, and though they came from similar backgrounds, he lived such a different life from Jenna that she never dreamed there might be any entanglement between them.

There certainly was now, and those long, tanned, hair-spattered legs made her all the more aware of it. She cleared her throat. "Yes. Well." Praying that driving would distract her from his imposing presence, she started the car. "Do you want to go back to the house and drop your things off?"

"I'd rather eat. I'm starved." He was scanning the stores and businesses that lined the road. "There used to be a terrific steak place around here—Terry's, Carrie's—"

"Corey's?"

"That's it. Is it still open?"

"Uh-huh. Want to go?"

"A-S-A-P."

In less than ten minutes, they were at the restaurant, but it was nearly forty minutes before they were seated and another forty minutes before their food arrived. Jenna saw the expectant looks Spencer sent their waitress and waited for him to explode at the delay the way some other men would have. But he didn't. He shifted in his seat and went through two baskets of rolls, but he didn't complain about the wait. Instead, he kept Jenna talking about McCue's, about people they both knew, about Caroline and the kids.

When the food arrived, he ate his own, plus half of what Jenna left on her plate. "I need all the energy I can get," he explained with a mischievous look.

"Spencer," she complained.

"What?"

"That's embarrassing."

"Sorry. I couldn't resist."

Wiping the smugness from his face, he finished eating. Jenna arched a brow when he refused dessert, but they both had coffee, and when the waitress brought the check, she reached for it first.

Spencer's hand flattened hers to the table. With his other hand, he pulled the check free. "I pay."

"That's not right. You're here on my account. I want to pay."

"I pay," he repeated in such a firm voice that she backed off. More gently, almost distractedly as he pulled out his charge card, he added, "Besides, I ate twice as much as you."

Not wanting to risk another reference to why that was so, Jenna sat silently while he settled the bill. It was dark outside by the time they returned to the car.

The darkness did nothing to ease her nerves. Spencer had said they would do it at night, and it was night. Jenna couldn't forget that for a minute during the drive to Little Compton. Hands tight at ten and two on the wheel, she kept picturing her house, picturing the bed she had freshened up for Spencer, then picturing her own bed and wondering which one they would use.

Spencer seemed deep in thought, as well. Once, passing beneath a streetlight, she saw that he had his elbow braced on the door and his forehead braced on his fingertips, and for an instant, she worried that he was changing his mind.

"Everything okay?" she asked.

"Yeah."

She hesitated, then said, "You sound angry."

"Not angry." He was silent for a minute. Then he sighed, dropped his hand to his thigh and looked out the windshield. "Unsure."

Her heart beat harder against her ribs. "Unsure about whether you want to go ahead with it?"

"Unsure about *how* to go ahead with it. I've seduced women plenty of times, but you don't want to be seduced. You want this to be businesslike. I've never done it that way."

On a ray of hope, she said, "Y'know, we could still do it my way. I'm sure my doctor would be willing to meet us in his office tomorrow—"

"Forget it," Spencer stated. He didn't have to elaborate. The finality of his tone said it all.

Jenna knew better than to ignore the message. Yes, she wished they were doing it her way, but still, Spencer was doing her a huge favor. He was helping her make a baby. A baby. She couldn't forget that.

"It shouldn't be difficult," she said in a deferential tone. If he didn't know what to do, it was really the blind leading the blind. "We both know the mechanics. Isn't that enough?"

He didn't answer. In fact, he didn't say anything for the rest of the drive, which saddened Jenna. Always in the past when she'd been with him, talk had been easy. She loved hearing about his travels, his adventures, his books, and as though sensing her interest, he relaxed in the telling. But the air between them was tense now. She had the awful thought that their relationship might be permanently changed, and prayed that wouldn't be so.

When she pulled up at the house, he grabbed his gear from the back seat and followed her in. She wavered for an instant in the hall before saying, "I'll, uh, show you to your room. You may want to unpack." She led him up the stairs and down the hall. The room she had chosen for him was nearly as large as her own, though at the opposite end of the house. At the door, she moved aside to let him pass.

He went in, dropped his things on the bed and stood with his hands on his hips and his back to her. His spine was straight, his displeasure evident.

"If you don't like this room…" she began, only to stop when he turned quickly. His face was dark, his eyes iridescent as they held her in their thrall.

"I think we should do it now, since neither of us will relax till it's done. I need a shower. I'll meet you in your room in ten minutes, okay?"

Jenna knew he was right. The longer they put it off, the more nervous she would be, and she was plenty nervous already. At his words, she had started to shake. It was all she could do not to let it show.

"Fifteen minutes," she bargained, then swallowed and explained, "It takes me longer. In the shower."

"Fifteen minutes," he agreed. His eyes held hers for a heart-stopping moment more before letting her go.

SPENCER TOOK HIS TIME in the shower. Long after he had soaped himself from head to toe, he stood with the hot spray concentrated on the tight muscles at the back of his neck. True, the mess with the manuscript had gotten him down, but he suspected that he might have handled it better if Jenna hadn't been weighing heavy on his mind.

No artificial insemination, he had told her with such smugness. *It's the real thing or nothing.* Such arrogance. *Sexual intercourse, between you and me.* Such cocksureness, and why the hell not? He was a handsome guy. He was a super lover. He would show little Jenna McCue the time of her life, and she'd get the baby she wanted, to boot.

He had believed all that up until several days earlier, when the reality of what he had arranged had hit him— and it wasn't the baby part that bothered him, as much as the Jenna part. She was Caroline's best friend, and he had always liked her. She was gentle and understanding. She accepted his way of life. She was also vulnerable where men were concerned, something he hadn't realized until she had put her proposal to him at his parents' anniversary party.

He wasn't used to vulnerable women, any more than he was used to petite women. He was used to women who were tall and shapely, who reveled in their sexuality, who came to him with confidence and hunger, and demanded as much as they gave.

Jenna wasn't like those women at all, but now he felt a responsibility for her. He wanted to please her, but he wasn't sure how best to do it. She wanted their coming together to be a simple, straightforward coupling for the sole purpose of producing a child. His body wanted more.

He shifted to put the force of the spray on the small of his back, then raised first one arm, then the other to stretch his muscles. He supposed he could find a compromise. He could be gentle, without dwelling on preliminaries. He could make her feel good if she let him. The question was whether she would.

Turning the water off, he reached for the towel and dried himself. He looked at his foggy reflection in the mirror, pushed his hair around a little, took a toothbrush from his grooming kit and set about brushing his teeth, and all the while he pictured Jenna in her own bathroom getting ready for him. By the time he'd rinsed his mouth, a slow heat was gathering between his legs.

No, getting it up wouldn't be a problem. Preparing Jenna to take it in might be.

He glanced at his watch. It was time. Knotting a dry towel around his waist, he left the bathroom and headed down the hall. Jenna's was the only other room lit. He assumed it had once been her parents' room, but he wasn't thinking about her parents when he came to stand at the door. A single low light glowed by the turned-down bed. She was beside it, with her back to him. She was wearing a robe that was long and white, and her head was bowed. Only when he came closer did he see that she was studying something in her hand.

"Whatcha got?" he asked softly.

She held up a tiny bracelet made of glass beads interspersed with ones of ivory that spelled out her name. "My parents had this made when I was a baby. I always loved it. If I have a little girl, I want to give her one with her name on it, too."

Spencer looked at the bracelet for a minute, before his gaze was drawn up to Jenna. Her hair was dark as the night, spilling softly around her face and onto her shoulders. Her skin was moist, her cheeks a pale pink. She smelled of spring flowers and looked incredibly young.

He touched her hair. "I think that sounds like a nice idea." He ran his fingers through the loose waves.

She tucked her chin lower. The gesture made him feel that much larger beside her and more protective. Gently he took the bracelet from her hand and set it on the table by the bed. While he was there, he switched off the light. "If it were up to me," he said, straightening close by her side, "I'd leave it on. But I think you'll be more comfortable this way."

"Yes," she whispered. "Thank you."

He touched her sleeve. "Is there a nightgown under this?"

She nodded.

He kept his voice low and gentle. "Want to take the robe off?"

Head still bent, she slipped the silky fabric from her shoulders. In a strained voice that sounded as if she were trying for humor but missed, she said, "Right about now, the nurse would be handing me a paper sheet, telling me to take everything off from the waist down and climb on the table."

"No table here. No paper sheet." Spencer paused. In an even lower voice, he said, "Is there anything you need to take off from the waist down?"

She shook her head.

That bit of information sent a spark from his brain to his groin. Needing to touch her, he curved a hand around her neck. At the same time, he lowered his head to her hair to breathe in the sweet scent of roses.

She slipped away from him. Climbing into bed, she moved to the far side and slid down against the pillow.

The room was dark, but Spencer's eyes had adjusted enough to see the tension in her body as she lay waiting for him. His first impulse was to stand there debating what to do next, but if he hesitated for long, she would remind him that they could go to the doctor's office in the morning, and he wouldn't, couldn't do that. It went against his grain. And his groin. He was already aroused.

Coming down on a knee, he crawled across the queen-size bed until his thigh met Jenna's hip. He touched her face and whispered, "There's nothing to be afraid of."

"I'm not afraid," she whispered back.

He traced her jaw. "Then tense."

"I just want this to work so badly."

"It will if you relax. I can help you do that." He slipped his hand to her neck, then her throat.

Her eyes were wide in the dark. "You don't have to, Spence. Really. I'm okay. I'm really fine."

"Well, I'm not," he said, taking a different tactic. Climbing under the bedcovers, he stretched out on his side, facing her. "I want you now, want you badly—"

"You don't have to say that."

"It's the truth." Needing to show her, he rolled on top of her and let her feel the full weight of his lower body. He knew he'd made his point when she took in a quick breath. "Believe me?"

"I believe you."

"Then relax your legs a little so I can feel you where I'm supposed to."

"This is so embarrassing, Spencer," she murmured, but she did as he asked. She caught in another breath when he settled more snugly against her.

"Feel okay?" he asked.

"Feels okay," she answered.

"I'm supposed to be on top, aren't I?"

"Yes. I'll lose...less. This is *so* embarrassing."

"No, it isn't. It's nice." He moved gently against her. "I don't know why I didn't think of it sooner."

Her voice was more breathy. "You didn't think of it because I'm not your type."

"If you're not my type, why am I so hard? And besides, how would you know what my type is?"

"Caroline tells me."

"Caroline knows diddly-squat." He was wondering if he knew much more, since he had known Jenna all these years without seeing the possibilities, but that was water over the dam. Carefully holding his upper body weight from her, he said, "I'm afraid I'll hurt you if you're not ready, so I'm going to touch you now, Jenna. Just a little.

I know you don't want to get into things this way, but if I hurt you, I won't be able to go on. I want you to feel good, too."

"I don't need that."

"But I do." He lowered his head to her neck and kissed the warm skin there, kissed it lightly, then, without planning to, more deeply, because her scent did something to him. That something was strong enough to startle him. His muscles were trembling faintly when he raised his head. "Jeez."

She was instantly alarmed. "What's wrong?"

He laughed, then growled. "Nothing." He buried his face against her neck and undulated helplessly against her. He couldn't believe how aroused he was. He supposed it could be because he hadn't had a woman in a while, but he'd had dry stretches before without this sudden, dire wanting. Against her neck, he warned, "I don't know how long I can hold off, Jenna."

Her arms, which had been lying still until then, crept around his back. Her fingers dug into his muscles. "Don't wait. Don't wait. Do it now."

But he had to know if she was ready. So he ran a hand down her side and came up under her nightgown. The feel of her smooth, bare thigh against his palm was like fire, but no more so than the unevenness of her breathing. That, too, had crept up on him. It was the most welcome sound in the world just then.

"Are you okay?" he whispered hoarsely.

Breathlessly, she whispered back, "I'm okay."

He touched her between her legs, and a tiny sound came from the back of her throat. "You're sweet," he murmured. "So sweet." He stroked her, gently finding his way deeper. Well after he had the answer he sought, he continued to rub her. "I want to kiss you, Jenna."

"No!"

"Your mouth." He lowered his head to hers, but her high-pitched plea stopped him short.

"Don't, Spencer, please don't. Kissing makes it something it's not." She paused and let out an involuntary kind of hum. At the same time, albeit in a motion so subtle as to be missed by a lesser lover, she moved her hips against his hand.

Spencer wanted to argue, but she was ready for him, and, Lord knew, he was ready for her. Taking his hands from her only long enough to drag the towel from his hips, he tangled his legs with hers, spreading them farther apart, and positioned himself at their notch. He reached for her hands and held them on either side of her head. Then he watched her closely while he pushed forward into her warmth.

She was tight. Wonderfully tight. He let out a sigh and grinned down at her. "How does it feel?"

"Full."

"It is that." His grin persisted. It stretched wider in an agony of pleasure when he withdrew and thrust forward again. He moaned this time and with a steady downward pressure deepened his penetration. "Jenna, oh, Lord, Jenna," he whispered. He wanted to laugh, or hug her, or yank up her nightgown and put his hands all over her. Instead, with another moan, he said, "This feels so good."

"I'm not too short?"

He did give a laugh then, a low, throaty sound. "Hell, no. We fit—" he took a shaky breath "—very well." As though to prove it, he slid against her inside and out.

She let out a tiny gasp. "I'm glad." Her hands came around to his front, palms grazing his nipples, then returning there when he sucked in a great gulp of air. "I want a baby, Spencer," she cried. "Give me one, please, give me one?"

The reminder of her purpose should have doused at least some of Spencer's flame, but it didn't. Quite the opposite happened. He felt a heat so sudden and intense that he nearly came apart. Yielding to the demand of his body, he moved against Jenna with a hard, driving rhythm that gained in speed and depth until, with a last, forceful thrust and a near-savage cry, he erupted inside her.

His orgasm went on and on. He was panting and damp with sweat when he finally collapsed on top of her, and even then, he kept his buttocks locked so that he could stay deep inside her until the last bit of pulsing pleasure was done. Finally, after several long, air-thirsty breaths, he rolled to the side.

Jenna was on her back, her head turned to look at him. Even in the dark, he could see the expectancy on her face. He knew she was thinking of the baby, and felt a glimmer of disappointment. His ego had wanted her to be bowled over by his lovemaking, so much so that she forgot the reason behind it. But, then, she had worked hard to keep that reason in her mind. Perhaps it was for the best.

With a gentle hand, he unbunched the nightgown from her waist and lowered it to her thighs. When that was done, he put his fingertips to her lips. Then he cleared his throat. "So. Did we do it? Did you feel that little spark when egg met sperm?"

She was lying so quietly and was so long in answering that he wondered if something was wrong. He was about to ask when, in a small voice, she said, "There isn't any little spark, at least not one I'd be able to feel."

"Do you feel any different?"

"I don't know."

"What does that mean?"

Lying very still, she said, "It means that I feel different, but I don't know whether it has to do with the baby or not."

"If not, what would it be from?"

It was a while before she said, in an even smaller voice, "What we just did."

Spencer felt a light jab inside. Rolling to his stomach, he propped himself on his elbows with his head inches from hers. "Was it any good, Jenna?"

"It was great," she said with a burst of enthusiasm. "You were incredible. I mean, if any man can make me pregnant—"

"For you," he interrupted, and put a hand on her stomach. "Was it good for you? Did you feel good down here?" He started to move his hand lower, but she grabbed it and held it still.

"It felt nice." She paused, then admitted, "Better than I thought it would."

"Why did you think it wouldn't?" he asked. He'd been wondering about that a lot, wondering why someone like Jenna hadn't had terrific experiences with men. "I told you once that it had to be the guys, and I believe that now more than ever, since I sure as hell can't find a thing wrong with *you*. But why were you expecting the worst with me?"

"I wasn't expecting the worst. It's just that I wasn't doing it for the pleasure of it."

"But there was some?"

"Yes," she said softly.

He was relieved to hear that. His own pleasure had been so intense that he was feeling very selfish. "I wish there had been more. Can I do it for you now?" He tried to move his hand lower, but she tightened her hold on it.

"No. I'm fine. Really, Spencer."

"I'd like to."

She gave a short shake of her head.

"Then let me hold you, at least," he said, and was reaching to pull her into his arms, when she gave a small cry and put a protesting hand on his chest.

"I'm supposed to lie flat for a few minutes. The less I move, the greater the chance of something getting where it's supposed to be."

Spencer could understand that argument, but he was feeling a need that wasn't to be denied. "Okay," he said agreeably, and hoisted himself up. He punched and pushed at the pillows until they were arranged to his satisfaction. Then he arranged himself in such a way that he could slip an arm under Jenna and bring her against him without moving her lower body an inch. "If the mountain won't come to Muhammad," he said with a sigh.

"You don't have to do this, Spencer. It's not part of the deal. You have work to do. Don't feel that you have to lie here—"

He covered her mouth with a hand. "If I wanted to work, I'd work. If I wanted to get up, I'd get up. Trust me, Jenna." He removed his hand.

"But—"

He put his hand right back. "Good Lord, you're like a broken record! Yes, I know that I'm only here to help you make a baby and that anything else is unnecessary, but I want to hold you—I just want to hold you. Unless you really don't want to be held. In which case I'll crawl off to the corner and lie there in a pathetic heap until I recover enough of my strength to crawl back down the hall. In case you've forgotten, I've just given you every bit of the life in me!"

Jenna relaxed against him. "Not every bit," she scolded, but with good humor. "You've got enough left to argue."

"Barely."

She made a sound against his chest. He felt her breath

stir the hair there, and was stunned when the stirring echoed deep inside him.

"Jenna?"

"Yes?"

"Are you feeling less embarrassed now?"

"A little."

"There was really nothing to be embarrassed about."

"There was. You're you."

"And you're you, but I'm not embarrassed."

"Men are more cavalier about things like this."

"Like having a baby? Are you kidding?"

"I was talking about having sex. You'll be able to go downstairs for breakfast tomorrow morning like nothing at all happened. It may be harder for me."

"And so it should. Something did happen. But that doesn't mean seeing each other has to be hard."

She drew in a deep, faintly shaky breath. When it left her, it stirred him again. "When you do that," he said in a low voice that held equal parts humor and warning, "I start thinking about all those things under your nightgown that I want to feel clearly but can't." He turned himself so that she could clearly feel what that thinking was doing to him. With his mouth by her ear, he said, "How long do you have to lie here?"

"A little longer."

"Can we do it again then?"

"No. We have to wait until Monday."

"But I want you again now."

"Spencer."

"I do. Can't you feel it?" he asked, knowing that she had to, since his arousal was heavy against her groin.

"We have to wait until Monday, Spencer. That way we'll be optimizing the chances of conception."

She was missing the point. She was deliberately turning a deaf ear to the fact that he found her attractive, and one part of Spencer wanted to shake her hard. The other part just wanted to make love to her again, to feel that intense pleasure again, to give her a taste of it this time.

Since neither part was going to win out—and since he did understand the importance of her lying still—he let it go. He could live until Monday, he supposed. He guessed he'd have to.

CHAPTER SIX

JENNA AWOKE ON SUNDAY morning to the lingering scent of Spencer in her bed. Burying her face in the pillow, she breathed it in. She rolled over, taking the pillow with her, and, eyes still closed, held it close as she remembered the events of the previous night.

Her insides tingled. She put her hand to her stomach and wondered whether, indeed, there was the beginnings of a baby inside. The thought brought her down to earth with a reminder of what she was supposed to be doing. Taking the thermometer from the night stand, she put it under her tongue. Five minutes later, satisfied, she returned it to its case.

The timing was right. Her ovaries were about to release an egg, and an army of sperm was waiting right there to fertilize it. The conditions were optimal. Her doctor would be pleased.

Smiling softly, she lay back, and in that instant, felt more peaceful than ever before. In the next moment, she felt a burst of energy. Pushing the sheets aside, she climbed out of bed and headed for the bathroom.

By the time she emerged, she had showered, knotted her hair back and made up her face—none of which she would normally have done on a lazy Sunday at home. But there was nothing normal about this Sunday. She had a house guest, one whom she wanted to impress with her poise, her maturity and her competence. To that end, she bypassed her usual shorts and T-shirt in favor of a more sophisticated pair of narrow white pants, a long navy blouse that she belted at the hip and navy flats.

She listened at the door for sounds of Spencer but heard nothing. He had been up late the night before—she had heard him moving around the house—and was still sleeping, she assumed. Grateful for that, she tiptoed down the stairs and into the kitchen, where, as quietly as possible, she put coffee on to brew. She had just closed the lid and was turning around, when the sudden sight of his large figure made her jump.

Gasping, she pressed a hand to her heart. "I didn't hear you."

He was standing barefooted in the doorway, wearing an old sweatshirt and sweatpants. A dark stubble covered his jaw, lessening the effect of his scar. He looked sleepy and mussed and thoroughly endearing. He also looked unabashedly masculine—so that even if she hadn't smelled him on her sheets, even if she hadn't thought of him during her shower, even if she *hadn't* been thoroughly intimate with him the night before, she would have felt his pull. It helped some that his eyes were half-lidded; if those electric blues had been open wide, she might have melted on the spot. Her cheeks were heated enough as it was.

In an attempt to buy time to calm down, she tugged open the refrigerator and peered inside. She had gone to the market on Saturday and was well stocked. "Would you like an omelet? I have some terrific Vermont cheddar to put in it. Or ham. Or onions. Or all of the above." She straightened, took a half step back and bumped into him. Her head shot around, eyes up to his. "Sorry. I didn't hear you come over." She ducked into the refrigerator. "If you'd rather have bagels and cream cheese, I have those, or you can have an omelet *and* a bagel—"

"Jenna."

She set a carton of orange juice on the counter. "Hmm?"

"Look at me, Jenna."

She darted him another quick glance before going back for the butter. "Pancakes, maybe?"

He put his hands on her shoulders and physically turned her. "Jenna, *look* at me."

That was the last thing she wanted to do. Looking at him would bring back the image of what they'd done in bed, and that image made her squirm. But she wasn't a coward. Mustering the composure that stood her well as president and chairman of the board of McCue's, she tipped up her chin and met his gaze.

"You're still embarrassed," he accused.

"A little."

"But why?"

She knew he was mystified. What was a little sex to him? He had made love to more women in his day than she had *dated* men. He was freer with his body, and more confident in it than she would ever be in hers. He wouldn't understand the discomfort she felt knowing he was Caroline's big brother, the awe she felt knowing he was a world-renowned adventurer and author. He was larger than life, and though she was successful and sophisticated within her own sphere, that sphere was narrow. His was not.

But she didn't want to go into all that. So she said, "The husband of one of my good friends is a gynecologist. Sharon can't understand why I don't use him, but there's no way I could. Some things demand detachment. If Don were my doctor, each and every time I saw him, whether it was at a cookout here, at a party somewhere else, at the movies, the post office or the supermarket, I'd know—we'd *both* know—what he'd seen and touched. I'd be mortified." She paused, then added, "Having sex with you is a little like that. You're not my lover. You're my...my...I don't know *what* to call you."

Spencer scowled. "I didn't see a hell of a lot. It was dark."

"You touched."

"And enjoyed." He gave her small shake. "So there's no cause for mortification. You should be proud, Jenna. What we did last night felt really good!"

She wanted to believe him. She wanted to believe that he wasn't just saying that to keep her spirits up. He was capable of it, she knew. She had seen the way he had buoyed Caroline when, soon after her wedding, she was convinced that her marriage was on the rocks. Ironic, given that he was against marriage for himself, but he had argued a wonderful case for patience, understanding and compromise. Caroline had listened and stuck with it. Her marriage had survived that rocky start and grown strong.

Oh, yes, Spencer could be convincing. Jenna wanted to believe every last word he said. Somehow, though, she didn't think it would be wise. A woman could become addicted to praise like that, and Spencer would soon be gone.

With that in mind, she said, "I'm really grateful for all you're doing, Spencer. I hope you know how much. My baby is going to be so wonderful, and I have you to thank."

His blue eyes scolded her for trying to change the subject. "You can thank me by relaxing when I'm around. You can also thank me by looking a little messy once in a while. You didn't have to get all spiffed up."

"I'm not all spiffed up."

He looked her over. "Silk blouse? Hair in a twist? Makeup?" He challenged her with an arched brow. "On a Sunday morning?"

She was silent in her guilt.

"I know what you're doing, Jenna. You're trying to keep this thing businesslike, but some things don't have anything to do with business, and this is one. Sure, what we're doing is unconventional. It's an arrangement, something we agreed to for a specific purpose, but that doesn't mean it has to be cold or matter-of-fact. You can't be detached when it comes to something like this. There are feelings and emotions involved." He gave her another gentle shake. "I won't have you stifling them, do you hear?"

"I can't help but hear," she said softly.

"But will you *listen?*"

"I'll try."

He stared at her for another minute before raising his hands in concession. "Okay. That sounds okay."

She hadn't expected him to let her off the hook so easily. The fact that he had, gave her a boost. "So what do you want for breakfast?"

Without a moment's thought, he reeled off, "One omelet loaded, plus a bagel, but no pancakes, and I can help make the omelet. I've been cooking for myself for years."

She wasn't surprised. Spencer was the most independent man she knew. "That may be, but you're in my house, as my guest, doing me a monumental favor. You wouldn't let me pay for dinner last night. The least I can do is to make you breakfast. Besides, if you don't let me do it, you'll never know what kind of a cook I'll be for your child."

She knew she'd made her point when he raised his hands again, this time in surrender. "Make me breakfast. I'll take a shower while you do. As soon as I eat, I have to work."

JENNA WASN'T SURE what she'd expected, but it certainly wasn't the doggedness with which Spencer sat in her office and worked on his book. She had thought he'd take breaks. She had thought he'd keep tabs on what she was doing. She had thought he would pace the floor, brooding over one passage or another. But he sat still, pencil in hand, barely moving from his chair all morning.

At first, she sat on the back patio reading the Sunday paper, expecting him to join her at any minute. She made sure that her blouse didn't bunch at the waist, that she wasn't caught reading the funnies, that her legs were gracefully arranged. When minutes became hours and she realized her efforts were wasted, she began doing the things she would normally do on a Sunday. She changed the sheets and put the old ones in the wash. She went through her closet for clothes to be dropped off at the dry cleaner the next day. She caught up on personal correspondence. She called her marketing director to discuss an upcoming advertising program.

She waited for Spencer to emerge at lunchtime. When he didn't, she brought him a large turkey sandwich and a soda. He finished both in record time, refused seconds, and left the office only long enough to use the bathroom before going back to work.

He did take time off for dinner, but not until eight o'clock that night and then only for pizza in the kitchen. Jenna was oddly disappointed. She had wanted to cook, but he argued that he was too preoccupied to appreciate the effort and that pizza would do just fine. So she called in an order and brought it home, then, while he ate, asked questions about his book. It was about a trek he had made through the rain forests of the Amazon in search of a tribe of Indians that was reportedly using medicinal plants to cure certain cancers. While the efficacy of those plants had yet to be proven, the core of Spencer's story consisted of the Indians' way of life.

"When can I read it?" Jenna asked. His enthusiasm, so rich in his tone and expression, was contagious.

"When it's published next spring."

"Not before?"

He shook his head. "No one reads it before, except my editor." He made a face. "Not that he's ever gonna like this one." He carried his plate to the sink. "I have a feeling he'll fight me all the way. He was looking for a treasure hunt. I gave him an anthropological study. He can say he doesn't like the way the story's organized, but that's just an excuse."

"What does he have against an anthropological study?"

"It's not a treasure hunt."

"But it could be fascinating."

"It *is* fascinating—" Spencer snorted "—but to convince him of that is something else." He added her plate to the dishwasher and closed the door. "Okay, I'm back to work."

"You've never done an anthropological study before," Jenna said, turning to let her voice follow him as he left the room.

"Yeah, well, it's time," he called back before he disappeared from sight.

She wanted to ask him more, but the office swallowed him up. So she brought him coffee and kept his cup refilled, then baked brownies and offered him those. By eleven, realizing that there wasn't much more she could do for him, she decided to go to bed. Going to the office door, she waited until he reached a break point and looked up. "I think I'll turn in. Should I put on a fresh pot of coffee?"

He sat back in his chair and regarded her with tired

eyes. "Nah. I've had enough to keep me up for a while. What time do you leave tomorrow?"

"Seven-fifteen. I have an appointment at eight. Will you be working here all day?"

With a despairing glance at the papers that covered the desk in clumps, he nodded. "When will you be back?"

A buzzing started in the pit of her stomach. Tomorrow night was the night. Again. "Five-thirty. Would you like to eat in or out?"

"Out. I'll be stir-crazy by then. But I don't want to bump into my parents or Caroline—" He interrupted himself to ask, "Does Caroline know I'm here?"

"I didn't tell her. I thought you would if you wanted to."

"That would have made you more uncomfortable. Has she asked you what I decided to do?"

"Yes, but I told her we were still discussing it."

"Once you're pregnant, will you tell her the truth?"

"I'm not sure," Jenna said, then added softly, "probably not. That might be easier all the way around." She went on before he could comment. "So where would you like to go to dinner?"

"Someplace where we won't bump into anyone who will want to talk for three hours. And I don't want to dress up. Any suggestions?"

"I'll think of a place," she promised, and raised a casual hand. "'Night." She slipped away from the door.

"Jenna?" She leaned back in to find his eyes suddenly less tired-looking than they had been moments earlier. They were warmer, more direct and penetrating. They sent an unmistakable message, which he followed up with "I'll look forward to it."

Keeping her poise, she simply nodded and left, but she thought about his words all the way back to her room. She thought of them later, when she lay in bed ignor-

ing the book on her lap. They were the last things she
thought about before she fell asleep and the first things
she thought about when she woke up in the morning.
When her thermometer told her that she was ovulating,
the words took on a more practical meaning. Even that,
though, she pushed from her mind when she set off for
work.

She was busy all morning, going from one meeting to
the next. When she had a break at noontime, she found
herself wondering how Spencer was doing. The telephone beckoned, but she resisted. Theirs was a business
relationship, she reminded herself, and she didn't call
business associates to see if they'd eaten lunch.

So she didn't call Spencer, but went back to work,
and for a while, she successfully immersed herself in
studying the company's latest spreadsheets. As the afternoon wore on, however, her mind began to wander,
and always in the same direction. She thought of Spencer coming to her again, of his touching her, of the heat
of his skin and the heaviness of his sex. She grew warm
inside, then trembly. She actually left the office early and
drove around for an hour to relax before going home.

Spencer was sound asleep when she arrived. After
searching the house for him, she found him on the patio,
sprawled facedown on the chaise longue. His bare feet
hung over the end. One arm was tucked under him, the
other bent to the flagstone, long fingers loosely splayed.
She debated waking him, but didn't have the heart. So
she called the restaurant—a dark, quiet place in Providence where neither of them would have been recognized—and canceled their reservations. Then she
changed into a casual sundress and, leaving a note on
the counter lest he wake up while she was gone, went to
the local market for a pound of fresh shrimp.

Spencer was still sleeping when she returned, which

pleased her tremendously. She liked the idea that he was getting the rest that he needed. She also liked the idea of making dinner, which was amusing in that she was a businesswoman, not a cook—but understandable given the maternal instincts that had taken her over in recent days. Granted, Spencer wasn't a child, but the urge to nurture was there. She looked on what she was doing as practice.

With three separate cookbooks open on the counter, she made shrimp curry, saffron rice and a cucumber salad. When Spencer slept on, she took out a fourth cookbook and whipped up a cold strawberry soup, and when she still had time to spare, she made an apple crunch for dessert. By then the sun had set, and she was wondering whether he was all right. So she went out to the darkened patio and knelt beside him. Only one eye was in sight, and it was closed. The scar running along his jaw was masked by the night and less threatening than usual. In fact, the whole of him looked less threatening than usual. He actually looked vulnerable.

Not sure whether she liked the vulnerable Spencer over the one who was in full command, she finger-combed the hair from his brow and rested a hand on his back. His skin was warm through his T-shirt, his muscles firm to the touch. "Spencer?" she called softly. "Spencer?"

He took a deep breath, then seemed to settle into sleep again.

She gave him a tiny shake. "Spencer?"

"Mmm."

She waited to see if he would rouse. Since he clearly wasn't unconscious, if he wanted to sleep longer, she couldn't deny him. Dinner would wait.

She was about to stand, when he took another deep breath, squeezed his eye shut, then opened it a crack. His gaze hit her shoulder and stayed there for as long as it took him to realize what he was looking at. Then it lifted slowly to her face.

He looked dazed. She couldn't help but smile. "I was beginning to think you'd contracted sleeping sickness in the jungle."

"Um-hum," he said, without moving his mouth.

"Were you working all day?"

"Umm."

"And last night?"

"Umm."

"Did you finish the revisions?"

"Almost." He yawned and shifted his head so that he could see her with both eyes. Pulling his free hand from the flagstone, he tucked it under his body. "What time is it?"

"Nearly nine."

He grunted. "You should have woken me sooner."

"You were tired."

"We were supposed to go to dinner."

"That's okay. We can eat here. I've been cooking—"

"After working all day?"

"I'm practicing. I'll have to cook for a baby whether I'm tired or not. Besides, I don't mind cooking. It's a change from my work. Of course, I can't guarantee the results."

"That omelet was great. You're a terrific cook."

"I'm still a novice. I haven't had much practice."

"You didn't do it when you were growing up?"

"We always had a cook."

"Why don't you now?"

"Because it'd be pretentious. And a waste of money. And unnecessary. I don't eat a whole lot."

"Clearly," he murmured. In the dark, his gaze dropped to her shoulders, then her breasts.

"I'm not too thin," she said in self-defense. "If I didn't watch what I eat, I'd get fat."

He frowned. "When you were younger, weren't you a little..."

"Fat?"

"Not fat."

"Chubby," she put in.

"Not chubby. Solid."

"That's, uh, one way to put it. Our cook was *too* good."

"Made brownies all the time, eh?" he asked.

She remembered the plate she'd brought to him the night before. When she'd left for work, there had been a few brownies left, but they were gone when she returned. Not that Spencer had to worry about his weight. He was lean but solid, which, on a man, was a wonderful thing.

"Yes, she made brownies," Jenna admitted with a sigh, "and lots of other incredibly fattening things. It wasn't until I got into college that I lost weight. By the time I got to graduate school, I was into healthy eating. I had my own apartment then, so it was easy. My tastes were simple. What cooking I did was elementary. It's not much fun cooking for one." Thinking about the pleasure she'd had earlier that night in the kitchen, she said, "It's more fun cooking for two." Then she realized that what she'd said could be taken the wrong way, so she added, "God help this baby if it doesn't like haute cuisine."

Spencer continued to lie quietly, looking at her. With the night muting the electric charge of his eyes, she felt surprisingly comfortable.

"The baby will like anything you make," he said.

"I hope so."

"You'll be a good mother."

She smiled. "I hope so."

The smile was still on her face when his hand came

from under him and went to the back of her head. It faded
when he tugged out a hairpin. "I like your hair down,"
he said in a deep voice as he pulled out a second pin.

Her pulse picked up. She wanted to tell him to stop,
but the words wouldn't come. She wanted to get up and
go back to the kitchen, but her legs wouldn't work. One
by one, he discarded hairpins until her hair spilled onto
her shoulders. He sifted through the waves, working out
small tangles, massaging the place on her scalp where
the pins had dug in.

Jenna felt suddenly warmer. "Maybe I should, uh,
check on the shrimp."

"Don't. I want you, not the shrimp."

"Me?" Her heart beat more loudly. "Now?"

He curved a hand around her neck. "Come here." A
slight pressure knocked her off balance. Taking immediate advantage of that, he pulled her forward, and though
she put out a hand to steady herself, before she could do
more, she was half under him on the cushion.

"Spencer…"

He touched her lips. "Shh." He slid his palm down her
throat to the neckline of her dress. "You look sexy."

"I didn't intend that," she said, then sucked in a breath
when he cupped her breast. "Spencer—"

"It's okay, honey, it's okay." He kneaded her right
through her sundress in a way that sent hot flashes
through her. She made a small sound when he brushed
her beaded nipple with a thumb. "That feels good, does
it?"

It felt *incredibly* good. "We can't."

"Can't what?"

She struggled to think. He had shifted to her other
breast. After delineating its shape, he opened his hand
wide and put his little finger and thumb to both nipples
at once. She was robbed of all but the smallest fragment

of breath and could only manage a faint "Can't do this here."

"Sure, we can. No one'll see. You own everything for acres around."

"But on the patio?" she cried on a pleading note, because his hand was moving down her body now, leaving fire in its wake. "It's not a bed."

He reached under her dress. "I never make love in the same place twice. Didn't I tell you that?"

"No." She nearly choked on a breath when he touched her where she was hot and wet. "Spencer!"

He grinned. All she could see of it was the gleam of his teeth, it was that dark, but she heard it clear as day in his whisper, and she knew its cause. "Oh, yes, you want me."

"I want a baby."

"Right now you want me." His hand left her to deal with his shorts. "The chemistry is right. You can't deny it."

"I didn't plan this."

"Some of the best things are unplanned." Having freed himself, he tugged at her panties. "Lift up."

She lifted. "I'm not comfortable doing this here."

"You will be when you look back on it." He tossed the panties aside and came down between her legs. Slipping his hands under her bottom, he pulled her to him. "When you have your baby, you'll think back to this and laugh."

"I'll think back and blush—Spencer!"

"There we go. Deep inside." He made a guttural sound that was halfway between a grunt and a hum. "Oh, Lord, oh, Lord, does that feel good."

"I don't believe this."

"Wrap your legs around me, honey. There, ohh, there, isn't that better?"

"On the *patio*."

"I'm not sure how slow I can go. Tell me if I hurt you, okay, sweetheart?"

Jenna didn't hear him at first. Her insides were aflame with a most intense pleasure. She held him tightly with her thighs, then with her arms when she felt she'd go up in smoke.

"You with me?" he asked in a thick rumble that was made ragged by the rhythmic movement of his hips.

Her voice was a wisp. "I shouldn't be."

"But you are. Jeez, what was that?"

"What?"

"You did something inside."

She clenched her muscles again. "This?"

He gave a tortured groan and thrust higher, and it was her turn to groan. The feeling inside her was new and intense. No man had ever excited her this way. She could barely think beyond his hardness, heat and size, and the scent she was coming to recognize as his, maybe theirs. Needing more, she strained against him. Her hands moved through the hair on his chest. She clutched his shoulders and began meeting his thrusts.

Burying his mouth against her throat, he bowed his back and quickened his pace. Wanting to feel him deeper, then deeper still, she raised her legs to his waist. Reality was beginning to slip away from her when, with a hoarse cry, Spencer climaxed.

Loving the triumphant sound of his cry and the feel of his pulsing inside her, Jenna held him tightly. Only with the ebbing of his orgasm did she become aware of an inner expectancy unfulfilled. Then, as though he'd read her mind and understood it, she felt his hand slide between their bodies to the place where they were still joined.

She whispered his name in protest.

"You won't lose anything," he whispered back. His

finger found what it was seeking and began to pluck that swollen flesh. "I'll stay inside you to stopper things up."

"No," she whispered, but reality started slipping again. She grabbed at his wrist, wanting to pull him away. Instead, the movement of his finger made her weak with wanting, so that she had to hold on tight or fall. The heat grew in her belly and spread through her body like a fog, dimming all thought of protest. Her breasts rose and fell. She arched mindlessly closer to Spencer, oblivious to the soft sounds of need that came from her throat until, with a choked cry, she exploded with a pleasure so total that the world went a brilliant, blinding white.

JENNA HAD NO IDEA how much later it was when Spencer finally lifted off her. She knew it had been a while. Her breathing was even; the dampness on her skin had dried. She wasn't sure whether she had actually dozed or whether she had simply floated in a stupor of satisfaction that was reinforced by the warmth of his body over hers. But she felt a loss the minute he moved.

"Stay put," he whispered, and groped around for her panties. After he had helped her put them on, he fixed his own pants. Then, before she had any inkling of what he planned, he scooped her into his arms.

She didn't say a word. She felt so lethargic that she wasn't sure she could have moved on her own, and besides, being held close and carried felt good. Too soon she was being set gently down on one of the kitchen chairs.

Spencer proceeded to reheat the dinner she had made and serve it. He claimed it was delicious and she supposed it was, though she was distracted. She was struggling to put the pleasure she had just felt into a context that had to do with the baby.

She hadn't bargained for pleasure. She hadn't expected

it, didn't *want* it. She didn't want to enjoy something enough to miss it when it was gone. After all, Spencer had done his job and was leaving the next day.

She knew he was aware of that, too, because what little conversation they had revolved around his manuscript, which would be ready with several more hours of work that night, and his plane, which was repaired and airworthy again. He was planning to fly to New York and drop the manuscript off, then continue south to Florida.

Because it seemed the only polite thing to do, she told him she would drive him to the airport. "It's only an hour," she pointed out when he frowned.

"I can take a cab."

"You could have taken a cab when you arrived, but you asked me to pick you up. So I can take you back." It was the least she could do, given how generous he'd been with his time.

Gruffly he said, "I thought we should talk then. There's no need for it now."

She knew that he was anxious to regain his freedom, and felt a twinge of hurt at the thought. But the hurt was good. It put a necessary wedge between them. Spencer had helped her with something she wanted, but that was where their involvement ended. The only thing left was to wind up their time together as cleanly as possible.

"I'm driving you," she said firmly.

"You have to work."

"I won't feel comfortable working until I know you're in the air."

"That eager to be rid of me, are you?"

She shot him a look of annoyance, and felt that annoyance all the way to her toes. She didn't know the answer to his question. Even aside from the sex, being with him hadn't been bad at all. It hadn't been as intimidating or anywhere near as awkward as she had thought it would be. But life had to go on, and that would mean reclaiming her office at home, stripping his bed of the sheets he had used and watching the calendar and her body for signs that what had happened in the dark of night between Spencer and her had worked.

They were in the Jaguar on their way to the airport Tuesday morning, with Jenna driving and Spencer brooding, when he asked her about that. "How soon will you know?"

She didn't equivocate. The baby was the only interest they had in each other now. "Thirteen days."

"I thought there were tests to tell you sooner."

"I don't trust them. If one said I was pregnant and it turned out I wasn't, I'd be devastated. I'd rather wait. If I'm a day late, I'll know. Then I can do the test to confirm it."

He was silent, staring out the side window. When they were within five minutes of the airport, he said, "I'll give you a call in two weeks to find out."

"I won't be here. I'll be in Hong Kong."

His head came around fast. "Hong Kong?" The silver in his blue eyes was alive, though whether from envy, curiosity or irritation she didn't know. "Why are you going to Hong Kong?"

"I'm touring the factories that make some of our things."

"Alone?"

She shook her head. "With a few of my people. We like to see things firsthand once or twice a year."

"You shouldn't be going now."

She pictured the front page of the newspaper as it had been that morning, and couldn't remember seeing Hong Kong listed among the world's current trouble spots. "Why not?"

His eyes flashed—quite definitely in irritation, she realized.

"Because you may be pregnant."

"If I am, what's happening inside me is so microscopic that going to Hong Kong won't affect it one way or another. Believe me," she said with a knowing chuckle and a protective hand on her stomach, "I would do *nothing* to endanger this child."

"I've done that trip many times. It's long and tiring. You don't call that a danger?"

"No. Neither does my doctor. Once I knew you'd help me, I asked him about it. He said that if an egg is going to be fertilized, it'll happen before I leave, and if it happens and is good, nothing about a trip like this can harm it."

"What if it isn't good? What if you have a miscarriage when you're halfway around the world?"

"A miscarriage at this stage is a period. I won't even know I was pregnant."

"What if you are, and you start getting morning sickness?"

"I won't. Morning sickness doesn't start until the fifth or sixth week at the earliest. If anything, this is the best time to go. If I'm here, I'll be looking at the calendar every day. If I'm there, I'll be distracted. The time will go faster." She took her eyes from the road long enough to see the doubt on his face. "Really, Spencer. It's not like I'm going there to party. Between the length of the flight and the fact that this trip is strictly business, I'll be getting plenty of sleep."

"*Will* you sleep on the flight?" he asked in such a way that she was momentarily shaken. She hadn't thought he would put two and two together where her emotions were concerned, but his tone was knowing enough to suggest just that.

She kept her eyes peeled for the airport turnoff. "I always sleep on airplanes. That's the only way I can make it through the flight. Actually, I've flown enough since my parents died to be over the worst of the fear. The statistics are in my favor. And Mom and Dad went down in a small, private plane, while I only fly in the largest commercial jets to be found."

"You'd love my plane," Spencer said tongue-in-cheek, and looked out the window again.

Jenna wouldn't step foot in his plane for all the tea in China, but that didn't mean she begrudged Spencer flying it. She could understand the convenience, even the pleasure. She could also understand that a person might feel more in command with his own hands at the controls, than with a stranger in charge. Personally, she wanted size and bulk around her. It might be a delusion, but she felt safer that way. She could also, with a determined stretch of the imagination, pretend she was simply sitting in a cabin-shaped transport moving along the ground from point A to point B.

Feeling a gnawing in the pit of her stomach that she was sure came from the dozens of small planes in sight, she pulled up at Hangar C, turned off the engine and launched into the speech she'd been preparing since dawn. "Thank you, Spencer. I can't begin to tell you how grateful I am for what you've done. You made the time to be here, when you had a pile of your own work to do, and I appreciate that. You were considerate and gentle. You made me feel less embarrassed than I might have. You were wonderful."

Slowly he turned to her, eyes piercing, jaw set. The look was intimidating. She wasn't sure what he was so angry about.

"I mean all that," she insisted.

"I'm sure you do."

"With any luck, I won't have to bother you again. I've already signed papers to the effect that I won't ask you for anything when it comes to this child. My lawyer has them. I'll have him send them to you by courier if that would make you feel better."

Spencer pushed the door open and climbed out. "What would make me feel better," he grumbled as he reached for his gear, "would be for you to stop thanking me as though I had just delivered a rush order of panty hose in time for your summer sale." He was leaning into the car, his eyes level with hers and narrowed. "What you and I did was fun. It was stimulating and satisfying. It was a nice diversion from my work." His voice sharpened. "And don't bother with a courier. I know where the papers are. When I need them, I'll get them." He straightened and slammed the door. Then he swung his duffel over his shoulder and walked off.

Jenna's eyes grew glassy. She blinked once, then again. She took a deep, shaky breath and let it out with a sigh, but she didn't move. She sat in the car until she saw Spencer come out of the hangar and approach one of the planes. It looked old and more battered than the rest. But his step didn't falter. He opened the door and threw his gear ahead of him before he climbed in. She saw him moving around the cockpit, then settling in behind the controls. After what seemed an eternity, the propellers started turning slowly, then faster. When they were little more than a round blur, the plane turned and headed away from the terminal. It advanced to the runway and paused. After a bit, it started forward again, gaining speed this time until, with a small bounce that made her gasp, it left the ground. She watched it gain altitude, watched it put distance between itself and her, watched until it was nothing but a speck in the sky.

Only then, with a vow to look nowhere but forward, did she start the car and head for work.

CHAPTER SEVEN

IN FACT, JENNA HAD GRILLED her doctor long and hard about the wisdom of going to Hong Kong. The trip had been planned six months earlier, when she hadn't known she'd be trying to make a baby. Knowing it now, she had been as skeptical as Spencer. But the doctor was right. If she was going to conceive that month, she would have conceived before takeoff. She would be flying first class, staying in a luxury hotel, eating in fine restaurants, taking taxis wherever she went. Anything that might happen under those conditions could just as easily happen at home, and for her peace of mind alone, she was better off busy than idle.

So, one week after Spencer flew south, she flew west, then west again, and to some extent she succeeded in not dwelling on whether there was a baby or not. From breakfast through dinner each day, she followed a comfortably busy schedule. Before breakfast, she prepared herself for those meetings; after dinner, she analyzed them. She only thought about the baby at night, when she was in bed awaiting sleep, and for the most part she was hopeful. During those times of doubt when she wished she had stayed home, where things were less eventful, she thought of the millions of unplanned pregnancies each year, of the women who went about their lives without realizing anything was amiss, who did things that were active, rigorous, even dangerous without losing their babies, and she was encouraged. Yes, she was active, but no more so than usual, and she didn't do anything that could even remotely be considered rigorous or dangerous.

Every morning, she took her temperature. From a low at the time of ovulation, it had risen to normal and was hovering there, which meant either that she would be getting her period or missing it.

She got it. Seven days into the trip, with three days to go before she flew home, she woke in the morning with proof that there wouldn't be a baby in April. The first thing she did was to burst into tears, but they didn't last long. She was too levelheaded to wallow in self-pity. After all, she and Spencer had only made love twice. Some couples tried for years before they succeeded. Hadn't her own doctor said it might take time? Hadn't he said she shouldn't be discouraged if she didn't immediately conceive?

They would try again. It was as simple as that.

Assuming Spencer was willing.

That thought haunted her through the final days of her trip. She found herself thinking about it not only at night, but when she was with other people, at meals and meetings. Spencer had been annoyed with her when he'd left. She assumed he had been feeling antsy after being stuck at her house for three full days. Granted he'd had to work on his book and probably would have been restless wherever he was, but he was at *her* house with *her*, so she took his restlessness personally.

He said he liked the sex. She wasn't sure she believed him, though she desperately wanted to. Sure, he climaxed, but for all she knew he was thinking of another woman when he did. It would be just like him to try to make her feel good. On the other hand, he had snapped when she'd mentioned the papers she'd signed, which told her that regardless of who was in his mind at the time, he liked the sex part more than the baby part.

Had the sex been good enough to bring him back for another round? It had been for her, good enough—terrific enough—for her to feel more than a shimmer of excitement at the thought of being with him again, but what did *she* know. Spencer was the most skilled man she'd ever been with. She seriously doubted the reverse was true, and if that was so, he had possibly moved on to another woman already.

She wanted him back. She wanted that baby. He was the only one who would do.

By the time she returned to Little Compton, she was dead tired. Ironically, that wouldn't have been so if she'd been pregnant. But between worrying about Spencer's reaction when she gave him the news, wondering about his willingness to try again and coping with her period, which took a toll on her strength in the best of times, she was washed out. Without bothering to phone either the office or her answering service, she went straight to bed. That was at five in the afternoon. By the time she got out of bed at nine the next morning, feeling far, far better than when she'd crawled in, she knew she owed Spencer an immediate call.

He wasn't home. Her answering service told her that he had tried her the day before. Her secretary at the office said the same thing. She tried him again, every hour on the hour, and with each unanswered call, she conjured up more disturbing reasons for his absence. All involved women.

Finally, at three that afternoon, he picked up the phone. Even before she spoke, he sounded hassled. "Yeah?"

"Spencer?"

There was a pause, then a tentative, "Is that you, Jenna?"

"Uh-huh."

"For *God's* sake, where have you been?" he thundered. "I thought you were due back yesterday. Did you decide you wanted an extra day in San Francisco, when you knew I was waiting to hear from you? That was a damned inconsiderate thing to do. There are phones in San Francisco. You could have called me from there." With barely a breath, he asked, "So are you, or aren't you?"

"I'm not," she said immediately. Clearly he was impatient to know if she was pregnant, though she didn't know whether he wanted her to be or not.

"You got your period?" His tone was calmer, but it gave nothing away.

"Right on time."

He was still for a minute. "Were you disappointed?"

"Very!" She thought that would be obvious. "I wanted the baby. And I didn't want to have to ask you to come up here again. I felt badly enough doing it the first time."

Cavalierly he said, "It wasn't any problem. I got the work done on my book, and I got my book to New York."

She wrapped the telephone cord around her hand. "Well, I'm glad of that, at least." She didn't know what else to say.

"Are you feeling okay?"

"A little jet-lagged, but one more night will fix that. Spencer, I didn't hang around San Francisco for an extra day. I had a two-hour layover at the airport and was on the first plane back here. By the time I got home, I was so tired I couldn't keep my head up."

"See? You shouldn't have gone in the first place. It was an exhausting trip."

"I felt great until I got my period," she said, but she

didn't see the point of elaborating, so she turned the tables. "Besides, I've been trying to call you all day. If you were so anxious to hear from me, you should have stuck around."

He suddenly sounded tired himself. "I've been with my lawyers all day. The court is still holding us up on these exploration rights, and time's running out. We've been trying to negotiate a compromise settlement with the other party, but so far it's a no-go."

"He won't give in at all?"

"Oh, he'll give in, but not as much as I need him to, to make it worth my time and effort to do the salvaging."

"What happens now?"

He sighed. "We wait for the court to reach a decision."

"How much time do you have?"

"Before hurricane season sets in? A few weeks. Even if the court was to hand down its decision tomorrow, we wouldn't have much time. I guess I'll be waiting until November to begin."

"What will you do in the meantime?" she asked. She was thinking that if he had time on his hands, he wouldn't mind making another trip north.

"I'll do research. Maybe fly down to the Yucatán and see what's happening there, or visit friends in Michigan. I don't know. It's frustrating."

Since she didn't think she'd have a better opening, she took a breath and forged ahead. "Would you—do you think you'd be willing to come up here again?"

"You mean, to try for the baby? Sure. I told you I'd help you."

So easy! She felt a weight lift from her heart. "Ahh. I was worried you'd had enough the first time."

"I made a commitment. I'll see it through—not that I've had a change of heart about wanting a kid of mine running around, but if there has to be one, I'd rather have it be yours than someone else's."

Jenna felt a thickening in her throat. It was a minute before she was able to produce sound, and then it was a soft "Thank you. Thank you, Spencer. You'll never be sorry, I promise you that. This baby will be the most special, special child in the world."

"That could be good or bad. For the time being, why don't we concentrate on getting it conceived. When should I fly up?"

"Uh, ten days, I think."

"You *think?*" He clucked his tongue and said in a teasing tone, "You're slipping, Jenna. Usually you know exactly when, why and for how long."

She felt instantly sheepish. "I know, but I haven't been thinking beyond getting you to agree to try again. If you want to hold on, I'll get my calendar."

"No need to do that now. I'll call you in a few days."

"But you'll want to make plans."

"Yeah, so I don't have a conflict with all the high action that's taking place here."

He was being facetious, of course. She could hear that, along with a note of disgust in his voice, and it occurred to her that a diversionary trip back to Rhode Island might be just what he needed to relieve the tedium of waiting for the court's decision on the salvage rights to his galleon.

"By the way," he said, "how was Hong Kong?"

"It was great, really. Our meetings went well, and the tours were interesting. We visited several factories that we're not using now but may be able to use next year. Our lawyers will start negotiating come fall."

"Will you have go back there then?"

"No. I'll make another visit in the spring."

"What if you're pregnant by then?"

"I won't go."

"Are you sorry you did this time?"

She had been half expecting the question. He had been against the trip from the start, had said it would be too tiring, and he had reminded her of that moments earlier. She didn't think she heard an I-told-you-so now, still she said with conviction, "If you're asking whether I feel that the trip had something to do with my not being pregnant, the answer is no. I got my period right on time, and it's been no heavier than usual. It's not a spontaneous abortion, just a period. I wasn't pregnant, that's all. Maybe if we'd done this in the doctor's office—"

"That wouldn't have worked."

"How do you know?"

"I just know," he said lightly. "Listen, don't worry about it. It'll happen this time. I'll call you soon to find out the date. Take care, Jenna."

THE LIGHTNESS IN Spencer's voice hadn't been for show. He was legitimately pleased to be seeing Jenna again. The timing was right; he had nothing better to do. She was easy to be with, and the sex had been great. The only thing that bugged him was when she started talking about signing papers. Hell, he trusted her. He didn't for a minute believe that she would turn around and sue him for child support, and even if she did, it wouldn't be the end of the world. He had plenty of money. He could easily establish a trust fund for the kid. In fact, he'd probably do it, anyway. Then he wouldn't feel guilty leading his own carefree life.

Great sex. He still couldn't believe it. Sure, he found Jenna attractive, but he found lots of women attractive. That didn't mean that when he took them to bed the world tipped and spun. It sure had with Jenna. He didn't know why, since some of those other women were more lush and sexy and *skilled* than her, but he wasn't analyzing it too deeply. All that mattered was that they were good in bed together.

Or good on the patio together.

Or good...where? He wondered where they'd do it next. He liked variety. It added spice. Jenna found it shocking, but that was part of the fun he had with her. She came to sex expecting nothing. Each bit of pleasure she felt stunned her. She was nearly as naive as a virgin, but there was a definite fire inside. His challenge was to draw it out.

That thought was foremost in his mind over the next few days. He wanted Jenna to loosen up with him, but he doubted she'd do that at home. Her life was too well structured, her mind too tied into the idea of getting pregnant. He wanted her to forget that, which meant, for starters, changing the scenery. Yeah, he liked that idea. When he let his imagination go, he could picture all sorts of super things happening.

He was thinking of some of those things when he called her later that week. Feeling buoyant, slightly aroused and very masculine, he said, "Hi, angel. How're you doin'?"

Jenna hesitated. "Spencer?"

"Who else would be calling you 'angel'?"

"I didn't think *you* would. Are you—is everything all right?"

"Everything's fine. Still holding even, no word from the courts, but I'm doing okay. Did you figure out when you'll be needing me next?" He conjured an image of a stallion being brought to stud, and stood a little straighter.

"Uh-huh. I'll be ovulating again on August 5. That's a Monday. So I guess the Saturday before would be good, just like before."

"That's fine. How about meeting me in Washington?"

"Washington?"

"D.C. I have research to do at the Smithsonian." Research that could actually wait for another time, but would serve the same purpose as the work on his manuscript had. It gave them an out if being together got to be a drag. "You'd have time to shop or museum-hop or do whatever you want."

"There isn't much shopping I'd do."

"You can check out the competition, then. Can you take Monday and Tuesday off from work?"

"I can," she said hesitantly.

"Then do it. We'll have fun."

He heard her sigh. "Spencer, I don't know—"

"Want me to fly there and pick you up?"

"Oh, no," she said quickly, "that won't be necessary."

He chuckled. "You do know that you're safer flying with me than with a commercial pilot, don't you?"

She harrumphed. "That's what every private pilot says."

"Well, it's true—assuming the private pilot is worth his salt. The guy who flew your parents that day wasn't. He didn't check out the plane the way he was supposed to, and if he had, he would have found that leak. If he hadn't died himself, the FAA would have brought him up on charges. But not me. I check everything out, and I do it carefully. Believe me. I love myself too much to risk my life."

"Then I guess I can be confident you'll make it to Washington safely. As for me, there's a nice DC-9 flying there from Providence three times a day. I'll book two rooms at the Capital Hilton."

"No, you won't. I'm not staying in anything big and impersonal." Nor did he want two rooms. "Let me make the reservations. I'll call you next week to tell you where."

"I'm paying."

"You're not paying."

"Having a baby was my idea."

"Going to Washington was my idea."

"But the baby is the point of the trip."

"No, it's not. Super sex is."

"We're not going there for super sex."

"I sure am."

"Spencer." She fell silent. He could picture her blushing and felt an unexpected swell of affection for her.

"Jenna," he said gently, "don't worry about it, okay? You'll get your baby, and I'll get my super sex, and we'll both be happy as pigs in—"

"Spencer!"

"Sorry. But it's true. Talk with you next week, angel. Ciao."

SPENCER FLEW INTO Washington's National Airport at noon on Saturday, the third of August. After securing his plane in the private hangar, he went to the commercial terminal to wait for Jenna's arrival at one. When the big plane rolled up, he felt a pleasant sense of expectation. He found himself breaking into a grin when Jenna finally came through the door.

She looked pretty. Her dark hair was in a bun, but he could excuse that because of the heat. The rest of her—in a pair of linen walking shorts the color of apricots, a matching cotton blouse and flats—was so easy on the eye in a chic kind of way that he felt pride when she walked up to him and not someone else. But that wasn't what made him grin. What made him grin was her expression.

"You look," he said, taking the carryon from her

shoulder, "like you can't decide whether to be relieved to be on the ground or terrified that you're here. Which is it?"

With a resigned twist of her lips, she said, "A little of both. My better judgment tells me we should be doing this back home."

"If we listened to your better judgment—" he put a light hand at her waist and started steering her through the crowd "—we'd have done it in the doctor's office, and just think of what we'd have missed."

She kept her eyes on where they were going.

He lowered his mouth to her ear. "No comment?"

"No comment."

Peering down into her face, he saw that she was blushing. He liked it when she did that. Blushing was a soft, feminine thing to do.

More important, though, she wasn't angry. And a "no comment" meant that she didn't disagree with him, which was an indirect acknowledgment of the pleasure she'd felt, which was a step in the right direction. By the time they were done making this baby of hers, he was determined to have her aware of the true joys of life.

He would go slow, however. That was half the fun. They had the weekend, plus Monday and part of Tuesday ahead of them. With a little luck, he might even convince her to stay longer, but he'd have to play that part by ear. He'd have to see if *he* wanted it. For all he knew, he'd be sick of her in two days, in which case he'd be the first one out of there on Tuesday morning.

But Tuesday morning was Tuesday morning. This was Saturday, and he had things planned. Jenna was still nervous about being with him—nowhere near as much as the previous month, but still nervous. So he intended to keep her busy. Well aside from his research, which he would tackle on Monday, there were things he wanted to do around the city. She could do them right along with him.

First, though, there was the hotel and a preliminary hurdle to be cleared. He had made reservations at Loweth Park, which was small and elegant and just right for a romantic interlude. Jenna must have sensed something of that when they entered the lobby, because she was crowding his elbow when the clerk passed over the reservation slip.

"Two rooms?" she whispered so that only Spencer could hear.

Concentrating on the paper before him, he whispered back, "A suite."

"Not a suite. Two separate rooms."

"The suite has two rooms." He took his wallet from his pants.

"Two bedrooms?"

"Waste of money."

"Spencer."

"I'll take the couch." With a smile for the clerk, he flattened a charge card on the paper and passed both across the counter. In full voice, he asked, "This room has a king-size bed?" He managed not to laugh when Jenna made a small sound of dismay beside him.

"That's right, sir. Just as you requested."

Jenna left his side. When he had finished checking in, he found her sitting in one of the large wing chairs, looking regal in a vulnerable way. He cocked a brow in the direction the bellboy was taking their bags. Slowly she rose from the chair and rejoined him.

"This isn't right," she said quietly.

He took her arm and spoke softly as they walked toward the elevator. "Sure, it is. Given what we're here for, it didn't make sense to take separate rooms—or to take a two-bedroom suite. The bed is big enough so we can have our own sides, and I really will take the sofa, if you want." Not that he expected it would come to that. Her problem was that she thought too much. When she wasn't thinking—like the last time, on her patio, after she'd had such a sweet climax—she was pliant. If they had been in a bed then, he would have stayed the night, and she wouldn't have fought him on it.

So he had to drive her out of her mind with pleasure. That was all.

CHAPTER EIGHT

THE ROOM WAS BEAUTIFUL. It was colonial in style, lushly done in rich burgundies and greens. The bed was king-size, indeed, and covered in velvet, as were a chair and love seat in the bedroom and more chairs and a sofa in the sitting room.

Though Jenna didn't comment on the decor, Spencer watched her run a hand along the velvet, linger before the oil paintings, carefully set her makeup case on the marble dressing table. She was used to fine things, he knew; still, she appreciated them. He liked that. He also liked the way wisps of her hair had come free of its knot, and he didn't want her tucking them back in. So, telling her that they had lots to do, he quickly ushered her from the suite.

They spent the rest of the afternoon walking. Spencer hadn't planned it that way; he had thought Jenna would tire long before he did, but she kept pace with him, and contentedly so. Neither of them were strangers to the city, so it wasn't a matter of sightseeing as much as catching the spirit of those around them who were visiting the city for the first time. They held hands as they walked, talked when the mood struck, smiled often. The day was sunny and warm enough to force regular stops for cold drinks, and that was fun, too. They hit all the tourist spots—the monuments and memorials, the Mall, Capitol Hill—and some out-of-the-way places that they both knew. Late in the afternoon, on impulse, they ducked into a theater to catch a movie neither of them had seen. By the time it was over, they were famished, so they stopped for dinner—all the way from appetizer to dessert—then were so stuffed that they had to walk more. It was after eleven when they finally returned to the hotel.

Spencer was all too aware of what they'd be doing once they reached their suite. He had spent the afternoon trying not to think about it and had succeeded simply because conversation with Jenna had been engrossing and diverting. But the movie had been a sexy one, and Jenna had looked so sweet sitting across from him in the restaurant that he waged a losing battle. Increasingly his mind had fast-forwarded. During those times, his hunger must have shown, because Jenna's cheeks had pinkened and her eyes grown evasive. She held his hand, though, during the walk back to the hotel and didn't let go when they passed through the lobby.

Once in the elevator, he tightened his grip. "You're not gonna get nervous on me, are you?"

She didn't pretend not to know what he meant. "Of course I am. I wouldn't be me if I didn't."

"I won't let you get away with it," he warned, and the instant they entered the suite, without switching on a light, he backed her to the door, caged her there with his body and took her face in his hands. "I'm kissing you this time."

She shook her head. "Don't."

He traced the corner of her mouth with his thumb. "Can you give me a good reason not to?"

She nodded. "We're not lovers."

"We sure as hell are." His thumb brushed her cheek.

"Not in the real sense. What we're doing is purely functional."

He shook his head and gave her more of his weight. "It

ceased to be purely functional way back on your patio. Maybe even before that, but you won't admit it."

"I can't."

He slid the back of his finger along her jaw, which was soft and smooth and delicate. "Why not?"

"Because it ends with the conception of this baby."

It occurred to Spencer just then that it didn't have to, that they could remain lovers longer if they wanted. Then he thought of the complications, the *far-reaching* complications, but they couldn't possibly be sorted out when he had sex on his mind. So, rather than argue, he cupped her chin in his hand and held her still for his kiss.

She caught her breath at the first touch—that tiny sound of surprised pleasure she often made, which he loved—and flattened a hand on his chest, but she didn't push him away. Giving her time, he drew back, but only for the space of a breath. He had felt the same surprised pleasure she had and wanted more. He touched her lips again, stroking them lightly, gentling her.

At first, aside from the quickening of her breathing, she was still. She didn't move her mouth, didn't move her body. He imagined she wanted to stop him but couldn't work her way through the pleasure she felt to do it. So he kept the pleasure going—it was easy enough to do, his heat was rising—made his kisses progressively deep and long. He slid both hands into her hair and tipped her face higher. He teased her tongue with his, then withdrew and dragged his mouth over her cheeks to her eyes, which he kissed closed. The brush of her lashes teased him, so whisper light against his skin that he began to shake with a greater need. Her lips were open when he returned to them, and with his hungry reclaiming, he felt her first, tentative response.

That response, so new and shy and sweet, brought him to near-full arousal. "Ahh, angel," he moaned against her hair, and lifted her into his arms. He carried her into the bedroom and pulled back the spread, then set her on the sheets.

She sat right up. "I...the bathroom."

"No," he whispered. Bracing himself on a knee, he caught her mouth and held it in a suctioning grip while he started unbuttoning his shirt.

"I want," she managed breathlessly, "my nightgown."

Tossing the shirt aside, he buried his face against her neck. "No, angel. I want to feel you."

But she slid out from under him, and was halfway across the room before he could reach her. Telling himself that there would be other times when she would be naked for him, he got rid of the rest of his clothes. He was waiting at the door to sweep her up again, nightgown and all, when she left the bathroom.

"So macho," she whispered.

But her arms were around his neck, and if she minded his gesture, she didn't let on. Nor did she object when his mouth covered hers before she hit the sheets, or when he made an immediate place for himself between her legs, or when he filled that part of that space with his hand and brought her to a heated climax. Her insides were still pulsing when he entered her, and if the white nightgown was any obstacle to pleasure, Spencer would have been hard put to say it, because, in exchange for leaving the garment on, she began moving her hands on his body. She had never participated quite that way before. Her touch was light and shy, with such devastating effect that his own climax came nearly as quickly and every bit as powerfully as hers had.

Then she slept in his arms as though it was the most natural thing in the world to do, as though there had never been talk of separate bedrooms or separate sides of a king-size bed or, heaven help them, his using the sofa.

True, when she awoke to daylight the next morning, she slid away, but he understood that. Relatively speaking, she had come a long way. If he was patient, she would come another long way yet. And he could be patient. For a treasure, he had all the patience in the world.

JENNA KNEW SHE was falling in love with Spencer. The knowledge hit her hard on Sunday morning when, after a late brunch in bed, he rented a car and drove them to visit friends of his in Virginia. Sitting in the passenger's seat for a two-hour blend of easy conversation and companionable silence, she had time to reflect on the previous day. She'd had a wonderful time with him—she couldn't deny it—and that included what they'd done in bed. Yes, what they'd done in bed. As a lover, Spencer was masterful. He had her wanting him the way she had never wanted another man, and it kept getting better and better. The wanting was with her even now. No matter that they were in bucket seats, separated by a storage bin and the gearshift, she felt his presence as though they were still in bed, nestled against each other, sleeping—or pretending to. *He* had been sleeping; she had heard the evenness of his heartbeat by her ear; but she had found something so pleasurable in lying with him that she hadn't wanted to miss it by sleeping for long.

Vividly she remembered the softness of his chest hair against her cheek, his clean scent, the firmness of his torso against hers, the length of the arm that circled her and held her in place. She remembered the way her leg had curved naturally over his, and the way he had slept with his face buried in her hair.

Oh, yes, she was falling in love. Try as she might to find things to hate about Spencer, she couldn't. She supposed she could take that as a tribute to her own judgment, that the man she had chosen to father her child was as close to perfect as a man could be. But it didn't bode well for her future, in which Spencer had no role at all.

So what was she to do? Was she to go back to pushing him away and trying to keep their lovemaking as uninvolved as possible? That made sense. At least if she could keep reminding herself of the reason they were together, she had a chance of keeping her feelings for him within bounds. The problem was that when she was with him, when they were doing things together, she had trouble thinking straight.

It was a good thing she didn't have to remember to use birth control, she mused. She'd be pregnant for sure then.

"What is it?" he asked, darting her short, repeated glances.

"What?"

"You chuckled."

She hadn't realized it. Blushing but unable to help it, she said, "It was nothing. A Murphy's Law kind of thing."

He reached over and took her hand. She liked it when he did that. His hand was large and strong, and made her feel protected. This time he anchored it to his thigh—clad in jeans today—and held it until they turned in at his friends' farm.

Jenna liked his friends. Spencer had gone to school years earlier with the female half of the couple, and he and the male half had subsequently become friends. The couple raised horses. Jenna, who had always wished Rhode Island were lush enough for that, loved seeing the stables, the paddock, the pastures. Though she had never ridden a horse previously, she was eager to try—then proud when she held her own on the albeit gentle mount they gave her. Spencer stayed by her side for all but the brief periods of time when he gave his own horse free rein. She didn't begrudge him those times. He needed the freedom himself, and besides, he was a heart-stopping sight on a horse.

It was dark before they left Virginia. Having slept only intermittently the previous night, Jenna managed to stay awake during the drive back, but she was in bed and sound asleep by the time Spencer returned after disposing of the car. She woke up several times during the night to an awareness of the warmth of his body beside her and, selfishly, didn't fight its pull. He would be gone soon enough, she knew, but before he left, she wanted the closeness he was so willing to offer. Somehow that didn't seem wrong.

So she curled against him in defiance of the fact that he was Caroline's brother, that he was a world-renowned adventurer and author, that he would be back to his own life before long. If nothing else, she reasoned, he would know that his baby's mother was a woman worthy of warmth and affection.

SPENCER WAS IN PAIN. The last thing he wanted to do was to climb out of bed on Monday morning, and it didn't have to do with the soreness of his thighs, but rather what lay hard and heavy between them. Morning desire had always been a problem for him, but waking up to a snuggling Jenna made the problem ten times worse. He shifted her in his arms and rubbed his lips against her forehead, then lay for a while wondering how much more he dared do. She wasn't a daylight lover. He would make her one yet, but he couldn't rush her. She was still thinking of the baby, and had her mind set on the night.

The night. *That* night. He wasn't sure if he could wait. Closing his eyes, he took a tortured breath.

"Spencer?" came a whisper from his chest.

"Umm?" He was afraid to say much, lest she move away.

"Are you okay?"

"Just fine."

"You sound uncomfortable." Before he could explain that the discomfort was a sweet agony, she rolled out of his arms and sat up on her side of the bed. Her hair was a tangle around her head. She pushed it back with a hand, sat that way for a minute, then freed herself of the sheet and swung her legs to the floor.

In her innocent white gown, with her slenderness apparent and her hair a dark, seductive cloud, she looked as exotic as the most delicate of South Seas beauties. Spencer would have given his right arm to lunge for her and drag her back to bed.

In a moment of pique that was directed as much at his own damnable self-control as at her, he said, "I wasn't just uncomfortable. I was—am—in excruciating pain."

She looked back at him in alarm, but the alarm faded when she caught sight of the shape of the sheet. "Oh," she said, and blushed.

He laughed in spite of himself and rolled away. "I would suggest," he called over a shoulder, "that we get dressed and out of here fast. Anything else, and I can't promise I'll behave." The next thing he heard was the soft click of the bathroom door.

Fifteen minutes later, she emerged fully dressed and ready to let him take his turn, and that, too, was torture. The bathroom was filled with the lingering warmth from her shower and the scent of her body lotion. He had to run the water at its coldest and stand under it for a bone-numbing ten minutes before he was finally under control.

They ate breakfast in the hotel dining room. Then Spencer set out for the Smithsonian. He asked Jenna if she wanted to come, but she was intent on museum-hopping, and it was just as well. He needed a break. She was a temptation to look at. He prayed that out of sight would be out of mind.

For the most part, it was. He spent the day poring through ancient records of vessels that had sailed at the time of his Spanish galleon. He traced their routes on yellowed maps and made notes of their cargo, as recorded in crude journals that demanded his close attention. There was referencing and cross-referencing to be done, papers of earlier researchers to study, and he found it all as intriguing as he'd known it would be. Then the mustiness of the air got to him. His mind slowed and started to wander. He felt not so much bored as drained of energy.

The office he was using was in the basement of one of the lesser buildings of the Smithsonian, and wasn't far from where the records he needed were stored. He had given Jenna the number of the room and told her that he would be there at least until six, and that if she finished early and wanted to join him, she could. By midafternoon, he was listening for her footsteps in the hall.

Shortly before six, he heard them. When she knocked on the door and poked her head in, he felt a return of the energy he had been lacking. He also felt a return of the desire, which, in his enervated state, hit him all the harder. Hoping action would diffuse it, he rose from the desk and quickly gathered together the books he'd been using.

"I'll wait if you want to work more," Jenna said, but he simply handed her a book to carry.

"I've had enough." He pushed his notes into a pile and put them in his briefcase. "If I were superstitious, I wouldn't be touching these records. The court still has to rule in my favor." He put the books on top of his briefcase and lifted the lot. "Let's get these returned." He shut off the light, locked the door and started down the hall. "How was your day?"

"Fun."

"Which museums did you hit?"

"The Portrait Gallery and the Hirschorn. I had lunch on the terrace at the Botanic Garden."

"You went to the Botanic Garden without me?" The Botanic Garden was his favorite. Being there was the next best thing to being on a tropical island.

She smiled him an apology. "Sorry. But I couldn't resist. I love that place."

"You should've saved it. You should've gone shopping, instead. That's what most women would have done." His words were gruff, offered in jest, but they made him think. Jenna wasn't like other women. He was just coming to realize that. She didn't follow a crowd, didn't cling to tradition for its own sake, didn't run from new experiences. She had walked all over Washington with him, had ducked into a movie theater on the spur of the moment, had bravely climbed up on that horse. She had decided that she wanted a baby, so she'd set out to get one. He respected that.

Now she sent him a chiding look, but it was no harsher than his tone had been, and he was struck once again by how pretty—no, how beautiful she was with her dark hair and her pale skin, how sweet and innocent, how sexy.

"Here we go," he said in a thick voice, and separated a key from the others. After using it, he shouldered open a door that took them out of the dimly lit hall and into a pitch-black storage room. He hit a switch with his elbow to give them light, dropped his briefcase on a table by the door, took his books and Jenna's and returned them to the shelves from which he'd removed them several hours earlier.

Jenna was leaning against the table by his briefcase. Her eyes smiled when he emerged from the stacks, and he felt a little flip-flop inside. From nowhere came a naughty thought. Actually it wasn't from nowhere; he'd been thinking naughty thoughts all his life. This one, though, he immediately pushed from mind. Jenna wasn't the type.

Then he remembered what he'd been thinking about her, that she wasn't any "type," and the naughty thought returned.

Pushing at the light switch, he plunged them into darkness, but it was Jenna he reached for, not the door. "I missed you today," he said, and brought her close. "Did you miss me, too?" His head was already descending, and before she could answer, he covered her mouth with his.

It was supposed to be a mischievous kiss, stolen in the black belly of the Smithsonian, but within seconds, it erupted with the hunger he had been feeling so strongly that morning. She tasted faintly of coffee and smelled of rare flowers, both of which pleased him, but it was the stealth of her arms winding around his neck that pleased him most of all.

He kissed her deeply, using his tongue to its utmost, but that wasn't enough. He caressed her back, brought his hands forward and caressed her breasts, but that wasn't enough, either. So he bent his head to her neck and planted wet kisses down that slender column to where the slim strap of her sundress lay on her shoulder.

Her arms were coiled around his neck. Taking encouragement from that, he reached behind her and unzipped her dress.

"Spence?" she whispered breathlessly.

He unhooked her bra and reached for her hands. "If I don't feel you, I'll die." Pulling her hands down, he drew the dress and bra from her breasts.

"Here?" she cried, then cried again when he took her warm flesh in his palms.

"Oh, yeah, here." He felt her swell and wished he could see her. Since he couldn't, he lowered his head.

"Someone could walk in—" She caught her breath sharply when he opened his mouth on her breast. She said his name again, pleadingly this time, and while he was waiting for her to push him away, she surprised him by fastening her fingers in his hair.

He drew her into his mouth, nipped her softly with his teeth, used his tongue to make her wet. His thumb rolled over that wetness while he moved to the other breast, and when it was as wet, he left both hands on her and rose to her mouth. For the first time, her kiss was as open, as deep, as hungry as his was.

Needing her more badly than he'd have imagined possible, he dragged his mouth away. "Help me," he whispered, and pulled up her dress.

"Are you sure we can do this?" she whispered back, but her hands helped his.

"The only thing I'm sure of," he said as he opened his pants, "is that we can't *not* do it."

She clutched his bare hips. "What if someone comes along?"

"I'll take that risk." He splayed his hands over her bottom and lifted her onto the table. When he felt her legs circle him, he captured her mouth and thrust into her.

He would never get over how tight she was, or how delicate, or how sweet smelling, or how right. She was made for him. Their fit was ideal. Again and again, he buried himself in her, only to withdraw for the sake of stroking the warm, wet walls that hugged him. He was thinking that nothing could be better when she started to come apart in his arms. Her first small cry sent him into a shattering orgasm.

Afterward, she was the first to speak. "My God, I don't believe this." There was, indeed, disbelief in her voice, but delight as well.

He was still breathing heavily. "The room?"

"Room, table, building—" She paused and in a smaller voice said, "That was the first time I've ever climaxed during intercourse."

He suspected she wouldn't have confessed in the light, and he knew the feeling. In a voice that wasn't so much small as humble and the tiniest bit awed, he said, "Do you know how rare it is for two people to come at the same time?"

She drew her head away from his shoulder. "Is it?"

"Yes. It's only happened to me once before in my life."

"I don't believe you."

"So help me God, it's true."

"But you're so *experienced.*"

"Yeah, well, not in the kind of thing we just shared." And that included the one other time he had climaxed at the same time as his lover. That time had been purely accidental. This time there had been deep emotions involved.

He stroked her legs all the way around to her ankles, then reluctantly eased them from his hips. "I guess we blew the missionary position, huh?"

"Guess so," she murmured. He could tell by the small, slithering sounds that she was putting on her bra.

"Are you gonna hate me in the morning for this?"

"Of course not."

He pulled up his pants. "Do we get to do it again tonight?"

"I don't know. We shouldn't."

"Because I won't be at full potency? Somehow I don't

think that's an issue here, and it's got nothing to do with ego." He zipped up. "You have a powerful effect on me, Jenna."

The sounds that had been telling him she was putting her dress back in place suddenly stopped. Hesitantly she asked, "Is that really true?"

"Can't you tell?"

"Words are words. A person can say what he or she thinks the other wants to hear. It's done a lot."

Annoyed that her earlier experience with men had been so deflating, he snapped, "Not by me." He gentled his tone. "And besides, it isn't only the words. It's the action that goes with them. Do you think I could make love to you the way I do if my attraction to you wasn't potent? And with nearly no foreplay!"

Jenna was quiet.

"Well?" he prodded.

"Okay."

"Okay, we can do it again tonight?"

"Okay, you're attracted to me."

He sighed. "Such enthusiasm."

She went back to dressing. "I'm pleased."

"Such *enthusiasm*."

It was her turn to sigh. "Enthusiasm can be a dangerous thing. We're leaving tomorrow."

"We don't have to," he said because it seemed like the time. "I'm pretty free right about now."

"I'm not. I have McCue's."

"And you're the boss." He ran his hands up her arms to her shoulders. "You're not punching a time clock." He reached behind to raise her zipper. "You can take another day off if you want." He barely had to move to put his mouth to her temple. "Do it, angel. Spend another day with me."

"Oh, Spencer," she whispered, and slipped her arms around his waist.

Once upon a time, Spencer would have heard that whisper and felt those arms, and turned and run in the opposite direction as fast and as far as he could. No woman had ever tied him down. He had never allowed or wanted one to. And he wasn't sure he did now. All he knew was that the sound of his name, whispered so sweetly by Jenna, made his heart swell, while the feel of her arms warmed something he hadn't realized was cold, until now.

What he felt was confusing. He and Jenna didn't have a future. Not in the long run. He had his travels; she had McCue's. And then there was the matter of the baby. She was vehement in her determination to raise it alone, and that was fine, because he didn't want to change diapers.

But, damn it, he liked being with Jenna.

"Stay," he whispered. "Just for the fun of it. One more day. I'll be a good boy and get on top, and I'll make sure you don't move for an hour afterward. I'll even do it in that bed again, though it goes against my better judgment to make love in the same place twice."

She growled in frustration. "Ugh, Spencer, you're impossible."

"But irresistible. Will you stay?"

"I'll stay."

"Until Wednesday morning?"

"Until Wednesday morning, but I *have* to leave then, and I mean it, Spencer. I have a board meeting on Thursday morning. I'm the chairman. I can't miss it."

"You won't." He tipped up her chin and planted a smacking kiss on her mouth. "Thank you, Jenna. You won't regret this."

JENNA DIDN'T, THOUGH if Spencer had told her what he'd intended, she might have had second thoughts.

He didn't make love to her on Monday night, which threw her off balance partly because she wanted him to. Rather, he came up with tickets to see the Kirov Ballet at Wolf Trap Farm, and hired a limousine to take them there. It occurred to her that he might try something risqué in the long back seat on the way home, but he didn't, and once in the hotel room, he settled her comfortably against him to watch a late movie that he swore was classic horror. Never a horror fan, she fell asleep as soon as she realized that he fully intended to watch.

She woke up in his arms on Tuesday morning. He shifted her against him. He stroked her back and kissed her softly. She knew he was aroused, could feel it in his body, yet he made no move to make love. Instead, in a lazy voice, he told her about his place in the Keys and what it was like to wake up to the sun spilling across the ocean.

"I know what it's like," she told him. "I see it, too."

"But you're up north where it's cold. In my neck of the woods, you can walk stark naked on the deck just about year-round."

"God help the neighbors."

"No neighbors close enough to care. Kind of like your patio. Only warmer."

That said, he climbed out of bed. He was naked—he always slept naked—and though she saw only his back as he went into the bathroom, that was enough. His hips were narrow, his buttocks tight. Both made his shoulders look all the broader. His back and legs were tanned a dark bronze. His walk was smooth and fluid.

Jenna had seen many a male model in her line of work, and while some had been younger and more handsome, none could hold a candle to Spencer for sheer virility.

When he emerged from the bathroom moments later, he was wearing a robe, but she couldn't forget what he looked like without it. The image haunted her, stirring her blood each time she gave in to it, which was often. She didn't have anything—like work—to divert her mind. And Spencer was there, never farther from her than a yell.

They had breakfast in the room. While he showered, she called her secretary to say that she wouldn't be back until the next day. Then she took her turn in the shower. When she was done, they set out for Georgetown.

Had it not been for the ache inside her, the day would have been as carefree as the others had been. But alongside that image of a naked Spencer was one of his small plane heading south in the morning. If she was pregnant, there wouldn't be any excuse for their meeting again. He might be attracted to her, but he didn't want anything to do with a baby, and she still wanted the baby—now more than ever. While Spencer chased after his adventures, she would have his baby to love.

But he wasn't gone yet. She was reminded of that time and time again—when he caught her hand in his, when he grinned at her, when he turned his blue eyes on her in a way that promised good things to come. He seemed oblivious to the women who looked at him, who were drawn either by those eyes or his height or his scar. He made Jenna feel as though she were the only one worthy of notice. No man had ever made her feel that way, which was why, by the time they'd had dinner that night and lingered over a third cup of coffee, Jenna was ready to follow him to the ends of the earth. When he asked if she wanted to go back to the room, she didn't trust herself to do anything but nod.

The hotel was quiet. They took the elevator to their floor and walked down the hall. Spencer unlocked the door and followed her in. Then, coming up behind, he wrapped her in his arms.

"Jenna?"

She closed her eyes and leaned back against him. "Yes?"

"I want you."

That much was becoming clearer by the minute, to her infinite relief. "You could have had me last night."

"I know. But I wanted to wait. I wanted you to feel the wanting, too."

Softly, clasping his wrist, she said, "I do."

"Will you do something for me, then?"

"That depends what it is."

"I want you to leave the nightgown in the bathroom. I won't put the light on, if that'll make it easier, but I want to feel all of you against me."

Two days earlier, Jenna might have balked, but two days earlier she hadn't known this awful wanting. Shyness was just fine, until it interfered with satisfaction, and satisfaction was what she needed from Spencer. He was her lover, yes, *her lover*. She couldn't deny it any longer. He wanted her naked against him. She wanted it, too.

"Okay," she said softly, and heard him drag in a rough breath.

"You will?"

"Yes."

Turning her in his arms, he kissed her with a tenderness that might have brought tears to her eyes if she hadn't been burning inside, burning inside already. That was what he did to her.

She was hanging on to the lapels of his shirt when he

released her mouth. "Will you undress, too?" she whispered.

"I always do."

"But when I do? At the same time?"

"If you want."

"I do."

He gave her another, even softer kiss, then began to unbutton his shirt. She stepped out of her flats and unfastened her belt. When it was discarded, she unzipped her walking shorts and slipped them off. Spencer was unfastening his pants, but his eyes were on her, and though the room was dark, she imagined those blue eyes saw everything. Once she would have found that daunting, and she still half expected a wave of modesty to hit, but it didn't. The night was a veil of emotion, telling her that what she was doing was right. So she drew her shirt over her head and dropped it, then did the same with her bra and panties. When she looked at Spencer, he was standing in the shadows, as straight and naked as she.

"Come here," he said quietly.

Her feet made no noise on the carpet. Heart pounding, she stood before him, half wishing she could see more of him, half grateful she couldn't. When he still didn't move, she touched his chest. "Spence?"

His voice was low when he said, "That's what I want. Touch me more, angel. Your hand feels like heaven."

For a minute, she didn't do anything. She had never been much of an activist where sex was concerned. But touching Spencer seemed as natural now as holding his hand had been earlier. It was satisfying in ways she hadn't expected. And stimulating.

Her hand trembled over his chest. She shaped her palm to his shoulder, and when the fit felt incredibly good, let the other palm do the same. His skin was smooth there. Seeking more texture, she dragged her hands down his hair-roughened chest, touching nipples that were tiny and tight. His breathing grew more ragged, but that goaded her on. Lightly her fingertips followed the wedge of dark hair that tapered into a thin line down his middle. She flattened her palms on his waist and slid them down his flanks, then to the front of his thighs.

He whispered her name in a sound of sheer pain. Her hands froze; her eyes flew to his. While she tried to read his feelings, he made another, more strangled sound. "Don't stop, angel. Don't stop now. Keep going. I need you to touch me there, too."

Jenna would have laughed in relief if she hadn't been so curious. She touched him where he had asked. He was stretched into silk—she was amazed at how sleek, and how hard, how erect. She explored him with one hand, then with both until his groan reminded her that the rest of him was still waiting. Slipping her arms around him, she came against him naked for the very first time.

That full-body touch was his undoing. Whatever restraint he'd had was suddenly gone. He kissed her and touched her like a man who couldn't get enough of either. He brought her to one climax before, then another when he was inside her, and after he had come himself, he stayed with her only until he had recovered his breath. Then, albeit careful to keep her on her back, he started all over again. This time, he kissed her everywhere. His mouth learned her body by inches, silencing the few protests she made without a word. Jenna was so stunned that anything could feel so good for so long, that she soon ceased protesting anything. She trusted that Spencer knew what he was doing, and put herself into his care.

She lost count of how many times they made love. She ceased to care about who was on top, how long she lay still afterward or whether Spencer's sperm count was depleted.

She didn't exactly feel a spark. In fact, by the time morning came, she was so pleasantly numb that she wasn't sure she would have felt a full-fledged explosion if it happened inside. But she knew. *She knew.* At some point that night, they had made a baby. All that was left was to wait two weeks for the proof.

CHAPTER NINE

SURE ENOUGH, JENNA didn't get her period on the day the calendar said she was due. She didn't feel bloated or achy, the way she normally did at that time of the month. And her home pregnancy test read positive.

She was elated. Secret smiles came often and lingered. She had badly wanted a baby; now she would have one. And *what* a baby. Spencer's child would be outstanding. She couldn't wait to feel it inside her, to see it, to hold it. A May baby. Nine months seemed an eternity to wait.

That night, standing unclothed at the bathroom mirror, she looked closely at her body. Nothing of the pregnancy showed. Her breasts were no fuller than before, her stomach just as flat. She assumed it would be several more weeks before she detected the first of the changes.

Later, lying in bed with the same soft smile that had been coming and going all day, she thought about that. She wasn't in a rush to look pregnant. All along, she had intended to keep early word of the pregnancy private, simply because it was her own sweet secret and to be savored as such. She had envisioned waiting to tell her board of directors about the baby until the second trimester, and then only when she started to show. Some would disapprove of her choice of single motherhood, but by then she would be far enough along—and have enough plans made—to still their worries.

So, the board could wait to hear the news. And Jenna's

friends could wait. Even Caroline could wait. But Spencer? He was the one she agonized over long into the night. He had called her the week before to see how she was doing—it was the highlight of her week—and had asked when her period was due. She had upped the date by a day, thinking that she wanted to be sure, *really* sure, before she told him she was pregnant.

Now she wasn't sure she wanted to tell him. She didn't want to give him the chance to say goodbye and never call again. She wanted another weekend with him. Just one more.

Was there harm in it? One little white lie? Not even a lie, but the failure to tell the whole truth? Was it so wrong, given how good he made her feel as a woman and how little of that feeling she'd had in her life? She was prepared to put being a mother above everything else, but before she did, would one last passionate fling be so awful?

She didn't think so, which was why, when he called her the following evening, she chose her words with care.

"Did you get it?" he asked after little more than a hello.

He didn't mince words, which was one of the things she loved about Spencer. He didn't hem and haw and beat around the bush like some of the men she knew. He had guts.

She hesitated just long enough to suggest pain, then spoke in a voice low enough to suggest apology. "I think we'll have to try again." She didn't elaborate. Understatement was better, silence even better than that.

"Ahh, angel, I'm sorry. Are you feeling lousy?"

"Not too bad."

"God, I'm sorry. I thought for sure something would have happened in Washington. I mean, we did it so much, and we were both so loose. What do you think the problem is?"

"I'm not sure there's any problem," she said firmly. She didn't want him worrying that there was something wrong with *him*. "Two months is nothing, really."

"I can't believe it's the position we use. I've been on top of you as much as under—and I refuse to believe it's because we did it too much—and don't even think that it might have worked if we'd done it in the doctor's office, because it wouldn't have. And even if it *might* have," he tacked on vehemently, "I wouldn't have missed the fun we had. It was good between us."

She felt the womanly parts of her coming alive. "I know."

"So we'll try again."

Softly she said, "If you don't mind."

"I don't mind." He sounded sober, but in no way put out.

"Thank you, Spencer. You're a good sport."

"Uh-huh. Yeah. Well, I have a new idea this time. If we were to follow past pattern, we'd be getting together in another two weeks. I think we ought to meet sooner, like in ten days, and I think you should plan to take a real vacation from work then. I have to be in New York right around that time. I could swing by and pick you up, then fly you down here. My place is perfect for a vacation."

"Your place?" She conjured up images of sunshine, seclusion and sand.

"It's warm and open. And relaxing. If there was ever a place to conceive a baby, this is it."

Jenna had no doubt that was true, though conception wasn't any longer a worry. The worry was her peace of mind. Seeing his home would make things harder when she had to forget him. Then again, she did want to see where he lived. "I suppose I could take a few days off," she conceded.

"Not a few days. I'm talking a real vacation."

She thought of the office and her appointment book for the next few weeks. The timing was actually fine. The end of August was the quietest time of the year. "I could take five days and a weekend," she suggested.

"I was thinking ten. Plus weekends. Two full weeks."

"I couldn't do that."

"Sure you could. Don't tell me much of anything gets done the week before or after Labor Day."

He had a point, she knew. "But I'm never gone from the office that long unless it's for business."

He paused for a minute before saying, "You'll be out longer than that when you have the baby."

"True, but I'll be close by and accessible by phone."

"Hey, I'm not talking a trip across the Sahara by camel. I'm talking the Florida Keys. We're civilized down here. We do have phones. If you were needed, someone could call. Come on, angel," he urged gently, "go for it."

He was right—about Labor Day, the phone, civilization—and she wanted to be with him. Thinking about it, she realized that she couldn't have asked for a better time or a nicer place. "Okay," she said. "But I'll meet you there. I can take a commercial flight into Miami, rent a car and drive down."

"I'll be in New York anyway. I want to fly you back."

"Your plane is too small."

"But it's my plane. I know it like the back of my hand. If there's anything wrong, I can sense it before it even shows up on the dials."

"Uh-huh. Seems to me you've had trouble with it in recent weeks."

"And the trouble was fixed well before I crashed."

"Obviously. If you'd crashed, you wouldn't be around to talk about it. Survival would have been impossible. That plane won't protect you from *anything*. I've seen it. It looks like it's held together by rubber bands."

"Rubber bands or not, in the past fifteen years I've criss-crossed this continent in that plane more times than you and I have fingers and toes combined. *Double* that. It's a safe plane, Jenna, and I'm a safe pilot."

"You may be, but I'm a basket case of a flyer. I'd drive you nuts before we ever got off the ground. Seriously, Spencer. It would be better for both of us if I just met you there."

He was quiet for a minute. Then, sounding surprisingly dejected, he said, "You don't trust me."

"I do. It's the plane I don't trust, and the weather."

Somberly he said, "I don't fly if either of those things are in question, which is more than I can say for the average commercial pilot. He has a schedule to keep. I don't. Do you honestly think I have a death wish?"

"Some people might think that, given the adventures you've had."

"But do you?"

After no more than a single heartbeat, she said, "No." He respected life. She could tell that from his books, and from everything she'd experienced with him.

"Then fly with me."

She squeezed her eyes shut. "Spencer, I'll be *so nervous*."

"No, you won't, because you'll be sitting right beside me watching what I do, and you'll know that I wouldn't do anything to endanger either you or the baby that may be someday—if we can do it right this time."

She didn't want to fly on his plane. She *really* didn't want to. But she felt guilty letting him think there was no baby yet, when there was, and if it was an issue of trust, there was no one she trusted more than Spencer.

"You'll be sorry," she warned. "I'll be the worst passenger you've ever had. I may even get sick and throw up all over your cabin." A brainstorm! She was covered in the event of morning sickness!

His tone picked up. "No sweat. I'll bring barf bags. Hey, this is great, Jenna. We'll have a terrific time. I'm really looking forward to it."

"Uh-huh. Well, I will, too, once we get there. What should I bring?"

Based on the answer he gave—a bathing suit, shorts and T-shirts and a sundress—Jenna surmised that life on Spencer's Key was thoroughly informal. Not that she expected or wanted anything different. Clothes were irrelevant. Being with Spencer was what mattered.

HE SENT HER FLOWERS, a dozen bright yellow roses. They arrived at her office early the next morning with a note that said, "Cheer up. The best things often take the most work. We'll make it this time. S." It was such a sweet, unnecessary thing to do—and made her feel so guilty— that she promptly burst into tears. She was abundantly grateful that she had beat most of her staff to work. She was the president of the company. Her people would be shocked to see her crying over a vase of roses.

But the roses stood proudly on her desk, giving her a tiny thrill each time she looked at them. When Spencer called two nights later, she thanked him profusely and assured him that the flowers had made her feel better. He called two nights after that to see if she was feeling all right, then three nights after that to make sure she hadn't had any trouble making vacation arrangements at the office, then, again, from New York the night before he picked her up, to make certain she was ready.

On the one hand, Jenna loved talking with him. On the other, she felt like a heel for deceiving him. So she decided that she would look her absolute spectacular best while she was with him. To that end, she had her hair conditioned and trimmed, had a facial, had a manicure and pedicure. Being a McCue, she also shopped. She visited five of her stores, scattered in three different states. All five were already filled with fall clothes, but each had fitness departments that were stocked with things like bathing suits, shorts and T-shirts year-round. She struck out when it came to a sundress, but she had enough of her own not to mind. Moreover, several of the T-shirts she bought were oversized enough to be belted into dresses this trip, then worn loose later, when she needed more room.

She had one large suitcase and a well-stuffed carryon waiting when Spencer picked her up at the house. "All for a bathing suit, a couple of T-shirts and shorts and a sundress?" he asked, eyeing the bags in dismay.

She didn't take offense. He was such a wonderful sight that she doubted she could have held much of anything against him—except the plane, which she was making a monumental effort to forget. "I knew how hot it would be down there and that I'd be sweating a lot. I wanted to have fresh clothes to change into."

"I could keep you naked. It'd be simpler." His eyes teased her with something indecent, and in spite of all they had shared, she felt a blush warm her cheeks. He laughed at that and picked up her bags. "Let's go."

She was fine on the way to the airstrip. She didn't allow herself to think that this flight would be any different from the others she'd taken. Her heart rose to her throat when she spotted the plane, but she pushed it back down. People flew on small planes every day, she told herself. She looked out over the other private planes that were moving in the area of the runway. She didn't expect any of those to crash. There was no reason for her to believe Spencer's would.

It struck her then that she was responsible not only for her own life, but for the baby's, too, and she felt a sudden need to tell Spencer that. But if she told him about the baby, he wouldn't feel impelled to take her anywhere, and she wanted so to be with him. Besides, when all was said and done, she trusted him with her life.

Holding that thought close, she stayed calm as she went with him into the flight office. After he had finished his business there, she walked with him onto the tarmac. The plane should have looked larger close up, but, if anything, the opposite was true. Still, she was composed. She trusted Spencer. He was a veteran pilot. He knew what he was doing. He wouldn't let anything happen to her.

When he stowed her luggage in the back, she widened her eyes on the other things stowed there, a full assortment of bags, boxes and cartons. "What's all that?"

"Supplies. Whenever I'm up here, I buy things to bring back for the house."

Two bags immediately caught her eye. They were a familiar purple color and were filled to the brim. "You were at McCue's?"

"I needed new towels and blankets."

Another bag—not from McCue's—held paper goods. Several others, actually four or five, she guessed, held groceries. She saw a large cooler, a bag filled with books, a combination radio/cassette player still in its box and a bag from Tower Records. "I thought you were in New York on business. From the looks of this, you spent the whole time shopping."

"I did do business."

"Is your manuscript okay now?" She knew that his

editor had made him do work even beyond what he had done that weekend at her house.

"Finally." He helped her into the plane, then slid around her into the pilot's seat. As soon as their seat belts were fastened, he began to flip switches. Nonchalantly he said, "You don't look nervous."

"You said I shouldn't be. You said I was safer in this plane than in a commercial jet. You said you were the best pilot around. I'm taking you at your word, Spencer. I'm trusting you with my life." Her voice was nearly as nonchalant as his had been, but her eyes sent him a pointed message.

If he was at all bothered by the responsibility, he didn't show it. "You're a wise woman," he said with confidence, which, under the circumstances, was the best thing he could have done.

Jenna fed off that confidence. It kept her steady during his preflight checks, during the conversation he held with the control tower, during the slow trip out to the runway. At each step, he told her what he was doing. He identified the noises she heard without her having to ask and reassured her that the bumps and vibrations she felt were totally normal.

With surprising ease, the plane was in the air and climbing, and though Jenna's heart was beating faster than normal, she was in no way panicked. Spencer clearly knew what he was doing. He seemed as comfortable at the controls as she was behind the wheel of her car.

"You're doing real well," he said. "I'm proud of you." He reached for her hand and brought it to his mouth for a kiss.

She quickly took it back. "Both hands on the controls, please. You're right, I'm doing real well, but only because you're concentrating fully on this. If you're going to start fooling around, I'll take the first parachute home."

"I don't have parachutes."

"What?"

He chuckled. "Just kidding. Not only do I have parachutes, but I packed them myself. I'm an experienced skydiver. Did I ever tell you that?"

"No, but I assumed you've done most everything along that line, like hang gliding, helicopter skiing, hot air ballooning."

His eyes lit up in enthusiasm, confirming the last. "Ever been in a hot air balloon?"

"No."

"You'd love it. It's smooth and silent. Incredibly peaceful."

"It looks a lot simpler than this," she mused with a lost look at the bank of switches and dials.

Spencer shrugged. "This isn't terribly complicated. You could fly it."

"No, thanks. I'll pass."

"I'm serious."

"So am I. You got me up here. Don't push your luck."

He chuckled again, and paid several minutes' attention to the control bank that she found so complex. "I have to say one thing. We got great weather. The flight path all the way down the coast is clear. This time last week Hurricane Chloe was threatening things right and left."

Jenna had followed Chloe's course closely. If the hurricane had gone anywhere near the Keys, she would have been a nervous wreck on Spencer's behalf. "You didn't get much more than rain, did you?"

"Nah."

"But you've lived through far worse."

"Don't you know it. This season is a tough one. If it isn't a hurricane, it's a tropical storm or gale winds or

driving rains. That's why salvaging now is out of the
question. When the seas get churned up, the dangers
multiply, and the seas get churned up this time of year
with disgusting regularity." He grunted. "So the judge
can take his sweet time coming down with the ruling.
We can't do a damn thing in the water until the weather
stabilizes." He tapped one of the dials.

Jenna's gaze flew to it. Her pulse faltered. "Any problem?"

"Nope."

"Is that reading okay?"

"It's great."

He sounded confident, which was enough for her. Her
pulse leveled. She relaxed as much as she ever relaxed in
an airplane, which meant that she was able to take a deep
breath, release her death grip on the sides of her seat and
quietly put her hands in her lap. The ride wasn't so bad,
actually. True, she felt more by way of ups and downs
than she would have felt in a larger plane, but Spencer was right, there was a sense of control. Then again,
maybe that sense of control came from her faith in him.
She doubted there was any other person who could have
gotten her on an airplane this size.

"Still with me?" he asked.

"Still with you."

"Not airsick?"

"Not airsick." She waited for him to say I-told-you-
so—just as she had waited once before, that first month,
when he had told her not to go to Hong Kong. But he
hadn't said it then, and he didn't say it now. He was special in that regard, too. Other men made a thing of ma-
chismo, of pride and superiority. Spencer didn't, though
Lord knew he had better cause to do so. The difference
was in self-confidence. Spencer had it. He had earned
it. He had proven himself ten times over in the things

that mattered to him. She felt such respect for him, *such respect*.

That respect grew even more during the next two hours. Spencer handled the plane as calmly and capably as he handled her. When he made changes at the controls, he told her what he was doing and why, and that included a landing in Savannah that Jenna hadn't realized they would be making. She wasn't pleased when he told her. Takeoffs and landings weren't her cup of tea even in jumbo jets; her travel agent had long since learned to book her a nonstop flight at any cost. But Spencer wasn't her travel agent, and he claimed that even if she didn't have to use the bathroom, the plane needed fuel. She couldn't argue with that.

So they landed in Savannah. He talked her down, then, after they'd availed themselves of the restrooms, the coffee shop and the fuel tanks, talked her back up into the air. She had to admit that it was easier the second time around, since the sound and feel of the plane were familiar. Still, she knew she wouldn't be completely comfortable until they landed on Spencer's Key. Once she was on the ground there, once she knew that she wouldn't be flying again for two full weeks, she would be able to relax and enjoy Spencer.

Prior to Savannah, they had hugged the coast. Now they flew over water. Jenna put her head back, closed her eyes and, as she always did for the purpose of escape, dozed off. When she awoke, they had just passed to the west of Grand Bahama Island.

It wasn't long after that when she saw a troubled look cross Spencer's face. She wasn't overly alarmed. Surviving four hours in the air, with two takeoffs and a landing, made her something of a veteran. "Something wrong?" she asked casually.

"Nah," he said, and returned his attention to the highway of the sky.

But something about the way he'd said "Nah," as though in annoyance more than conviction, kept her darting him regular looks. Sure enough, several minutes later, he tapped the same dial again and frowned.

"What is it, Spencer? You can tell me. I'm prepared for the worst."

"No worst. This dial has been giving me trouble for the past six months. I've had it replaced twice, but it's still giving cockeyed readings."

"You told me this was a safe plane."

"It is."

"You told me you could sense if anything was wrong even before it showed up on the dials. Do you sense anything wrong?"

"No," he said reasonably. "The plane's flying great. But I also told you I'm a safe pilot, and a safe pilot doesn't ignore a cockeyed reading. We're going in." With the shift of a throttle and the flip of two switches, the plane began to descend.

"In? Where?" Up to then, Jenna had been remarkably calm. Now some of her calmness began to erode. "All I see is water."

"We're coming up on an island." He pointed with a finger that was perfectly steady. "Over there. See it?"

She could make out something vague, barely. "It's a mirage."

"No, it's an island."

"What island is it?" The blob she saw didn't look big enough to allow for a landing, much less repairs on the plane.

"It's just north of Bimini."

"What's it called?"

"Private Island #457."

She stared at him. "Are you serious?"

"Could be #483 or #421. It's hard to tell with these little ones. Did you know that there are seven hundred islands in the Bahamas, and that only thirty of them are inhabited?"

Jenna had a perfectly awful thought. "Are you trying to tell me something, Spencer?"

He grinned. "Yeah, I guess I am. I'm trying to tell you that assuming there's a reasonable stretch of beach, I'm putting down on that little island, and if I do, it's very possible we'll be the only ones there."

"We're putting down on an uninhabited island?" She swallowed hard. "With no runway?"

"A beach is a great runway."

"Spencer," she complained. He didn't seem the least bit upset, which should have been reassuring but wasn't. Her nightmare was coming true.

"Come on, angel," he coaxed gently. "We're in no danger. If this island isn't appropriate to land on, I'll find another. Once we're down, I'll see whether there's any problem. If there is, either I'll fix it myself or radio for help, and if there isn't, we'll take off again with nothing lost but a few minutes."

Jenna was back to gripping the side of her seat, though only with one hand this time. The other hand rested protectively on her stomach. "I should have taken a commercial flight. That was what I wanted to do."

"But you agreed to come with me because you trusted me, and I'm saying that you can trust me still. Do you think dials don't go haywire on commercial jets? Sure they do. But commercial jets can't land on beaches, so they continue on to their destination and a mechanic may take a quick look at the dial between flights. I'm playing it safe."

"By landing on a beach?"

He held up a finger. "Only if the beach looks right. I told you I didn't have a death wish, and I meant it. I also told you that I wouldn't do anything to endanger you, and I meant that, too." He chucked her under the chin. "This is an adventure, angel. Think of what you'll be able to tell your grandchildren someday."

"Uh-huh," Jenna said with the only energy she had to spare. The rest was being directed toward willing the plane to stay in the air until it reached the island. She imagined she heard all kinds of strange noises coming from the engine. She imagined the air in the cabin felt different. She imagined the plane was losing speed at such an alarming rate that they'd have to put down in the water, which, no doubt, was infested with sharks.

Silently she began to pray. She promised to be good, so good, if only the plane didn't crash. Her life was just beginning. She had so much to live for. She didn't want to die the way her parents had, and she *especially* didn't want to die before she'd had a child. Could fate be that cruel?

"Hanging in there?" Spencer asked.

"Do I have any choice?" she returned in a high-pitched voice.

"Yeah. You could be scrambling around in back hooking on a parachute."

Her eyes widened. "Should I be doing that?"

"Of course not. There's no need for a parachute when we have a perfectly good beach to land on."

She looked out the window. The island had solidified into something resembling a chocolate kiss, but in green. Rimming it was a healthy band of sand. "Are these landings difficult?"

"Nah. Piece a' cake."

She went back to praying. It was either that or yell at Spencer for endangering her life, but that would be counterproductive. He had to concentrate on landing. Then she'd yell.

"Okay," he said with a breath, "now, this landing is going to be exactly the same as the one we made in Savannah." He banked the plane, sending it into an arc that would bring them into alignment with the beach, and he kept talking, just as he'd done during that earlier approach.

Jenna's heart rose to her throat and stayed there this time. Pictures of her life passed before her as the stretch of sand came closer. She thought of her parents, and wondered what they had been thinking in the minutes before their plane had crashed. She thought of her friends and of the people at McCue's, and wondered what would become of the store. She thought about the baby that had such potential—and of *Spencer*, who was so full of life and had so much laughing yet to do. If she hadn't been paralyzed by fright, she might have cried at the loss.

The plane descended the last hundred feet and skimmed the beach for a second before touching down. It bounced once, then a second and third time in quick succession before it finally remained on the ground.

Jenna sat still as stone.

"You can breath now," Spencer said softly. Releasing her seat belt, he drew her rigid body into his arms. "I'm sorry, angel. I know that was tough on you."

"Tough?" she said weakly, then caught a wave of returning strength and said more loudly, "Tough? It was *horrible!*" She struggled out of his arms and glared at him. "How could you *do* this to me, Spencer Smith? You *know* I'm terrified of small planes. You should never have suggested I come on this thing in the *first* place!" Pushing her door open, she scrambled down over the wing and hit the sand at an angry stride.

"Where are you going?" Spencer called, following her out.

"Where *can* I go?" she cried, and kept walking. She had to put space between herself and that plane. She had to gather her wits. So she strode down the beach to an outcrop of large rocks, climbed onto the largest, put her back to Spencer and the plane and sat staring angrily out at sea.

Some time later, Spencer joined her. He didn't touch her, didn't even sit on the rock abutting hers. He chose one that left room between them, which was wise, Jenna realized. Given what he went on to say, had he been closer she would surely have hit him.

"We have a problem," he began.

She pressed her forearms to her thighs.

"The reading on that dial was faulty, all right. There wasn't anything wrong with the hydraulic system. The problem is electrical, which is why that dial was going wild."

She planted her chin on the heels of her hands and gritted her teeth.

"Unfortunately," he went on, "when I turned the engine off just now, the problem that affected the dial caused a larger short circuit that's now affecting far more than one dial. So it looks like we won't be taking right off. That's the good news," he said just as she was thinking it herself. "The bad news is that I don't have the parts I need to fix it. We won't be taking of *at all* until some-one gets them to us."

She let out a breath and returned her forearms to her thighs. "How long will it take?"

"That depends," he said in such a hesitant way that her eyes went to his.

"On what?"

"On when we're spotted."

"What do you mean, 'when we're spotted'? Can't you just radio in an alarm?"

He shook his head. "The electrical system is gone."

"Right. That's what you have to tell them."

"I can't tell them. I can't get through. I have no way to contact anyone. The radio is part of the electrical system, and the electrical system is gone. The radio is useless."

Jenna stared at him. "Useless?"

"Nonfunctional. Out of order. Dead."

"I don't believe it," she said.

"Would I kid you about something like that?"

No, she supposed he wouldn't. Slowly the meaning of what he said began to sink in. "Then we're stuck here?"

"'Fraid so."

"For as long as it takes for someone to spot the plane on the beach?"

"Looks that way."

She swallowed. "How long will that be?"

"I don't know. Could be a day or two. Could be longer."

"Longer?"

"A week. Maybe more."

Jenna thought about the last possibility. More than a week could mean a month or two or five. If they were stuck longer than that, she would be significantly pregnant by the time they were found, and all that time, she would be without medical care. She didn't know what she'd do if anything happened to the baby.

"Can we survive here?" she asked nervously.

Spencer didn't look at all nervous, nor did he sound it. "Easily. We've got food. We've got shelter. We've got clothes. We've even got towels and blankets."

"This is the hurricane season. What if it storms?"

"Then we'll sit it out. This island has survived more storms than you and I can count."

"But there's no one alive here. Maybe there's a message in that."

"There's no one alive here because there's nothing to do here."

"What'll *we* do here?"

"We'll eat the food I brought. We'll read the books I bought. We'll lie in the sun. We'll swim." His eyes suddenly sparkled. "I can think of a few other things we can do."

Jenna could, too, and wanted to hit him for reminding her. It was inappropriate to be thinking about sex when their lives were at stake.

She considered telling him she was pregnant. He had a right to know. He had to share the responsibility for the baby's well-being. Then she realized that he didn't have to share the responsibility at all! Papers to that effect, signed by her, were in her lawyer's office. From the first, she had promised she would ask nothing of him but his sperm. She intended to stand by that promise.

So she wouldn't tell him about the baby because it wasn't his responsibility. And because it wouldn't make any difference to their chances for rescue. And because he would be furious that she'd deceived him.

"I should have flown Delta," she muttered.

"Yeah, and you'd have arrived at my place and waited and waited, and I'd still be on this island. So which is better—" he stood "—being alone there waiting or being here with me?" He sauntered off, back in the direction of the plane.

In a fit of fury that was no doubt a legacy of the terror she'd felt during their landing on the beach, she yelled after him, "*There*, Spencer, I'd rather be *there*, and if you're so *arrogant* as to believe it's not true, you're deluding yourself!" She rose with her hands on her hips. "You and your plane have taken ten years off my life. I'll have nightmares about that landing for days, and now I have to worry about surviving to be rescued. Well, let me tell you something, when that rescue plane comes, I don't care if it *does* bring you the parts you need to fix your crate, I'm going back with the rescuers!" She was breathing hard, feeling emotionally strung out. When he kept walking, she yelled louder, "You're not only *arrogant*, you're *sly*. You *conned* me into flying with you. You wanted me to trust you, and I did, and where did it get me?" Even louder. "I'm stuck on a deserted island in the middle of the ocean with a man who spends his life living out his childhood fantasies! *Grow up,* Spencer! Life isn't all Spanish galleons, sparkling gold and sex!"

By the time she ran out of strength and breath, he had stopped walking. He stood with his head bowed for a minute before slowly turning. Just as slowly but with purpose, he started back toward her, and the closer he came, the more uneasy she grew. He looked furious. She was grateful that she stood on her rock, which gave her a small height advantage. Then she wondered whether even that would help. With his black hair strewn over his forehead, his brows drawn together and his jaw set in such a way that his scar seemed to pulse, he looked like an angry man, indeed.

Had her pride allowed it, she would have stepped back. But she was Jenna McCue, president and chairman of the board of McCue's. She was a woman of reason and, perhaps, momentary temper, but she was also the mother-to-be of Spencer Smith's child—even if he didn't know it yet—and she refused to cower. She tipped up her chin and met his gaze as bravely as she could.

Halting at the base of her rock, he stared at her for a minute. Then, before she realized what he planned and could ward him off, he ducked his shoulder and swung her over it. Stunned, she had to fight to catch her breath, but by the time she could launch a protest, he was striding boldly back to the plane.

CHAPTER TEN

"PUT ME DOWN!" she cried. "Spencer, you can't do this! Put me down!"

He kept walking.

The blood was rushing to her head, making it feel thick and heavy. "I mean it, Spencer!" She clutched fistfuls of his shirt to keep from bouncing with his stride. "Put me down!"

His arm was an unyielding band behind her knees. It held her firmly and, at the same time, prevented her from kicking. Not that she'd have done that. She was suddenly very upset—upset that the plane wouldn't fly, upset that they couldn't call for help, upset that Spencer was angry, upset that she'd said such awful things. She was upset about the baby, too, because the last thing she wanted was to expose it to risk, but she had. It was her fault, all her fault. If she hadn't lied to Spencer, he wouldn't have invited her south, and if he hadn't invited her south, they wouldn't be stranded on a uninhabited island with no rescue in sight.

Feeling dizzy and overwhelmed, she started to cry. She pressed her cheek to his back. "Please—Spencer—I'm sorry."

The words were barely out of her mouth, when he bent forward and let her slip from his shoulder. When he saw her tears, he swore. He lifted her in his arms this time, and, while she pressed her face to his throat, carried her to the inland edge of the beach where the sea grass began. Palm trees grew there, curving upward. An umbrella of fronds spread at their tops, while their bottoms swirled around and broadened into inviting benches. Spencer straddled one, seating Jenna between his legs. He kept an arm curved around her, holding her close.

"Don't cry on me, angel," he said in a gruff voice. "I can't take it when you cry. I swear, I'd rather listen to the chant of a band of headhunters than to hear that sobbing. Shh. Come on, Jenna. Shh. You've gone teary eyed on me twice before, once when you thought I wouldn't donate my sperm, then again when I told you I would, and both times the sight of those tears got to me. Now it's the whole shebang. But hell, I'm the one who should be upset. I'm the one who was called all kinds of names."

"I know." She brushed the tears away. "I'm sorry. I shouldn't have called you those names. I was wrong." Her eyes filled again. She pressed her face more tightly to his shirt so that he wouldn't have to see.

Still gruffly, he said, "There's no need to be upset. We aren't in any danger."

"We're marooned."

"We're probably less than one hundred miles from Miami."

"But we can't get there."

"So? We're safe, and we have supplies."

"But for how long? Oh, Spencer, if it hadn't been for me, you wouldn't be here."

"How do you figure that? I was in New York, anyway. I had to fly home."

"But you'd have ignored that dial, and you'd have gotten home just fine. The electrical system didn't blow out until you landed. The plane was flying well until then. You only took it down to prove to me what a cautious pilot you were." When he didn't say anything, she said, "Isn't that so?"

"Yeah, but it's water over the dam. I'm not upset we're here, Jenna."

"But we could be here *forever.*" She had visions of giving birth to the baby on the beach without knowing what to do. She was a businesswoman by training, not a midwife. All the reading she'd done had dealt with getting pregnant, not giving birth. She hadn't been to the doctor since she'd missed her period. She certainly hadn't started childbirth classes yet.

"We won't be here forever," Spencer scolded.

"How do you know?"

"Because I know these islands. Planes fly over them all the time. Cruise boats sail past them. Charters work through these waters and put in at islands like this one for cookouts on the beach."

"During hurricane season?" she asked skeptically.

"During every season if the money is right. Okay, if there's a hurricane brewing, they don't go. But there's no hurricane brewing this week, so someone will find us."

"Before we run out of food?"

"We won't ever run out of food. Between bananas and fish, we have an endless supply."

"Bananas?"

"In the forest. And I have brand-new fishing gear in the plane."

Jenna figured a baby might like bananas, but there was *no way* it would like fish. She had hated it for the first twenty-three years of her life. Of course, she planned to breast-feed the baby for a good long time, and since she liked both bananas and fish just fine now, perhaps the issue of starvation was moot. Other issues were not.

"What about everyone back home?" she asked.

"They'll assume we crashed. Can you imagine what that will do to Caroline, and your parents? And the company? They'll hold memorial services." She moaned. "It would be *awful*."

He gave her a squeeze. "Don't rush things, angel. Your people aren't expecting you back for two weeks, so they won't start worrying until then, and my people know not to miss me for a lot longer than that. I've disappeared before and shown up alive too many times for anyone to think twice, and that *especially* means my family. Caroline knows you're with me." Jenna had told her they were spending some time together. "She'll assume I did exactly what I did—that I set down on an uninhabited island so that I could have you to myself for two weeks."

Jenna wiped her eyes on his shirt. "I wish you wouldn't say things like that."

"Why not?"

"Because they're sweet. But you're not supposed to be sweet. You're supposed to be a brash swashbuckler."

His arms relaxed. "Sorry to disappoint you, angel. Hey, why don't you come exploring with me? I want to see what we're working with. Are you game?"

She raised her eyes. If Spencer was at all worried about getting back to civilization, there was no evidence of it on his face. He looked as though he'd merely stopped by the island for an afternoon's adventure. But, then, adventuring was his thing. He was good at it. He loved doing it.

To please him, she said, "Okay."

He wiped the last traces of tears from her face and grinned. "That's my girl." Helping her to her feet, he led her off down the beach.

They passed the plane with its engine open where he had been working. They passed a dozen palms like the one they had been sitting on. Spencer stopped occasionally to peer toward the thicker growth, but it wasn't until they'd reached the end of the beach that he led her in.

Jenna wanted the woods to be breathtakingly beautiful, which was the way woods should be, she reasoned, if one had to be marooned near them. But these woods weren't beautiful. She wasn't even sure she could call them woods. The shrubbery was about Spencer's height and nondescript. Other than the palm trees, she might have been back in Rhode Island.

As they advanced inland, however, things began to grow. The path started to steepen. The trees greened and spread skyward. Though Spencer held her hand, Jenna kept watch underfoot for vines that were easily tripped on. She also kept watch for snakes and other crawling things that, once seen, would surely keep her from sleeping. When Spencer saw the vigilant way she was walking and asked, she bluntly told him her fear. He assured her that there would be no snakes, and that if there were lizards about, they were harmless. As though to make his point, he indicated the disappearing tail of one such creature, which, he claimed, was more afraid of them then they could ever be of it. Jenna wasn't so sure, but she nodded.

They walked on. Their sneakers made little noise on the forest floor, compared to the buzz of insects and the occasional cry of a bird. Spencer pointed out various forms of vegetation, but he seemed to be listening. When they came to a clearing, he broke into a grin. Victoriously he said, "I thought I smelled water." Sure enough, the clearing was bisected by a tiny stream.

"Smelled?"

"It's distinct." He knelt beside the stream, cupped a handful of water and sipped it. With his eyes, he invited Jenna to join him.

She was thirsty and very warm. Kneeling, she drank

her fill of the clear, fresh water, then patted it to her face, neck, throat and wrists. It felt heavenly.

Spencer watched her. "It's hot in here. The air doesn't move as much as it does on the beach. Want to head back?"

"Not if you want to explore more." She refused to slow him down, and, in truth, it felt good to walk. She would walk, rather than fly, any day. On this particular day, walking worked the tension of the flight and its premature landing from her body.

But Spencer seemed bent on turning back. "I'll explore more another time. I'm hungry."

"You're always hungry," she said, but looking at his long, lean shape through his clothes, remembering the feel of his bare body in the dark, she doubted he carried an ounce of fat.

"Aren't you?" he asked.

"Not always."

"Are you now?"

"A little." Actually, she was more than a little. She was famished. She wondered if it had anything to do with the baby and prayed that it didn't. Their supply of food was limited. Despite Spencer's claim of unlimited bananas and fish, she was going to have to watch what she ate. If she ate wisely and as balanced a diet as possible, the baby would be fine.

The return trip to the beach seemed shorter. The fact that it was downhill helped, as did the breeze, which gusted toward them more often as they neared the water, lessening the effect of the heat.

Spencer declared himself chef. Claiming that certain of the foods he'd brought would only keep a short time without refrigeration, he made two overstuffed ham-and-cheese sandwiches—on croissants from a Manhattan bakery, no less, Jenna mused. For dessert, he produced a chocolate cake from the cooler, which also held six-packs of beer and Evian water.

"Boy," Jenna said, studying the cooler and its contents, "when you get marooned, you do it in style." And in style, they did it. They ate on a large beach towel beneath the shade of a cluster of palm trees whose fronds rippled in the breeze. The sound was as peaceful as the gently rhythmic one of the sea rolling onto the shore. Closing her eyes and listening, Jenna could almost forget that she was stranded on an uninhabited island for the indefinite future.

Almost. But not quite. Each time she thought of it, she felt renewed unease. It would be one thing if she knew she was here for, say, three days or even a week. She could handle that. But indefinitely? That was a frightening thought.

Spencer apparently didn't share her fear. As soon as he had had his fill of lunch, he stretched out on his back with his shoulder touching her thigh, laced his hands on his middle, crossed his ankles and went to sleep. He looked perfectly calm, totally relaxed and eminently content.

While he slept, Jenna studied him, as she had never had quite the occasion to do before. She admired his feet, which were bare now. Her gaze climbed his long, hair-roughened legs to his shorts, which lay on his lean hips in such a way that his sex was pronounced. Her eyes lingered there for a long time, before she dragged them over his T-shirt, which broadened with his chest, to his neck, then his face. The beginnings of a dark shadow had appeared on his jaw. She wondered whether he would shave while they were there. She wondered whether he would bathe in the ocean. She wondered whether he would have her cut his hair when it grew shaggy and long.

But damn it, she wasn't a barber any more than she

was a midwife. She had never been a Girl Scout. She had never gone camping. When it came to outdoor things, she had enthusiasm but little experience. In that respect, the thought of what lay ahead in the next few days, perhaps weeks or months, was thoroughly daunting.

It galled her that Spencer didn't feel any of that. He had simply eaten his lunch and gone to sleep as though he had nothing better to do. But he did! He could be working on the plane. He claimed he didn't have the parts to repair it, but maybe with enough tinkering, something would start. He could *try,* at least.

And if he didn't want to work on the engine, he could be taking inventory of their supplies for the purpose of rationing. It was one thing to have huge sandwiches and chocolate cake on the first day they were marooned, if for no other reason than to boost their spirits. But if they continued to eat so freely, they might be very sorry two or three weeks down the road.

And if he didn't want to be taking inventory, he could be building a shelter. The plane might be fine for protection during a brief rainstorm, but they couldn't very well sleep there. They wouldn't be able to stretch out. For a prolonged period, they needed more room. She would go at it herself if she had any idea what to do, but she didn't. Roughing it was Spencer's specialty, not hers. But Spencer was sleeping as soundly as a child, and for the life of her she couldn't wake him.

So she brooded. She glared at his serene features and wondered how a man could so lackadaisically accept his fate. She shifted her gaze to the sea and scanned the horizon. Cruise ships passed by, he had said. Charters came for cookouts. But she didn't see anything that remotely resembled a boat, and as for airplanes passing overhead, the sky was clear blue and empty. It occurred to her that since they had landed nearly three hours before, she hadn't heard even a single drone of another airplane.

So much for airplanes flying overhead all the time!

And Spencer slept on.

Needing to do something, Jenna bounded up and started down the beach. She walked along the lip of the sand, just shy of the beach grass, where pieces of driftwood had gathered. She collected them until her arms were filled, then carried them back and formed a pile on the highest spot of sand near the airplane, where the tide wouldn't go. If a boat or a plane passed by at dawn, at dusk or during the night, they'd need a bonfire. Even a noncamper knew that. Spencer had matches. Now they had wood.

Sending intermittent scowls Spencer's way, she took strength from self-righteous efficiency. Back and forth she went until she had a sizable pile of wood, at which point the unfortunate realization hit that if it rained, the wood would get wet and be useless. So she transferred it, armload by armload, into a haphazard pile under the plane. By this time her shorts and shirt were dirty, she had chipped the polish off the tips of two fingernails, her hair was fast falling from its pins and she was sweaty. But at least *someone* had done something practical, she mused, then whirled around when Spencer's booming voice broke the island's peace.

"What are you *doing?*" He was bounding to his feet with a furious look on his face. "Just because the electrical system's bad doesn't mean the whole thing's no good. What in the hell will you accomplish by *burning* it?"

"I'm not burning it," Jenna snapped, "though I should for all the good it's done us. I was gathering wood, and that seemed like the only place to store it where it won't get wet if it rains. If anything passes nearby, we'll need a signal fire."

His anger faded instantly. He ran a hand over his face, as though belatedly waking up, then pushed that hand through his hair. "Good thinking." He eyed her more closely and with a touch of a smile. "That really was good thinking. I'm proud of you, Jenna."

She didn't like his smile. It suggested surprise that she had a head on her shoulders, and was as chauvinistic as anything she'd seen him do. "Well, someone has to think around here." She tossed a hand toward the towel. "You eat until you're stuffed, then fall into a sleep so deep that it would take an army to wake you, and in the meantime, our rescuers would have come and gone."

He let out a breath. "Uh-oh, you're worked up again?"

"Someone has to be, or we'll never get out of here."

"What's your rush?"

She pointed in the direction she thought home might be, though in fact she couldn't have said where north was. "I have a life back there. I have things to do. I can't spend the next few years of my life eating fish and bananas on a tropical island."

He let out a bored sigh. "It's not tropical. We're not even in the Caribbean. This is the Atlantic."

She arched a brow. "Are people rescued from the Atlantic more often than from the Caribbean?"

"Come on, Jenna."

"I want to be rescued," she stated. "I'm not the hardened adventurer you are. I'm not used to being in precarious situations like you are. You love the mystery of it, the challenge, but not me. I like security. I like stability. I *like* knowing where I'll be a month from now." She gave a short headshake. "I can't take things like this in stride the way you can. I can't just turn over and go to sleep and wait for fate to happen. I have to *do* something."

He ducked his head until he was on eye level with her

and said in an exasperated way, "But there isn't anything *to* do."

"We can build a fire."

"Not in broad daylight. Besides, I have a flare gun
in the plane. A single shot'll do it if anything passes
nearby."

She was still for a minute. "You have a flare gun.
I've spent half my afternoon gathering wood for a fire,
and you have a flare gun. That's just great!" Whirling
around, she stalked past the towel. "You could have told
me." She plopped down on the base of the palm.

He followed her. "You didn't ask."

"How could I ask? You went to sleep."

"Well, I was tired. You think you're the only one who
feels tension? Maybe, just maybe that landing was hard
on me, too."

Jenna wasn't in the mood to feel sorry for him. "I
don't buy that. You thrive on danger. For the ten years I
lost during that landing, you probably gained five."

"If I did, you're taking them away real quick. For
God's sake, Jenna, ease up," he muttered, and started
unbuttoning his shirt. "This isn't the end of the world."

Her eyes fell to his chest, which was fast appearing.
"What are you doing?"

"Going swimming. In case you haven't noticed, it's
hot here."

"And you've been working so hard."

"I don't work hard unless there's good reason to work
hard, and there isn't. Not here. Not now." He pulled his
arms from the sleeves and tossed the shirt aside. "We
have supplies and shelter, and all the time in the world."
He undid his shorts. "If you want to scurry around seeing
to all kinds of little domestic chores, be my guest." He
pushed down the shorts and his briefs and stepped out
of them. "Just don't ask me to help." Stark naked and to-

tally unselfconscious, he cocked his hands on his hips. "I'll be the first one to fix a meal or set up a tarp or dig a latrine, but I refuse to go looking for other work. I don't need routine. I don't need chores to keep me happy. If I'm stuck here, I intend to make the most of it. I intend to have fun."

Jenna swallowed and shifted in her seat. She was trying desperately to keep her eyes above his neck, but she was abundantly aware of what lay below. She had touched it. She knew the texture of the hair there, and the firmness of his flesh when he was aroused.

"Go ahead," he goaded. "Look. I'm not shy."

"That's obvious," she said, but she kept her eyes on his. What she saw there was nearly as unsettling as what she was seeing below his waist. Those blue eyes gleamed. They were suddenly filled with a brand of mischief that had danger etched in silver, and they were coming closer. With smooth, deliberate movements, he approached, leaned over and propped his hands on either side of her hips.

His breath was gentle against her cheek. "I dare you, Jenna. I dare you to look at me." He remained bent that way, letting his lips play by her ear.

Unable to resist, she looked down at his body. Her chest tightened at the sight of him. He was large and bold, suspended so beautifully that he might have been sculpted by a master—which indeed he had been, she mused. By way of resisting the urge to touch him, she pressed her hands to the palm trunk.

Slowly he straightened and took a step back. She kept looking at him, curious and fascinated, impressed, aroused.

"I dare you, Jenna" came his low voice. "Dare you to take off your clothes and swim with me." Her eyes flew to his face, and everything she saw there reinforced the dare. "Dare you to let me see you naked."

Her heart was beating soft and fast, a tiny animal caught between danger and desire. She swallowed again. Her eyes were wide on his.

Then he gave her the indolent blink of a tomcat, turned and set off toward the water, calling calmly over his shoulder, "You know where to find me."

She sat there trembling, watching him go. She had seen him naked from behind before, but not with the sun glancing off his bronzed skin and not with the sparkle of the water setting his tall, tapering shape into stark relief. The sheer magnificence of him took her breath away.

In an attempt to restore it, she leaned forward and hugged her knees. From that position, she watched him enter the water. He waded until the waves reached his thighs, then dove shallowly and began a strong overarm stroke away from shore.

He was right, she knew. She hated to admit it, because her own success in life had come from analyzing a situation and taking action, but in this situation there wasn't much action to take. If Spencer felt that tinkering with the engine would get them anywhere, he would do it. She did believe that he knew his plane forward and backward. If he said they were grounded until he got parts, it was true.

So what were they to do in the meantime? Not much. They could sit and fret over their situation, or make the most of it. Dragging her eyes from his dark head and the arms that stroked steadily through the water, she took stock of the setting. In its own way, the island was beautiful. Though it wasn't as lush as some of the islands she'd visited, it had a natural appeal. It was quiet and peaceful. Its sand was soft and white, its water a translucent turquoise. The air was clean, the breeze refreshing. If she had ever wanted a private setting in which to be with Spencer, she couldn't have asked for one more so.

The danger was there, the same danger that had been present since the day Spencer had announced he would father her child. Jenna had always been slightly in awe of him. From the first night they had come together, she had feared that the awe might grow into something deeper. And it had—so much so, that she who never lied had lied about not being pregnant so that she could have more time with him.

Should the lie go to waste? Should she fritter away her time with him worrying about getting back to civilization? Or should she give him her ultimate trust, take his word that they'd get back and have a good time with him here?

She could end up loving him more. That was the danger now. If it happened, her suffering would be even worse than it would already be when their time here was done and they went their own ways. Then again, if it happened, she would have memories to cherish, memories to someday pass on to her child about the atmosphere in which it had been made.

She looked back at the water. Spencer was swimming parallel to the shore now, doing a strong breast stroke. As she watched, he turned onto his back. One muscled arm followed the other in confident overarm rhythm. He was clearly relaxed and enjoying himself. She wanted to be relaxed, too. She wanted to enjoy herself. If the most she could have was memories, damn it, she wanted them.

Pushing herself to her feet, she began to undress. She put her clothes in a neat pile, thinking about habits that were hard to break, like neatness and modesty. Spencer was doing the front crawl again, so he couldn't see her, still the touch of the breeze on her bare skin made her acutely aware of her nakedness, as did the kiss of the sun on virgin curves as she set out for the water. She went faster than Spencer had, seeking the shelter of the waves. The water was bathtub warm. She dove under and came up with her head back. Her hair streamed away from her forehead and down her shoulders, those few pins that had remained in it lost to the surf. She stroked away from shore, then treaded water until she caught sight of Spencer. He was swimming toward her, his head above water, his arms beneath. The surf helped him along. He kept his eyes on her.

She continued to tread water. When he was an arm's length away, he let his feet sink until he, too, was upright in the water. As they bobbed gently before each other, his eyes asked a silent question, then lowered to the water's surface in search of the answer. Jenna had only to look through the waves herself at the hair clearly visible midway down his chest to know what he was seeing.

Guiding himself with purposeful scissor kicks, he came closer and ran his hands from her shoulders, down her back and over her buttocks. With the revelation that she wasn't wearing even bikini bottoms, his blue eyes seemed to take on the life of the sea. She kept hers fastened to them, taking encouragement as it was needed.

"Hold on to my shoulders," he urged. At the same time, he gave her hips a gentle push toward the surface. When she was prone, he began a breast stroke that propelled her backward. Not once did his eyes leave hers.

She knew the instant he was able to stand. He touched a foot to the ocean floor, then kicked off again and swam on a little longer so that when he stood this time, the water came to midchest. Just as her own legs started to sink, he brought her against him.

She wrapped her arms tightly around his neck and closed her eyes. This was what she wanted—the closeness, the feel of his body against her, the strength of his arms around her. She felt secure and savored. She felt wanted for who she was as she had come to him, totally unadorned.

He continued to walk until the water lapped at his waist. Reaching back, he took her arms from around his neck and eased her down to her feet. His gaze fell to her breasts, which floated just above the waterline. His face darkened with desire.

He didn't say a word. He didn't have to. His eyes touched her with a reverence that gave her the courage to let him look his fill, and where courage left off, pleasure picked up. That surprised her. She hadn't anticipated feeling pleasure when he looked at her. She hadn't expected to feel proud or aroused, yet she felt both.

Drawing his hands from the water, he touched her breasts with his fingertips. He traced her roundness, then cupped her fullness with his palm and gave his thumbs free rein. They slid over her wet flesh first on the outer swell of her, then progressively inward until, just when Jenna was about to go wild with frustration, they covered her nipples.

She didn't even try to contain the sound of aching pleasure that came from her throat. Spencer looked at her as though she was a woman. He touched her as though she was a woman. The fact that she cried out like one was normal and acceptable, even desirable, if the expression of satisfaction on his face meant anything. Moving his hands to her hips, he walked her backward until the water fell away from first her ribs, then her waist, then her navel. He paused to watch the sea skim her. He spread his fingers, moved his palms. He walked her backward another few steps until her thighs emerged, and stood for the longest time with his gaze locked on the dark triangle at their apex. Then, taking a slow route that caressed her at each stop, his eyes rose to hers.

"Don't ever hide from me again, Jenna," he murmured. "You're too beautiful to play that game."

She couldn't speak, couldn't take her eyes from his face. The look there was everything she could have ever wanted, and though she didn't fool herself into thinking that it would last longer than their stay on the island, she basked in it now. It gave her the confidence to rise on her toes and initiate the kind of long, soul kiss that she hadn't liked from other men, much less been able to give.

He rewarded her by sinking to his knees in the surf and bringing her down over his lap. She felt him rise inside her to fill the aching void that had been, and there, with the ocean playing gently around their legs, he loved her as she had never dreamed to be loved. She touched him and offered herself to be touched. She opened her mouth wide to his, opened her body wide to his. She couldn't seem to get or give enough, and when they both climaxed, when their sharp gasps had mellowed into softer pants of satisfaction, she knew that she'd made the right decision.

For as long as they were on the island, she was Spencer's. He was the fantasy she had never dared entertain, and even if there would be pain at the end, she was going for the pleasure now. She owed it to Spencer as a thank-you for giving her a child. She owed it to the child as a source of memories of its father to warm long winter nights. Mostly, though, she owed it to herself. She was a woman. Mothering a child would be one source of fulfillment. Being with Spencer was another.

CHAPTER ELEVEN

PARADISE WAS AN uninhabited island, after all, Jenna decided several nights later as she lay in Spencer's arms. He had made a bed by scattering fern fronds on the sand, covering them with towels and rolling blankets into pillows. He had even stretched a tarp from the body of the plane to its wing to provide shelter should it rain during the night.

It had rained that afternoon, a quick island rain that came for an hour and left when the dark cloud passed by. Rather than taking shelter, they had walked the beach. When their clothes had been drenched, they'd taken them off and continued on naked. Jenna had never done anything like that before and was still stunned by the sense of ultimate freedom in it. She doubted she'd forget that, or the caress of the rain on her bare skin, for as long as she lived.

At the moment, though, rain seemed unlikely. A half-moon was shimmering over the water, silvering the linings of the occasional clouds that passed by. The sea lapped the shore with fair-weather ease. It was a calm, quiet night.

They had cooked dinner—steak from the cooler and potatoes—over a fire made with Jenna's wood. The flame had long since died, leaving an orange glow on the sand not far from where they lay. She was on her side against him, with her cheek on his chest and a leg between his, while he held her close with a single firm arm. Though she wore one of his shirts and he wore shorts, the memory of flesh against flesh, as it had been so often in the three days since they'd landed on the beach, kept them warm.

It occurred to Jenna that she had never felt so peaceful or content in her life, which was particularly remarkable since there had been no sign of a cruise ship, a sailboat or a rescue plane. She should have been worried. But she wasn't. It was too early to worry. She was having too fine a time with Spencer.

"What are you thinking?" he asked against her hair.

"How far away Rhode Island feels. Not just physically. Emotionally. Like it's another world. Like I've been through a time warp."

"That was the trauma of the landing."

"The landing wasn't so bad," she said because he sounded disturbed. Yes, she'd been upset. In hindsight, though, there hadn't been a point when she had truly believed they would crash. Spencer had been in control of the plane the entire time. "I think it's more the difference between here and there. Here, there's no sense of time. Life is slow and leisurely. We do what we want, when we want. There, life goes according to schedule."

"Tell me more about that life, Jenna. About what a day is like."

She moved her cheek against his chest, loving the feel of the hair there, loving the firmness of his flesh, loving the way he asked questions. As an adventurer, he was naturally curious, but she'd never thought his curiosity would extend to the details of her life. Yet this wasn't the first time he'd asked.

"My day is very organized," she began. "My secretary types up a schedule before she leaves the office each day, so that when I arrive the next morning, I know just what to do. Sometimes I have reports to read. Mostly I'm busy with meetings and phone calls."

"Where are the meetings?"

"Sometimes in my office. Sometimes in our conference room. Sometimes in restaurants. *Often* in restaurants," she amended dryly. "Businessmen love an excuse to eat in style and deduct the meal."

"Business*men*. What about business*women?*"

"Not us. We're always on diets. We'd be just as happy to meet in our offices. That's the safest place."

"Because of the food?"

"Because of the men. In an office, clear lines are drawn. I sit at my desk—whoever I'm meeting sits on the other side. In a restaurant, those lines become blurred. I feel more threatened with men in restaurants."

"That's because you're single."

"I assume."

"Which still amazes me. I can't believe some terrific guy hasn't come along and swept you off your feet."

She sputtered out a soft laugh. "The terrific guys aren't sitting around the city wangling meals on expense accounts. They're in the Himalayas looking for Noah's ark, or retracing Peary's expedition over the Pole, or exploring the Amazon." She gave him a teasing pinch.

He didn't laugh. Soberly he asked, "What makes those guys terrific?"

"They're activists. They're nonconformists. They're interesting." She sighed, knowing what she had to say next. "And they're off-limits, which makes them all the more attractive. But going after them is like trying to catch the wind. Stopping them would be like caging a wild bird." Which was just how she felt. She was head over heels in love with Spencer, but she would never ground him, much less try. She knew how he resented his parents. She refused to make the mistakes they'd made.

Spencer's adventures were too important to him to even *hint* that he give them up.

Besides, just because she was madly in love with him, that didn't mean he felt anything beyond attraction and affection for her.

She forced out a sigh. "Anyway, I told you at the start that I wasn't looking for a husband. I don't need one. I have my life under control."

He was quiet for a minute. "I wonder how we're doing with the baby stuff. We've thrown your rules out the window."

"I know." They had been making love whenever and in whatever position they wanted, with no thought at all to what was best for conception. But, then, Jenna knew it didn't matter. Likewise, she hadn't brought her thermometer along. When Spencer had asked her about it, she had said—sheepishly—that she'd known they would be making love often during their time together, so knowing the exact day she was ovulating didn't matter. In truth, she hadn't wanted Spencer to see that her temperature hadn't dipped at all that month. As close as she could guess, she was four weeks pregnant.

"You're not worried it won't happen, are you?" he asked.

"It'll happen."

He was quiet again for a time before asking, with a kind of reluctant curiosity, "Do you think about the baby much? I mean, not about getting pregnant, but about the baby itself?"

She was surprised and pleased that he'd asked. "I think about it a lot."

"Do you want a boy or a girl?"

She tipped her head back to meet his eyes. "I'm supposed to say that it doesn't matter as long as the baby is healthy, and the largest part of me truly feels that way."

"The other part?"

"Wants a girl."

"Why?"

She returned her cheek to his chest. Lightly, so that he wouldn't think she was complaining, criticizing or, worse, making a subtle suggestion, she said, "For one thing, I imagine it would be harder raising a boy without a father figure around. Not impossible. Just harder. For another, there's the issue of companionship. There's mutual identity with a child of the same sex."

"There's also competition. Caroline and my mother used to go at it for hours. Didn't you and your mother argue?"

"Sometimes. It wasn't so bad. I guess because I was an only child, she indulged me. And because they were gone a lot."

"Where did they go?"

"Here and there. They traveled for the business, and whenever they could they tacked on a few extra days. Second honeymoons, they called them." She smiled. "I think they must have had a hundred second honeymoons over the years. They were very much in love. They were each other's best friends." Her smile faded into pensiveness. "I suppose if they had to die early, they were better off dying together. If one had been left without the other, the pain would have been unbearable."

"It's rare to find two people who love like that."

"Mmm."

"Did you ever wish for something similar?"

"All I want is a baby."

"Right now. But other times. Have you ever dreamed of finding that kind of love?"

His natural curiosity notwithstanding, Jenna was still surprised to find Spencer talking about love. Most men didn't. Most men were uncomfortable discussing it. They used the term, usually in bed before or after sex, but when a woman asked what they meant, they closed up like clams. Spencer, on the other hand, was pursuing the discussion. She felt she owed him an honest answer.

"I've dreamed of finding love," she said quietly. "I used to dream of it all the time. Then it didn't come, so I told myself I could do without."

"Can you?"

"I'll have to, won't I?" she said with a laugh that was supposed to be nonchalant but fell short.

Spencer didn't answer. When he finally spoke, he asked another question. "Will the rest of your life be enough to compensate?"

"If I have a baby, it will."

He was skeptical. "Even with a baby?"

"Yes."

"And when the baby grows up and moves out?"

They had touched on that issue in one of their earliest talks, back in Rhode Island, when Jenna was trying to explain why she wanted a baby so badly. Since then she had fallen in love with Spencer. He would be leaving her, too, which made the question and its answer even more apt. "When the baby—child—adult moves out, I'll still have the business, but it's not like I'll cease being a parent. There's a saying to the effect that a parent is a parent for the rest of her life. I'll certainly always love this child. I'll always feel a responsibility for it. With a little luck, he or she and I will always be close."

"Would you want another one?"

She caught her breath. "Ahh. A pregnant question if ever there was one."

"Would you? If you had that love of your life so that finding a sperm donor wasn't an issue, would you have more than one child?"

Without hesitancy, she said, "Yes. I'd have at least two

or three. If I had that love of my life, I'd want to go off with him, too, but I wouldn't want a child of mine to feel the loneliness I felt. Not that I'm criticizing my parents. They always left me well attended. But I missed them when they were gone. If I'd had a brother or sister, it mightn't have been so bad." She sighed. "But that really is beside the point. I'll be content with one child. We'll keep each other company."

SEVERAL DAYS LATER, Spencer surprised her by raising the issue of the baby again. They were sitting in the wet sand at the water's edge, playing with small shells and seaweed, not so much drawing pictures as doodling. The fun came when every few minutes a strong wave washed over their markings, leaving behind something far more interesting and attractive than what they'd started with. Of course, it was changed again with the next wave, and diminished with each successive one, but that didn't matter. They simply started all over again.

"When you think about the baby," he asked, "do you think about doing things like this?"

She hadn't been thinking about the baby then. She hadn't even been thinking about Spencer, though he was her partner in art. She had been engrossed in the activity, feeling lighthearted and carefree. Would she do things like this with the baby? "I'd love to. Children are fascinated with the way the sand changes." She laughed when a new wave rolled in. "*I'm* fascinated with it. Look." She bent a knee to let the surf roll past and watched the new design emerging in the sand.

"You live on the shore. You see this all the time."

"But you know our sand. It's different. Harder. Besides, I don't think I've ever sat like this at home. I've never taken the time. Once the baby comes, I will." Assuming she made it back to Rhode Island. The fact that not even the smallest sailboat had passed by made her uneasy from time to time. But Spencer said they would be rescued, so they would be rescued. If he wasn't worried, she wouldn't be, either. It was far more fun to set new shells in her sand design.

Oddly enough, he seemed worried about the baby. "Won't it make you nervous raising a small child so close to the water?"

"You were raised close to the water. So was I. Neither of us drowned."

"I came damned close more than once. My parents never let me forget it. They claim they should have known what kind of person I'd grow up to be when I kept tempting fate that way. What if you have a little boy like me?"

She grinned at him. "I'd love to have a little boy like you."

"He'll give you gray hair."

"Maybe not. Maybe he'll keep me young."

"You are young. Very young."

"Only six years younger than you."

"Right now, you look about twelve years old." His gaze touched her breasts. "Make that fourteen." He frowned and pushed himself to his feet. "You're turning red. I'll get the sunblock." He headed back toward the plane.

Jenna watched him for a minute. She was glad his swim trunks weren't the miniscule swatches of fabric he'd worn on Crete years before. Skimpy bikinis were fine on teenagers and men in their twenties, but Spencer's stature called for something more classy. The bathing suit he wore was that. It was like a pair of snug-fitting boxers and did his body proud.

Boy, was he right about her, though. The preparations she had made for the trip—manicure and pedi-

cure, facial, haircut—might never have been. Had it
not been for her breasts, she would have looked much
younger indeed, and she didn't need a mirror to tell her.
She wore no makeup, no jewelry. On her head, to shade
her eyes from the sun, was Spencer's baseball cap, with
her ponytail spilling through the hole in the back. Her
bikini—of which she wore only the bottom—was from
the junior department, and why not? She was making up
for lost time. When she'd been a teenager, she'd been too
plump to wear anything brief. For a long time after she'd
slimmed down, she had continued to *feel* fat, imagining
folds in her skin where her friends assured her there were
none. Gradually she had grown comfortable in higher-
cut one-piece suits. Only in the past few years had she
worn bikinis, and then only in select company.

Spencer was as select as company got. He had seen
her in nothing at all more times now than she could
count. He didn't leer. He simply enjoyed looking at her.
She had the impression that what he enjoyed nearly as
much as seeing her body was her having the confidence
to show it unclothed.

She'd come a long way, she thought with a smile, and
watched him return to her over the sand. He squatted so
that she was between his knees, dabbed sunblock across
her shoulder blades, recapped the tube, then began to rub
the cream into her skin.

"You take good care of me," she said, feeling pam-
pered.

"Sun poisoning isn't any fun."

"I thought I was turning brown."

"You are. Under the red."

His able hands kneaded, spreading the sunblock over
her shoulders, back and chest. He lingered long enough
on her breasts to stir her deeper. In an achy voice, she
said, "Are you trying to tell me something, Spencer?"

His slightest touch made her ready for love, and it didn't matter whether it was midnight or high noon. She had grown positively shameless.

He rubbed his forearm under her breasts, lifting them slightly. "These always surprise me. I knew from touching them that they were firm, but I hadn't pictured them as being as big as they are."

They were bigger than they'd been the month before, and Jenna knew why. Her stomach was as flat as ever, though, which meant that Spencer wouldn't guess her condition. When she didn't get her period in ten days, he would know, but that was fine. It would be the best way for him to find out. After all, he wouldn't know if the baby came a month early. He wouldn't be around then.

"When you touch me," she said softly, "I swell. When you're anywhere *near* me, I swell."

He pressed his mouth to her nape. His palms moved in large, stroking circles, one on her back, one on her stomach. After a minute, he drew in a shuddering breath. "Oh, God."

Something in his tone frightened her, and it went beyond the pain of arousal. She looked up. "What's wrong?"

His silver-blue eyes flashed. "I want you. I always want you. I should be getting past this, but I'm not."

As admissions went, it was heartstopping because there was bewilderment in it, and bewilderment wasn't something Jenna normally associated with Spencer. He was always strong and sure. His bewilderment was unsettling.

But, then, there was what he had said, and that made her heart sing.

She wanted to tell him she loved him so badly that she could taste the words in her mouth. But she couldn't say them. She didn't dare. He didn't want to hear them.

The time might come—she allowed herself to think it for a single minute before pushing it out of her mind—when he wanted those words the same way he wanted her body. Until then, she could only do the second-best thing, which was to love him out of his mind with her mouth, her hands and the body that he'd trained for the purpose so well.

THERE WAS NO RESCUE plane. There was no cruise ship, no sailboat, no charter. They had been on the island for ten days, and even Spencer was having his moments of doubt. He tried to hide them from her, but she saw the worried look he sometimes got when he sat on the beach gazing out to sea, with his legs bent and his elbows on his knees. She had stopped asking about it, in part because he never admitted to concern, in part because she didn't *want* him to admit to it—because the rest of their time was heavenly.

Jenna had taken vacations before, but never one like this. Neither of them wore a watch. They woke in the morning when they were rested, and went to sleep at night when they were tired. Their days were filled with walking, swimming and sunning. They read a lot; between the books Spencer had brought and those Jenna had packed, there was no shortage, particularly since their tastes were similar enough for them to exchange favorites. Occasionally they listened to his battery-operated cassette player, though they both agreed that the island's natural music was preferable.

As far as the necessities went, they were faring better than she'd ever have expected. They had gone through first the fresh food Spencer had brought, then the frozen things that had slowly defrosted in the cooler. They were into canned and freeze-dried food now, of which the latter's presence had surprised her. Spencer told her that he used freeze-dried foods in his travels and that the best source for them was located in New York, which was why he'd had a supply along. She thought it a fortunate coincidence. The freeze-dried foods, which were packed in boilable bags, were meals in themselves. He had enough to last them through a month of steady eating, and they weren't even eating them steadily. Once a day, Spencer waded into the water on the end of the island that was banded by a shallow reef and caught fish. He cleaned them and cooked them. Jenna had never tasted anything as fresh or as good. Some of this she knew was due to the island ambiance. She felt part of the environment there, one more living creature struggling to survive.

No. Not struggling. Spencer had been right about that. They had food and shelter. They were in no danger. Indeed, worry about rescue notwithstanding, she was having the time of her life. She knew the island now, so that even those parts she had once considered shabby had taken on beauty. And then there were those spots that had been beautiful from the start.

The waterfall was one such place. It was located at the highest point on the island. They had discovered it the second day they were there, when they had followed the stream up the hill to where it first gurgled out through large rock formations. And a more Edenic spot Jenna couldn't have imagined. The trees were high and green here, the ground carpeted with moss. The rocks were smooth, some tall, some flat, and the water that spilled over the highest of them was more gentle and refreshing than any shower she had ever stood under. They had taken to climbing the hill at the end of each day, not only to clean themselves of the salt and the sand that clung to their bodies, but to watch the sun settle slowly into the ocean.

On this day, Jenna particularly enjoyed the curtain of water that fell from her hair to her shoulders and over her body. She had woken that morning feeling muzzy, and as the day had progressed, the heat had bothered her more than usual. Now, letting the soap stream off her, she felt renewed.

Spencer had finished his own shower. He was faster at it than her on even the best of days, but he never hurried her along. Rather, when he was done, he stretched out on the largest and flattest of the rocks and watched her. In time, she joined him. She wiped her face with a towel while he made a gentle twist of her hair and squeezed the water from it.

"If you have a daughter, she'll have hair just like this. Do you ever think about that? Do you ever picture what our child will look like?"

Jenna didn't immediately answer. The "our" reverberated in her mind. He hadn't used it before, not in any of the other questions he had asked. And he had asked. For a man who proclaimed to want nothing to do with a baby, Spencer had developed a puzzling interest in Jenna's. But he hadn't said "our" before.

It was like the phrase "having sex," she mused. Somewhere along the line, that had become "making love," and it made sense, since she was in love. But Spencer had used the term first, and he wasn't in love—or if he was, it was a love that came in a far second to his work, which was the love of his life.

She pictured him going off in November to salvage his Spanish galleon. Then she pictured him going off the following year to explore something else. By then the baby would be born. She pictured it, too, and felt a pulse of serenity.

"Curls," she said. "I had curls when I was little. Boy

or girl, it'll have curls. And, yes, dark hair. We both have that. Likewise, skin the color of cream."

"I don't have skin like that."

"You do."

"Where?"

She turned her head and eyed him boldly. "Your groin."

"You've been observant."

"Uh-huh." Actually "observant" didn't begin to explain what she'd been. She suspected she knew Spencer's body better than she knew her own. She could certainly see most of it more easily, particularly when he stretched out and let her look, which he did often. The only rule he had was that she not stop at looking. She hadn't broken it once.

Now he frowned. "If it's a girl, she'll be a knockout. Guys will be after her all the time. You'll have to be careful, Jenna. I know what guys do. I was damned randy when I was a kid."

"When you were a *kid?*" she murmured facetiously. If he heard, he didn't let on.

"Everyone talks about safe sex, but kids still think they're immortal."

Jenna couldn't think years ahead, when she had so much to go through first. She blotted the rest of the water from her body, then reached for the lotion she always carried. He had laughed the first time she'd done it, telling her that body lotion was totally out of place at an island waterfall, but he'd been the one to remind her to take it the next time they'd gone.

"It's tough raising a child these days," he went on. "Even in a two-parent family. Are you sure you'll be able to do it alone?"

"Uh-huh." She rubbed the lotion into her legs, squeezed out more and applied it to her stomach.

"Babies are totally dependent. They need constant care. Won't it be tough on you?"

"No tougher than on any new mother."

"How will you go places with it? Babies cry at the drop of a hat."

"They cry if they're tired or hungry or wet. I'll make sure mine isn't any of those things—at least, not for long and not if I'm taking it somewhere." She spread lotion on her shoulders.

"Will you put it on your back in one of those carriers?"

She grinned. "That sounds like fun."

"But how will you manage it? Don't you need two people to get it up there?"

She looked at him again. "Do you need help putting *your* pack on your back?"

"No."

She arched a brow, then returned to lotion her arms, but her thoughts remained on his questions. Something was going on in his mind. If he was trying to suggest that she needed a husband, he was barking up the wrong tree. If he was trying to convince himself that babies were more work than they were worth and he was therefore right in wanting no part of them, he wouldn't get any encouragement from her. And if he was trying to discourage her from having the baby at all, it was a little too late.

"You can't have a baby where I go," he declared.

She kneaded lotion into her hands.

"You can't have a *woman* where I go," he added.

She drew dabs of cream from between her fingers.

"Sometimes I'm miles from civilization," he continued piously. "There aren't any phones, there aren't any baths, there aren't any beds."

Jenna could have sworn he was trying to justify his lack of a wife and family, but what he described was nothing different than what they had here. Granted, she wasn't his wife, but she wasn't minding life here. She hadn't complained once.

"If you get sick," he argued, "you can't run to the drugstore for an antihistamine. You can't run to a restaurant for dinner if you get tired of cooking. You can't go to a movie if you're bored, or run to the bookstore for something to read."

"That sounds like a very difficult life," Jenna said.

"It *is* difficult. There are days when I trek miles and miles with a heavy pack on my back. A woman couldn't do that, much less with a baby." He snorted. "I can just see you stopping in the middle of the tundra to nurse." He went still. "You are planning to nurse, aren't you?"

"Yes."

"Well, you can't nurse where I go. We rough it out there. We're often on the go twelve hours a day." He snorted again, louder this time. "Can you even begin to imagine what that kind of life would be like for a woman at the end of her pregnancy?"

Quietly, she answered, "I can't begin to imagine what *any* kind of life would be like for a woman at the end of her pregnancy, since this one's my first." The words were barely out, when her heart began to thud. She wondered if she'd given herself away. Had he caught it?

When he didn't answer, she glanced over her shoulder. He looked troubled. Her heart beat louder.

"Are you frightened?" he asked.

"Frightened?"

"Of the last month."

She let out a tiny breath. "A little."

"I wonder how big you'll get." He reached for her arm and drew her around. His eyes touched her breasts, then fell to her stomach. His hand followed. He rubbed his knuckles over the soft skin below her navel. His voice was a gritty whisper when he said, "There were pregnant girls in that Indian tribe I studied. They wore no more clothes than anyone else, so you could see their bellies. Sometimes, an elbow or knee poked at them from inside. I used to be fascinated by that." His hand slid lower, knuckles brushing the spot so close to where Jenna's baby would emerge. "They let me watch a birth once. It was incredible."

Jenna swallowed. Her heart had swelled to twice its normal size, which was why she said without thinking, "You could watch the birth of our baby if you want to."

His hand came to a gradual stop, then fell away. He flattened it on the stone, straightened his shoulders and raised his eyes to hers. "The agreement was that I'd make you pregnant. That's all."

She was stung. Quickly, she said, "I know, and I can do just fine on my own, but you said that you found watching a birth to be incredible, so I thought—"

"Just think pregnant." He rose to his feet. "When will you know?"

She forced away her hurt. "Five days. Or six." She wasn't sure. Keeping track of the time had become difficult. One day blended into the next.

He nodded and turned away to scoop up his towel. Without waiting for her to join him, he started back down the hill.

JENNA AWOKE THE next morning feeling nauseous. It passed as soon as she'd had breakfast, so Spencer knew nothing of it. She was infinitely grateful for that. He hadn't been in the best of moods when they'd returned to the plane the night before, and though he held her closely through the night and seemed calmer this morning, she didn't want to risk setting him off again.

The nausea returned late that afternoon. She snacked on a handful of crackers. That helped.

The following morning, though, she wasn't as lucky. Again she awoke nauseous. Ignoring it only worked until she left the cover of the tarp and was headed for the latrine. Halfway there, she turned off the path and lost the contents of her stomach in the woods.

Spencer was on the path when she returned. "What's wrong?"

"I'm not feeling great," she said. Passing him, she went quickly back toward the beach, wanting only to bathe her face and rinse out her mouth.

He was right behind her. "Did you throw up?"

"Yes."

"Was it something you ate?"

"I don't know."

"Did you feel sick during the night?"

"No."

She broadened her stride on the sand. When she reached the water, she sank to her knees and immediately scooped a handful of water to her face.

He hunkered down beside her. "Jenna?"

"Give me a minute," she murmured weakly. She was still feeling queasy, though there wasn't anything left in her stomach to heave.

"It's too soon to be morning sickness, isn't it?"

She didn't answer. She was weak and suddenly tired of keeping the secret.

"Isn't it, Jenna?"

"I don't know."

"You said morning sickness wouldn't begin until five or six weeks at the earliest. You told me that before you went to Hong Kong, remember?"

She nodded. The water was helping. She scooped more to her forehead, her mouth, the back of her neck.

"If you became pregnant while we were here, you'd only be a week and a half along."

"Maybe this is an aberration."

"Maybe you were pregnant before you stepped foot on my plane. That would explain why your breasts were bigger than I remembered them feeling."

She splashed her face one last time and hid behind her hands.

"Jenna?"

She didn't know what to say.

"Damn it, Jenna," he growled in warning, then with dawning awareness. "It's true, isn't it?" He took her wrists and pulled her hands from her face. "Are you pregnant?"

CHAPTER TWELVE

JENNA COULDN'T LIE. Not anymore. "Yes, I'm pregnant," she said, and kept her eyes wide on Spencer's to gauge his reaction.

He looked at her stomach, swallowed and looked back up. "It happened in Washington?"

She nodded.

"But you *denied* it."

"I know."

"Why?"

She could have lied again and said that she hadn't been sure she was pregnant, but she ruled out that thought in a second. She wasn't a deceitful person. She hadn't wanted to lie in the first place, but she'd seen no choice. Now the dismay on Spencer's face gave her pain. It was time for the truth. "I was selfish," she said, feeling the burden of her guilt. "I wanted to be with you again. I knew it would be the last time, and thought there wouldn't be any harm done."

"No *harm* done?" he bellowed. In a flare of the temper that Jenna knew existed but had been so rarely directed at her, his face was suddenly darker, his hands tighter around her wrists. "You came on my plane knowing that you had a mortal fear of it, knowing that the flight would be traumatic—"

"Not traumatic—"

"Frightening enough so that you might have lost the baby."

"I didn't lose the baby. I never thought I would."

"You didn't say anything when we landed. You let me go on thinking you weren't pregnant. I led you up and down, all over and around this island. I had you walking in the rain and sleeping on the ground and eating dried biscuits and freeze-dried beef, and through it all, you kept your mouth shut, when you should have been home seeing a doctor and eating fresh food and taking vitamins." His fingers dug into her skin. "I thought you *wanted* this baby."

"I do," she cried, "I *do*." Tears sprang to her eyes. "It's the most precious thing in the world to me!"

"If that's so, *why didn't you tell me you were pregnant?*"

"Because it wouldn't have changed anything!" Defensively, she explained, "There was nothing wrong with my climbing all over the island or walking in the rain or sleeping on the ground or eating what I ate. Those things are all fine—I've made sure they are. But if I'd told you the truth, you'd have been angry and worried, just as you are now, when there's no point! All the anger and worry in the world won't get us off this island! Your plane won't fly! You can't *change* that, Spencer!"

He stared at her long and hard. Finally, in a defiant voice, he said, "I sure as hell can."

She didn't understand, but before she could ask what he meant, he had dropped her wrists and was stalking across the sand, headed straight for the plane. When he was halfway there, he did an abrupt about-face, returned to where she still knelt and took her hand. "Come on. We're packing up."

"Now?"

"We're leaving." He drew her up and set off. His grip was firm, his voice tight.

"But how?" she asked, confused.

"My plane."

"You need parts."

"Not by a long shot."

"But you said we couldn't fly without them."

"I lied."

"What?"

"I lied."

She dragged her feet in the sand. "Lied how?"

"There's nothing wrong with the plane. We can fly."

"Nothing wrong?"

"That's right."

"No electrical problem? No *radio* problem?"

"Nope."

"I don't believe you."

"Believe what you want. You're going to have something to eat while I dismantle this camp. Then we're taking off."

She was still trying to grasp what he'd said. For eleven days they had been marooned on an island waiting for rescue. Or so she'd thought. "We're leaving, just like that?"

"I want you back in Rhode Island where everything is safe and predictable. I want you seeing your doctor. Hell, prenatal care is all you read about nowadays."

Jenna didn't give a damn about prenatal care just then. "You *lied* to me, Spencer?"

"Yeah, I lied."

Furious, she pulled her hand from his and took a step away. "You planned this accident, knowing that my parents died in one just like it? How *could* you?"

He climbed aboard the plane and called over his shoulder, "It was about time you got over that fear. Besides, there wasn't any accident. I kept telling you I knew what I was doing. Our landing here was a carefully planned maneuver."

"But we landed on a beach!"

He was rummaging in the food boxes. "I've landed on this beach dozens of times. The island is owned by a friend of mine. He knew we'd be here. That's why no one else dropped by."

Her fury rose. "You knew we wouldn't need a bonfire? You knew we wouldn't need your flare gun? You knew no one would come looking? I'll bet you even told Caroline where we were going!"

"Sure did. I didn't want anyone up there worrying." He emerged with a juice box and tossed her one. She caught it on reflex and angrily threw it back. It missed him, hit the door and fell to the ground.

"All those supplies—you bought them with this in mind." Not coincidence at all, but careful planning. She should have known. She'd read every one of his books. He planned his adventures well. "You had just enough fresh food to be eaten before it spoiled, just enough ice packs to keep the frozen food frozen until the fresh food was gone. You had soap and towels and toilet paper. You had books and a cassette player. You even had sunblock."

"So did you," he said, and retrieved the juice box.

"Of course I did. I thought I was going to the Keys!" The extent of his deceit cut her to the quick. "I should have guessed. It was too pat. But I trusted you!"

"The way I trusted you."

"Hold on, Spencer. There's a difference. I never actually lied. I never actually said I wasn't pregnant. I misled you, and then I didn't correct you when you assumed I wasn't. But you—you contrived an entire story, one outright lie after the next. That's *indefensible*."

He handed her a chocolate-covered breakfast bar—

which he had previously claimed he'd brought along because he loved munching on the things at home. "Eat
this. And the juice."

She ignored the offering. "How *dare* you do this to
me, Spencer! How *dare* you decide I should get over my
fear of flying! How *dare* you take my entire life in your
hands without giving me a say!"

"Oh, please," he muttered, then said more loudly,
"take the food, for God's sake."

"I don't want it. I want to know how long you were
planning to keep me here."

His dark brows were drawn tightly together. "You
sound like it was a prison. Were you unhappy? Were
you mistreated?"

"I was deprived of the freedom to leave."

"Did you want to leave?"

"That's not the point. The point is that I had a right to
know the truth!"

His eyes drilled hers. "So did I!"

"You'd have known the truth when I missed my
period," she said, feeling suddenly defeated. Her stomach was starting to churn again. "All along I knew I'd be
telling you then. So when did *you* plan to tell *me?*"

"Long before now, I gotta say." He smirked. "I never
thought you'd last here. I thought you'd be tearing your
hair out after a week. I thought you'd be sick of the sand,
sick of the bugs, sick of the heat. You've been a trooper,
angel." He held out the food. "Take this."

"I don't want it!" She turned away. "I feel sick." Not
knowing what else to do, she walked down the beach to
the same rocks she'd sat on that very first day. She'd been
feeling highly emotional then. She was feeling highly
emotional now. And nauseous.

Spencer came up from behind and reached around to
offer her a handful of crackers. "I should have known

what was up when you were munching on these things," he grumbled. "How many days have you been feeling sick?"

"Two."

Swearing under his breath, he nudged the crackers at her hand until she finally took them. Then he went back to the plane.

For several minutes, Jenna stared at the crackers. She felt miserable. They would help her stomach, but she didn't know what would help her mind. She didn't have to look back to know that Spencer was packing the plane. He was taking her home. Their time together was over.

Tucking her face to her knees, she began to cry. Deep, soft sobs welled from within. She wanted to stop— Spencer hated tears—but the emotion behind them was too strong. So, hugging her legs, she let them come. In time, they eased. Hiccuping, she turned her cheek to her thigh and looked out to sea.

It would be good to go home, she told herself. It would be good to have a hot bath, to brush her hair until it was smooth, to put on real clothes. But Lord, she'd miss Spencer. All along, she had known love might be a problem, but she had underestimated its scope. Forgetting him was going to be impossible. She would see him every time she passed the room he'd slept in at her house, every time she watched a movie on television, every time she read a book or ate a piece of steak or saw an airplane, every time she kissed his baby good-night. Letting him go was going to be like severing a part of her heart. Already she felt the pain.

Her throat tightened into another knot. She swallowed, forcing its release. Taking a full breath, she straightened. Crying wouldn't accomplish anything. She was an accommodator. Life went on. She would survive—more than survive—do well. After all, she had a baby coming.

Who wanted an adventurer, anyway? Adventurers might be exciting, but they wouldn't be around when you wanted them most. They'd be off chasing dreams of their own. Besides, they were scheming, bald-faced liars.

Slowly she ate one cracker, then a second. Crumbling the remaining few in her hand, she tossed them toward the water for the terns that dove nearby. She pushed herself from the rock and went to the water's edge to cleanse her face of the ravages of her tears. Then, knowing that the next few hours would be the most painful of her life but that they had to be endured, she went to join Spencer at the plane.

He was nearly ready. The tarp was down, the towels and blankets stowed, those personal effects that had been lying on a makeshift table of driftwood cleared off and packed. The beach that had been their little home looked so tragically bare that Jenna felt the threat of tears yet again, but she refused to let them flow. Life was full of heartache, she told herself. She'd get past this. She would.

"Are you less nauseous?" Spencer asked with a scowl.

"Yes."

"Then eat these." He handed her a banana and a single-serving bag of granola.

She didn't want to talk or argue or do anything that would prolong the agony of their parting. The sooner she was back in Rhode Island, the better. So, though she had no intention of eating, she took the food.

He stood watching her with his hands on his hips, seeming to know exactly what she had in mind. "Go on."

"I'll eat while you pack."

"I'm done. Eat before we take off."

He was nagging. She didn't like it. "Have you eaten?"

"I'm not hungry."

"Well, neither am I."

"Eat for the baby, then."

"I'll eat for the baby later," she snapped, thinking how impossible overbearing men could be. "I don't *feel* like eating now."

"Some mother *you're* gonna make."

"And what difference is it to you? You didn't want this baby to begin with. You didn't want the responsibility. So I'm telling you not to take it. Let *me* worry about the baby."

He stared at her then, and his eyes shook her. She'd seen anger in them before, but she'd never seen the kind of cold fury that turned the silver in them to ice. She felt the chill all the way to her toes.

It was just as well, she reasoned, though her heart broke a little bit more. She and Spencer could never be just friends again. Their feelings were too strong for that. If they couldn't love each other, they'd have to hate each other—a tall order on her part and one she would have to work at, but it was the only way. The only way.

As though he had reached the same conclusion, Spencer gestured her into the plane with an angry toss of his head. He climbed in after her and strapped himself in, then started flipping switches. In no time the propellers started to turn.

"You bastard," she muttered.

"Yup."

She clamped her teeth together and stared blindly ahead. She didn't look at Spencer when he maneuvered the plane to the end of the beach and turned around. She didn't look at their camp when they accelerated past it. She was too heartsick to be frightened when the wheels left the ground and the plane slowly rose into the air.

All she wanted was to go home. It would be an hour and a half to Savannah, then two and a half to Rhode Island. She willed the time to pass quickly. After a few minutes, in hopes of helping it along, she looked out the side window.

"What's that land mass?" It extended forward and back for as far as she could see and looked suspiciously like the mainland.

"Florida," he said tersely.

"If we're heading north, what's it doing on my side of the plane?"

"We're heading south."

"But I live north."

He didn't respond to that other than to clench his jaw, which made his profile even harder than it already was. He was more tense than she'd ever seen him, and angry, very angry. Well, Jenna thought, so was she, and she didn't like what she was reading between the lines. "I thought you were taking me home."

"I am."

"To *my* home."

He flexed a muscle in his jaw, which looked tight enough to snap.

"Enough, Spencer," she declared, sitting ramrod straight behind her seat belt. "You decided we'd go to that island, so we went. Now it's my turn to decide, and I decide that you deliver me back to Rhode Island."

"I'm not flying all the way up there now," he snapped.

"Why not? You have nothing better to do until November. You told me so yourself."

"I have to think. I need time. I don't know what to do."

"I'll tell you what to do. Fly me to Rhode Island, drop me off and let me be."

"I can't do that."

"Why not?"

"Because we're not finished."

Jenna felt the slow twist of a screw inside her. The pain was unbearable. "We are—we are! You did your part. You gave me my baby. There is nothing else you have to do. I signed papers to that effect."

"Well, *I* didn't sign any papers!" he thundered. "And you can take yours and burn them, for all I care! They don't mean squat to me!"

Jenna stared at him in disbelief.

He went on angrily. "I *told* you I was going to have trouble with this. I *told* you I couldn't father a child and not care about it. I warned you, Jenna, but you seemed to feel that those papers were some kind of protection. Well, they're not! I can't just ignore the fact that my baby's growing inside you. I can't just go off and forget it. Hell, don't you think I wonder what it looks like, too?" He drove a hand through his hair. The other was white-knuckling the throttle.

Jenna was afraid to think ahead.

"Yeah, I planned this trip," he went on. His eyes were focused on the horizon. His tone was one of brassy self-mockery. "I thought to myself, okay, Spence, the woman turns you on. She was real easy to be with in Little Compton. She was real easy to be with in D.C. She should be real easy to be with in the Keys. Then I thought about the island, and I thought, what an adventure! She's used to marble and velvet. Let's see what she makes of seaweed and sweat." He added softly, "I didn't fool myself too much. Sure, I wanted to see if you'd crumble, but in the meantime I wanted to enjoy you. And it wasn't just the sex. It was the being together."

He pursed his lips. His nostrils flared when he took a breath. "That's been driving me nuts, the being together. The *enjoying* being together. The looking *forward* to being together. I've never felt that for another woman, and I didn't want to feel it for you. But I went ahead and made plans to maroon us for a couple of weeks on the island because I couldn't resist. And was it ever fun buying supplies! I felt like I'd been gathering knowledge for years and was finally putting it to good use for the very first time. Can you imagine that?"

He sounded as if he couldn't. Jenna pressed her fingertips to her mouth.

He swore softly and shook his head. "Hell, it was good. Everything about it was good. I mean, you didn't crumble. You didn't complain. You were having just as much fun as I was, and you were doing it in my kind of style." His voice faltered. "I don't think I'll ever forget the way you looked sitting there in the surf with nothing on but your bikini bottoms and my baseball cap. I mean, talk about tugging at heartstrings." He swore again, and she thought she saw something wet and glimmering in his eyes. "I could've stayed there forever. Do you know that? I don't think I've stayed anywhere for more than six months in the past twenty-three years, but I'd have stayed on that island forever. Or at least until we'd run out of food." He grunted. "Or until you'd gotten pregnant. Boy, it didn't take long, did it?"

Jenna wanted to speak, but her throat was too tight. Her heart was wedged there, along with her hopes and dreams.

"And now I don't know what in the hell to do," he sputtered. "Okay, so I've got you off the island and on your way back to civilization, but if that means I won't see you again, I can't do it—I just can't do it. I feel too much. I want too much. I can't just drop you back there and fly off, and only some of that has to do with the baby. Most of it has to do with you. When we were making love, I wasn't thinking of the baby. When you told me you weren't pregnant last month, I was disappointed for you but not for me. I wouldn't have been upset if we'd had to keep trying for months, because it would have given me time to figure things out. But you're pregnant now, damn it. So I don't have that time. And I don't know what to do."

Jenna was daring to hope. "What do you *want* to do?"

He shot her a terrified look. "Marry you. Have you ever heard anything so crazy? I mean, here I am running all over the world, and I want to marry you. I want you legally bound to me. I want to know you'll be waiting when I come home. I want to send you flowers again, and rub sunscreen on you again, and carry your shoes and your bags and your books. I want to knot my tie around your hair again. I want our kid to have my name." He shot her another look, no less terrified than the first. "But you don't want any of that, and I don't blame you. You're a capable woman. You have your own corporation, your own house and now your own baby. You don't need me." This time when he looked at her, he scowled. "Put that back on, Jenna."

She had unbuckled her seat belt and was climbing toward him. When her bottom touched his thigh, she wound her arms around his neck. "You're wrong, you're wrong, you're wrong," she whispered, and started to cry. "I do…need you. So…much."

"Oh, God, don't cry. Jenna, please." His voice broke. "You don't know what that does to me." He wrapped an arm around her and held her convulsively close.

"I love you," she sobbed.

"Oh, God."

"I do…and I lied about something else. Back on the island…I said that the baby was…the most precious thing in the world to me. It isn't true—it was once, but it isn't anymore. You're…just as precious to me as the baby… but I can't hold you back, Spencer. If I did, you'd resent me the way you resent your parents. That would *kill* me."

His arm tightened around her. "Oh, Jenna."

"I love you," she whispered. Now that she'd said it, she couldn't say it enough. "I love you."

He let out a ragged moan. "Ahh, angel." The hand that was wound around her pulled her hair back from her ear so that he could put his lips there. In a tortured whisper, he said, "I don't want to be living out childhood fantasies when I'm old and gray. I want life to hold more than Spanish galleons, sparkling gold and sex."

"I was *awful* to say those things."

"You were right to say them."

"But your life is terrific."

"It's not enough. I keep running so I don't miss things, but I miss them, anyway. I want warmth, angel. I want a home."

Jenna had never thought to hear those words. Her tears came again. "What should we do?"

"Think. We should think. And you should sit down and put that seat belt back on. You're making me nervous."

"I trust your flying."

"Yeah, well, you may not in a few minutes if you don't strap yourself in. I'm feeling the need to do more than hold you."

"Oh." She drew her head back and looked up at him. "But nothing's been settled."

He kissed the tears from her cheeks. "One thing has." His voice was heart-stoppingly tender, as achingly warm as the silver in his eyes. "There's love here. Somehow we'll find a way to make things work."

FOR AS LONG as he lived, Spencer would never believe how simple it was, but that was because, never having been in love before, he hadn't known its power.

Jenna had insisted on passing the presidency of McCue's to her vice president. Spencer protested, but she claimed that she would likely have done it, anyway, once the baby was born. She wanted more time for her family, she said, and besides, she was still chairman of the board, and the company's controlling stockholder.

They were married on the Thanksgiving weekend. Spencer's parents were pleased as punch with the union—then appalled when Spencer promptly took Jenna to the South Seas for three months. Even Caroline was miffed, complaining that instead of regaining a brother she was losing a sister-in-law. But Jenna had insisted on the trip. She had known Spencer wanted to go, had gotten full clearance from her doctor, and told anyone who argued that since Spencer had won his court case but was waiting to salvage his galleon until after the baby was born, this was *definitely* the time to go.

And Spencer thought *he* had wanderlust! She had been as enthusiastic as he every step of the way, ballooning belly and all.

Now, ballooning belly and all, they were back to await the birth. After spending time in Rhode Island to make sure all was well with McCue's, they had rented a cottage on the Maine coast, far enough from Spencer's parents to let him breathe, yet close enough to a top-notch hospital should the baby come early.

It was late March and still cool enough for Spencer to light a fire in the fieldstone hearth. With flames crackling around the logs, he sat on the floor, against the sofa. Jenna was straddling his lap. Her arms were looped around his neck; her eyes were level with his; a sweet smile softened her lips.

"You're a very handsome man, Mr. Smith," she said.

"Scar and all?"

She touched his jaw. "Scar and all."

"Did you know that was one of the first things I loved about you? You weren't fixated on the damn scar."

"It's just a scar. It's been part of you so long that I rarely notice it."

"Know how I got it?"

"Uh-huh. In a jeep accident in Kenya."

"Usually I tell women I was gored by an elephant."

"You don't."

"I do. It's more dramatic."

She rolled her eyes. "More drama I can do without." She grinned. "I still can't believe you're mine."

He took her hand to his mouth and kissed the diamond wedding band he'd so proudly given her. "I'm yours." Leaving her hand on his neck, he slipped his under her sweater. She was due in six weeks, but there were times when he wondered whether she would explode before then. Every bit of weight she'd gained was in her stomach, which protruded from her front like a great, fallen nose. From behind she looked as slim as ever, and he did enjoy her behind, but this was what he loved, this warm, smooth, tautly stretched belly that was glasslike and alive. "Feeling okay?"

She nodded. "Feeling great. I love it here."

"So do I. Maybe we could come back after the baby is born."

She shook her head. "We're going south. Your ship awaits."

"You're really looking forward to that, aren't you?"

"You bet. I've never worked with a salvaging crew before."

"Jenna, you're not working with my crew. How many times do I have to tell you that?"

"I know, I know. I'll be in your boat with a full-time captain aboard, but we'll be near the workboats, so I'll be able to see what's brought up. Are you sure your men won't resent my presence?"

Spencer wasn't sure of it at all. The boat he had bought

for Jenna and him was far more luxurious than the one the men would be living on. Some envy was inevitable. If that envy reached an uncomfortable level in any of his crew, that man would have a quick, one-way trip to shore.

"My men will be fine. I'm the one who may have the problem."

"With resentment?"

"With distraction." His eyes widened. His voice dropped to an excited murmur. "It's moving. Whoa, feel that?" He had both hands on her stomach, fingers splayed to feel the nudge of a tiny arm or leg.

Jenna laughed. "Such wonder. Your expression is priceless. But you've felt that before."

"It's still the most incredible thing in the world." He kept his hands where they were. He liked thinking that the baby recognized his touch. He liked thinking that the most primitive form of bonding was taking place.

It probably wasn't. But he liked thinking it.

"Spencer?"

He looked up to find her eyes suddenly deep and intense. "What, angel?"

"I'm glad you're here."

"Where else would I be?" No other place in the world held half the challenge and a fraction of the reward.

"I mean, I'm glad you're doing this with me."

"I'm your husband."

"But you weren't my husband when I got pregnant, and I said I could do this alone. I think I was wrong. This wouldn't have been anywhere near as easy or exciting an experience if you hadn't been sharing it with me—"

He kissed her silent, then wrapped his arms around her and closed his eyes when she sighed in contentment against his cheek. He was always amazed to hear her say things like that, since *he* was the one who had been so wrong about being independent and self-sufficient.

Sure, he could be both. So could she. And they were fine things to be if one had to. If one didn't, ahh, that was where true joy lay.

Since he'd been with Jenna, even the smallest things in life had taken on new meaning. Her reaction was important to him. Her enthusiasm sparked his, and vice versa.

When he thought of traveling, he thought of ways he could do it with Jenna. And with the baby. The baby was coming along, too. He was thinking of spacing out his travels, actually. *Actually,* he was thinking of going back to school. He and Jenna had spent hours talking about his experiences with the Indians in the Amazon, and it had occurred to him that a degree in anthropology might be nice. It had occurred to him that if he went on for a doctorate, he might teach one day. He could intersperse classroom work with fieldwork. He could have a life that would be exciting and diverse, yet stable enough for a wife and child. And children.

He wanted all that. More important, Jenna wanted it, and her happiness meant the world to him. She was a treasure, fallen right into his hands. Now that he'd found her, he wasn't letting her go.

* * * * *

T.L.C.

CHAPTER ONE

UNDER NORMAL CIRCUMSTANCES, Karen Drew would have found the article intriguing. She was a devoted armchair traveler—the more exotic the locale the better—and the tropical Seychelles, with their gentle breezes and sun-tipped turquoise seas, sounded perfectly idyllic compared to upstate New York in February.

Today, though, visions of coco-de-mer palms, giant tortoises and white sand beaches just weren't doing it for her. Her energies were concentrated on seeing the words on the magazine page, speaking them aloud in a relatively normal manner and, in the process, breathing as little as possible on Rowena Carlin.

Karen was sick. She'd been fighting a cold for nearly three weeks. It had flared up, died down, looked to be going away, only to rear its stubborn head in renewed bouts of sniffling and coughing. Now it had settled in her chest. No battery of antihistamines, decongestants or expectorants was budging it. Though Karen had fortified herself enough to temporarily mask the symptoms, each breath she took was an effort.

She couldn't afford to be sick. Thought of it sent her into a tailspin. Midterms were coming. Even without those, she had research to do for Professor McGuire and, even beyond that, tables to wait at the Pepper Mill. Paychecks weren't given for nothing, and Karen needed the money. So she'd spent the last three weeks ignoring the germ that plagued her. Unfortunately, it wasn't going away. It had slowly but surely sapped her, leaving her fighting for the tiniest shreds of energy.

On the tail of one such shred, she shifted the glossy magazine from which she'd been reading onto the plaid blanket that covered the older woman's small lap. "See, Rowena?" she asked. "Isn't it beautiful?"

Rowena, who had been raptly studying Karen's face, lowered her eyes to look at the magazine, but no sooner did they reach their destination than they started right back up again. The look they held made Karen brace herself. If she'd learned one thing in the eight months she'd been visiting Rowena, it was that the woman missed very little and let even less pass without comment.

Rowena was eighty-one and sharp. A spinal injury had hindered her mobility, a subsequent stroke had affected her speech. Nothing, though, had affected her mind—or her eyes, which said far more far faster than her tongue could. Those eyes held concern even as the small, wizened mouth went to work.

"S-s-something is…wrong," she announced. Her speech was faltering, yet far better than it had been even three months before. Karen was amazed at her improvement—both in speech and movement. Rowena approached physical therapy with a will to succeed, and she was doing just that. The fact that her arms and legs were slowly coming back to life was a tribute to sheer determination. Karen followed her example and answered as confidently as she could.

"No, no. Nothing's wrong."

"Y-y-you're under the…w-w-weather."

Karen crinkled her nose and gave a quick shake of her head, which was a mistake. When her head turned right, her awareness stayed left, and when her head turned left, she felt as though she'd bumped into herself at the pass. The air in the small parlor seemed suddenly warmer.

It was a minute before she regained her equilibrium and a minute after that before she quelled the urge to cough. When she spoke, her voice was husky. "I'm just a little tired. It's a busy time. Midterms begin in two weeks." She paused when she saw Rowena's mouth working again. Patiently she waited, giving the woman the time she needed to form the words.

"Will y-y-you have a rest…then?"

If only, Karen thought. "A little," she said. "I'll have two weeks without classes, so it'll just be a matter of working."

"F-f-for…McGuire?"

"Uh-huh."

"And the…r-r-restaurant?"

"That's right."

"Karen?"

"Uh-huh?"

"Take a…v-v-vacation."

Karen's eyes held a wistful look. "I wish I could."

"Y-y-you…can if…you…want."

"No. My hours at the restaurant will be shortened since most of the customers will be gone, but I'm committed to working full-time for Professor McGuire during those weeks."

"And visiting me. It's…t-t-too much."

"But I *enjoy* visiting you."

"D-d-do you enjoy…y-y-your work, too?"

Karen desperately wanted to say that she did, but she couldn't do so unequivocally. While she found her work for Professor McGuire to be intellectually rewarding, the only reward she gleaned from her work at the Pepper

Mill was a pocketful of tips. The restaurant was heavily patronized by students, and deep down, she had trouble dealing with them. Some were in her classes; others she knew only in passing. Theoretically, she might have shared in the camaraderie.

But she didn't. For one thing, there was the age difference. At twenty-nine, she was a good ten years older than many of them. For another, there was the socioeconomic difference. These were wealthy kids. They weren't working two jobs on top of classes, as she was. They weren't living on shoestring budgets in small rooms off campus, either; they were well enough off to pass up the dining hall food their parents paid for in favor of regular meals at the Pepper Mill.

In small groups they were fine—inoffensive, even congenial. Often, though, groups of five, six or more came in, and at those times, Karen wished them on any other waitress but herself. Large groups tended to be boisterous and demanding, sometimes even obnoxious.

But that was the downside. Looking to the upside, she said, "My work isn't all that bad. Professor McGuire has me researching the lives of obscure artists, several of whom, I'm sure, won't be obscure too much longer—" she pressed her lips tightly together to ward off a sneeze, and when it had passed, went on "—and the Pepper Mill makes super nachos."

"Y-y-you eat there?"

"Dinner every night that I work." Which was five days a week.

"Do they…make you…p-p-pay?"

"No. The owners are generous about that."

Rowena's concern just then wasn't with the owners. "Nachos…aren't…n-n-nourishing."

"Maybe not, but they sure taste good."

"Too...thin."

Karen knew Rowena wasn't referring to the nachos. "Me? Nah. Thin is in." Her n's were growing more dense, which meant that the nasal spray she'd used before she'd left home had begun to wear off, which meant she had just a few minutes left before she'd be stopped up.

"T-t-too...thin," Rowena repeated firmly.

Not up to arguing, Karen retrieved the magazine and read on for several more minutes, but her eyes grew progressively heavy and her cheeks progressively hot. She found the room increasingly stuffy in spite of the chill that seeped from the window behind her. Her voice sounded tighter, her chest felt tighter, and her body had begun to ache in spots it hadn't ached before. The aspirin was wearing off, too, she realized. She felt horrid.

Gently closing the magazine, she sent Rowena an apologetic glance. "I think," she said tentatively, "that I ought to head home. I'm working tonight."

Rowena's gaze slid from Karen's face to the window. Something in her look made Karen turn.

Not only had it begun to snow, but it was snowing hard. "Oh dear," she murmured under her breath. Home was in Syracuse, which was a forty-five-minute drive from the nursing home under normal conditions. Over snowy roads it was bound to take longer. If she were feeling fine, that wouldn't be much of a problem. But she wasn't feeling fine. She wasn't looking forward to stepping foot outside the nursing home, let alone tackling the storm in her aging Chevy.

But it had to be done. "I'll be okay," she said, brows knitting as she tucked the magazine into her shoulder pouch. Taking a slow breath for strength, she stood, then reached for the coat she'd dropped on a nearby chair when she'd arrived.

A momentary wave of dizziness hit her. Bracing her legs against the side of the chair in which she'd been sitting, she took several shallow breaths and willed the dizziness away. Mercifully, it went.

"Driving...c-c-could be bad," Rowena warned.

Karen felt a chill even through the wool of her topcoat. Fingers slightly unsteady, she worked the last two buttons through their holes and tried to sound philosophical. "Actually, I've been impressed. People up here take the snow in stride. The highway crews are pretty good about keeping the roads plowed and sanded." She wrapped a long wool scarf around her neck once, then a second time. "Besides, it's been a snowy winter, which makes me a veteran. I'd probably be more nervous if I were back in New York."

"Do you...m-m-miss it?"

"The city?" She stuffed one hand into a mitten and curled her fingers around the wool in a blind search for warmth. "Not really. It was—is—so hectic."

"Your life here is...hectic."

Pulling on her second mitten, Karen shot Rowena a gently chiding glance. "You're not supposed to know that. You're supposed to think I'm a woman of leisure."

Rowena's eyes made mockery of the idea. "Y-y-you wouldn't...ever be a...w-w-woman of leisure."

Karen didn't have to ask how she knew. She and Rowena were kindred souls—both curious, both strong-willed, both dreamers. From the start they'd hit it off. Karen would easily bet that Rowena had never in her life been a woman of leisure. And neither had she.

"Do you mean to say," she ventured in as playful a tone as she could muster, "that I don't look totally laid back—calm, cool and collected?" When Rowena simply pursed her lips, Karen made a tiny face. "I look frazzled?"

"Sick."

She supposed sick was better than frazzled and perhaps more correct at the moment. "I'm tired."

"Go...home."

Aware that her head was beginning to throb, Karen hoisted her bag to her shoulder. "If I didn't know better," she managed to tease hoarsely, "I'd think you were trying to get rid of me." She held up a mittened hand. "I'm going. I'm going." Then she dropped all pretense of teasing. She hated leaving Rowena. The woman gave her a kind of comfort that she couldn't quite explain. "I'll see you Tuesday, okay?"

"Only if...y-y-you're...f-f-feeling better."

"I'll be fine."

"D-d-drive slowly."

"I don't think I'll have a choice today."

Rowena's eyes, riveted to Karen's face, grew more worried. "Maybe...you should...s-s-stay here."

All the nursing home needed, Karen mused, was a bundle of germs in its midst. She felt badly enough being near Rowena, but she couldn't have not come. Twice weekly she visited. Those visits had become as vital a part of her schedule as anything else she did.

"No, Rowena," she said gently. "I have to drive home."

"Then...w-w-wait awhile."

Casting a glance out the window, Karen considered that, only to reluctantly veto the idea. "The longer I wait, the worse the driving may be. They're expecting me at the restaurant later, and when I'm done there, I have a history paper to start. I was planning to spend most of tomorrow finishing it."

"Tomorrow is...S-S-Saturday. N-n-no date?"

"Nope," Karen said with deliberate nonchalance. "I'm working the late shift."

"You don't usually."

"I know, but Saturday nights are busy, which means good money. And since things will be quieting down really soon…" She let her words trail off, realizing that it was taking more and more of an effort to force them out. "Gotta run, Rowena. Really." She bent forward to tug the blanket a little higher on Rowena's lap. "You take care now. Anything special I can bring on Tuesday?"

She always asked, she was always refused—as she was now with a look. Rowena Carlin was an independent soul, but Karen could appreciate that, too.

"Take…c-c-care of *your*self," Rowena advised.

"Will do," Karen said. She gave the older woman's shoulder a gentle touch before starting for the door. There she stopped for a final, fond glance back. "See you Tuesday," she promised and forced herself on.

Once clear of the parlor arch and Rowena's all-seeing gaze, she paused, lowered her head and closed her eyes for an instant, then took a stuffy breath and went on. When she reached the desk just inside the front door, she paused again, this time to speak softly to the receptionist.

"Judy, I've just left Mrs. Carlin. Will you see that someone gets her?"

Judy smiled. She was a young girl, a high school junior who spent her afternoons at the nursing home. She knew Rowena nearly as well as Karen did and understood that the elderly woman wouldn't have stood for being "gotten" in Karen's presence.

"Sure thing, Ms. Drew."

Karen nodded her thanks as she turned to look through the window at the fast-falling snow. She couldn't contain a husky moan.

Judy was in instant sympathy. "I only live two blocks from here. You've driven a ways. I'm surprised you did it today. They've been talking about snow since last night."

"I didn't know."

"What do you listen to?"

"What what?"

"Radio station. In the car?"

"I don't."

Judy stared at her in genuine disbelief. "Don't you get bored? I'd go out of my mind without music, especially driving the distance you do."

"Unfortunately," Karen said with a weak sigh, "I don't have a radio—well, I have one but it hasn't worked since I bought the car, and I couldn't see spending the money to fix it when there were so many more critical repairs to be done."

"Sounds like you bought a clunker."

"No. It's just seen better days."

Judy's young face lit up. "Want my brother to take a look at it? He's great with cars."

"I'll remember that if I run into trouble," Karen said, casting another worried glance at the snow. "Which may be very soon."

Judy followed Karen's glance. "Are you sure you want to go out in that?"

Karen started to sigh but broke into a low, thick cough. She covered her mouth, turned her head, controlled the cough, then said, "I don't have much choice."

"You could stick around for a while, see if it lets up, y'know?"

"Is that what the forecast says it's going to do?"

"No."

"How much are we in for?"

"Eight to twelve inches."

Bowing her head, Karen pressed wool-sheathed fingertips to the aching spot between her eyes. Actually, she was aching all over. Her fingers felt like ice inside the mittens. At the same time, her nose was beaded with sweat. The sooner she got home, the better.

Tightening the scarf around her neck, she tucked her shoulder bag firmly beneath her arm, gave Judy a quick wave, and forced herself out the door.

She was hit in the face by the snow. Hard little nuggets of cold stuff, tiny ice pellets driven by the wind felt like needles against her hot cheeks. Ducking her head and slitting her eyes, she focused on her feet. She took one step, a second, a third in rapid and steady succession. Her boots sank into no more than an inch of snow, yet she felt she was trudging through a foot. The fourth step required more of an effort than the third had, the fifth more than the fourth.

She plugged on. Tucking her head even lower against the frigid gusts, she hastened her step. At least she thought that was what she was doing, but the walk seemed endless. She put a shoulder to the wind and led with it, at the same time glancing back at the nursing home. It seemed far away, separated from her by a wall of sheeting snow.

Finally reaching the end of the walk, she skidded onto the driveway and half slid, half trotted to her car. Snow had started to mount on the windshield, but the wind had prevented it from doing so elsewhere. She batted a mittened hand across the slight accumulation, then tugged off the mitten, reached in her pocket for the key, opened the door and threw herself inside. The slam of the door beside her was accompanied by a heavy cough. She sat still for a minute, breathing shallowly, with her head against the headrest and her eyes closed.

But that wasn't going to get her home, and home was where she wanted to be. So though her head felt like a brick, she raised it and turned the key in the ignition.

Nothing happened.

Shoving the scarf away from her face, she tried again. Still nothing happened. The motor didn't even turn over.

This time when she closed her eyes, she bowed her head to the steering wheel and moaned. It was the battery. She knew it was. For weeks now, the car had been giving her little messages, hinting that something inside it was getting tired and worn. She hadn't listened because she'd felt tired and worn herself. She hadn't had energy to spend on the car, much less time or money.

That had been short-sighted of her.

Raising her head, she forced herself to think clearly. Her eyes felt dry and hot, but she trained them on the gearshift. She was in park. The car should start. Hands shaking, she removed the key from the ignition, checked to see that she had the right one, reinserted it, turned it.

She stepped on the gas pedal once, slowly, then turned the key again. She stepped on the gas a second time, then a third and a fourth while she flicked the ignition switch from off to on, back and forth with a breath in between.

She reached for the broken radio to make sure it was off. She turned off the heat. She checked to make sure the windshield wipers were off. She turned the key again.

Shivering now from the cold, she peered at the fuel gauge and felt a wave of relief. The needle was on empty. She was out of gas. Then it occurred to her that the needle was always on empty when the engine was off. And she'd filled the car three days before.

Swallowing painfully, she cast a helpless gaze skyward. A dead battery in the middle of a snowstorm. Swell.

Simply because she didn't have the strength to move, she sat where she was for the course of a minute, which was long enough for her to realize that if she remained much longer, she'd freeze. Snow was pelting the windshield. The swathe she'd brushed clear had been covered again. Even worse, gusts of wind rocked the car, sending the chill to her bones.

Having no recourse, she tucked the keys back in her pocket, put her mitten on and climbed from the car. The force of the wind made her stagger for an instant. She pulled the scarf higher to cover her hair, but the wind quickly blew it back down, so she ducked her head as she'd done before and set out over her own fast-fading footprints.

She didn't get far before another wave of dizziness hit. This time she didn't have a chair to rest against, so she stood swaying in the storm, taking shallow breaths, which was all her congested lungs would allow. She was hot on the inside, cold on the outside. Her knees felt rubbery, and she wanted nothing more than to lie down for just a few minutes. She'd do that while she waited for someone to jump start her car. Just a few minute's rest and she'd be fine.

The problem was getting back to the nursing home. Her legs didn't seem to want to work, and the dizziness wasn't going away. Her body wasn't cooperating, she realized in dismay. But she had to get inside. She had to do it quickly. The world was growing whiter and whiter. She'd never feared the snow, but there was something strange about it now. It was growing too thick, becoming a wooly blanket that could either freeze or suffocate her. And the noise…she hadn't thought snow made that kind of buzzing sound.…

BRICE CARLIN HAD PULLED into a parking space just as Karen was leaving the nursing home. Turning off his engine, he watched her fight her way through the storm to the car beside his. Still comfortable in the slow-ebbing heat, he sat for a minute longer. When she remained motionless, he wondered why she didn't start her car. When she dropped her forehead to the wheel, he felt perverse satisfaction.

So she felt bad? Good. She *should* feel bad.

But rather than leaving his car and showing his disdain by stalking past her into the nursing home, he continued to watch. He couldn't understand what she was doing, why she didn't start her car if for no other reason than to turn on the heat. It was freezing. The windchill factor had tumbled the temperature to zero. Yet she simply sat there, leaning slightly forward, seemingly preoccupied with the dashboard.

At last she settled back in the seat, inert for the space of a minute. Through the snow-studded glass, Brice could make out most of her profile, and what he couldn't make out he remembered. He remembered well. For two days he'd studied her with neither car windows nor snow to fog his view. He remembered well the wide eyes, the straight nose, the gentle lips. He remembered well her look of innocence, which had annoyed him, and of worry, which had given him a measure of comfort. That comfort had disappeared on the day she'd been acquitted.

Jaw tighter than it had been moments before, he saw her move. He waited to hear the rev of her engine, but instead she climbed from the car and started back toward the home. He assumed she'd forgotten something and glanced at the digital display on his dashboard. It was nearly four o'clock. He didn't want to sit there forever. Then again, if he left the car and went inside, he'd risk a head-on confrontation, and he wasn't sure he trusted himself for that. So he sat and monitored her progress.

It slowed, then came to a halt.

He was beginning to think that she was screwy on top of everything else when she swayed. She seemed about to fall, then caught herself, and he assumed she'd been taken off guard by the wind. Then she swayed again. She was halfway to the ground when it suddenly hit him that she wasn't well.

Without another thought, he threw open his door and bolted from the car. Karen was in a limp heap, dead to the world when he reached her. Scooping her into his arms, he lifted her from the snow and started toward the nursing home only to stop and press his lips together, then do an about-face. Moments later he was depositing her into the passenger seat of his car, where he took a minute to examine her. Her forehead and cheeks were hot to the touch. Her skin had an unearthly pallor. Her breathing was quick, shallow and labored.

Having seen enough, he closed the door, rounded the car to the driver's side, slid behind the wheel and took off.

Very slowly, Karen returned to awareness. She felt cold and hot and achy. She also felt light, as though she'd been floating and had just touched down. Only she was still moving. Or something was moving under her. It came to her gradually that she was going to have to open her eyes.

The first thing she saw when she did so was a dashboard with a strange display of buttons, gauges, dials and readouts. She felt more disoriented than ever. Needing a familiar point of reference, she raised her gaze to the windshield. Snow was hitting it—that rang a familiar bell—but the wipers were working, and hers hadn't been. Her car hadn't been working, period. This one was. And even if it had been her car, she wasn't driving.

Blinking once, then again, she tipped her head just the slightest bit and looked at the driver. That was when stark fear hit.

His profile was unfamiliar and totally intimidating. His hair was dark, his features chiseled and tight. The collar of his topcoat stood up against his nape and was as dark as the insides of the car.

With a strength born of panic, she grabbed the handle of the door and tugged it. She would have tumbled out had not an arm snagged her middle and hauled her back. Simultaneously the car swerved to the side of the road, missing a large tree by inches before coming to a stop on the snowy shoulder.

"What in the *hell* was that for?" the dark voice above her bellowed.

Karen tried to pry the arm from her waist, but it was like steel. "Let me go," she croaked, twisting as much as the arm would allow, which was little.

"And have you run out in that mess?"

She kept twisting, kept grabbing the arm, trying to loosen it. "You can't keep me here…I don't want to be here…kidnapping is a capital offense…" The burst of words ended in a fit of thick coughing that hurt her head, her chest, her stomach.

Brice took advantage of her momentary weakness to reach across her and tug the car door closed. He'd no sooner straightened when, coughing behind closed lips, she reached for the handle again. He returned an arm to her waist and pinned her back against the seat.

"I am not kidnapping you," he said in an angry growl.

Karen felt trembly and weak. Her voice reflected it. "I want to get out."

"Not now. Not here."

Head against the headrest, eyes on the road, she was panting shallowly. "Then where?"

"My house."

Her eyes flew to his in alarm. It was the first time she'd viewed him head-on, and if she'd been intimidated before, when she'd thought him a stranger, she was even more so now. Recognition was instantaneous. It didn't matter how many months had passed. She'd never forget those dark, piercing eyes.

Swallowing hard, she tried to sink deeper into the seat of the car, but plush as the leather was, it only gave so much. She held still, very still, suddenly afraid to move or speak.

"You know who I am?" he probed in that same deep voice, but less angrily. He had no qualms about frightening her; she deserved that. Terrorizing her was another story.

She nodded.

"You passed out back there."

She stared at him silently.

"I'd say you're sick," his tone hardened, "so your visiting Rowena was a really dumb thing to do. Do you know how dangerous it would be for her to catch something at her age?"

Again Karen nodded.

Very slowly, Brice withdrew the bond of his arm. There was no further need to physically restrain her. The force of his gaze did that on its own. "So why did you have to see her today? You didn't develop that cough this afternoon. It sounds like it's been in your chest for a while. Didn't it occur to you to skip a visit, or did you think she depended solely on you for human companionship?"

His sarcasm cut into Karen nearly as sharply as the accusation itself. She knew she'd been selfish. If Rowena got sick she'd never forgive herself. Still, she'd needed to come, and the need was her own more than Rowena's. But could she explain that to Brice?

"I was wrong," she admitted quietly, hoarsely. She didn't move other than to take those short breaths, and she wasn't taking her eyes from Brice. She didn't know him. Though they'd seen each other before, this was the very first time they'd talked. He had good reason to hate her. If he wanted revenge, she was in poor shape to defend herself.

"Is that all you have to say?"

"I don't feel well. If you could take me back to my car…" She swallowed the rest of the thought in a lump as the facts of the situation settled on her shoulders. Her car was dead. She was sick. A snowstorm was in full blow. And Brice Carlin was, theoretically, in a position to do with her as he wished. "A cab," she whispered because it took less effort. "There must be one." But the cab fare to Syracuse would be prohibitive. "Or the bus stop. If you could just drop me—"

"Your car?"

"It died."

"That's why you were going back into the nursing home?"

She nodded, feeling suddenly stranded and very cold. Earlier she'd been shaking with fear. That had stopped when Brice's identity had sunk in. He was Rowena's grandson. He wouldn't physically harm her. When she began to tremble now, it was from a chill.

Brice shot a glance at the road, then looked back at Karen and spoke in the slow, deliberate tone of one expecting obedience. "I am going to start driving again." Very carefully, he shifted into gear. "I don't want you to reach for the door because if it opens again and I don't catch you on time, you could get yourself killed." With a look over his shoulder, he pulled back onto the road. "Or you could get both of us killed if I have to swerve off the road again. In case you hadn't noticed, the driving is tricky."

She said nothing because she was feeling dizzy again. So she closed her eyes and tried to take slow, even breaths. But her chest hurt with each one.

"Put your head between your knees."

"I can't."

He raised his voice to a tone of greater command. "Put your head between your knees."

"It takes too much effort." She was beginning to shiver more noticeably.

"How long have you been this way?"

"Not long."

"How long?"

She opened her eyes, thinking that her head would be better if she could see the world. "A week, maybe a little longer." She could see the world, all right, but it wasn't one she recognized. "Are you taking me back to the nursing home?"

"What would be the point of that? The only thing you'd accomplish there would be to infect a few more innocent people."

His words stung, but Karen was feeling too weak to hurt as much as she might otherwise have. "I was careful with Rowena."

"You instructed the germs to behave?"

Sinking lower in the seat, she turned slightly to rest her hot cheek against the leather. "Yes. Are you taking me to a bus?"

"You won't get a bus in this weather. Things are closing down right and left. I told you, I'm taking you to my house, which is about five minutes from here." When she made a sound of protest, he added, "It's either my house or a hospital."

Karen wrapped her arms around her middle in a futile attempt to still the shakes. "I can't afford a hospital."

"I know," he said, but she didn't hear. She had curled into herself, feeling sick and confused. He glanced at her face, what little of it showed above the collar of her coat. Her skin was ashen and damp with sweat. She was clearly sick. He would have no idea how sick until he got her home and took a look. If he decided then that she needed the hospital he wouldn't hesitate to take her there.

For the duration of the drive, Karen drifted in a state of semiawareness. She vacillated between fearing Brice as Rowena's grandson and finding comfort in that fact, but for the most part he was relegated to the periphery of her consciousness. She didn't have the strength to bring him forward, when her primary thought was of escape from her body's misery.

Five minutes stretched to ten when Brice slowed the car to avoid skidding on the ice that slicked the roads. He began to worry. The sensible thing, he knew, would have been to have carried Karen into the nursing home when she'd collapsed. If he had an accident with her in the car, he'd be in trouble.

But he'd come too far to turn back. His house would do fine, he supposed. And after all, he and Karen weren't *total* strangers.

Turning off the main road at last, he directed the car down the short drive and was relieved when the familiar shape of his home emerged through the driving snow. He worked his way carefully over the accumulation on the circular drive and came to a halt immediately in front of the door.

Karen was shivering in her sleep.

Hitching his collar higher, he forged out in the snow, circled the car to the passenger's side, opened the door and lifted her with ease, as he'd done earlier. In several long strides, he was at the front door, then inside.

Karen stirred when he shifted position to kick the door shut behind them. She stared groggily at the oak of the entry hall ceiling, then at Brice, and her eyes widened a fraction. "You can let me down," she whispered hoarsely.

Ignoring her, he entered the larger front hall, crossed directly to the living room and deposited her on a sofa. She immediately put her feet on the floor and sat up.

A cab, she thought. She should call a cab. She looked around the room for a phone, but there was none and she didn't have the strength to go in search of one just yet. She was very cold. Her hands and feet felt like ice, and her insides were shaking. Only by clenching her jaw did she keep her teeth from chattering.

Brice, meanwhile, had tossed his overcoat onto a chair and was hunkered down before the huge fireplace arranging logs for a fire.

Even without the dark topcoat he was intimidating, Karen realized. It could have been his size; he was above average in height, lean but solid. It could have been his clothing; he wore navy slacks and a navy sweater, with only a pale gray shirt collar showing to lighten the effect. It could have been the aura of command he exuded; he placed each log with confidence, almost casually tossed kindling between them, touched a match to the wood and the fire caught.

Probably, she decided, it was his face. Stern. Brooding. Craggy in the way of a man in his prime who had seen—or chosen to see—the dark side of life too often.

She would have wondered about that had she been given the time, but Brice was rising and turning to her with his hands on his hips and annoyance in his eyes.

Karen did her best not to cower, but that became harder as the minutes passed with no sound breaking the silence but the snap and hiss of the growing flame and her own faintly rattling breath. She still wore her coat, scarf and mittens, so her shaking wasn't visible, but for good measure she clamped her hands between her thighs. When Brice continued to stare at her, she averted her gaze. Like a magnet, though, he drew her back before she'd gone far.

She cleared her throat. "I'll be on my way as soon as the snow stops."

The hard lines of his mouth barely yielded when he spoke. "It won't be letting up before morning, and only then if we're lucky. I wouldn't count on the roads being clear for a while."

"A while?" she echoed in a raspy voice as she realized the extent of her predicament. "But…but I can't stay here."

Brice dropped his hands from his hips. "It looks like you haven't got much choice." He reached for his coat. "I'm going to put the car in the garage. I have no intention of driving again."

"You were on your way to see Rowena."

"She wasn't expecting me. She won't worry."

"But I can't stay here." She darted a worried glance at the approximate spot where her watch would be, under her layers of clothing. "I'm supposed to be back in Syracuse. I have to work, and after that I have a paper to write. I *can't* stay here."

Brice studied her for a minute more. Beneath the layers of wool, she was sick, trembling, cold, exhausted and weak, which was all pretty pathetic in his estimation. And still she argued.

But if she thought she could win her case this time, she was mistaken.

With a mirthless smile, he shrugged. "You can't leave." Calmly pulling up his collar, he left the room.

CHAPTER TWO

KAREN DIDN'T LIKE that smile. She didn't like the tone of voice. She didn't like the man.

True, he was Rowena's grandson, and she trusted that he wouldn't cause her harm, but there was harm and there was harm. It didn't take a genius to interpret that smile. Brice Carlin might not take a hand to her physically, but that smile said he wouldn't be averse to a little psychological torture.

Karen wasn't sitting still for any kind of torture.

Inching to the edge of the sofa, she took a breath and pushed herself to her feet. She found her shaky way back to the hall, crossed it and entered a room that was the twin of the other. There she began to feel dizzy. So she rested a hip against the worn leather sofa and bowed her head until the brief wave had passed, then moved on into the next room. It boasted more of the same dark woodwork, including an elegant mahogany table and chairs, and was clearly the dining room. Crossing through that, she reached a huge butler's pantry and, finally, the kitchen.

A telephone sat on the tiled countertop. Lifting the receiver, she called directory assistance, and within a minute was talking with an agent at the bus station.

Brice was right. Nothing was running.

Desperate, she placed another call, this one to the dispatcher of one of the local cab companies. His language was more colorful than the bus station attendant's had been, but the message was the same.

"They're not crazy," Brice said from the door. Glassy-eyed, Karen turned in time to see him toss his gloves to the counter. Crystals of snow dotted his hair and shoulders. "They wouldn't be caught dead out there."

Which was pretty much what the dispatcher had said. "I'll try another company," she said and coughed.

"Try five. You won't get anywhere. The roads are treacherous. Visibility is next to nil."

She pressed the phone to her ear and squeezed her eyes shut. "Some driver has to want the money badly enough." But when she opened her eyes to dial another number, she found that the world had tilted. She swayed and caught herself on the edge of the counter. In the process she dropped the phone.

Brice smoothly scooped it up and set it in its cradle, but his smoothness faltered when he turned back to Karen. She was wearing an expression so helpless that the healer in him was pricked.

"I think," he said in a lordly voice, "that you ought to lie down by the fire." He curved a large hand around her upper arm and took a step, only to stop when she didn't move. He looked down at her. He gave a small tug with his hand.

Karen returned to the living room with him, not because she was giving up the fight but because she knew when to regroup. He was right. She ought to lie down by the fire, at least until she warmed up. She was so cold. So hot. So tired. Besides, there were no buses running. No cabbies were willing to pick her up. She'd tried.

Her knees gave way just as she lowered herself to the sofa. Unable to help herself, she leaned sideways until her head hit the armrest, which was soft, covered in the same plush corduroy as the rest of the piece. She barely noticed when Brice raised her legs, but quickly curled them beneath her in a bid for warmth.

A cool hand felt her forehead, her cheek. A brusque voice said, "You're burning up."

"I'm cold."

"That's the fever. Don't move. I'll be back."

Karen didn't care whether he returned or not. She had withdrawn into herself and was concentrating once more on escaping the misery. Sleep wasn't coming so quickly this time, though. She opened her eyes to see the fire, closed them to see sparks behind her lids. She tucked her hands between her knees, shifted a little, moaned.

Then Brice was back, unwrapping the scarf from her neck.

She clamped a hand to the scarf. "Don't do that. I'm cold."

"Your things are damp from the snow," he said tightly. "I have blankets. You'll be warmer in them."

Something of what he said made sense. Karen removed her hand from the scarf and was about to lift her head to help him when he did it for her. Gently, firmly, efficiently. In the same manner, he removed her mittens, then her coat. She was sitting up by this time, feeling awkward and not so much cold as hot. Brice was squatting before her, tugging at her high boots.

"I can do that," she insisted, but feebly, and he had the boots off before she could muster the strength.

Closing a hand around her foot, which felt cold even through the wool tights she wore, he looked up at her. "How long did you say this has been going on?"

She lifted one shoulder in a shrug. "A little while."

"How little a while?"

"A week. Maybe two."

He was studying her eyes in a strange way. She was

trying to figure out what he saw there when he suddenly raised his hand and began to touch her neck.

With a hoarse cry, she shrank out of his reach. "What are you doing?"

"Checking for swollen glands. Did that hurt?"

"I don't know."

He shifted to sit on the sofa, and his hand was back, fingers probing efficiently, before Karen could escape. "Hurt?"

"No!" she protested, then promptly started to cough. When she'd caught her breath, she said, "Persistent, aren't you? Where did you get your medical degree? Sears and Roebuck?"

Brice dropped his hand and said stiffly, "Yale, actually. Then Sloan-Kettering."

Karen's jaw dropped.

He was almost as surprised. "You didn't know I was a doctor?"

She shook her head.

"Rowena never told you?"

She shook her head again.

He frowned. "How much *do* you know about me?"

"Just that you're Rowena's grandson, that you visit her often and that you have no cause to like me."

"Right on all three counts," he said, then narrowed an eye. "And she never said I was a doctor?"

Karen wanted to lie down again. Her head felt like lead, her eyes like hot pokers, her chest like a trough of mud, her stomach like quicksand. "I've answered that twice," she said, and not caring that Brice was sitting right there, keeled over and curled up. She broke into several deep, hacking coughs, then murmured weakly, "I don't understand it." Her eyes were closed, one arm thrown over her face. "It was a cold. Just a cold."

"When did it start?"

"Three weeks ago."

"Three."

"It's been coming and going ever since."

"Did you pamper it at all?"

She didn't answer at first. Her breathing was audible over the crackle of the flames. Finally she said, "I tried taking naps, but I couldn't sleep."

"You must have stayed home from school."

She shifted, moaned, murmured, "How do you know I go to school?"

Brice propped his elbows on his knees, but there was nothing casual about his expression. His features were hard. "I know you go to school because I did some snooping when I found out you were visiting my grandmother. You're a second-semester freshman. You're on half-scholarship. You pay the rest by doing research for Arnold McGuire and waiting tables at the Pepper Mill."

Karen suddenly felt exposed. She began to shake again. "You said you had blankets," she whispered, not looking at Brice. Within moments, a light weight covered her body, then a second weight joined the first. Still she trembled.

If she'd been sitting up, facing him, showing the slightest semblance of strength, Brice might have continued his questioning. But she was such a miserable figure that he couldn't. Without thinking beyond warming her up, he began to rub her back. She tried to escape his touch at first, but when his hand persisted in following her, she gave in.

She was too thin, Brice realized. He'd caught sight of her on other occasions when she'd visited Rowena and she'd always given the impression of slenderness. Now he felt it with his hands. He chafed her back, slowed the pace to rub her arms and legs. He wondered how much weight she'd lost to her illness.

"Are you taking any medicine?" he asked evenly.

She didn't answer. Seconds later, she sent him a dazed frown and croaked, "I didn't…did you ask something?"

"Are you taking any medicine?"

"Mmm." In a thin, cracked voice she listed an antihistamine, a nasal spray and a cough syrup by brand. All were over-the-counter remedies that, Brice knew, were akin to putting a finger in the dyke.

"When did you take them last?"

She was drifting in and out. "This morning—no, noon—mmm, before I left to see Rowena."

He continued his rubbing until her tremors had eased. Then he felt her cheek with the back of his hand and rose from the sofa. Several minutes later, he was back.

"Karen?" He pushed a tangle of hair from her forehead.

With effort, she opened her eyes.

"I have to know your temperature. Can you put this under your tongue?"

Obediently she opened her mouth, then closed it on the cool, slim instrument.

"Have you seen a doctor at all?"

She made a small, negative movement with her head.

"Are you taking any medication other than what you just told me?"

She repeated the negative gesture.

"Has there been any nausea along with the cold?"

No.

"You've had dizziness, though. Any fainting spells before today?"

No.

"Are you pregnant?"

The headshake came a little faster this time. With the thermometer still in her mouth, she coughed, then winced and pressed her head to the cushions.

"That hurt?"

She gave a single nod.

"Your head or your chest?" She was trying to figure out how to answer when he simplified things by asking, "Both?"

She nodded.

He left her alone for a minute, and she gratefully faded out. Then he was back, this time disturbing the blankets. She yielded the thermometer to Brice just before he drew her sweater over her head. Then she fell back to the sofa and looked up at him. She might have protested had she not been feeling warm again. The air felt good on her neck, and her pullover had been too warm anyway.

"Is it hot in here, or is it me?" she asked in a raw whisper.

"It's you," Brice answered. He flicked open the first few buttons of her blouse, warmed the stethoscope on his thigh for a second, then slid it against her skin. When he'd heard enough, he flicked open two more buttons and eased the blouse away from her shoulders to gain access to her back. At length, he folded the instrument and set it aside. Then he drew the blankets back to her chin.

Karen waited for him to speak. As disoriented as she felt, she sensed something in his silence, and along with the sensing came fear. To be examined by a doctor was to admit to sickness, but she didn't have the time to be sick. She couldn't *afford* to be sick.

But she was. On top of whatever germ lurked in her body, she was overworked, overtired, overwrought. It wasn't fair, when she was trying so hard to do it all and succeed. And she thought she *had* been succeeding— until now. Suddenly her world seemed to be caving in.

Unable to help herself, she began to cry.

Brice hadn't expected that. She'd been remarkably composed up to then. He'd thought her too hard for tears.

But there they came, trickling down her cheeks with the slow cadence of near-silent sobs.

His first thought was that she wanted something, that she was playing on his sympathy to achieve her own ends. But there was something about the way she was hiding her head, shrinking into herself as though she were mortified. She looked very uncomfortable, very unhappy and very alone.

He could identify with all three.

"You'll be okay," he assured her gruffly. He raised a hand to stroke her hair but stopped short and, instead, cupped her shoulder. "There's no need for a hospital. I can treat you myself."

He had no idea if she heard him. The soft crying continued.

Feeling oddly helpless, he moved his hand to her back and began to rub it as he'd been doing earlier. "It's all right, Karen. You'll be fine once you've had the right medication and some rest."

She sniffled and used her hands to wipe the tears.

"Are you allergic to penicillin?"

"No," she whispered without looking at him.

"You've had it before?"

She gave a quick nod.

"Good," he said. His hand had stopped on her shoulder. He gave it a squeeze, then rose from the sofa and left the room.

Without knowing why, Karen started crying again, but she regained control of herself sooner this time and, other than the intermittent cough, was lying quietly when he returned.

"I'm going to give you a shot," he said, moving the blankets only as much as was necessary. "That way the medicine will get into your system faster."

She barely felt the sting of the needle. It was lost

among the rest of her aches, and even if it hadn't been she would have welcomed anything that promised to bring her relief. When the blankets were tucked around her once more, she settled into them and, with surprising speed, fell asleep.

"KAREN?"

She gave a closed-mouth cough.

"Karen?" Brice raised her until she was nearly sitting. "I want you to swallow some aspirin for the fever."

She struggled to open her eyes and whispered a hoarse, "What time is it?"

"Dinnertime," he said in that same low voice that wasn't quite hostile, wasn't quite friendly. "Are you hungry?"

She shook her head, opened her mouth to take in the two tablets he pressed there, then washed them down with several sips of water.

He tapped her bottom lip with the edge of the cup. "Finish it. You need the liquid."

"I have to go to the bathroom."

"When you finish the water."

She finished the water because she was thirsty. Then wrapping the blankets securely over her shoulders, she gripped the edge of the sofa and tried to push herself up, only to lose her balance and sink right back down.

She moaned but held up a hand to stop Brice when he would have lifted her. "I'm okay." This time she made it to her feet and managed to weave halfway across the floor before wavering. Brice was there to catch her.

"If there's one thing I can't stand," he muttered as he carried her through the hall, "it's a bullheaded woman."

"Do you know many?"

He frowned down at her. "My grandmother and you.

Two peas in a pod, only *you* can't blame it on senility like she does."

"She's not senile."

"Damn right she's not, but she's wily enough to use it as an excuse." He set her down inside a warmly lit powder room and asked in a voice edged with sarcasm, "Can you manage, or should I stay here and hold you?"

Karen pointed a shaky finger toward the hall. She shut the door firmly the instant he was out, then quickly dropped the blankets and collapsed on the commode.

Brice settled himself on the stairway nearby. It wasn't that he didn't respect Karen's right to privacy, simply that he was worried she'd fall and hurt herself. Not that he cared, on one level. She could hurt herself if she pleased, but on her own time. While she was in his home, she was his responsibility, and he took his responsibilities seriously.

Apparently so did Karen, but she'd gone off the deep end this time. She was weak and shaky, feverish and congested. It galled him that she'd gone to visit Rowena in that condition. Then again, it amazed him that she'd been able to pull it off. Sheer willpower must have kept her on her feet.

Sheer willpower, he didn't mind. He respected independence. Same thing with determination. But he had little patience with bullheadedness. Karen had been crazy not to pay attention to her health. She must have suspected that she had more than a cold when she was still feeling lousy after two weeks. Nevertheless, she hadn't taken time off from school, she hadn't taken time off from work, she hadn't seen a doctor…and she'd continued to visit Rowena.

His features darkened each time he thought of that. She had no business risking Rowena's health. He wondered why she had. Was it selfishness? Or bullheadedness, a refusal to admit she was sick? Or was it guilt that brought her two times a week, week after week to Rowena's side?

The bathroom door opened slowly. Karen emerged holding tightly to the knob with one hand, to the blankets with the other. Her face was damp, as though she'd splashed it with water, and the wet tendrils of hair that framed it gave her a fragile look. In the dim light of the hall the shadows beneath her eyes were more pronounced. Wrappings and all, she looked as if a gust of wind would blow her over.

Brice Carlin was a sucker for people in need. He'd always been that way, which was why he found his profession so rewarding. When people were sick, they were in need. When they came to him, he did everything in his power to treat the need, heal the wound, cure the illness. It wasn't always possible, and those cases made him ache. The thought of his grandmother, once such an active woman, now sidelined, made him ache. He couldn't cure her ills, and she fought him right and left, which didn't help.

Karen wasn't fighting him—at least not at the moment. Swathed in a mass of blankets, with only her head showing above and her stockinged feet showing beneath, she was looking at him as though she was lost and in need of direction. Moreover, she seemed to be relying on him for that direction and would be willing to do whatever he said.

It should have been heady, that sense of power, particularly feeling it over Karen Drew. Strangely, though, it wasn't as satisfying as he would have thought.

Rising from the stairs, he approached her. "Everything okay?"

She nodded. He saw the tremor at her shoulders that said she was shivering.

"Want to go back in the living room?"

She nodded again.

He didn't wait for her to crumple this time. Nor did he lift her from the ground. Rather, he curved an arm around her waist and provided the little bit of extra steam she needed to walk.

Once back on the living room sofa, she immediately put down her head and closed her eyes. Brice was standing there just looking at her when she said in a small, nasal voice, "They were expecting me at the Pepper Mill. I have to call."

"I'll do it."

Eyes still closed, she gave a single short nod. She didn't thank him, nor did she offer the number, but Brice didn't expect either. He knew that she was totally drained and could well imagine the energy it took for her to speak.

Without another word, he went into the kitchen and called the restaurant. Then he made himself a sandwich, poured a glass of milk and carried both back into the living room to eat before the fire.

Exhausted, Karen slept through his meal, but it was a fitful sleep. She didn't thrash around; she was too weak for that. Rather, she moved an arm, then rested, moved a leg, then rested, turned her head on the armrest, rested, coughed, rested, inched the blankets higher on her neck.

Brice watched her. He thought back to how he'd picked her up from the snow, and though technically it all made sense, there was something odd about her being in his home. Part of it was that he wasn't used to having a woman around. He wasn't used to having anyone around. He was a solitary man, a man who, after hours, liked his home and his time to himself.

He didn't feel like reading a book now, though. He didn't feel like listening to music or proofing the article he'd written or watching a basketball game. He felt like sitting and watching Karen.

Which was what was so strange. Karen Drew. Of all people. That she was in his living room, huddled beneath blankets on his sofa, entrusting herself to his care was incredible. That he had invited her to do so was even more bizarre.

She came to with a start. She gasped, coughed, peered at him over a corner of the blanket, then dropped her head and fell back to sleep.

"Karen?" He lowered the blanket from her face to find that her cheeks were still flushed, her skin hot. Settling on the edge of the sofa, he propped her up against his chest. "More aspirin."

Her eyes flickered. They didn't exactly open, but he sensed she saw something because she opened her mouth just when he reached it with the pills.

"Another shot?" she asked in a scratchy whisper after the pills were gone.

"You slept through it."

She seemed content with that. "What time is it?"

"Eleven."

She did come to life then, opening her eyes wide, struggling to sit up on her own. "Eleven at night?" The darkness of the room attested to it. The flame in the hearth provided the sole light. "Is it still snowing?"

"Yes."

With a whimper, she sank back against him. "I have to get home."

"Not tonight, you don't."

"I can't *stay* here."

"I thought we settled that."

With another whimper, she rolled toward the back of the sofa, where she murmured to the thick corduroy, "I have so much to do. I can't stay. I can't."

Brice's patience began to wane. "You can't go any-where until the snow ends and the roads are cleared."

"If I were home, I could work on my paper."

"Uh-uh. You're sick."

"I could still work," she argued. Her voice was dis-tant, its throaty sound absorbed by the corduroy. "I could bundle myself up in bed and write."

"How would you do that," he asked sharply, "when you can't keep your head up for more than five seconds at a stretch?"

"I could do it."

He considered the possibility, then said with disdain, "I suppose you could. It's probably nothing more than you've been doing for the past three weeks. Tell me. How much sleep do you get a night?" When she shrugged, he prodded. "How much?"

She shrugged again, but this time she followed it up with a subdued, "Five hours, maybe."

"And you think that's enough? Hasn't it occurred to you that you may be run-down? That if you'd taken care of yourself when you'd first caught cold, you'd be fine now?"

Karen's will to argue was petering out. "You sound like a doctor."

"I *am* a doctor."

"And a self-righteous one at that," she mumbled, but he heard it.

Rising to his feet, he stared down at her back. "Self-righteous or not, I'm right, and if you have any brains, little lady, you'll admit it. You may be great at jam-packing your life with a million and one things to do, but there comes a time when you have to slow down, and if you can't see that, you're in big trouble." Bent on get-ting the last word, he strode from the room, but by the time he reached the kitchen, he was growling to himself.

"Bullheaded woman." He grabbed a saucepan, filled it with water and put it on the stove none too gently. As soon as the gas was dancing beneath it, he opened a nearby cabinet. "Why do I waste my breath? She won't listen. She'll do the same thing again." He put a large mug on the counter. "And so what if she does? It's no sweat off my back. What in the hell is she to me?" Taking a tea bag from a cannister, he tossed it into the mug, then raised both hands in surrender. "Want to kill yourself, go ahead. I'm not your keeper."

Karen didn't respond, of course. Back in the living room, she couldn't hear a word he said. She was fully awake, though, and aware of how awful she felt—most immediately, how hot. Pushing the blankets aside, she sat up and plucked her blouse from her sweat-dampened skin. It was already free of her skirt, but the skirt was a heavy wool number that was at the moment unwanted. So she pushed it off her hips and out of the way.

Her blouse covered her from neck to thigh, her wool tights from waist to toe. Folding her legs Indian-style with the blouse draped sedately between, she sat forward. The change of position felt nice for a minute, but she was still too warm.

So she put a hand to her hair. The long curls that she'd secured from crown to nape in a series of barrettes had long since escaped their bonds. Removing the barrettes, she combed her fingers through the wayward tangles, lifted them and let them fall over the top of the sofa as she sat back. Then, hands lying limply by her hips, she closed her eyes and tried to think cool.

That was how Brice found her when he returned. He was carrying the mug of tea, expecting that she'd be lying as he'd left her with her back to the fire, and he came to a sudden halt when he saw it wasn't so.

For a minute he simply stood there. She was an elf

in loden green, wispy and petite. She was also sexy as hell, but the instant he heard the thought, he denied it. She wasn't sexy; she was sick.

Armed with that deliberate reminder, he continued into the room. Karen didn't move until he crossed in front of the fire, alerting her to his presence. Whether it was his shadow or the deflection of heat with his passing, he didn't know, but she opened her eyes, stared at him blankly for a minute, then suddenly realized what she was wearing and how she was sitting. Quick as a flash, she shifted her weight, brought her legs together and grabbed the blanket.

"I was hot," she murmured without looking at him. Homing in on one of the barrettes she'd discarded, she gathered her hair and shakily secured it into a high ponytail.

Brice set the tea on the end table within easy reach of her hand and said, "Drink this." Then he hunkered down by the hearth and added another log to the fire. "It may make you sweat more, but it'll loosen up what's in your chest."

Karen cast a dubious glance at the mug and asked quietly, "Is it poison?"

"I didn't have the guts."

"Then it must be tea. Almost as bad." Turning sideways, she drew her knees in and covered them with the blanket. "I've had so much tea in the past three weeks that I should be sprouting tags."

Brice found the thought vaguely amusing, but he didn't crack a smile. He had other things on his mind. Swiveling, he faced her. "I wasn't trying to be self-righteous before. I was trying to get across the message that if you hope to get better, you'll have to take a breather from that schedule of yours."

She moved her cheek against the sofa and fiddled with

the blanket binding. "What's wrong with me?" she asked almost idly.

"Bronchial pneumonia, I'd guess."

She closed her eyes, only then aware that she'd been frightened. She'd lived through years of illness with her parents, but bronchial pneumonia wasn't so bad. "Are you sure?"

Brice frowned. "Were you expecting something else?"

"No," she answered quickly. "I just wondered."

"I don't think you have cause for worry. Assuming," he added sternly, "that you take care of yourself. This looks like a classic case. I can't know for sure unless you're X-rayed, and I don't have the equipment here. If the penicillin works, it won't be necessary."

"How long will it take to work?"

"A day, maybe two."

She tipped back her head, closed her eyes and whispered, "Two days. Oh, hell."

Her head lowered, but her eyes stayed shut. Brice thought of reminding her that it was a weekend, that she couldn't have picked a better time to be sick, that by the first of the week she'd be feeling a whole lot better, but he thought twice and remained still. She would argue that her weekends were precious, that she had to work at the restaurant, that she had to write her paper. He remembered the grind. He'd been through it himself. But that had been when he'd been young and pompous, when he'd felt he was God's gift to the ill.

When had he changed, and why? He wasn't sure. It hadn't been anything traumatic, simply the passage of time, the reaching of maturity. Somewhere in his early thirties—just about the age Karen was reaching—he'd realized that there was more to life than work. That was when he'd bought his home and set up shop in Ithaca, when he'd rediscovered books and music, when he'd begun to travel.

It was also when he'd learned about loneliness.

Taking the chair not far from the sofa, he slid low in it, extended his legs, crossed his ankles, folded his hands on his chest and watched Karen sleep.

IT WAS NEARLY TWO in the morning when she awoke. The room was darker than before. The fire had burned down to a layer of smoldering embers that could barely produce enough heat to warm the room. That didn't bother her, though. She was burning up again, dripping with sweat. Pushing the blanket aside, she sat up, only to lie right back down when her head protested the sudden movement. It was from that position that she looked for Brice.

He was a long dark form sprawled in the chair.

"Brice?" she whispered, not sure if he was asleep.

He didn't answer.

She rose gingerly this time, pushed herself to her feet and crossed the room. After pausing to steady herself at the door, she continued on into the bathroom. Several minutes later, she was leaning heavily against the sink with a wet towel over her eyes when a knock came at the door, followed closely by an imperative, "Are you all right?"

Blindly she reached for the door and pulled it open. "I'm okay," she croaked.

Brice took one look at the way she was standing—as though the only things keeping her upright were a pair of locked knees and the sink—and eased her down to the toilet seat. Her head and shoulder came to rest against his hip with something akin to finality.

"You should have woken me," he said—irritably, because he felt bad and didn't want to.

She gave the tiniest of headshakes against his hip.

"How long have you been up?" he asked.

"A couple of minutes."

"Don't feel so hot?"

"I feel *too* hot. That's the problem."

Brice saw the way strands of hair were plastered to her neck. He brushed his fingers under the back collar of her blouse; the skin there was wet with sweat. "Has the towel helped?"

"A little."

"Want to sponge off more?"

"I want a bath."

He tried to decide whether it was petulance he heard or simply bluntness. He supposed it didn't matter. "Do you feel strong enough?"

"It doesn't take strength to lie in a tub."

"It does if you want to keep from drowning."

She moaned. "Maybe I'll just go back to sleep."

Brice let her consider the options for a minute, during which time she coughed once but didn't otherwise move. He leaned forward to see if she'd fallen asleep.

"Karen?"

After a minute, she gave a nasal, "Hmm?"

"I'm taking you upstairs. There's a bath. And a bed."

"Not yours," she said with surprising fierceness.

"No."

Her fierceness vanished. "Okay."

Slipping an arm beneath her knees and one around her back, he carried her into the hall, then up the winding stairs. There were four spare bedrooms, only one of which was furnished. He took her there. With only the lamp from the hall to light his way, he set her gently on the four-poster bed. Then he entered the adjoining bathroom and ran a warm bath before returning for her.

And it hit him again. Something about her as she sat

on the edge of the bed. Something that touched him for no apparent reason.

Women didn't usually touch him, not in the emotional sense. But Karen did.

Unsurely she turned her head to him. Then, painstakingly, she got up from the bed and crossed to the bathroom. He stood aside.

"Can you handle it?" he asked without a trace of sarcasm.

She nodded.

"Yell if there's a problem."

Again she nodded, then shut the door.

Frowning, Brice went to the window. The room looked out on the front of the house, the circular drive, the short road to the street. A lamppost stood at the point where the road met the drive. It was lit. He left it lit all night, every night, a sign that he was home if someone needed him.

Tonight it lit a particularly beautiful scene. Snow was still falling, blanketing not only the lawn but the surrounding stands of juniper, hemlock and pine. The light bathed them gently, the effect was one of charm, of peace.

Taking a bit of that peace inside him, he went to the bed, drew back the hand-quilted coverlet, straightened the pillow. He glanced at the small line of light that escaped from beneath the bathroom door, listened, heard nothing. So he called, "Are you okay, Karen?"

"Uh-huh," came her weak reply.

For another minute he stood with his hands on his hips, wondering what he could do. Then he left the room and went down the hall to his own, where he found the largest, softest shirt he owned.

Back at the bathroom door, he called, "Still awake?"

"Uh-huh," came the same weak reply.

After several minutes, he heard a splash, then the soft rush of water down the drain. Bracing his back against the wall, he waited for her to dry off, then waited through an even longer period of total silence. Finally it was broken by the hesitant call of his name.

He opened the door to find her wrapped in a towel, sitting on the edge of the tub. Her face was washed out, her tired eyes sending him a frantic message. Her shoulders were bare, very pale, very thin. And she was shaking.

Wishing he could say something sharp about helpless women but unable to utter a word, he helped her into the shirt, buttoning it down to her thighs before tugging the towel from underneath. Then he scooped her up and put her in bed before returning to tidy the bathroom.

When he emerged, she was sleeping. He touched her skin; it was cooler than before. He brushed several long, wispy curls from her cheek, ran his thumb very, very lightly over the line of her jaw to her chin. He took a spare blanket from the closet and layered it over the quilt. Then, leaving a slim sliver of light coming from the bathroom and the door to the hall open, he returned to his room to lie awake for hours trying to summon up suitable contempt for Karen Drew.

CHAPTER THREE

KAREN HAD BEEN driving the car that had hit Rowena two years before. The night had been dark, the road narrow. Rowena had had no business riding a bicycle without reflectors at that time of night, Karen's lawyer had argued, and the judge had agreed. Allegations that Karen had been speeding had been impossible to prove.

Brice had been furious.

His fury had toned down some since the day of the verdict, but it had far from disappeared. He knew that he couldn't blame Karen for Rowena's stroke, but he blamed her for most else, which was why he'd been livid the month before, when he'd arrived to visit Rowena and first seen Karen there. He'd raised hell with the administrators of the home, particularly when they told him Karen had been a regular visitor since shortly after Rowena had arrived. He'd gone so far as to forbid them to let her in again, but they'd calmly told him that the matter wasn't his to decide. Rowena was in the nursing home by her own choice and at her own expense. Hardest to accept was their claim that Rowena looked forward to Karen's visits, though he could almost believe it—his grandmother was a sunny, forgiving sort.

He was not.

He had to remember that.

KAREN SLEPT SOUNDLY for a time, then more fitfully as dawn approached. She coughed often, coughs that shook her slender frame from within and left her weak. She was more comfortable in bed, where the sheets were smooth and cool against her skin, and the large shirt she wore was a definite improvement over a sweaty blouse and wool tights, but her head felt twice its normal size, and the rest of her ached.

She was aware of the occasional ring of a distant phone and of Brice's periodic, professional ministrations. He left the room dark and rarely spoke, and when he did he said little, which was fine with her, as she wasn't up to talking.

Even through the haze of her illness, though, she thought him a contradiction. He didn't like her, and with good reason. Yet while his voice was cool, his hands were gentle. He was conscientious in his care of her, and she couldn't imagine why. She couldn't imagine why he hadn't left her lying in the snow the afternoon before.

It was late in the morning when she awoke for more than a groggy minute or two. Shifting position, she raised an arm to sweep her ponytail off her neck and left her wrist propped limply on her head as she looked around the room. For the first time she registered the early American charm of its decor, but that was an overall impression. She didn't have time to examine the details because Brice caught her eye.

He was sitting in a wooden rocker, not rocking, just staring. It seemed the simplest thing for her to stare right back.

He was a very serious man. His hair was dark and on the long side. His eyes were dark also, though she couldn't tell their color over the distance. His features had a ruggedness to them that seemed somehow mismatched with the preppiness of his clothes—a fresh version of the shirt, sweater and cords he'd worn the day before.

She guessed him to be forty, though whether the stoniness of his expression made him look older than he actually was she didn't know. Etched into that stone was a crease between his eyes. He was a very serious man, indeed.

The very serious man spoke. "How do you feel?"

"Okay," she said in a strained non-sound.

"That tells me nothing, and you sound like hell. Do you feel better or worse?"

She thought about that for a minute. "Better, I guess. My bones don't hurt as much." The gaze she turned to the window grew worried. "It's still snowing, isn't it?"

"Yes."

"The roads haven't been plowed?"

"They have—several times—but it keeps piling up."

"Maybe the next time the plows come around—"

He knew just what she was thinking, could see it in the slight, hopeful rise of her brows. He was quick to set her straight. "The plows can't help you. They don't come near the house, and my own man won't be by until the snow stops."

"But you're a doctor," she argued in that same would-be voice. "You have to get out."

"My office is here."

"Then patients have to get in."

"They know to try the hospital in weather like this. If there was a severe emergency, the police would come for me."

She closed her eyes and swallowed hard, then looked at the ceiling. "I can't stay here all day." She dropped her gaze to his relentlessly unwavering one. "You can't want me to stay."

"You're wasting your voice."

"I'm the *last* person you want in your home."

Brice's expression was grim. "I don't have any more

choice in the matter than you do. I can't turn off the snow. In fact, the snow just turned off the electricity, so now the town crews have something else to worry about besides plowing."

Karen greeted that news with a look of despair, but she didn't say anything. Talking was a definite effort. Sinking deeper into the pillow, she closed her eyes and thought of her apartment in Syracuse, thought of the books waiting on her desk, thought of her job at the Pepper Mill and wondered if they'd hold it for her when she failed to show two days in a row. Rolling to her side, she gave a helpless moan and clutched her stomach.

Brice's hand was on her forehead nearly before the moan had died. She was still warm, but not as hot as she'd been. He hadn't expected the beads of sweat that suddenly dotted her nose.

Concerned in spite of himself, he asked, "What is it?"

"Nothing," she whispered.

"Are you feeling worse?"

She didn't answer.

"Karen."

"It's my mind," she mumbled.

"Explain that."

She opened her eyes to his and wondered if a man like him, a man who seemed to be totally controlled, could possibly understand. "When I think about everything I should be doing, I get an awful feeling. Like something's holding me down, smothering me. Like something's inside trying to get out. Antsy. Almost panicky."

Brice understood, all right, but rather than launch into a repeat of his repent-or-suffer speech, he straightened. "I haven't got any medicine for that. You're right. It's psychological."

She snorted, then realized the error of that when she started to cough. After she'd caught her breath, she closed her eyes again and whispered, "Don't you have something that can knock me out until the snow stops and I can leave?"

He studied her ashen face. "Is that what you want?"

She was silent, then said in a defeated whisper, "I just want to get up and walk out and go back to doing everything that has to be done."

"Karen, the world will still be there when you recover."

She gave a skeptical "Hmph," which was all she could garner the strength for. She'd zapped herself again.

Sensing that, Brice said, "You must be hungry."

"No more tea," she whispered.

"I was thinking of eggs and toast."

Turning to her other side, she snuggled into the quilt. "Maybe later."

"You should eat."

"Later."

Frowning, he stared at her. Then his frown became a scowl. He felt as though he'd been dismissed. It was a disconcerting feeling, one he didn't particularly like. People didn't usually turn down his services.

Not that he'd offered this particular service to many people. There was Karen, and Rowena. Rowena had refused it, too. That had been years before, when he'd still been in the city, and she'd taken time out from her endless stream of activities to pay him a visit. He'd thought himself rather gallant to have offered, and he'd been hurt when she'd turned him down flat.

"I've seen how you make your eggs, Brice Carlin," she'd said in a knowing tone. "*Hard*. You want them to obey you. You want them to stay just so on the plate. Well, I like my eggs soft. I like them doing their own thing. I like having to chase them a little. Soft eggs make life interesting."

At the time he'd simply scowled and yielded the kitchen to her, but he'd thought about her message afterward and gradually he'd begun to make his eggs softer. Somehow, though, he'd never had the opportunity to offer Rowena breakfast again. She'd been always on the go, and when she visited him, she insisted on taking over his kitchen.

Now, of course, she couldn't do that.

Hardened by the thought, and still annoyed that Karen hadn't jumped at his offer, he headed straight for the kitchen, where he proceeded to cook the breakfast that she was going to eat. When he returned to her room, she was sleeping.

Twice he reached for her, intent on waking her up. Twice he drew back and straightened. Then, glaring at her tucked form, he grabbed the tray from where he'd set it, returned to the kitchen and, with a pithy oath, dumped the soft, perfectly cooked eggs into the sink.

KAREN WAS HUNGRY when she woke up, and Brice was nowhere in sight, which disconcerted her. He had the strangest capacity to make her feel safe. She supposed it was the aura of command he projected. He had certainly taken over when she'd collapsed in the snow, and she had to admit she could have done far worse than landing in a warm house with her own personal physician. It wasn't like he was keeping her there against her wishes. The snow was doing that.

Slowly, she sat up, dropped her feet to the floor and steadied herself, then padded silently to the window. Still snowing. She glanced down at her watch, only to remember she'd left it in the bathroom when she'd bathed. After retrieving it, she looked around.

Her clothes were nowhere in sight or she'd have surely put them on, if only to tell herself she was on her way home. Not that anything she saw out the window suggested she *was* on her way home, but whenever she thought of the time that was passing, she felt that restlessness bordering on panic that she'd described to Brice.

Pushing panic from mind, she straightened in front of the bathroom mirror and took stock of herself. That was even more discouraging, and her legs had begun to wobble, so she returned to the bedroom, this time sliding into the rocking chair Brice had occupied earlier.

Slowly she rocked. Slowly she looked around the room. As prisons went, it was quite charming, she mused. The four-poster was early American, as was the dresser. The quilt on the bed matched the dust ruffle and the drapes, all done in a coordinated variety of small country prints. The colors were mauve and pale blue, and were picked up as solids in a cornice over the window, as well as in the frame of a mirror and those of several small pieces of what looked to be original art.

A decorator had obviously done the room, she decided. Brice was a doctor. He didn't have the time to spend on collecting and placing such things as the matched pitcher and basin that stood on the bureau. She doubted he'd have the inclination, either. He looked to be a clinician, a man who diagnosed and treated, diagnosed and treated, diagnosed and treated, with a slew of paperwork in between. Not an artistic man at all.

Still, the room was lovely. Emotionally warm. Physically cold. She was eyeing the blanket on the bed, wondering if it was worth the effort of getting out of the chair, when Brice appeared at the door.

He took one look at her, and his expression darkened. Striding to the bed, he snatched up the blanket. He didn't ask her to rise; the hand he placed on her arm did it in no uncertain terms. As soon as she was upright, he wrapped the blanket around her, pressed her back into the chair and knelt to tuck the wool around her feet.

"In case you hadn't noticed," he muttered, "the temperature in here is dropping."

Feeling foolish, she said nothing, but he wasn't satisfied with that. So he eyed her accusingly. "You didn't feel cold?"

"A little, but I figured I'd be sweating in another minute." She endured his silent study of her face for a minute before asking, "Where are my clothes?"

"Downstairs."

She waited for him to say that he'd get them for her. When he didn't she asked as sweetly as she could, given the rasping of her voice, "Am I allowed to have them?"

"No."

The sweetness disappeared. "Why not?"

"Because you're sick. If I give you your clothes, you're apt to think you're better and go running out the door, and if you do that, I'll have to go out after you, and it's still snowing."

Karen eyed him in disbelief. "You're keeping me here by keeping me naked?"

"You're not naked."

"Close to it."

"I know."

He hadn't smiled. The inflection of his voice hadn't varied from its usual evenness, but there was something of a sudden glimmer in his eyes that pricked Karen inside. She decided that the prick was a hunger pang, since that was what she'd felt before, and, besides, she had the sinking feeling that another discussion with Brice about when she could leave would get her nowhere but tired.

She wanted to discuss food—in particular, how she could get a little of it—but she hesitated. She felt like a parasite. She'd taken shelter, warmth, even clothing from Brice, when in essence she was the enemy.

So she simply sat there and looked at him, waiting for him to ask again if she was hungry."

"How do you feel?" he asked instead.

"Weak," she answered, hoping he'd take the hint.

He didn't. Thrusting a hand in the pocket of his slacks, he asked, "When was the last time you slept as much as this?"

"When I was four months old. According to my mother, I only got up for meals." Another hint tossed out.

Another hint missed. "Is your mother still living?"

"No."

Brice took his hand from his pocket and ran it around the back of his neck. He tried to remember if he'd seen anyone with her during the trial. He didn't think he had. "Do you have any family?"

"No." She paused, asked cautiously, "How about you?"

"Just Rowena."

She tried again. "You live here alone, then? No house-keeper…cook…?"

"A woman comes in on weekdays."

"To cook?" She didn't think she could be more blunt.

"Mostly to clean. I'm not a fussy eater."

"Neither am I," Karen said.

She paused, waited, was just about to give up when Brice informed her, "You really ought to eat. Even if you're not hungry. You have to build yourself up."

"I'm *hungry*," she said without further ado.

His expression turned indignant. "Why didn't you say so?"

"Because I've imposed on you too much already."

"So what's a little more? I think I can spare a couple of eggs."

"A piece of toast will be plenty."

"No, it won't. You're not much more than skin and bones."

"Thanks," she whispered, feeling hurt for no valid reason. She knew she was thin, and Brice had done nothing more than use a common figure of speech. Why she suddenly felt like a living scarecrow—and why it mattered to her—was the puzzlement. She wondered if it had something to do with the contrasting hardiness of his physique.

Eyes averted, she started to rise from the chair. "Actually, I'd be glad to help myself—"

"Sit," Brice growled.

She sat.

"Better still, get back in bed."

But Karen didn't like being ordered around. "I'll sit here," she said with as much dignity as she could muster given the rusty sound of her voice and her ridiculously swathed shape. She did hold her chin steady, and her eyes were firm on his. Apparently she succeeded in conveying the strength of her intent, because after staring at her for several long, silent moments, Brice turned on his heel and left the room.

Only when Karen heard his footsteps recede to a safe enough distance did she get up from the chair and return to bed, which was where he found her when he returned fifteen minutes later. Because she was lying on her side facing the window, she didn't see the way he paused for an instant at the door. Nor did she see the self-satisfied look that passed over his face in that instant. When he suddenly appeared in her line of vision, she slowly raised her eyes.

He gave a short toss of his chin. In response, she struggled up and propped both pillows behind her back. He set the tray across her knees, then stepped away and settled into the rocker to watch her eat.

Unfortunately, her general grogginess didn't prevent her from feeling awkward. She wasn't a performer. She didn't like being the center of attention. Some people called her shy, and once upon a time that had been true. Now she was simply a private person. She did her own thing, went her own way. Even if she hadn't been too busy to cultivate large groups of friends, that wasn't her style. She was a loner, she supposed even more so of late.

She wasn't used to eating under anyone's watchful eyes, let alone those of a man like Brice Carlin, whose gaze was sharp and critical.

Still, she ate. Hunger could overcome dozens of inhibitions, she decided. Not that she tasted all she ate. But the juice was just smooth enough, the eggs just soft enough, the toast just crisp enough...which raised an immediate question.

"How did you make the toast?"

"Under the broiler."

She'd tried that once when her toaster had been on the blink. The toast had burned. Apparently Brice had the knack she didn't.

"Did you make the jam?" she asked. It was strawberry, and delicious.

He shook his head. And sat. He had one long leg loosely folded over the other, his elbows on the arms of the chair, his fingers laced. He would have looked perfectly relaxed had not his mouth been so firmly set. And his eyes didn't let up on her for a minute.

By the time she'd finished a little more than half of what he'd served, she set down her fork and frowned at Brice. "What are you staring at?"

He replied with a soft, swift intake of breath, as though she'd brought him out of a trance. Raising both brows, he shrugged.

"You've done it before," she said. "I feel like I'm on display."

"You are."

"Why?"

He wasn't about to say that she fascinated him, because he didn't want to admit it to himself, much less to her. But there was something about her looks that made him want to look again, and the oddness of that commanded his thought.

She was skinny. Her skin was pale, her eyes shadowed. Her hair was too long, too curly, too dull. So what was he looking at?

He was looking at the smoothness of her pale skin, the dark amber of her shadowed eyes. He was looking at the way one of those too-long curls was caught between the collar of his shirt and her neck, and he was thinking that it was a shade lighter than some, a shade darker than others of those curls, and that if she were in good health it would probably shine. He was also looking at the way his shirt fell over her shoulders, making them look delicate, and the way her breasts made themselves known beneath the slope of soft fabric in front. He was thinking that there was something secretly seductive about the woman—either that or he'd gone soft in the brain.

Sure it was the latter, he snapped himself out of his thoughts and put on a hard face. "You're on display because you're the only woman around."

"If there were others, would they be on display, too?"

"That'd depend. I'm a one-woman man."

"So you'd pick the one who irked you most and focus your stare on her?"

"Probably."

Pushing the tray aside, she slid lower on the pillows. "Has it ever occurred to you that staring that way is unsettling?"

"Uh-huh."

"And that it's impolite?"

"The only people who think that are the ones who are unsettled, and they're only unsettled if they have something to hide."

Turning onto her side, she tugged up the quilt. "A very pointed statement."

"If you take it that way."

"You knew I would. But I'm really not up for it just yet." She closed her eyes. "Maybe later."

LATER, THOUGH, SHE SLEPT. With a little food in her stomach to quell her hunger, and regular doses of penicillin and aspirin to work on her illness, she slept deeply.

Shortly after dusk, when the room was cast in darkness, Brice bundled her up and carried her downstairs. She awoke briefly during the trip.

"The bedroom's too cold without heat," he explained in response to her look of confusion. "You'll be better off by the fire until the power comes back on."

She didn't argue, and the minute they reached the living room she knew he was right. The warmth in the air was a stark contrast to the chill upstairs. And then he made her so comfortable on cushions on the floor, and wrapped the quilt so snugly around her that the most natural thing was to close her eyes and go back to sleep.

When next she awoke, the room was darker. She coughed and blearily looked around. The first thing she noticed was that the fire had burned down, the second was that Brice was asleep beside her. Easing out of the quilt, she took several logs from the wood box and placed them over the red-hot embers. They began to smolder, then flame. Returning to the quilt, she tucked herself under it, closed her eyes and willed herself back to sleep. But the chill she'd felt when she'd left the quilt remained with her, and the slight activity of adding logs to the fire had woken her completely.

Lacking anything better to do, she turned her head and studied Brice. He lay on his side facing her. A thick afghan covered him to his ribs; a turtleneck sweater covered the rest. His arms were crossed in front of him, one hand braced on the rug, the other splayed loosely on the opposite shoulder.

She looked at those splayed fingers. Though they were long and lean, there was no delicacy to them, nothing to suggest that he was an artist, or as the case would be, a surgeon. For the first time it struck her that she had no idea what his specialty was.

Not that it mattered.

But she was curious.

Eyes creeping to his face, she studied it for the softening that sleep should have brought. There was little. His jaw was as firm, his mouth as straight, the small line between his brows as marked. In fact, the sole softening came from the fact that his eyes—eyes that could pierce so easily—were closed. Aside from that, he seemed on call.

Hit suddenly by a cough, Karen turned her head away. When she turned back, his eyes were open. Other than tugging the quilt higher, she didn't move. Brice looked at her. She looked right back.

"Have you been up long?" he asked. His voice was thicker, not quite as awake as his eyes.

She shook her head.

He glanced at the fire, saw that she'd added logs. "How do you feel?"

"Better."

"In what way?"

"It doesn't hurt so much when I cough."

"That's good."

During the ensuing silence, it struck Karen that he wasn't a bad-looking man at all. His hair was mussed. He didn't look as stiff. And he wasn't looming over her.

"Are you cold?" he asked.

"I'm okay."

"Are you *cold*?"

"A little."

He sat up, then knelt forward and added another log to those Karen had already fed the fire. She was surprised to see him wearing sweatpants, far softer than the corduroy jeans he'd worn up to then. He hadn't struck her as the soft type. Not that she'd pictured him wearing cords to bed. She hadn't pictured him going to bed at all. Not that he was in bed now. But still. Sweatpants. They looked well worn and fell familiarly over his flanks to outline narrow hips, leanly muscled thighs and a tight butt.

Shocked by her own unexpected analysis, she squeezed her eyes shut. Lying on her side that way, she heard the swish of the afghan as Brice got up, the dull pad of his feet as he left the room. When he returned with several more blankets, she couldn't resist opening her eyes.

"Can you get up?" he asked quietly. "Take the quilt with you."

She managed to stand and move aside while he spread one of the blankets over the cushions. He motioned for her to lie down again, but when she'd settled as she'd been before with her feet closest to the flames, he leaned over and turned her, pillow and all, so that she lay on her side, parallel to the hearth.

"Now I'm hogging the warmth," she protested as he dropped another blanket over her.

"I have more of my own than you do," he stated in a

deep, vibrant voice. Stretching out behind her, he drew
the afghan to his chest. "Are you warm enough now?"

"I'm okay."

"Are you *warm* enough?"

"Yes." It wasn't exactly true, but she assumed it would
be soon. Already the heat of the fire was reaching out to
her. She closed her eyes and concentrated on that welcome warmth, but her concentration was broken by her
awareness of Brice.

And the realization that he looked very good in sweatpants.

Swallowing hard at the inappropriateness of the
thought, she tucked her legs up and twined her bare feet
in the quilt. A minute later, she shifted again, this time to
layer one foot over the other, but when that didn't seem
to produce the warmth she needed, she shifted again.

"What are you doing?" Brice asked darkly.

"My feet are cold."

"Rub them together."

She tried that, but for the short time she had the
strength to keep it up, it didn't do much good.

"Still cold?" he asked.

"Yes."

With a sigh, he moved and before Karen could antic-
ipate his intent, he had joined her under the quilt. "Put
your feet between my legs," he instructed.

"Uh, I don't think—"

"Between my legs," he repeated less patiently.

Seconds later, her feet were sandwiched between his
calves.

"Better?"

"This is really not—"

"Better?"

"Yes."

"Good."

Karen had to admit that it was good. Not only were her feet beginning to thaw, but the rest of her was likewise benefiting from Brice's body heat. As though hearing her thoughts, he wrapped an arm around her waist and pulled her closer.

She stiffened. "Brice?"

"Mmmm?" The hum was muffled by her hair.

She tried to put distance between them, but his arm prevented the movement. "Let me go, Brice," she whispered.

But he wasn't about to. He was oddly comfortable. Without pausing to analyze that comfort, he said, "I won't hurt you. Given that there's no heat and that the fire didn't do the trick, this is the only way I know of to warm you up."

"I'm really *okay,*" she said, clutching at his forearm much as she'd done the day before in the car, with similar results. That forearm was made of steel and it wasn't moving.

"Don't fight it, Karen."

"This is unnecessary," she whispered, then began to cough. He brought an arm up between her breasts to support her during the wracking hacks and left it there, hand splayed over her collar bone even after she'd quieted.

And she did quiet. Completely. Her slender body was rigid in his arms.

"Relax," he ordered in a whisper.

She didn't respond in any way.

"Karen?"

"What?"

"I want you to relax."

"I can't."

"I said I wouldn't hurt you."

"I know."

"Then what's the problem?"

"This is very awkward."

"Only because you're so damned stiff. If you'd let go a little, let your body relax back against mine, you'd be fine."

"I was fine before."

"You were cold. Now relax."

She tried, really she did. But the heat emanating from Brice was oddly electric. It sent little tingles up and down the line where his body touched hers. She found it far more unsettling than his stare had ever been.

She tried to wiggle away to sever that bodily contact and ease the tingles, but Brice wasn't having it. "Lie still."

"I can't."

"Why not?"

"I don't know. Maybe you put something in my medicine."

"I did not." He shifted a bit, nestling her more comfortably in his arms.

"Brice," she protested.

"Take a deep breath and let it out very slowly."

She took a deep breath and began to cough. "I'm not good at this," she whispered.

"At what?"

Her whisper grew more frantic. "Touching. I'm not a toucher. I've never slept with a man in my life."

He took a clipped breath. "You're a virgin?"

"I didn't say that. I said I've never slept with a man."

He sighed. "Well, I can understand it. You don't have an awful lot for a man to cuddle up to." When she made a spasmodic move to escape, he held her close and growled, "Stay put."

She did, but she was more tense than ever, because unbidden images were flitting through her mind—images of Brice embracing her in another context, rising over her, possessing her. They were sexual images. She didn't know where they'd come from, only knew that they were wrong. Still they came with startling intensity and persistence. In their shadow, she realized that between the storm and her illness, she was more vulnerable than she'd ever been in her life.

Brice was thinking many of the same things, most notably that if he wanted revenge it was his. Karen couldn't escape him. He could turn her, twist her, terrify her to his heart's content.

If only he were a cruel man.

He'd been accused in his day of being sullen, strange, curt, cold and arrogant, but never cruel. Some of the comments he'd made to Karen had probably come as close to cruel as he'd ever come, but each time he felt badly. As he did now.

She wasn't all *that* scrawny. She had curves in the right places. He could feel those that were cradled against his hips and those that his forearm brushed. He could also feel her fear, and he wondered about it. He wondered why she didn't like touching, why she'd never spent the night with a man, why she'd never married.

But his wondering took a back seat to her fear.

Loosening his arms, he put the space of several inches between their bodies. "Turn around, Karen," he instructed, but gently.

She didn't move at first.

"Karen."

She turned. His face lay half in her shadow, but that half that was lit by the fire seemed less harsh than usual.

"I won't hurt you," he said quietly. "I told you that at the start, and I've told you several times since, but still you're scared. Why?"

Her answer came in a broken whisper. "I haven't ever

felt as helpless as this before. I don't like feeling help-less."

"No one does."

"Some people tolerate it better than others, especially if they…if they…"

"If they what?"

"If they have someone to lean on. Someone to trust."

"And you don't trust me."

She hesitated, then said, "I don't know you."

"But you know my grandmother. You trust her. Don't I stand to inherit some of that trust?"

Karen closed her eyes. She was feeling confused, increasingly weak and tired. "I don't know."

"Okay. Look at it this way. We've been stuck here together now for better than a day. In that time, have I done anything you'd consider untrustworthy?"

"Only…only…"

"Taking you in my arms a little while ago? Karen, I was trying to *warm* you. It's freezing outside, there's no heat inside, and you're sick."

"I know," she wailed softly.

"So why was what I did so bad?"

"It wasn't, I guess."

"Then why were you trembling?"

"I don't know!"

He let out a frustrated breath. "Well, I don't, either."

The fire snapped and sizzled then quieted, and for what seemed an eternity, silence yawned in the darkness between them. But his words echoed and lingered in Karen's mind, bringing her an odd comfort. Knowing that he didn't have all the answers made him seem a bit less powerful, which in turn made her feel a bit less helpless.

Without deliberate intent, she began to relax. She also

began to feel sleepy, but then suddenly it seemed important that she tell him something.

"Brice?" she whispered, rushing on before he could answer, "I didn't mean to hurt Rowena. It was so dark that night. I honestly didn't see her. If I could take back what happened, I'd do it in a minute. In a minute. You have no idea—" Her voice cracked. She stopped. When Brice said nothing, she turned over, closed her eyes and prayed that he'd believe her.

For some reason, that mattered to her very much.

CHAPTER FOUR

KAREN SLEPT UNDISTURBED until dawn's first light slipped through the living room drapes. She stirred groggily and coughed, then snuggled more neatly into the warmth that framed her back. After a minute she half opened one eye to focus blearily on the fire that was blazing healthily before her. After another minute she opened both eyes to an understanding of the warmth behind.

"Don't," came Brice's deep order. It was rough with sleep and accompanied the faint movement of his chin on the top of her head.

She held her breath and whispered, "Don't what?"

"Don't freeze up. I just got back. I'm tired."

"Got back?"

"From the hospital."

Karen's first thought was that she was delirious. But she didn't feel feverishly hot, and though she was still stuffed up, the congestion wasn't as heavy.

Her second thought was that Brice was talking in his sleep, because what he said made no sense. "You weren't at the hospital."

"I was."

But that would have meant she'd been alone. The thought was strangely disconcerting. "I didn't hear you leave."

"I got an emergency call," he mumbled. "You slept through it."

She couldn't argue with him. How could she possibly know what had happened while she'd slept? Then another thought dawned. If Brice had been to the hospital and back.... "The storm's over?"

"Mm." He yawned. Karen felt it—the expansion of his chest, the slight elongation of his body—along the length of her spine.

She didn't move. It was a minute before she dared speak. "Are the roads cleared?"

"The main ones," he murmured. "Not mine yet. I hitched a ride in a cruiser."

The main roads were all she needed. She could easily make it down the drive. "Then I'll be able to go home."

"No."

"Why not?"

"Ask me later. I'm too tired now."

It had been a long night for Brice. First he'd lain awake looking at Karen's bundled form and wondering why in the devil he couldn't turn his back on her. Then, just when he'd finally fallen asleep, the hospital had called to say that one of his patients had been brought in with burns suffered in a wood stove mishap.

Burns were the pits. Pain and scarring. He could never become hardened to that, particularly when the victim was a child.

He hadn't returned home seeking comfort in Karen's arms. He'd barely thought of her while he'd been gone. But when he'd walked in and seen her buried beneath the blankets, he'd suddenly felt chilled. He'd no sooner lain down and drawn her to his body when the chills had disappeared and he'd fallen asleep.

It was only natural that he awaken when she moved. For one thing, the internal alarm that had been honed during his internship days was fine-tuned to pick up the slightest noise—the ring of the telephone, a knock at the door, Karen's cough. For another, Karen wasn't the only one who normally slept alone. She moved; he awoke. But he easily fell back to sleep. Given that he'd been up most of Friday night, and then Saturday night watching Karen and that he'd lost the early hours of Sunday to third-degree burns, he was bushed.

Karen could feel that. What she'd initially heard in his voice was reinforced by the laxness of his body. Oh, his heat was there. It ran from the top of her head, where his chin lay, to her feet, which were somehow wound up in his, and, of course, there was the matter of the arm that lay heavily over her waist.

She wasn't bound to him by force, though, and that made the difference between her wanting to bolt and her pausing to consider the positive aspects of her position.

Aside from her face, which was exposed to the air, she was toasty. The quilts and Brice's body heat did that.

She was also surprisingly comfortable. Brice's body was large; she wouldn't have expected it to conform snugly to hers, but it did. With her head on a pillow, her side on cushions and her back supported by his front, she was feeling no pain.

Moreover, she felt unexpectedly safe. Protected. Sheltered. He had a way of doing that to her. It was an illusion, she knew, but still she had no desire to move.

She wasn't sure what Brice thought of the last words she'd whispered to him the night before. She wasn't sure whether he'd even heard them; he'd made no response. But she'd said them, and still he offered his warmth. That had to mean something.

On a note of hope, she fell back to sleep.

WITHOUT QUITE UNDERSTANDING how it happened, she slept through most of the day. It seemed that with the edge of pneumonia eased by penicillin, the exhaustion that had tailed her for far longer than three weeks was taking its due. When she awoke, it was but briefly. Brice brought her light meals—eggs, soup, pudding, cocoa—but she had trouble eating much. Her stomach seemed to have shrunk. She was frighteningly weak. As soon as he freed her of the small tray across her lap, she slid down to the pillow and fell back to sleep.

At some point during the afternoon, the electricity returned, but she remained before the fire on the living room sofa, wrapped in blankets. Each time she stirred, she made feeble sounds about needing to go home, but Brice repeatedly put her off. It wasn't until early evening that she mustered the strength to confront him.

She'd been lying alone for a while when that strength hit. Or maybe it was panic that hit. She was thinking of all she wasn't accomplishing, and the psychological restlessness had built and built until it reached fever pitch. So she wrapped herself in a blanket and went in search of Brice.

Finding him took some doing. He was in neither of the rooms on the other side of the hall. The kitchen and pantry were likewise empty. She was wondering if she had the strength to take her search up the stairs, when her eye fell on the entry to what she'd assumed to be a storage room. Closer inspection showed it to be the entry to a whole other wing of the house.

Brice was in a room off the paneled hall that looked to be his private den. The walls were lined from ceiling to floor with dark maple bookshelves, which were in turn lined with books. What little open wall space there was was filled with small and varied works of art, rather than diplomas. An Oriental rug overspread the floor, providing a cushion for an aged leather sofa and a sturdy oak desk.

Brice had his heels on the desk, ankles crossed. He

was leaning back in the chair with his fingers laced on his middle, and though his gaze met hers the minute she appeared at the door, he said nothing.

If Karen had worried about facing him in a second-floor bedroom, her fears were doubled here. She had the distinct feeling that she had fallen upon sacred ground. The room was Brice. It was serious and complex, dark and silent. She sensed that this was where he spent a good deal of his free time and that if she were to examine the books packed on the shelves she'd find them as well worn and diverse as they were revealing. In that sense, the room was incredibly intimate.

For a fleeting instant she recalled the way Brice's body had warmed hers during the night. Then the instant passed, leaving tingles in its wake.

Clearing her throat, she ran an eye around the room and said in a quietly sincere, sandy voice, "I'm impressed."

Brice had recalled that warming, too. He'd thought about it a lot since it had happened, had tried to make sense of it. But he couldn't. Now he looked at Karen and wondered about the satisfaction he'd felt when he'd held her in his arms.

In answer to both her comment and his thoughts, he gave a slow, begrudging shrug.

"Have you read them all?" she asked.

"Most."

"When do you read?"

"Evenings. Weekends."

"You have the time?"

"Of course."

She was envious. She was also puzzled. "I wouldn't have thought it—your being a doctor and all."

"Doctors don't work round the clock. They have lives like everyone else."

"But there are so many books up there." She scanned the shelves. "So many hours of involvement." Her gaze met his. "Were you always an avid reader?"

He hesitated. He wasn't used to being questioned about himself. The town knew him as a fine doctor who was intensely private. He was comfortable with the combination. Those few people who had tried to penetrate the private man behind the stethoscope had been quickly, even rudely put off. They hadn't tried again.

He wasn't quite sure what category to put Karen in. She wasn't a townsperson. Nor, at that moment, was she a patient. He would have called her a friend of Rowena's if the circumstances of that friendship weren't so odd, and on that score he had his own questions to ask. Karen wasn't the only one who was curious.

But she'd asked first. And he had nothing to lose by answering. "I used to read a lot as a kid. When I was in med school, I barely had time to breathe, much less read."

Karen tried to picture a younger Brice Carlin, sweeping up and down the corridors of a hospital in the crisp white garb of an intern. It was hard to imagine him in as busy a setting. He seemed so dark, so quiet, so solitary. Yes, the phone rang on occasion, and there had been the trip to the hospital he'd made early that morning, but she couldn't picture him as part of a team, dealing with other doctors, nurses and technicians, much less patients and their families.

She could picture him studying, though, leaning over a deskful of books with his dark hair falling on his brow and his eyes unwavering on the page. Then she pictured herself studying, leaning over a deskful of books with her eyes unwavering on the page and she was hit by the edginess that had brought her in search of her host.

Drawing herself as straight as she could, she looked

him in the eye and said in her firmest voice, "I have to leave, Brice. I appreciate all you've done for me, but I can't stay any longer." The words tumbled out with increasing speed. "The roads are passable. Your driveway's been plowed. There has to be someone I can call to take a look at my car." Feeling winded, she sucked in her lower lip, then watched in dismay as, without taking his eyes from hers, Brice slowly but firmly shook his head. Somewhere in the back of her mind, she'd expected it, but that didn't make it any easier to take. She wasn't feeling up to par. She didn't really want to fight him.

"Why not?" she asked with caution.

He unlaced his hands enough to run one flat palm over his chest. He was wearing another sweater—this one with a cable that ran up the left front—and the way his hand glided over it suggested it was made of cashmere. Karen wished he were an iota as soft as the fabric.

He wasn't.

"For one thing," he began with a bluntness bordering on the blasé, "no one is going to look at your car tonight. The people who could fix it are the same ones who have been digging this town out of the snow for the past twenty-four hours. If I were to call, they'd laugh—*if* they were home, which I doubt they are—but I wouldn't think of calling."

"I'll call."

"Same difference. Those guys are exhausted. Their work is far from done."

"A dead battery isn't part of their work?"

"Not this weekend. There's fifteen inches of snow out there, more where it's drifted. That's a hell of a lot to shovel."

"I'm just asking for a jump start. I'd think that would be a break for them."

"Think again. A break is being indoors, drinking hot

coffee laced with something strong enough to preserve the heat. Your car is under the same fifteen inches of snow as the road. It has to be shoveled out before the hood can even be raised. And besides, how do you know a jump start is all it needs? From the looks of that car, the battery may be hopeless. If the problem is with the battery. Are you sure it is?"

She was beginning to feel a little shaky. "No."

"If it's not the battery, the car will have to be towed, and believe me, you'll have trouble finding a tow truck that isn't plowing. And even if you get someone to tow you to a station," he went on in that same deep, infuriatingly placid voice, "it'll be at least another day or two before someone will take a look at the car. The high school kid who pumps gas—if he's there at all in this weather—won't know what to do with a car that doesn't start."

Karen wanted to cry. She was as frustrated by the situation as she was annoyed by Brice's blunt summarization. If he'd sounded at all smug she'd probably have hurled a book at him. But he hadn't sounded smug, just hard, and she doubted she'd have been able to hurl a book far. Feeling a dire need to sit, she stumbled to the sofa.

"How about a cab or a bus?" she asked as she sank gratefully into the pliant leather folds. She tucked up her knees and rewrapped the blanket so that all of her was covered.

Brice shrugged a single brow. "I doubt you'll get either." He had his fingers laced again and was studying her more intently. "Why the rush? Most of the world looks outside, sees the snow and rejoices at an unexpected holiday. If you can't go anywhere, you can't go anywhere. There's no sense beating your head against a brick wall."

"But is it a brick wall? That's what I need to know. If there's some way for me to get home, I'd like to take it."

"What's so special at home? Do you have a cat to feed?"

"I have work to do."

"And you're well enough to do it?"

She hugged her knees tight. "You don't understand. I *have* to do it. Classes may be canceled for a day or two—" her eyes widened in sudden alarm and she came forward "—I don't even know if they will be. For all I know, the storm was *nothing* in Syracuse!"

"It was worse."

She let out a breath. "Thank goodness." When Brice snorted, she added a hasty, "I don't mean to sound callous. But if it was business as usual, I'd be in hot water." Her brows met in a look of panic. "As it is, I'll probably lose my job."

"You won't lose your job," Brice said. "I talked with the owner of the Pepper Mill and explained that you were sick. He suggested you take off until after vacation."

Karen went very still. "Excuse me?"

"I talked with Jason Grant. You were supposed to work last night, weren't you?"

She didn't answer his question but sank weakly back into the sofa. "I don't believe you called Jason. I don't believe you said I wouldn't be in until after vacation." Silently she cursed herself for having been out of it for the past forty-eight hours. Less silently she cursed Brice for having taken over her life. "Damn it, you shouldn't have done that. You had no right. I have to work! I need the money!"

Brice had expected her anger. He supposed, when he thought about it, that he'd have been disappointed if she'd sat back and let him take over without a peep. If she'd done that, he'd have guessed she'd accept whatever charity he was willing to offer.

He was a generous man. Over the course of a year, he gave as much to charity as many people made for a living. But he picked and chose his causes, and a woman had never been one of them.

He'd already decided that Karen was independent, and while her occasional bullheadedness riled him, he was oddly assured by her show of pride now. It said that she wouldn't take advantage of him. Perversely, her self-sufficiency made it all that much more rewarding for him to do for her. Yes, he was pleased that he'd spoken with Jason Grant. He was pleased that he'd bought a little rest time for Karen. Given the condition she'd been in when he'd found her in the snow, she needed it.

All he had to do was to convince *her* of that.

Removing his feet from the desk, he crossed an ankle over his knee. "You won't be able to work at all unless you take care of yourself. You've been very sick and you're a long way from cured. How do you feel now?"

"Fine," she said on a single breath of boldness.

"How?" he repeated.

The boldness faded. "Okay."

"Is that why you dragged yourself away from the door and collapsed on the sofa?"

"I didn't drag and I didn't collapse."

He would have laughed at her disgruntled expression if he'd been the laughing type, but he wasn't. "Sure looked it to me."

"You saw what you wanted to see," she argued. She was feeling contrary, but her voice was weakening. "You're a doctor. If people were well all the time, you'd be out of business."

The small muscle at Brice's temple twitched. "That was a stupid thing to say."

She surprised him by looking contrite. "I think it came out wrong. What I meant was that you're attuned to seeing illness, therefore it's possible you see illness where there really is none."

"Are you saying you're perfectly all right now? That you're well? Feeling one-hundred percent?"

"No."

"You do admit that there's still something a little foreign running around in your system?"

She hesitated, then murmured a reluctant, "Yes."

"If that's true, should you be waitressing?" His eyes sharpened on her. "Don't think of yourself, Karen. Think of the people you'd be waiting on. If you were working in an accounting office, or sitting behind a computer all day, it'd be one thing for you to work through a cold—not that I'd recommend it, but that would be different from being sick and waitressing. You handle the food people eat."

"I know," she said. She hated him for being so sensible.

"And you still think you should be working?"

"No…" she admitted, and took in a breath to argue, only to be beaten to it by Brice.

"But you need the money."

She let out the breath. "Yes." She rested her head against the sofa and eyed the ceiling. Brice's voice came to her more gently then.

"How do you feel now?"

"Discouraged."

"Physically, how do you feel? I want to know where we stand for treatment."

She closed her eyes and tried to separate psychological edginess from the purely physical symptoms. "I feel tired," she said in a small voice. "I don't hurt as much. I'm not swinging hot to cold. But my legs don't seem to want to carry me far. I feel—" she searched for another word, but the first one she'd used seemed to sum it all up "—tired."

"You need rest."

"I've *had* rest. I've done little more than sleep for the past forty-eight hours."

"That sleep was for the infection. The sleep you need now is for you, and above and beyond that you need rest. There's a difference."

She heard what he said, understood what he meant, but the facts didn't change. "I don't have the time."

"Make the time."

"That's easier said than done," she wailed softly. "I agree that I should take time off from the Pepper Mill, but I still have papers and midterms, and Professor McGuire will be expecting me in his office tomorrow afternoon. I have to get back to Syracuse."

There was a pregnant silence. Karen saw something in Brice's eyes that she didn't like. Her pulse tripped.

"I spoke to McGuire," he told her.

"Oh, no." She squeezed her eyes shut. "I enjoyed that job, Brice. Professor McGuire was as interesting as his work."

"Why the past tense?"

She opened her eyes. "Because he has deadlines to meet and there are *dozens* of students willing to work for him. I'm sure he's hired someone else by now."

"He hasn't."

"How do you know?" she asked indignantly.

"I know. You still have the job."

Her indignation vanished. "I do?" When he nodded, she rushed on. "But he needs the work done."

"In time. He'll be away over vacation, anyway. Skiing in the Alps."

She stared, then murmured, "Oh."

"He said he'll meet with you when classes reconvene."

Turning sideways, Karen closed her eyes.

"Aren't you pleased?" Brice asked. He was rather proud of himself for having arranged things so well. "You have your job and a vacation." She remained still. "Karen?"

She sighed, looked at him, then said in a meek voice, "Thank you."

For the first time, Brice was roused from his pose of total control. Uncrossing his legs, he set his forearms on the desk. "I had better thanks from the kid I diagnosed as having chicken pox on the day before he was to leave for Disney World. But that's okay. I wasn't looking for your thanks. I was looking to buy you a breather from the hell of a schedule you've got. When was the last time you had a vacation?"

"I don't know."

"When?"

"I can't remember."

"What do you *do* with yourself?"

"I work."

"All the time? You're not *that* hard up for money, are you?"

She was resting her head on the soft leather, feeling very tired again. Perhaps for that reason, her defenses were down. The pride that might have kept her silent wasn't on guard. In a voice that was less nasal than it had been, but still hoarse and very soft, she said, "The earliest memories I have are of tension in my family. I couldn't have been more than three or four years old, but I remember it. My dad couldn't hold down a job. My mom never criticized him for it, but there was constant worry about how she was going to pay the bills."

Brice didn't want to hear her story, didn't want to feel for her. He opened his mouth to tell her to stop, then closed it again. He wanted to hear every word. He had to know more. He told himself it was the doctor in him needing a history, which was far easier to swallow than the idea that the man in him was the one in need.

So he didn't say a word. And Karen, seeming tired and weak but determined to talk, went on.

"My father had been in construction and had planned to start his own company. Then there was an accident. His legs were crushed under a wall of concrete. The doctors managed to rebuild them, but by the time that was done, whatever money he'd saved had gone for medical bills. There was a small settlement from a lawsuit, but he went through that almost as quickly, because by that time he was addicted to painkillers and they cost a bundle."

"Did your mother work?"

"She took in other children and called it babysitting, though she was really running a daycare center from our house. I thought it was great. I didn't have any brothers or sisters, and there were suddenly lots of kids around. Then the state got fussy about licensing. Mom couldn't get a license because we didn't have the money to make the repairs that would have been required. So she was reduced to really doing babysitting—for no more than one or two kids at a time—and the money that brought in wasn't enough to support the three of us. When I started school, she went to work as a secretary in a small law office. The pay helped, but it was never spectacular. She could type. She couldn't take dictation because she didn't know shorthand, and she didn't have the time or money to go to school for it."

Karen recalled her mother's frustration. Even at nine, ten, eleven years of age she could understand what it meant to want to earn a living and not be able to.

"Was your dad at home for you after school?" Brice asked.

"Sometimes."

"Was he...kind to you?"

That brought a spark. Her head came up a fraction, eyes focusing more clearly on Brice. "He was never a cruel man. He was frustrated and unhappy, went from one job to the next in the hope that the newest would be the best, but there was always the physical pain and the need for drugs. He never touched alcohol. He was never violent. But he was totally unreliable. Spaced out. Foggy. A couple of times he fell into a coma. He was rushed to the hospital and the doctors said all the right words about weaning him from the habit, but he signed himself out before it could be done. My mother tried to convince him to enroll in this or that program, but he argued that he couldn't if he wanted to help support his family. So he went from one job to the next. It was a Catch-22."

She dropped her head back again and fell silent, remembering the nights she'd lain in bed listening to the soft sounds of her mother crying. The woman suffered pain on all sides. Karen had vowed to help wherever she could.

"As soon as I graduated from high school, I went to work full-time." She paused, frowned. "I thought I was doing my parents a favor, but sometimes I wonder if my working didn't bring my mother more pain than relief. She wanted me to go to college. She saw women with lucrative careers, and that was what she wanted for me. She was a bright woman, but her only training was as a housewife, and there was no pay for that." Again Karen paused. Again she frowned. "It was a Catch-22 for me, too. Mom wanted me to stop working and go to college for the education that would have guaranteed me a better income, but I didn't have that luxury because we needed the money right then. Dad was in and out of the hospital more often; he had kidney problems and liver problems. The bills kept coming in."

She closed her eyes and sank lower into her blanket while Brice watched tiny lines of pain etch her brow. His heart went out to her, while the cynic in him had a fleeting moment's rise. If she'd set out to spin a heart-wrenching tale, she'd succeeded well.

Then he remembered how she'd begun crying on the first day he'd brought her to his house, how she'd withdrawn into herself, seeming mortified. Though there was no mortification now, there was the same kind of pained withdrawal, the same kind of introversion. Now, as then, she refused to look at him.

Rising from his chair, he tucked his hands deep in the pockets of his cords and walked slowly, almost idly around the desk. He stopped several feet from the sofa when she began to speak again. She was frowning at her thumb, picking its nail.

"When I was nineteen, I met a man. Boy—man—he was twenty-three. He was an artist, or thought himself one, though to this day he hasn't hit the big time. I was doing odd jobs—typing, filing, telephoning—for the curator of a small museum in New Haven, not far from where we lived. I loved art."

Her expression softened, though she didn't look up. "I met Tim at the museum and I loved him, too. He was everything I'd never known—carefree, lighthearted, fun-loving. I felt like a different person when I was with him." She frowned at her hand. "But I was living a dual life—working hard, counting my pennies, giving every spare cent to my parents, then going off with Tim for an afternoon picnic or an evening with his friends or a weekend on a secluded beach where he was supposed to be inspired."

"Was he?"

She gave a sad little laugh. "Not usually. We just… had…fun."

Brice felt a vague tightening around his heart. It wasn't that he was jealous of the man, because he had no claim on Karen, but there was something about that soft look on her face, something about the sadness in her laughter and the fact that it had been the first laughter of any kind that he'd heard pass her lips, that touched him deeply. Her skin was smooth, her face lined by nothing but fatigue and the occasional frown. He'd never seen her smile. It was a shame.

"What happened to him?"

She'd been thinking back to those fun times, remembering how nice it had been to forget her worries, if only for a short time. Brice's question brought her back to the present with a start. "Tim? Uh, we parted ways."

Brice had never been a gossip-monger, but he couldn't believe she'd leave him high and dry that way. So he asked, "Why?"

She shrugged. "I wasn't what he thought."

"What do you mean?"

"He thought I had money."

For a minute there was silence. Then Brice said, "Go on."

Head back against the sofa, she closed her eyes. Her voice was weary. "He was looking for someone to bankroll his career. Someone to support him while he sketched. Somehow he got the impression that I was wealthy. Maybe it was the way I dressed. I had an eye for style and could take a nothing piece of clothing and wrap it or knot it or belt it into something interesting. Or maybe it was the way I walked or talked. He said I sounded aristocratic. Cultured. He assumed there was money attached. I never took him home with me. I didn't want to blur the lines between my two worlds. Besides, my parents would have hated him on sight."

"So how did he find out?"

"I think," she said more slowly, "that he was beginning to ask himself whether I was worth the investment of his energy, and the only way he could know that was to see how I lived." She took a stuffy breath. "He found out, all right. The apartment we lived in was nice enough, but it was an apartment and it was small and it wasn't in the greatest of neighborhoods." Still, she remembered that apartment with fondness, because it was the place she'd called home for twenty-three years. Tim had felt no fondness for it at all. "We broke up soon after that."

Brice felt a flare of anger—at both Karen and her beau—and when he was angry, he was blunt. "How could you have fallen for him?"

Hurt, she looked up. "I didn't know what he was after."

"It should have been obvious. Was he that great an actor that he could pretend feelings he didn't have?"

Karen was the one to be angry then. Her anger gave her the strength to sit straight. "I wasn't blind or dumb, Brice. Tim wasn't pretending. He really did like me. He just wanted more." Shifting the blankets, she stood. "He was totally up-front about things when we broke up. I'm not sure that made it any easier for me, but when a guy is blunt like that about something so basic, what can you say?" She turned and moved toward one of the book-lined walls. "My heart wasn't broken, so I couldn't have been that desperately in love, either. But I was disillusioned. I think I'd have preferred to break up for any other reason than that."

Sighing, she absently fingered the camera that lay on one of the shelves. "The only thing was, the experi-

ence burned me a little. So there weren't any other men
like Tim, and I kept on working. I did love my work. I
loved—still do love—sitting in a room where I'm sur-
rounded by fine pieces of art."

Brice could believe that about her. She looked the
type. Rowena certainly was the type. For that matter, *he*
was the type. He appreciated solitude and silence, and
he appreciated artistic skill. "Do you draw or paint?"

"No. I can't do either. That's why I'm in art history
instead of fine arts."

But that was getting ahead of her story, and Brice
wanted to hear the whole thing. So, standing across from
her with his hands in his pockets, he asked, "What finally happened to your parents?"

Tugging the blanket around her shoulder, she stared
unseeingly at the books on the shelves. She was tired, but
something inside made her speak. "My dad died when
I was twenty-one. He left lots of bills. Mom and I were
chipping away at them—doing pretty well, actually—
when she got sick. I was twenty-three when she died.
It was two more years before I'd paid off the last of the
bills."

"Was that when you decided to go back to school?"

She gave a small headshake. "I had decided that years
ago. It was just a question of when I could swing it. After
the bills were paid, I started building a kitty so I could
study full-time." She lowered her chin to her chest.
"Then I hit Rowena. You know the rest."

Brice didn't know the rest, but he could piece it together. She'd needed that kitty to pay her lawyer, and by
the time she'd finished, she was back to square one. "So
you put togther an impossible program for yourself," he
said darkly. He wasn't sure who most annoyed him at that
moment—Karen for speeding down a dark country road,
Rowena for bicycling without reflectors, fate for putting

the two women at the same spot at the same time, or himself for hurting for them both. "You're pushing yourself at a pace that would try even the hardiest of people."

She turned a pleading look his way. "I have no choice. Don't you see? I've been caught in the same bind for so long that the only way I can escape it is to make it through these four years. Once they're done, I'll be able to breathe free."

"Because you'll be earning good money?"

He didn't understand. That hurt. "It's not only the money," she cried. "If it were, I'd be after a degree in business, rather than one in art history." Averting her gaze, she made for the door, but Brice was suddenly before her, blocking her escape.

"What is it, then?"

She looked into his eyes. They were as dark as ever, but involved. They challenged her. "It's getting out from under the heap. Being on top. Calling the shots, rather than having the shots call me. I don't need millions to live on. My tastes aren't extravagant. All I want is to be able to go to bed at night knowing that I've paid my bills. Is that too much to ask?"

Her gaze dropped to his mouth as she waited for him to respond. His lips were firm, boldly cut, masculine. They pressed together and she felt it. She raised her eyes in a hurry and they collided with his. They were dark. Sensual. They stunned her.

"Rowena was worried about you," he said distractedly as he tried to decide whether Karen's eyes were amber or brown.

"About me?"

"She called to tell me that your car was still in the lot. She wanted me to call the police."

Charcoal gray, Karen decided, and slightly lighter in

the center. His eyes were captivating. "Did you tell her I was here?"

"Uh-huh. She was relieved. She knew you were sick."

"She shouldn't have worried."

His gaze fell to her mouth. "She likes you."

"I like her, too."

"Is that why you visit her twice a week?"

"That's...one of the reasons," Karen said, but her voice was shaky. She had the strangest urge to touch Brice's face, the strangest urge to see what that dark shadow on his jaw felt like. It was taking all her strength not to give in to those strangest of urges, and she didn't have much strength to begin with. "I think...I'd better sit down," she whispered.

"Tell me the other reasons," Brice said thickly. He was fascinated by the small blush that lit her cheeks. It was a world away from the fever touch he'd seen before.

She could have moved, but she didn't. Her eyes were locked with his, her voice wispy. "Please...I'd like to sit."

He slid his hands down her arms as they were outlined under the blanket, but the small support that movement gave was offset by the greater weakness his touch inspired. Karen wasn't so faint or ill or out of practice that she didn't recognize the weakness for desire. She was attracted to Brice. That frightened her.

"What are the other reasons you visit Rowena?" he asked. It wasn't weakness he was feeling but the opposite, and in a totally unexpected part of his body. Just then he wanted to hold Karen close. But he couldn't. He wasn't supposed to like her.

"We have fun together," Karen murmured.

"You read to her."

"We both like that."

"But twice a week—that's three hours of driving."

"I don't mind."

"I'd think you wouldn't have the time," he said. He was thinking that he wanted to kiss her.

"I make the time."

He couldn't kiss her. "Gas costs."

"I pay gladly."

He couldn't like her. His fascination had to stop. "Is it guilt?"

She stiffened, then felt a wave of weakness that had nothing to do with desire. "No."

The soft infusion of warmth had washed from her face. Brice was relieved. He didn't want her looking kissable. "Guilt would be the normal thing to feel."

Karen knew that a special moment had passed and didn't understand what had happened. In addition to weak, she felt raw. Her response to Brice was defensive. "It started out as that, but it isn't now."

"You don't feel *any* guilt?"

"I didn't say that."

"Do you feel it?"

"Yes. I live with it all the time. I blame myself for not having somehow seen Rowena that night. I blame myself for not having concentrated more closely on the road that night, for not having cleaned my headlights, for not having driven way over on the right-hand shoulder of the road. I feel guilt. But that's not why I visit Rowena."

"Are you admitting that you were to blame that night?"

Tears gathered in her eyes. "No!"

"But you just said—"

"That I blame myself. That's different from admitting I was responsible for the accident." Trembling, she tried to pull back from his grasp, but he wasn't easing up. "I didn't lie during the trial, Brice. You sat there. You heard what I said. I wasn't speeding. I don't drink or do drugs." Her voice was getting more and more hoarse. "I didn't break any law that night, so I fought the charges you brought against me—"

"I didn't—"

"The district attorney did, but you were behind it, and you were wrong. I can understand what you did. She's your grandmother and you love her. But you were wrong. It wasn't fair—" Her voice broke, but she was determined to say it, so she started again, this time sniffling from the tears that were trickling down her cheeks. "It wasn't right that after everything I'd been through I should have been f-further penalized because Rowena and I were on that road together that night." His face was a dark blur through her tears, but she raced on. "If it's some consolation to you, I've suffered anyway. Each time I see her I remember that it was *my* car that put her where she is."

She tipped her face sideways into the blanket at her shoulder and cried softly, wishing Brice would let her go, wishing she could break away, wishing she were anywhere else at that moment. Absurdly, she murmured, "Sh-she's the grandmother I never had. I l-love her, too."

Closing his eyes, Brice brought her into his arms. He didn't care what he was supposed to feel or what he wasn't. She wasn't well. And now she was hurting more.

Cupping her head, he held it to his chest while he supported her with an arm around her waist. He could feel her body trembling, could hear her soft weeping. He sensed her getting weaker with each passing minute, and lest she fall, he lifted her and carried her to the sofa. Then he sat with her on his lap and shifted the blankets so that he could hold her closer. He stroked her hair, restrained in its barrette. He stroked her slender back, rubbed her neck, her arms. He held her until she'd stopped crying. Then he carried her, sound asleep, to the second floor bedroom he'd come to think of as hers, tucked her into bed and left the room.

CHAPTER FIVE

WHEN KAREN AWOKE, it was morning. Turning over in bed, she slowly opened her eyes to a winter sun whose rays were all the brighter for their own reflection on the snow. The drapes were gilded, the floor bathed in light. It was a cheery welcome to the day and went a long way toward compensating for the face of her watch, which proclaimed the time to be 9:40.

She couldn't believe that she'd slept the night through after having slept away the day before. A little voice told her that Brice had been right, that she was exhausted, that her body not only needed but demanded the rest. She listened to that little voice for as long as it took for the events of the evening before to return. Then she turned over again, bunched the pillow under her head and tried to understand what she felt.

It was a tall order, because Brice was an enigma. She had never pictured herself with the dark, silent type. Tim had been slim and fair. By comparison, physically and otherwise, Brice was more substantial.

What had happened the night before in his den? She'd been talking with him, telling him about her family. He'd been looking interested and very attractive. They'd come to be standing close, and she'd felt warm and excited. She had felt wanted.

Then Brice had gone cold. He'd turned off the appeal

by steering the conversation to Rowena and jabbing her with it. Karen felt as though she'd been punished.

Perhaps it was just as well, though. She had no time for a man, especially not now when she was on the verge of solvency. She couldn't be distracted, which was why she had to get back to Syracuse. McGuire and the Pepper Mill could be put off with little more than a loss of wages. But if she didn't write her paper, if she didn't start studying for midterms she'd be up a creek. There were no refunds for failed courses.

Tossing aside the covers, she quickly sat up, then steadied herself with a hand by each hip. She felt strange. Dizzy. But her head was clearer than it had been. She closed her eyes until the dizziness passed. She sniffed several times to find that her stuffiness had eased. She coughed. It was still a heavy cough, but nowhere near as bad as it had been, and it brought no pain. She was definitely on the mend.

Then she lowered her feet to the floor and stood—and quickly sat back down. Her legs felt like rubber. Her entire body felt disjointed.

"All from one weekend's disuse," she murmured, but she knew it wasn't true. The enervation she felt was the result not of disuse but abuse. She'd been driving herself too hard. She'd known it, but she'd had no other choice.

Thanks to Brice, she'd had another choice over the weekend and she'd taken it—perhaps not willingly, but she'd done it. She'd slept. Rested. Healed. But even if the healing process wasn't done, the weekend was. She had to get going.

More slowly shifting her weight to her feet, she stood. Closely circling the bedposts, she walked to the window.

The scene before her sparkled. Though the snow had been no ally, it was beautiful. Of course, it had something to work with; Brice's land was spectacular. Much of the landscaping was ancient, evident from the incredible size of the pines. The newer plantings weren't as large, but they were full and healthy, and had been craftily sculpted into the land.

The driveway had been plowed. Pressing her nose to the glass, she followed its curve around, past the front door toward the area she assumed to be his office. She couldn't see the entrance, but she could see the small plowed spot where several cars were parked.

Brice was at work.

Curious to get a look at one or two of his patients, she lingered at the window for a minute. But her legs quickly tired, so she sank into the rocker and tried to decide what to do next.

She had to find her clothes, take a cab back to the nursing home, call someone to repair her car and get back to Syracuse. But part of her didn't want to do any of that. Part of her wanted to stay where she was, enjoying the comfort of the house, the warmth of the room, the overall ambiance, cozy and relaxed. Part of her, she realized with a shock, wanted to stay and be taken care of by Brice.

That couldn't happen.

So she set her mind to thinking of what *could* happen and when. She had barely reached the point of wishing for a bath when she heard the sound of footsteps in the hall. Her heart skipped a beat, then sped. But the footsteps were too light to be Brice's, and besides, he was working. Eyes on the door, she watched it open a crack. The small face that peered through was female and was framed by thin, smooth blond shoulder-length hair. A slight tapping sound edged the door open wider. The girl carried Karen's breakfast tray, but she stood at the door unsurely.

Karen had never seen as delicate-looking a creature.

At first glance, she couldn't believe that the girl could be Brice's maid. At second glance, she realized that the girl was a woman—probably in her early twenties. She wore sneakers, a pair of pencil-slim, worn jeans and a large, heavy Irish knit sweater. And she was waiting, eyeing Karen nervously, in need of direction.

Karen made a small beckoning motion with her hand. That seemed to be what the girl needed, because she promptly cleared the threshold and crossed to the rocker. She started to lower the tray to Karen's lap, then drew it back and looked over her shoulder at the bed.

"It would be more stable there," Karen said gently.

The blond-haired creature quickly looked at her, both eyebrows raised in question.

Karen rephrased the thought. "Whatever's on your tray may spill if I rock by mistake. I think I'd be better in bed." Rising from the chair, she climbed back under the covers and smoothed a section beside her for the tray.

The girl set it down and shyly stepped away, but rather than leaving, she backed toward the foot of the bed. After tucking a lock of gossamer hair behind her ear, she wrapped an arm around the bedpost. She looked at Karen, then the floor, then Karen again. Finally, and with some nervousness, she asked, "How are you feeling?"

They were the first words she'd offered, and Karen instantly knew why. Yes, Brice's maid was young and shy. She was also severely hard of hearing. The heavily nasal quality of her voice—totally different from the nasality of a cold—and her slightly aberrant diction suggested it. With that clue and a single glance, Karen detected a hearing aid in her ear.

"I'm feeling better," she said, noting that the girl's eyes followed her lips. "Thank you." She looked down at the tray. It held a glass of orange juice, a plate filled with scrambled eggs, sausage and potato, two pieces of toast with a dollop of jam, and a mug of hot chocolate. "This looks delicious. I'm hungry."

The girl looked relieved. "Dr. Carlin said to make lots and to be sure you ate it. He said you needed to gain weight." She paused, shy again. "I don't think so. I think you're perfect."

Karen looked up in time to catch a blush on the girl's face. "You're very kind," she said in a tone suggesting she thought of herself as anything but perfect. "What's your name?"

"Meg."

"Mine's Karen."

"I know."

Karen took a drink of juice, found it to be fresh squeezed and took another, longer drink. Her taste buds were responding; it was the first time in weeks that she'd truly savored something.

She looked up to find Meg's eyes large and watchful. Holding up the glass, she asked, "Did you squeeze it yourself?"

Meg nodded, but made no move to leave, which put Karen in a bind. She was ignorant of the protocol involving household help. She wasn't sure whether she was expected to eat, talk or do neither. Somehow saying, "You can go now," didn't seem right at all.

Curiosity was the deciding factor. If Meg worked for Brice, she had to know something about him. So Karen asked, "Have you worked for Dr. Carlin long?"

"Two years."

"How did you meet up with him?"

"He knows my husband's family."

It hadn't occurred to Karen that Meg might be married. She seemed too young, too innocent. But, looking, Karen saw the thin platinum band that circled the ring finger of the girl's left hand. "When?" she asked, tossing her chin toward the ring. Then she looked up, prepared to state the full question if Meg hadn't been able to read her verbal shorthand.

Meg read it. She blushed again and smiled. "Two years ago. I was working in a daycare center in Schenectady when Richie—that's my husband—came to do some work. He's an electrician. He brought me here to live just when Dr. Carlin was needing help. The woman before me had been with him for a long time, but I guess they argued a lot. He finally got tired of the arguments." She looked puzzled. "I don't know what they argued about. I've never found anything to argue about with him. He's a nice, quiet man."

Karen could have argued with that; she'd seen a different side of the man. He could be domineering, sharp, sarcastic. But he seemed to take to the wounded. When she'd been feeling at her worst over the weekend, he'd been gentle. When she'd been upset last night, he'd been gentle. He was apparently gentle with Meg. She guessed that he'd be gentle with his patients.

"What kind of practice does he have?" she asked.

But Meg was worriedly eyeing the tray and didn't hear. "That's your penicillin pill in the little cup. You'd better take it."

If for no other reason than to erase that look of worry, Karen promptly took the pill with a swallow of juice. Then, lifting her fork, she started in on the eggs. The first mouthful went down so pleasantly that she went on to a second, then sampled the sausage and potatoes in turn.

"I hope you know," she paused to say, "that I feel decadent having breakfast in bed. You'd think I was one of the idle rich."

Meg was suspiciously silent. Looking up, Karen saw a face filled with confusion.

"I'm not rich," she assured her. "I'm not usually idle, either."

The confusion remained. "Are you a relative of Dr. Carlin's?"

"No."

"A friend, then?"

Karen considered that. Three days before she'd never have put Brice in the category of friend, but a lot had happened since then. On some level, they remained adversaries. On another level, though, yes, they were friends. At least, she thought that way.

"Actually," she answered on a note of greater sureness, "I'm a friend of Dr. Carlin's grandmother. I was visiting her when I took sick."

Meg nodded her understanding, but she seemed disappointed. Belatedly, it occurred to Karen that Meg had been speculating on the relationship being a romantic one, particularly with Karen wearing what was so obviously Brice's shirt.

"Is Dr. Carlin's grandmother's name Rowena?" she asked.

"Yes."

She grew sheepish. "I wasn't sure if that was his mother or a sister or ex-wife."

Ex-wife. A new thought. Karen wasn't sure she liked it.

"No. Rowena is his grandmother."

"I've taken calls from her sometimes—there's an amplifier of the phone downstairs. Well, they're not really from her but from someone announcing that she's calling. I have orders to put those calls right through to the office." She paused, offered a hesitant half smile. "I've always pictured Rowena Carlin as a rich lady whose personal secretary places the calls. Am I right?"

Karen knew that Rowena had always been a free spirit, that she had always traveled, that she appreciated a fine wine and was sophisticated in her way. In truth, though, Karen had no idea whether Rowena was wealthy. She did know that the calls coming in weren't made by a personal secretary.

What stunned her, though, was that Meg didn't know about Rowena—either that she was Brice's grandmother or that she was confined in a nursing home. Karen couldn't understand the rationale behind it. If Meg had been with him for a week or a month, she could see where something like that might have slipped through. But the girl had been with him for two years. She was shy; perhaps she'd never asked. Or was Brice ashamed? Embarrassed? Or simply that private a person?

Whatever the case, Karen wasn't about to betray his trust. Particularly when they were getting along. Particularly when she still needed his help.

So the dilemma was what to tell Meg. "Rowena is a lovely woman. I don't think she has a personal secretary…unless she's been hiding things from me all this time." Intent on redirecting the discussion, she asked, "What else does Dr. Carlin have you do—" she dropped her eyes to the tray "—besides making great breakfasts?"

Meg looked around the room. "I do laundry, dust, vacuum…." Her gaze lit on the dresser, the small table by the chair, the nightstand, and she frowned. "Where are your things?" She looked quickly back to read Karen's answer.

"At home. I hadn't planned on being sick."

"Where's home?"

"Syracuse."

Meg nodded, then frowned when she glanced down at the tray. "You're not eating."

"I'm talking."

"I'd leave you alone, but Dr. Carlin said I was to stay and make sure you finish. Maybe if I just sit here," she left the bedpost and went to the rocker, "and look out the window, you can do it."

Sure enough, she sat and looked out the window. Karen knew that if she were to speak, Meg's hearing aid would pick up the sound and the girl would turn around to read her lips. But Karen didn't speak. Dismaying as it was, she was actually feeling fatigued. Her voice was less hoarse than it had been, but it wasn't back to normal. Producing sound still took some effort, and she'd made enough of that for a while.

So she let the silence ride and concentrated on eating. It didn't take many forkfuls to fill her, but still she ate more. She didn't want to disappoint Meg, or suggest that the food wasn't good, or worse, risk Meg having to report to Brice that she'd failed at the job he'd given her.

In time, though, she reached her limit. "Meg?"

The girl's head came around, eyebrows raised in that same "pardon me" expression Karen had seen before. Then she stood and went to the bed to study the single sausage, half slice of toast and shreds of potato that remained on the plate. "That'll do until lunch."

"Lunch?" Karen echoed. The amount she'd just eaten for breakfast was more than she usually had for breakfast and lunch combined.

Meg didn't catch the dismay in her voice. "Dr. Carlin doesn't ask me to cook much, but I love doing it. While you're here, I'll have an excuse."

"Uh, please, Meg, don't plan. I don't know how long I can stay."

"Dr. Carlin said you'd be here for a while."

"Dr. Carlin may be wrong."

"I hope not. I really do like cooking. I was thinking of making quiche for lunch. I had some on my honeymoon—Richie took me to Atlantic City—but he says quiche isn't a man's food." She picked up the tray and continued to talk as she turned. "Man's food, woman's food—the cookbook says to use eggs and cheese and bacon, and those things would be nourishing for anybody—"

"Meg?" Karen said, but the young woman went on.

"—whether it's a man or a woman. But since Richie doesn't want it, you and I can—"

"Meg." This time, Meg turned. Knowing that the girl could see her lips, Karen lowered her voice. "How are the roads?"

"Wet. The sun is melting the snow."

"Is everything getting back to normal?"

"I think so."

"Do you think I would be able to get a cab?"

"I know you would. I passed two this morning."

Karen sank back against the pillows. There was one more critical question to ask. "Have you seen my clothes?"

Meg eyed her blankly. "Your clothes? No, I haven't seen them."

Karen's mind instantly replayed the theory that Brice was holding her prisoner by keeping her naked—or nearly so. She was going to have to confront him again. "I'm sure they're around," she mumbled, then said more clearly, "Thanks for the breakfast. It was delicious."

With a smile and the tiniest curtsy, Meg left the room.

KAREN SLEPT. SHE AWOKE at noon wanting a bath, but not wanting to exert the energy to take one. The matter was solved when Meg came in with lunch—indeed a quiche that was quite good. Karen didn't have the heart to mention the number of eggs she'd eaten that day. There was also fresh-baked bread and a salad, and Karen felt so full afterward that she rolled right over and went back to sleep.

She awoke at three o'clock perfectly disgusted with herself for having accomplished absolutely nothing. Pushing herself up against the pillows, she brooded, and the longer she did that, the more disgusted she felt. Not only had she accomplished nothing, but Brice hadn't been in once to see her.

She wondered why. He'd been so attentive over the weekend. She knew that he was working, but it wasn't as though his office was in town. It was in the other wing of the house. If he'd wanted to, he could have easily stopped up between appointments to check on her.

So much for country doctors making house calls, she mused a bit petulantly. For all *he* knew she was worse. In fact, she did feel warmer than she had at noon and suspected that her temperature was back up, though not by much. But Brice didn't know that. For all he knew she was burning up with fever. For all *he* knew, she'd gotten dressed and left the house!

Of course, he had her clothes—or knew where they were.

But she wasn't fussy. She didn't have to wear her own clothes to leave.

With the gears of her mind starting to turn, she climbed from bed, went out into the hall and looked both ways. There were doors to either side, lots of doors. She spent only a minute wondering why a man who lived alone would have a house with so many rooms. Then she started to explore.

The first door opened into a room that was totally empty. The second door likewise. The third door opened into Brice's room. It was larger than the others—including hers—by nearly double. A speedy look at the placement of doors and windows told her that he had indeed combined two rooms to form this one.

Done in navies and grays with a far simpler decor than the guest room, his bedroom was as masculine as the man himself. The bed, which was covered with a plaid quilt, was large and low. A lacquered headboard extended from the left nightstand to the right one. On that right one, was a telephone.

Making straight for it, she raised the receiver, brought it to her ear, lowered it to her chest for a minute, then set it down. There was no point calling a cab until she knew she had something to wear. So she returned her attention to the room.

The carpet was gray and plush. Navy Levelors covered the windows and were pulled high to let in the light of the day. There was a low dresser and an armoire, both of the same navy as the bed set. But the rest of the closets were built in—an entire wall's worth.

Karen headed for that wall. Drawing one door open, she found a sparse collection of suits and dress shoes. Closing that and moving to the next, she found shelves for shirts that were neatly pressed and folded. She figured that she could easily take one without it being missed, but she couldn't quite get herself to do it. They looked so neat, so proper, so starched. Closing that section of the closet, she opened the next. It held a television and a VCR, and the shelf above was filled with video cassettes. Unable to resist, she tipped her head and read some of the titles. There were classics and contemporaries, most of a serious or artsy bent. It was an impressive collection—as was the musical one on a lower shelf below the stereo.

But she felt too much like a thief to browse. Hastily

shutting that door, she moved along to find shelves of sweaters. After a quick perusal, she took what appeared to be one of the older ones and hugged it to her chest while she examined the next section, which held the corduroy jeans Brice wore all the time.

She stared at the jeans. That was it. Jeans, a sweater, maybe a pair of socks. She was sure she'd find her boots and coat in the closet downstairs. It would be very simple. She'd dress and be gone.

Still she stood. And as she stood, she found that the thought of sneaking out of Brice's home wasn't half as appealing, now that she had the means, as it had been before. She wanted her own clothes, her own car.

And she wanted Brice's blessing.

Of course, she wouldn't get it, she decided. He would remind her that she was still sick, remind her of how she'd fainted in the snow, remind her of her buried car and her deferred jobs. He wouldn't remind her about the midterms that were on the horizon, because that would defeat his purpose. But he would be very sane, very sensible, very dogmatic about the rest.

Still she wanted to see him.

Disappointed that she didn't have the guts, but knowing that she couldn't function any other way, she silently returned the sweater to its shelf, checked to see that the closet doors were all closed, gave a last wistful glance at the phone and left the room.

She was standing in the middle of her own, wondering what kind of fool she was, when Meg knocked and entered. She carried a small tray this time, with more hot chocolate, an orange cut into slices and three very large oatmeal-raisin cookies. A shopping bag was dangling from her elbow.

Ignoring the fact that Karen stood stock still in the

middle of the room, she set the tray down on the night-stand, then held out the bag.

"From Dr. Carlin."

Karen stared at the bag and frowned, at which point Meg went to her and pressed the twine handles into her palm.

"He went to Chelsea's," she said excitedly.

Karen could see where he'd been. The distinctive pale green and violet bag could have come from no other store. She couldn't count the number of times she'd admired the window of the Syracuse branch. She'd never gone in, though. The prices were exorbitant.

Meg rolled to her tiptoes and made a peeking movement toward the bag, silently urging Karen to open it. Karen did. Inside were several items, each wrapped in pale green tissue that matched the bag. She opened the first to find a hairbrush, but it was like none she'd ever owned. It was imported and of the finest boar bristles set in a sterling silver body with a handle to match.

Meg made soft ooo-ing sounds.

Karen was more cautious. She didn't know what to make of the gift. Brice had already done enough. She felt awkward.

Brush in one hand and bag in the other, she sat down on the edge of the bed. For another minute, she admired the brush's beauty. Then she gently set it down and looked into the bag again. This time she unwrapped a pair of deep red, fuzzy slippers.

Draped around the bedpost now, Meg clapped her hands.

Karen ran her fingers through the soft fur, brought it to her cheek for a minute, then set the slippers down beside the brush. The next package was small and light. She held her breath, deathly afraid that she'd find a lacy nightgown, and if that were the case, she couldn't pos-sibly keep it. The suggestiveness would be too much.

Rather than a lacy nightgown, though, she eased aside the tissue to find a lightweight knit nightshirt with Mickey Mouse on the front.

"How fun!" Meg cried.

Karen was more confused than ever. A sterling silver hairbrush was very much Brice's style. Furry slippers and a Mickey Mouse nightshirt weren't. Doubly curi-ous, she dug into the bag for the largest and last bundle. It contained a deep red terry velour robe to match the slippers.

"Try them on," Meg begged. "See how they look."

Karen was sitting on the bed, head bowed, eyes on the gifts. "Why did he do this?" she asked no one in particu-lar.

Meg touched her shoulder with a single finger, then crouched down, silently asking that Karen repeat what she'd said so that she could read her lips.

"I think I'd like to take a bath first," Karen said.

Meg's gaze traveled to the tray on the nightstand, for-gotten in the excitement.

"I think I'll take a bath second," Karen amended when she was sure Meg could see. "First I'll eat."

She was buying time. Before she put on the things Brice had bought, she had to be sure she was doing the right thing. So she nibbled at the cookies and sipped the cocoa and thought. She sucked out an orange slice, took another bite of cookie and thought. She sipped more, nibbled more, sucked more. But no amount of thinking could provide a definitive answer to her dilemma for the simple reason that she didn't know Brice's mind. She had no idea why he'd bought her anything, much less such lovely gifts. The hairbrush, the robe and slippers spoke for themselves. But she thought the Mickey Mouse night-

shirt lovely, too. It was fun and carefree in a way she'd
been only for one short time in her life. It made her want
to be that way again.

Meg left on the pretense of ironing sheets. Needing
a diversion from her thoughts, Karen went in search of
the bath she'd been thinking about. She ended up taking
a shower, because the glass-enclosed stall was too much
to resist, as was the promise of endless hot water. Her
own apartment had a showerless tub, and more often
than not, the hot water was used up by the landlord, who
lived below her with his wife and four kids and *did* have
a shower, which was constantly in use. Brice's shower,
on the other hand, was divine. It was large and bright,
and the water pressure couldn't have been better. When
she emerged she felt as though she'd been handled by a
personal masseuse.

She was back in bed, toweling her hair, when Meg
returned. Without a word, the girl picked up the brush,
gently nudged Karen's hands aside and went to work.

If the shower had been heaven, that brushing was a
step beyond. Karen had taken showers before. But it had
been years, *years* since anyone had leisurely brushed her
hair. Eyes closed, she savored one long stroke after the
next until she was sure she'd liquify.

She didn't liquify, though. She fell asleep as soon as
Meg left. This time when she awoke, Brice was there.

She was lying halfway on her side, with her cheek on
the pillow and her upper arm stretched out on the quilt.
As soon as she stirred, she sensed his presence, a large
immovable object by her hip.

Slowly she opened her eyes. He was sitting on the side
of the bed, with his elbows on his knees, hands hanging
loosely between. Only his head was turned her way, and
though the pose should have been awkward, he looked as

though he'd been there a while and could well sit a while longer.

She didn't know what to do. The last time she'd seen him had been the evening before, and the heat that had passed between them was as fresh in her mind as if she'd dreamed it that minute. In fact, she wondered if she had. The air around her felt charged with the same sensual awareness. It didn't help that he was so close, or that he was looking dark and mysterious in a black sweater and charcoal cords. Dark and mysterious was handsome—with the slight shadow of a beard on his cheek, very handsome. And he was just sitting there, watching her, thinking his own dark and mysterious and private thoughts.

She had no way of knowing that the reason he didn't move was because he didn't know what to do, either.

He had been stunned when he'd entered the room to find her sleeping. She was wearing the nightshirt he'd bought, and the robe was at the foot of the bed, the slippers on the floor—all of which gave him a feeling of satisfaction. But what stunned him was her looks. In all his years as a doctor, he'd never seen quite the change that three days of rest could make as he saw in Karen. Her skin was soft and smooth, still pale but more naturally so. The bags under her eyes had shrunk to shadows. Her features had relaxed. But her hair was what stopped him dead. It was breathtaking.

For one thing, it fell in long, thick curls over her shoulders to her back. For another it shone. For a third, whatever she'd used to wash it had brought out golden highlights on a field of pecan. The whole thing looked lighter. It looked alive.

In point of fact it scared him a little, but he'd be damned if he'd let that show. He had to have the upper hand when it came to Karen. So he schooled his expression to one of complete control.

Karen, meanwhile, was feeling awkward. "Thank you for the things," she said in a quiet voice. "You didn't have to do that."

"You needed a brush."

"A five-and-dime model would have been fine."

"Don't you like the silver one?"

"Yes, but it's too much."

"I can't return it now. You've already used it."

"I know." She felt his gaze on her hair, smoothing, stroking, separating the long curls, exploring them. Her scalp hummed. It boggled her mind to think what would happen if he actually touched her hair with his hand. He'd done it the night before, but in offer of comfort when she'd been upset. She had something else in mind now.

And that wasn't right at all. She had to leave.

Annoyed at herself, her tone was suitably cross. "You've avoided me so I wouldn't be able to nag you about leaving."

That was only one of the reasons Brice had avoided her. The other was that he'd felt too much when he'd faced her the night before. It was one thing to be touched by her helplessness, to feel sorry that she was ill, to do whatever he could to ease her physical distress. It was another to desire her. He'd wanted to make some sense of that in his mind before he faced her again. So he'd sent Meg with her food, her pills, the things he'd bought her in town. And he'd checked by for regular reports—but from Meg, not Karen.

At some point in the course of the afternoon, though, he'd realized that if he didn't face Karen, she was apt to walk out. He was surprised she hadn't tried it already. The fact that he'd taken her clothes would stall her, but not stop her. If she was like Rowena, she'd find a way to do whatever she set her mind to. He intended to stay one step ahead of that.

Without acknowledging her accusation one way or the other, he asked, "How are you feeling?"

"Better."

"Meg said you were warm again this afternoon."

"Meg has sharp eyes."

"Were you?"

"A little. I'm fine now."

He could see it. Her skin was the color of cream and very soft. He also saw the way her lips were slightly parted, the way her eyes were alert. She hadn't moved since she'd awoken and seemed as wary of him as he was of himself. That meant she remembered what had passed between them, too. He wondered what she'd do if he did reach out to touch her.

Brice fell back to the one sure thing in his life. "A slight rise in temperature isn't unusual with something like this, especially late in the afternoon. It may go up and down for several days."

"Then it's something I can monitor myself." Rolling to her back, she eyed him in earnest. "I have to get home, Brice. Meg says the roads are melting, so someone should be able to get at my car. The receptionist at the nursing home—Judy—said that her brother is great with cars and that if I ever have a problem, she'll be glad to have him take a look."

Brice was focusing on her face, but still he noticed the swell of her breasts beneath the nightshirt. "It was the battery. It couldn't be salvaged, so I had them put in a new one, and if you can't afford it, I can."

"I can afford it."

"I thought you were poor."

"Not that poor. I have an emergency fund."

"If you have an emergency fund, why your panic at the thought of not working for a while?"

"Because an emergency fund should be used only in an emergency. Not working to lie around in bed isn't an emergency."

"Not working to recover from pneumonia and exhaustion is an emergency."

"So I realized," she said quietly and was rewarded for her humility when Brice was momentarily without a comeback. She took the advantage to press her point. "That doesn't mean I can stay here. I have too much work to do. If I were home, I could be reading, writing my paper, studying."

He was quick to rally. "That's exactly what you'd be doing if you were home. You'd be pushing yourself harder than ever to catch up, then get ahead, and you still need sleep. I've been sitting here for half an hour. You were dead to the world."

"Half an hour?" The thought of his watching her made her uneasy. "That must have been boring."

"No."

She waited for him to go on. He didn't. His gaze dropped, leaving a trail of tingles from her chin, down her neck and chest to the small black bulb of Mickey Mouse's nose. Beneath that bulb was her nipple. It tightened instantly.

Dismayed, Karen debated her options. She could either draw the quilt to her throat, or sit up. If Brice was in a lecherous mood, he'd know exactly what she was doing and why. Then again, she'd never seen him in a lecherous mood. Dangerous, yes. Angry and frustrated, yes. Even sexually aware…

She sat up *and* tugged the quilt higher, deciding that she'd rather be safe than sorry. She also decided that it was time she stated her intent. "I'd like to stay the night, but if you'll give me my things, I can write you a check and be on my way in the morning."

He straightened, flexed his shoulders, closed his eyes, rocked his head around on his neck. Karen thought he looked like a fighter preparing for the next round. She was surprised when, rather than attacking her, he gave the floor a contemplative look. "Rowena called wanting to know how you were. She told me I wasn't to let you leave until you were completely well."

"Do you always do what she tells you to do?"

He looked at her in a way that left no doubt as to his answer. He was not the obedient type.

But Karen had sensed that from the start. "Then she won't be shocked when you discharge me early," she said.

"I'm not discharging you. If you leave, it will be against my wishes."

She thought about that for a minute, then offered a quiet, if unrepentant, "I'm sorry."

"What if I don't give you your clothes?"

"I'll take yours. You have a whole stack of sweaters. You could spare one for a day or two."

He turned to face her, his eyes dark, unreadable. "You were in my bedroom."

She swallowed. He was so close. So large. "That's right."

"What did you think?"

"What did I think?" she echoed dumbly.

"Of the bedroom."

"You mean, what did I think of the way it looked?"

"What else would I mean?" he asked impatiently.

She'd been prepared to defend herself against charges of trespassing. Taken off guard, she shrugged and sat back against the headboard. "I thought it was very neat and clean."

"The decoration."

"Oh. That. It was nice. Your wall of closets is fantastic. That whole room used to be two, didn't it?"

He gave a quick nod. "This used to be a tavern."

"Really?" she asked, instantly charmed. It made sense, now that she thought about it—the setup of rooms downstairs, their abundance on the second floor and in the wing.

Brice was entranced by the tiny curl at the corner of her mouth. It was rare, tempting. So while his eyes didn't budge from that spot, he went on a little about the house.

"It's certified. I have papers. This place used to be a famous watering hole."

"For humans."

"And horses."

"Not inside."

"Obviously. The public part of the tavern was in the three large rooms downstairs. The rooms up here were… I'm not sure…rented out, I guess."

There was an undercurrent to his vagueness that gave Karen pause. There was also the flicker of something in his eyes—she thought maybe it was discomfort, though it was fast gone. She tried to picture the house as a tavern, tried to imagine the downstairs rooms filled with carousers and the upstairs rooms, one after another along the hall, filled with…filled with…people…doing… what?

Her face lit up as she proudly announced, "It was a brothel, wasn't it?"

"I didn't say that."

"But it was."

He could swear he saw a smile. It was small, crooked, even rusty. But it did look like a smile. And it set off a burst of heat in his veins. "Does that please you?"

Her eye twinkled. "It's an…amusing idea. You're so dark and serious and straight. The good doctor. A pillar of the community. The thought of your living in a whore-house—"

"Former whorehouse."

"Former whorehouse." Her smile didn't widen, and it was still crooked, but her lips were more relaxed, as though they were getting used to it. "That's rich."

If she was laughing at him, Brice didn't mind. Two could play the game as well as one. "If it's true, do you know what it means?"

"Sure." She looked around the room. "It means that the decor in here must have been a sight different then than it is now."

"Uh-huh. Flashier. Sleazier. Lots of furniture, maybe a folding screen in the corner with flimsy little outfits hanging over the top."

Or mirrors on the ceiling, Karen thought, shooting a glance in that direction.

Brice followed her thought with ease. "It means that this room has seen its share of action." He flattened a hand on the bed on the far side of her hips, penning her in. "Think about it, Karen. All that loving in this bed."

Karen's smile was fading fast. He was too close. Too real. Too large. Too manly. "Not loving. Sex."

"Okay. Sex."

"And not in this bed."

He conceded that with a negligent, one-shouldered shrug. There was nothing negligent about his expression. "Okay, another bed. But in this spot. Wild, hot sex. Over and over, night after night."

"You have an incredible imagination," she murmured, but her breath caught, because his eyes weren't to be believed. They were dark, hypnotic, seductive. He was looking at her as though she could have been the object of that wild, hot sex. "Don't look at me that way," she whispered.

"What way?" His voice was a little hoarse. It rubbed against her, heightening the sexual tension she felt.

"That way."

"I'm just looking at you."

"You're hungry."

"My, we're direct."

Flattening herself against the headboard, she hugged her arms to her chest and murmured a bit frantically, "I need room, Brice. You're crowding me."

But Brice moved closer. He was feeling an irresistible urge to kiss her, and this time he wasn't going to deny himself. She was determined to leave; he wanted to taste her before she did. And besides, he could swear, could swear that despite her protests, she was hungry, too.

"Brice…"

He took her wrists and, uncrossing her arms, drew her forward.

"Brice…please, Brice. I'm not well," she reasoned, but her voice was without force. "Haven't you been saying so for days on end?"

He drew her closer. "Not days on end. Three days. And for far too much of that time I've been wondering about this." Bracing her back with his forearm, he took her face in his hand. Then, just when Karen was opening her mouth to protest, he covered it with his own.

CHAPTER SIX

KAREN FOUGHT HIM. Calling on what little strength she had, she tried to push him away, but he was rock solid. She twisted her body, tried to turn her head, but he held it firm. She whimpered into his mouth, but he didn't yield.

Then she went still. Since fighting hadn't worked, she decided she had nothing to lose by stopping, lying motionless in his arms, holding her mouth rigid beneath his. No man wanted to kiss a stone.

That was the plan, and in theory it was sound. But it was self-defeating, because without fighting, her senses were open to what Brice was doing.

He was very slowly, very purposefully caressing her mouth. His touch was firm and willful, but gentle in an oddly masculine kind of way. He slanted his lips across hers, opening them to draw her soft flesh to his warmth. He sipped. He sucked. He tasted her as he would a fine wine, swirling her lips in his mouth, savoring their bouquet.

Karen had never been savored quite that way before. Her breath came faster. Without conscious thought, she relaxed her lips. Her skin warmed. The fine network of nerve ends that radiated outward from her mouth was reinforced at each spot where her body touched his. But the starburst went deeper. She felt a heat she'd never known in her very core. The urge to melt was terrifying.

That was what Brice saw in her eyes when he reluctantly freed her mouth. His face was inches above hers, his gaze fixed on those eyes before falling to her lips, which were soft, faintly swollen and moist. He wanted to taste more; the need was alive in every pore of his body. But that look of fear in her eyes kept him from it.

He didn't want her afraid when he kissed her. He wanted her warm and eager. For that matter, he wanted her warm and eager for life in general, yet she wasn't. She was running on a treadmill, too busy keeping the pace to consider what it was worth.

She never smiled. He wanted to see her smile—and not smugly at the thought of his house having once been a brothel. He wanted to see her smile in pure delight. In innocent pleasure, sheer fun, unadulterated joy.

Splaying his fingers on either side of her head, he spoke in a deep, rumbling voice that held quiet command. "You're staying here, Karen. I promised Rowena I'd care for you, and I mean to do it. Early tomorrow morning, I'll drive you back to Syracuse. You can pick up your books, pens, papers, clothes, anything else you need to have to function here for a while."

"But—"

He covered her lips with his thumbs. "I have a typewriter and a computer if you want either. You know as well as I do that you can get class notes from someone else, but if you insist on going to classes yourself, I'll have you driven there and back. It should be no worse than the trips you've made to the nursing home, and with someone else driving, you can rest. You can study for midterms; you can go back and take them. Then you have a vacation. I want you here till it's over."

"I can't—"

He renewed the pressure of his thumbs. "You can. And you will." His dark eyes held hers for a minute longer, reinforcing the order. Then he released her and rose from the bed. He didn't look back on his way to the door. He didn't say another word.

Nor did Karen as she silently watched his tall frame pass from sight. Only when the rapid tattoo of his footsteps on the stairs faded did she release her breath. She put her fingertips to her lips. She dropped her gaze to the floor. A bewildered look appeared on her face.

She should have spoken up. She should have argued. But she hadn't, and she knew why.

She wanted to stay.

Lifting her gaze, she sent it slowly around the room, touching on each piece of furniture, each small decorative item. Her mind's eye wandered down the stairs to the living room, with its corduroy sofa and its blazing hearth, then to the other rooms, with their warm, dark wood, then to the kitchen with ultramodern amenities that were somehow traditionalized.

It would be so easy to stay, she mused. Whorehouse or not, she loved what she'd seen of the house. Even the powder room, which she'd seen only when she'd been so sick, left an impression of burgundy and cream in paisley walls, ceramic fixtures and stained glass sconces. It was warm here. Quiet. She'd never spent any time in a home that was quite as comfortable.

Then there was the fact that Brice made her feel safe. But he also threatened her. She couldn't stay if he planned to remind her of the accident at every turn. She couldn't stay if he planned to lecture her about her lifestyle. And she *certainly* couldn't stay if he planned to kiss her often—or could she? He had given her a taste of delicious feelings. She wondered where they'd lead.

Swinging her legs over the side of the bed, she slid her feet into her slippers, freshened up in the bathroom, secured her hair with its customary barrettes, then wrapped herself in the deep red robe and went looking for Brice.

It was easy this time. Not only was the noise in the kitchen a dead giveaway, but she could smell something cooking. It was strong—either that or she was greatly improved, because whatever it was successfully penetrated her nasal passages. It was also Italian and tempting enough to make her salivate.

Brice spared her little more than a glance when she appeared at the kitchen door. He had a mitt on his hand and was busily shifting things around in the wall oven. Karen, whose father had never gone near a stove, was intrigued. She wasn't sure how Brice could manage to cook and look masculine at the same time, but he did.

Then she remembered how he'd kissed her. She hadn't watched him while he was doing it, so she didn't know how he'd looked, but she'd felt him. She'd felt his firm mouth on hers, felt his large hands holding her face, felt his muscled chest exerting pressure on her breasts. He'd felt plenty masculine then.

She was unaware of the flare of pink on her cheeks, but Brice wasn't. Nor was he unaware of how captivating she looked in the robe he'd bought—or how quickly his body could respond to both the flare and the captivation. He never should have kissed her, *never* should have kissed her, but he'd been provoked. He'd been a little curious, a little belligerent, a little aroused. Unfortunately, now he was a little confused. And a lot horny.

So he concentrated on getting supper. With the garlic bread stowed beside the lasagna, he closed the oven door and went to take plates from an overhead cabinet. He shot a glance at Karen. She was standing with her arms around her waist and her eyes on the floor. He followed her gaze, thinking that maybe he'd spilled something, but the adobe tile was as clean as it had been after Meg had mopped it that afternoon.

"You should be in bed," he said gruffly. Putting the plates on the counter, he opened another cabinet.

She looked up. "We have to talk."

"That's not a good idea." He set down two glasses and closed the cabinet. "We don't see eye to eye on many things."

"Brice, you can't just give orders and have them obeyed."

He rummaged around in the silverware drawer. "Why not?"

"Because thinking people don't take to dictatorships."

Two forks slid over the counter to the plates. "It didn't strike me that you were doing much thinking when you worked yourself into pneumonia, then went to visit Rowena and passed out in the snow. Besides, this isn't a dictatorship. It's a democracy that is temporarily under martial law. I'm the doctor. I know what's best."

"Oh, please," Karen muttered.

He met her gaze. "I do."

"You know what's best for *you,* but that may not be what's best for me. And don't tell me that the AMA would approve of your prescription in this case, because I doubt it would."

Brice crossed to the refrigerator, which took him close enough to Karen for her to have to look up. He opened the door, then paused and eyed her. "Are you planning to report me to the AMA?"

"Of course not."

"That's good, because you wouldn't have much of a case." Turning his attention back to the refrigerator, he removed a large salad bowl and set it on the counter. "What's happening between us is personal."

Karen didn't waste her breath with denials. "That's why we have to talk. You're asking me to live here with you for the next month, but how can I do that, when I barely know you?"

"Dressing?"

She blinked. "Excuse me?"

"Do you take your salad with dressing?"

"Of course."

"What kind?"

"I'm not fussy."

"What kind?"

"Whatever you're having."

"What kind?"

"Thousand Island."

"Thank you," he said. He took a bottle of Thousand Island dressing from the shelf on the inside of the refrigerator door, then closed the door and turned to the counter. There he busied himself filling two salad plates from the larger bowl. He was using his hands; they worked far better than salad tongs.

Karen had no objection to that, but as she stood watching him work, she realized that her legs were tiring. She glanced at the kitchen table. It was oak and inlaid with tiles. Four chairs, two on a side, were of the same oak with sturdy rush seats. She made her way to one and sat down.

"Are you sure you're up to this?" Brice asked without turning.

"Yes. That's why your insisting that I stay here for a month is so bizarre. I'm fine. Really."

"Don't give me that."

"It's true. Okay, I'm not one hundred percent, but I'm on the mend. I'm no worse now than if I had a bad cold."

Mitts in hand, Brice took the lasagna from the oven and set it on the counter. "You're weaker, and that won't go away in a day. You'll be tired over the next few weeks. Your temperature may go up and down. Your cough should be watched." He tossed the mitts into a drawer. "Do you know what would happen if you stopped taking penicillin?"

"I'd get sick again."

He nodded.

"But I don't have to stop taking it," Karen pointed out. "You could give me a prescription. I'm not even contagious anymore."

Taking a bottle of milk from the refrigerator, he filled the glasses and put them on the table. They were followed shortly by the salad, replete with healthy toppings of dressing. Closemouthed and stony-eyed, he started doling out the lasagna.

At that point, Karen sensed that he had no intention of arguing further. He'd decided what should be done; he felt added discussion unnecessary. In a way, that was fine with her. She hadn't come downstairs to argue. She'd come to learn about the man who had appointed himself her guardian.

Starting with something relatively neutral, she asked, "How long have you lived here?"

Brice tried to find a catch to the question. At length he decided it was innocent enough. "Nine years."

"Was it a home when you bought it?"

He set a serving of lasagna before her. "You mean, as opposed to a whorehouse?"

So much for neutrality. "I was only guessing about that. Was someone living here when you bought it?"

"Yes."

She waited. Instead of elaborating, he retrieved the garlic bread from the oven. So she bluntly asked, "Who?"

He made a production of peeling back the foil, cutting the bread into slices, piling them in a basket. "The Walkers."

"The Walkers. Ahh. That says it all."

He shot her a wry glance. "The Walkers were a professional couple, both teaching at Cornell. They had seven kids and two maids. The house was perfect for them." Tossing the basket on the table, he went back to the counter for his own plate.

"Seven kids. Incredible. Why did they sell?"

"They received appointments at Stanford."

"Why did you buy?"

He sat down directly across from her. "Because I liked the place. I liked the location, I liked the land, I liked the house."

"But it's so big. You don't have seven kids and two maids. You don't have a wife, for that matter."

"I have an office. And a large practice." He raised his milk. "That requires a certain amount of space." He took a healthy drink.

Karen didn't miss the gentle bob of his Adam's apple when the milk went down. His neck was solid, not thick, but nicely developed. She wondered if he worked out.

"Were you practicing here in Ithaca before you bought the house?" she asked.

He picked up his fork. "I had an office in town and was living in an apartment not far from there."

"But you had a dream," she said anticipatorily.

"Don't we all?"

She wondered about his somberness, but sensed there'd be a better time to explore it. "We don't all get to fulfill our dreams. You did. You dreamed of working out of your home. Now you are."

Brice set down the fork and stared at her straight. "I worked hard to get where I am. The one break I had was that I didn't graduate from med school in debt. Rowena saw to that. But she couldn't wave a magic wand and make a successful practice appear. I had to work my butt off for that."

"I'm sure you did," Karen replied in a conciliatory voice, but he wasn't done.

"I started out in hospitals and clinics. Three or four times a week I spent my nights in emergency rooms. I covered for every other doctor in the area until, little by little, my name spread. I've paid my dues. I've earned more regular hours and the right to leave my own patients with a covering physician and go away several times a year."

Apparently, she'd struck a raw chord. She hadn't meant to do that, but it was interesting—a little clue as to what made the man tick. It seemed he was sensitive about what he had and what he'd had to do to get it. He was proud of his achievements—as rightly he should be, she reflected. But he was also defensive. She wondered why.

But she wasn't up to asking. That was sure to bring on a fight, and she didn't want one. So she settled for a sincere, "I think it's wonderful that you were able to buy this house."

Brice stared at his plate for a long minute before lifting his fork and starting to eat. After several more minutes, he took a breath and said more quietly, "Anyway, when this place came on the market, I knew the setup was right. Separate wing, separate entrance for my patients. Plenty of room for me."

"And Rowena?"

He leveled her a stare. "What about Rowena?"

She weathered the stare as best she could, while she asked herself why innocent comments should set him off. "Did she ever live here with you?"

"No."

"Or visit?"

"Sometimes."

The obvious question, of course, was why Rowena

wasn't with him now. Brice had the money to hire a nurse, and he had room to house them both. If he cared as much for his grandmother as he implied he did, why was she in a nursing home?

Karen knew better than to ask. "Do you entertain much?"

"No."

"Have out-of-town friends in to visit?"

"No." .

"Oh." She couldn't quite figure out what he wanted with all the upstairs rooms. The obvious answer was that he was planning on having a family of his own one day. But if that were true, what was he waiting for? He had a huge house and a successful practice. And he wasn't getting any younger.

"Have you ever been married?" she asked.

He set down his fork again and looked pointedly at hers, which she hadn't touched. "Aren't you going to eat?"

"I will."

"Not if you're talking. Doesn't your mouth ever stop?"

"I'm only asking questions."

"Well, can it."

"Why?"

"Because it's annoying. Shut your mouth for a change."

Karen didn't feel she deserved his sharpness, but if he could shell it out, so could she. "How do you propose I get food in if I do that?"

"You'll find a way."

Sitting back in her chair, she looked at him in dismay. "I hope you know that your personality leaves something to be desired."

"So I've been told."

"It's not critical that I eat right now. You just didn't want to answer my question."

"If you don't eat now, the lasagna will get cold. Meg made it for you."

"And for you."

But he shook his head. "She knows that I don't care one way or another what I eat."

"Poor Meg. She should be working someplace where she can be appreciated. I hope you don't tell her that the sauce is too thin."

"I don't, because it's not, and if it were, I wouldn't say a thing. Meg is special."

That was what Karen had figured. She rather envied Meg her "special" status. The sharpness of Brice's tongue smarted. Karen could still feel its sting. If Meg was spared that, she was blessed.

"It was kind of you to hire her," Karen said, thinking the comment innocent and sincere. She was startled when Brice bristled.

"Kind? It was practical. I needed someone; she was there. Believe me, she earns her wages."

"All right," Karen murmured hastily. "All right." Feeling more weary than she had moments before, she looked down at her food and began to eat. In the periphery of her vision, she saw Brice doing the same. She'd taken two mouthfuls of lasagna to his four when he set down his fork.

"I'm not angry at you," he said, frowning.

"Could've fooled me," she replied without looking up.

"I'm not. I just…get that way sometimes."

"Mmm. Angry."

"Not at you."

She did look up in challenge then. "You've been angry at me. Don't deny it. And what was so awful about my asking whether you've ever been married? Is it a state secret? Rowena would tell me if I asked. And, by the way," she went on brashly, "tomorrow's my day to visit her. I'm going."

For several minutes, Brice said nothing. He stared at her, then calmly returned to his dinner. Only after he'd made his way through better than half of his meal did he look up again, shocking her this time with the shadow of a smile. "You have spunk."

"I have to have *something* to deal with you."

"Most people turn and run."

"Believe me, I would if I could, but I'm not exactly in shape. You'd catch me in a minute. And I can't run out in this weather wearing nothing but a robe. You have my clothes."

"The dry cleaner has them."

"Same difference." She snatched up a piece of bread, tore off a corner and ate it, but there the small burst of frustration-induced energy seemed to wane. Sitting back, she chewed more slowly.

"You're feeling tired, aren't you?" Brice asked.

"I'm okay."

His tone sharpened. "Are you feeling tired?"

She met his gaze, but sadly, not defiantly. "Yes."

"Do you want to go back to bed?" he asked on a gentler note.

"Soon." She took a small drink of milk, then nudged a piece of lettuce around the edge of her salad. When it hit a cherry tomato, she abandoned it and forked a small piece of lasagna toward the side of the dish. And all the while she was trying to decide whether Brice disliked her because she had hit Rowena or…just…because.

"How's the food?"

Her head came up with a start. "Just fine."

"Don't you like lasagna?"

"I love lasagna."

"Is it too spicy?"

"No, it's great."

"Then why are you picking at it like it's liver?"

With carefully controlled movements, she set down her fork. With as carefully controlled movements, she raised her head. And when she spoke, her voice was as carefully controlled as her movements had been.

"I'm picking," she said quietly, "because you've upset my stomach. I'm not used to eating, let alone in a war zone. I can understand why you live alone. If you do to other people what you do to me, not even a fool would want to be with you."

Her throat felt tight. She looked down at her lap, then back up. There was more to say. "What I don't understand is how you can be a doctor—" She held up a hand. "No, I take that back. I can understand it. You warm up to the sick just fine. How the *families* of the sick can stand you is beyond me, but maybe they're desperate enough for medical help that they can excuse the rudeness."

She took a quick breath. "I can't, Brice. I can't live with it, even if it's only for a month. For twenty-one years, I lived in a house filled with constant tension. I don't want that. I'd rather be alone." To her chagrin, her eyes began to tear. Swearing softly, she bowed her head and covered her face with a hand.

Brice sat very still. He watched her struggle for control and though he felt an intense urge to help her, he couldn't move. He hadn't meant to cause her pain—or maybe he had, but if so, he was sorry. He no longer saw her solely as the woman who had put Rowena in a wheelchair; she had feelings and a personality, both of which he found himself drawn to.

But if he'd wanted to get her to stay, he'd gone about it the wrong way. "Karen?"

Her head remained bowed. "I'm okay."

He opened his mouth, then closed it and swallowed. Then he tried again, this time producing quiet sound. "I'm a jackass."

"You can say that again."

"No. It was hard enough the first time. I'm not used to apologizing."

"That must be why you have so many friends."

"I'm not good with people."

"Sure," was her facetious reply. "You're a doctor and you're not good with people."

"I'm not."

She fiddled with the belt of her robe. "I could buy that if you were in research. But you have a successful practice. You said so yourself. So how do you do it? Are your patients masochists?"

"My patients are kids. I'm good with kids. Not adults."

Karen looked up in disbelief. "Kids?"

He nodded.

"You're a pediatrician?"

He had his forearms on the table. His fingers were curled, not fisted but tense. He wore a look of vulnerability, which only added to her disbelief.

"I am a pediatrician," he stated. "Is that so hard to believe?"

"Yes! I mean, children are the most helpless creatures in the world. You can't be gruff with them. You can't issue orders and walk out. You can't come across like a block of ice."

"I don't."

She raised her shoulders while her eyes darted blindly around the kitchen. "I assumed you were a general practitioner, an internist, maybe a dermatologist—"

He sputtered his opinion of that.

"But a pediatrician. That's incredible."

"I'm a good doctor."

She didn't doubt it for a minute. "But a *pediatrician!*"

He was sitting straighter, beginning to look offended. "You don't have to act as though I'm the least likely candidate for the job, because I assure you I'm not. There are less likely candidates on the staff of every major children's hospital in the country. And I'm not that unlikely a candidate. I know what I'm doing medically, and I like kids.

"And what's more," he went on vehemently, "they like me. They don't have preconceived notions of what a doctor should be. They don't give a damn whether I belong to the university club or go to the local charity ball or pick up the award for 'Mr. Congeniality' at the state fair each year. They don't fault me because I choose to live alone. They don't ask for one iota more than I can give, which is the best medical care possible."

Karen continued to study him, now with a bemused look on her face. "A pediatrician," she murmured. It took some getting used to, but the more she turned it over and around in her mind, the more she liked it. A slow, tentative smile touched her lips. "I think that's just fine," she said.

The smile, oh, the smile. It made Brice forget about being offended, made him forget about defending his specialty. That smile was a soothing balm flowing through his veins. It warmed his insides, made him want to bloom.

"Do you treat kids of all ages?" Karen asked softly.

He nodded.

"Even newborns?" she asked with a bit of awe. When he nodded again, she tried to picture him holding a tiny bundle of life. At first, she couldn't. Then she tried harder and slowly formed the image of his large hands cradling an infant. It was an unexpectedly beautiful idea and held her momentarily speechless.

"I've always had a laid-back approach to medicine," Brice said. "I know when to be alarmed, but I'm not an alarmist. I assume that's why mothers bring their kids to me."

Karen nodded.

"I mean," he went on with a sudden breath, "I can relate to kids. I can sympathize with what they're feeling. They're guileless. Spontaneous. They say what's on their minds. They're honest without being malicious. I guess that's it. They can tell you they hate you. And at a particular moment—like when you've just given them a shot—they do, but they're not trying to hurt you back. They're not sophisticated enough for that." His mouth thinned. "They don't learn that till they're older."

He was suddenly dark again. Karen looked away, trying to retain in her mind's eye the warmer expression he'd been wearing when he'd been talking about his kids. And they were his kids. He saw them as his family. He hadn't said as much, but she'd heard it. His days were filled with the care of his kids, then he returned to his empty rooms at night.

It didn't make sense.

Lifting her fork, she picked at the lasagna for several minutes, but ate little. She was tired, no longer hungry, the lasagna was cold and Brice had her thoroughly confused.

"Brice?" Her eyes went to his. "Why do you dislike adults?"

He shrugged.

She pushed. "Why?"

"Because they dislike me."

"But why? I don't understand it."

"That's not what you said a minute ago."

"A minute ago I was angry. Now I don't know what to be."

He sighed. "Look, Karen, it's no big thing. I like kids, so I work with kids."

"What about their parents?"

"What about them?"

"Children don't just walk into your office on their own. They're accompanied by adults, and those adults are the ones you converse with. How do you deal with them?"

"I deal with them. They bring their kids for medical care; I provide it. It's as simple as that."

Karen knew it wasn't, and her look told him so. "There's more to pediatrics than diagnosis and treatment. There are emotional issues in the rearing of a child. Doesn't a pediatrician have to address those, too?"

"I do."

"By telling a mother all she's doing wrong?"

"More often by telling her all she's doing right."

That shut Karen up for a minute. She hadn't expected that he'd give such a perfect answer. "What happens when a mother brings a child in with real behavioral problems?"

"I can tell pretty quickly whether I can help, and if I can't, I refer them to a specialist."

She couldn't find fault with that answer, either. "What about the mother who runs to your office every time her child sneezes? Or the one who refuses to follow the instructions you give her for the care of her child?"

"I can handle them, Karen. I may not like them, but I'm not a total social misfit. I know what's expected, and I give my version of it. I don't patronize. I don't sweet-talk. And if they don't like that, they go elsewhere."

Apparently, Karen realized, they did like it, if Brice's practice was as successful as he said. He circumvented his dislike of adults by dealing principally with children; his love for and understanding of those children soothed over any rough spots he might have with their parents. What could be better?

She looked off toward the window. It was dark out. Feeling a chill, she crossed her arms over her waist and tucked her hands inside.

"Karen?"

Her gaze swung back.

"Are you all right?"

She nodded, but strange emotions whispered through her as she looked at him. It occurred to her that the stony expression he so often wore was part of a barrier, part of a wall he erected to keep others away and protect himself. Somewhere along the line he'd been hurt. She felt badly.

"Your color's gone again," he observed.

"I'm okay."

"I think you should go back to bed."

"In a minute." In an odd way, she was enjoying sitting with him. Yes, she felt tired. But she didn't want to go back to bed just yet. "I'm the first woman who's ever stayed here, aren't I?" she asked softly.

Brice didn't blink. "Yes."

"Why?"

"Why you? Or why no others?"

She shrugged, moved her head from side to side indicating that he could answer either or both.

Brice was feeling mellow. His kitchen was plenty big for two people, and he was finding that he liked Karen's company. He'd given her a hard time and still she stayed. Even after he'd told her to go to bed, she hadn't…and not out of defiance, either. Perhaps her illness had worn her down, but she'd softened. He almost got the impression that she liked his company, too, which was truly a miracle. He felt he owed her something for her perseverence.

"I was married once," he said in a voice that was only the slightest bit defensive. "It was right after I finished my residency. I figured that since I was going into private practice, it was time."

"Who was she?"

"An executive secretary at the hospital. I guess she figured it was time, too, and I was better than nothing."

"What an awful thing to say. Maybe she loved you."

"She thought she did."

"Did you love her?"

He considered that as he leaned back in his chair with one hand in his lap, the other on the table. He was giving the edge of his plate little flicks that rotated it by degrees. His features weren't as relaxed as the pose. "I thought I did, but I loved my work more. That frustrated her, so she made greater demands on my time and affection. We argued a lot. I took refuge in my work, and happily so. The divorce was amicable. She'd met someone else and wanted the quickest, cleanest split."

"Oh."

His eyes met hers. "What does that mean—'oh'?"

Karen shrugged. "I don't know. I'd say I'm sorry, but you don't seem to be."

"I'm not."

"But what about a family?"

"What about it?"

"You're a pediatrician. You love children. Don't you want to have some of your own?"

"Do you?" he asked.

She sank deeper in her chair simply because her body didn't want to hold her up. "Someday."

"You're not getting any younger."

"I was thinking the same about you. You're in a better

position to have children than I am. You've made it. I still
have a long way to go." She hooked a tired hand over her
shoulder.

Brice couldn't help but note the limpness of that hand.
"I think you should go up."

She closed her eyes for the space of several breaths.
"I'm not sure I can move from this chair."

"Should I carry you?"

Her eyes opened, and she shook her head. "I'd better
be able to handle your stairs if I'm going to be able to
manage three flights of mine tomorrow morning."

Pushing his chair back, Brice stood, stacked the
dishes, set the glasses on top and carried them all to the
sink. "So. What's the decision?" he asked with his back
to her as he directed a spray of water toward the plates.
His voice was rougher. "Will you be staying here, or
what?"

Karen studied his broad back, saw straight lines that
verged on the rigid. "I didn't think you were giving me
a choice."

He paused. "You have a choice."

"Do you want me to stay?"

"That's a dumb question," he barked. "Why else
would I ask?"

"I don't know. But then, I don't know why you picked
me up from the snow in the first place. Or why you've
taken care of me for three days. Or why you bought me
a nightshirt with Mickey Mouse on the front—why did
you?"

Slowly he turned. "Would you have preferred something sexy?"

She shook her head.

"That's what I figured."

"So why Mickey Mouse?"

His gaze slid to her chest, settling on the spot where,

beneath the deep red robe, the mouse's face would be. "Because it was sweet. And silly." His eyes rose and he rubbed the inside of his wrist against his pants. "Dumb, huh?"

She was more touched than she'd have believed possible. "No. I love it."

"But it hasn't made you smile."

"Maybe because it's more sweet than silly," she said, then gave him the smile he wanted. It was shy, not too big, but it was a smile nonetheless. "Thank you," she whispered. "I do love the nightshirt."

Not trusting his voice, Brice gave a single slow nod. At that moment, as he looked at Karen, he could find nothing, nothing to fault her on. The fury he'd once felt was forgotten. She was kind and gentle, and, in her innocence, sexy as hell.

He turned quickly back to the sink, but her image remained: soft wisps of pecan-colored hair framing her face; warm, amber eyes; delicate shoulders; gentle breasts. A heat rose in his body with stunning speed. Bowing his head, he gritted his teeth against it.

That was when her voice came to him softly, almost timidly. "What time shall I be ready tomorrow?"

It was a minute before he could relax his jaw, and then he wasn't sure if the tension in his voice was sexual or not. She still hadn't said if she'd return with him. "I'll wake you." He heard her slide back her chair and get up. "Karen?" Turning, he found her with her hand on the jamb and her back to him. "Will you be coming back with me?"

An hour or two before, she'd probably have refused him. One part of her would have regretted it, but she'd have felt she was doing the right thing. Now, she wasn't sure what the right thing was. Brice didn't seem the grump he once had. Oh, yes, he still had his moods, but

with each tidbit she picked up about the man behind the
moods, she became more and more intrigued. He was a
puzzle; she had a handful of pieces, but she wanted the
rest. There was only one way to get them.

Bowing her head, she whispered, "Yes. I'll be coming
back with you." Then she left the room before she had
second thoughts.

CHAPTER SEVEN

ITHACA WAS PITCH BLACK when a hand on Karen's shoulder shook her awake. She opened an eye, then flipped over in fright to look up into Brice's shadowed face. The only light was that which spilled in from the hall and silhouetted his large, looming form.

"Time to get up," he said.

She couldn't imagine why, at first. Though her fright quickly passed, it was a minute before her mind began to function. "What time is it?"

"Six. I have to be back at the hospital by nine."

She immediately pushed herself up. "Okay. I'll be ready."

"Your pill's in the bathroom. Ten minutes?"

She nodded and was swinging her feet to the floor as he left. She looked up in time to see him clear the door and disappear. He was wearing a running suit. She wondered whether that was what he planned to wear in the car, then wondered what *she* planned to wear in the car. She turned the light on and was in the process of contemplating that when Brice returned.

In two strides he was across the floor, placing a fleecy bundle in her arms. "Sweat suit. Warm and comfortable." He was back at the door in another two strides, but there he paused. Without turning, he said, "Your own clothes are in the hall closet downstairs. If you'd rather wear those—"

"These will be fine," Karen said.

He hesitated, nodded, then was gone.

Ten minutes later, he stood in the front hall watching Karen come down the stairs. His gaze slipped over her body. She looked adorable; he didn't know whether to laugh or cry. Reluctant to do either, he said, "You look like a deflated chipmunk."

She *felt* like a deflated chipmunk, because Brice looked like anything but. In those ten minutes he had somehow managed to shower, shave and toss on a shirt, sweater and cords. He looked fresh and ready to face the day in style.

Karen, too, had showered, but she didn't feel as fresh and ready as he looked. She knew that had something to do with her illness; she still felt weak and, because she was sleeping so soundly, a little hung over. She had to believe that she'd feel better—more herself psychologically—once she got some of her own things from home.

Not that she minded the feel of Brice's sweat suit. The fact that at some point he'd worn it himself made her feel all warm inside.

Averting her gaze, she spotted her boots by the closet door. She took them to the stairs, sat on the third step and pulled them on over the wool socks Brice had enclosed— along with her underwear—in the sweat suit. Returning, she let him help her on with her coat.

With a hand at her back, he ushered her through the kitchen and into the garage. His black BMW stood there, slightly spattered from the weather's recent inclemency. Beside it, looking less spattered but more battered, was her Chevy.

Coming to a halt at the BMW's nose, Brice trained his eyes on the Chevy and asked, "Do you want to take your car?"

Karen understood that he was giving her a last chance

to change her mind about returning, and while she had no intention of doing so, she appreciated the gesture. "My heating system is lousy."

"I had it fixed."

"Oh."

"So?"

She thought for a minute, then wrinkled up her nose. "Nah. The windshield wipers are broken."

"Not anymore."

"You didn't fix the radio, too, did you? I'm not a listener, which is why I didn't care whether it worked or not. I hope you didn't spend money on *that*—"

"No. I didn't feel there was a safety factor involved."

Karen bit her lip. The accusation was subtle, but it was there. She looked sharply at Brice, prepared to defend herself, if need be. But he wasn't looking at her. He was looking in the opposite direction, awaiting her answer.

"No, I don't want to take my car," she said with spirit. "I like yours better." And with that, she went straight to the passenger's side, opened the door and slid in.

The drive was a quiet one. Once Karen settled down after that little rise, she relaxed and found that she *did* like Brice's car better than hers. The seats were more plush, the ride silent and smooth. Given the lack of traffic at that early hour, they made good time. The day was dawning gray and cool when they pulled up at the wood frame house in Syracuse that Karen called home.

For the first time, looking at it as Brice would see it, the shabbiness of the place hit her. As she led him to the door at the back that led to the stairs that led to her third-floor apartment, she was thinking that the house badly needed a paint job. Actually, she decided as she pulled and tugged, pulled and tugged until the door finally opened, the house needed more than a paint job.

The three flights were long and narrow. She was visibly winded by the time they reached the top and she'd opened the door to her apartment.

"Sit," Brice instructed.

The instruction was unnecessary. Karen was already en route to the desk chair. The instant she reached it, she sank gratefully onto its canvas sling.

Hands buried in the pockets of his cords so that they pushed his topcoat aside, Brice looked around the room. The apartment was, in fact, a garret, though somehow that designation made it sound more luxurious than it was. It was an attic. A bathroom had been built at one end, and a small kitchenette stood at the other, but it was still an attic—doubtlessly converted for the sake of the rent.

Brice turned, then turned again.

"Pretty bad, huh?" Karen said self-consciously.

It was pretty bad, but he didn't say so. He'd decided to make an attempt to be less abrasive. It was going to take some effort; old habits died hard. He'd nearly blown it with the deflated chipmunk comment, though she hadn't taken offense at that. But he thought he'd done quite well in not calling her car a rattletrap, and he was determined to keep his opinion of her apartment to himself.

Actually, the more he looked, the less bad it did look. True, the rafters were water-stained and warped and had nails sticking out every which way in odd places. The floor was covered with vintage linoleum that curled at the edges. The sink was ancient, the stove even worse.

But the place was clean. The walls were painted white, and the miscellaneous pieces of furniture and their coverings—a comforter on the bed, café curtains on the windows, a recycled dresser, nightstand and desk, the deck chair she sat in—were all of bright and varied colors. Brice guessed that Karen had spent many a free hour painting when she'd first moved in. She'd come close to creating a rainbow.

"Not bad," he said and glanced at her. She was wrapped in her coat, seeming chilled. He looked for a thermostat, found none, then spotted a radiator and within seconds was trying to twist its knob.

"It's on," Karen said quickly. "When I left on Friday, I had no idea I wouldn't be back, and since I wasn't feeling great, I wanted the place to stay warm. If I turn off the heat for even a few hours, the temperature in here drops something awful."

Forgetting his resolution, Brice growled, "The temperature in here is something awful even with it on. Is this the best your landlord can do?"

"I guess so."

"What do you mean, 'you guess so'? Haven't you told him you're cold?"

She raised one shoulder and huddled into it. "I asked him if the radiator was working, and he said it was. That was last December, when it was really cold. It's not so bad now. If I've made it through this far, I'll make it to spring."

"You nearly didn't make it," Brice pointed out with a scowl. "If you'd had proper heat in here, you might not have been as sick. I have a mind to report this place to the board of health."

Karen straightened in her seat. "If you do that," she said quietly, looking him in the eye, "the landlord will fix the radiator and raise the rent to compensate, and I won't be able to afford it, so I'll have to move. Please don't, Brice."

The sheer quiet of her voice was a powerful plea. Brice stared at her for a minute, then raised both palms in a hands-off gesture. By the time he dropped his hands, she'd risen from the chair and was on her knees, tugging a large duffel bag from under the bed.

Brice hauled her unceremoniously back to her feet. "What are you doing?"

"Getting something to put clothes into."

"You're not supposed to be working. What do you think I'm here for?"

"To drive me back and forth."

"To help you pack."

"But you don't know where things are."

"So tell me." Bending from the waist, he swept the bag onto the bed. "Now, sit." He pointed to a spot by the duffel bag and waited until she'd complied, then he opened the bag wide and rubbed his hands together.

Karen didn't appreciate being treated like a dim-witted child. She decided that she was just offended enough, just defiant enough, just rubber-kneed enough to sit like a queen and give orders. So, crossing one leg over the other, she pointed to the closet. "Open the door." He did. "I want the sneakers and the black flats. They're on the floor beside the sewing machine."

"I can see where they are."

"Put them at the bottom of the bag. They're the heaviest."

He gave her a look as he carried the footwear to the bed. "I've packed bags before."

"That's good," she said brightly and waited until he'd stowed the shoes. "Now go back to the closet and get my jeans." He retraced his steps. "There are two pairs on hangers—" she watched him run a seeking hand along the edge of her clothes "—no, not those—there, that's right—and the ones beside them." He started back toward the bed. "Oh, wait—my belt—it's on the hook at the side."

"You don't need a belt with jeans."

"I do if I want to blouse up a sweater."

He recalled the comment she'd made about being able to take unnotable clothing and make it notable, and without further question he went back for the belt. When it had been stowed beside the jeans, Karen sent him back to the closet for sweaters.

"They're up on those shelves—see them?" He put a hand to the proper spot. "Take the gray one on the bottom, the brown one above it and the cream one in the next pile."

Each was large and heavy. Stacking them in his arms, Brice returned to the bag. There, holding them, he frowned at Karen. "Why gray, brown and cream?" He looked at the two sweaters left on the shelf; they were black and white. "Why not red, green or blue?"

"I don't have any sweaters in those colors."

"But why not? You obviously like those colors. Look at this place."

Quite unnecessarily, she looked around. Her eyes were still on the dresser, which was a rich moss green with white trim, when she answered. "This place is for me. No one sees it, so I can go a little wild with the colors. My wardrobe is something else. I like to buy a few things of high quality, but if I do that, unless I want to wear the same two or three outfits over and over again, everything has to blend so I can mix and match. That means sticking to neutral colors."

Brice was remembering how pretty she'd looked in the red robe he'd bought her, when she snapped her fingers, pointed to the sweaters he held, then to the duffel.

"I'll need turtlenecks, too. They're—"

"Hold it." He was spreading the sweaters over the jeans, trying to even out their bulk. "Turtlenecks? Under these? You'll *roast* in my house."

He had a point. "Mmm, maybe you should forget the turtlenecks. How about a few blouses?" He started back toward the closet. "No, I'd really prefer the turtlenecks. They're more comfortable." He turned. She pointed toward the dresser. He headed that way. "Then again, I would be awfully warm." He stopped, put his hands on his hips and glared. She held her breath for a minute before offering a contrite, "Then again, a turtleneck may be good to wear alone. I think I should take a few. Third drawer down in the dresser."

Brice removed three knit turtlenecks in muted shades from the drawer and added them to the fast filling duffel. But by then, she'd remembered that she needed a skirt or two.

"For what?" he demanded.

"Classes."

"I thought most college kids wore jeans."

"I'm a little older than most college kids. Sometimes I like wearing skirts. And I always wear skirts when I visit Rowena," she added with the slight uptilt of her chin. "Are you going to give me trouble about that?"

"Give you trouble? Hah! You don't know what I've been getting from Rowena. She doesn't give a damn how I am, only how you are. She doesn't believe me when I say that you're better. You're right—you're not contagious anymore. So be my guest. Go see her."

Karen smiled broadly. "Thank you."

Brice stood utterly motionless for a minute. He didn't understand how a simple smile could take his breath away, but Karen's smiles did. They lit her face, then his insides. It had happened enough times now for him to know the feeling, but rather than growing used to it, he felt harder hit each time.

She should only know the power she held, he mused. She should only know what he'd do for that smile.

Turning toward the closet, he said gruffly, "Tell me which skirts." She did. They were soon packed. "Now what?"

While he'd been doing the skirts, his dark head bent over the duffel bag, she'd been debating. By rights, she should tell him that the rest was personal. But she didn't want to. He'd been so overbearing when he'd told her to sit and let him work that she figured she ought to do just that. There was, of course, the issue of her own self-consciousness. But she figured she could overcome that. Watching the big man handle the little things would be worth it.

"Second drawer of the dresser," she said.

Brice opened it and found himself confronting a wild assortment of panty hose. Inhaling sharply at the oddly erotic sight, he caught a wisp of jasmine. "Swell," he muttered, gritting his teeth.

"Hmmm?"

"What happened in here?"

Envisioning the invasion of some form of pest, Karen slid from the bed and ran to the dresser. "What do you mean?"

"It's a mess!"

She looked into the drawer. She looked up at Brice. "It looks fine to me."

"It's a mess!"

"You just said that, but what do you expect with things like these?" Dipping a finger into the drawer, she hooked a pair of sheer somethings and held them up. "Have you ever tried neatly arranging legs like these?"

"Of course, I haven't. I don't wear stockings."

"Ahh."

"Karen..."

"They slither all over the place, Brice. There's no good way to fold them that stays. It's just easiest dropping everything in the drawer." Which was exactly what she did with what she'd hooked. Then she returned to the bed.

Brice toyed with the idea of letting her take over, but there was something of a challenge in the way she'd flounced away. She didn't think he could do it. Well, she was wrong. "Which of these…things do you want?"

She was sitting with deliberate primness, hands folded in her lap. "Just grab two or three. There are some wool ones farther back in the drawer. I'll need two or three of those, and several pairs of knee socks. They should be by the wool tights."

Pulling one pair of panty hose from the mess, Brice drew it up until its legs came free, then did the same with a second pair and a third. He felt like he was serving spaghetti—only spaghetti had never stirred his libido the way the touch of Karen's nylons was doing. With a less steady hand, he grabbed some wool tights and several pairs of knee socks. Returning to the bed, he quickly deposited them in the bag.

Karen was entranced, then emboldened by the color that had stolen to his cheeks. "Now the top drawer," she instructed.

Even before opening the drawer, Brice knew what he would find. She had to wear something beneath her clothes. The problem was that he'd already had a glimpse of her underthings—neatly folded, after they'd been washed by Meg—and that glimpse hadn't helped. He'd initially pegged Karen as the plain cotton panty type. She wasn't.

Before him was a sweet gathering of nylon and lace. Pressing his lips together hard, he tried to convince himself that he was at the lingerie counter of a department store. It didn't work. This was Karen's drawer. Each of the things in it she'd worn—not only worn, but worn intimately.

"Any problem, Brice?" she asked innocently.

He shot a glance at her through the mirror. If it hadn't been for that innocent tone, he mightn't have thought twice about the innocence of her expression. But the two together were a bit much. It suddenly struck him that she was enjoying herself.

"No problem," he said with a revival of control. Holding her gaze, he asked, "How many pairs of panties should I pack?"

"They don't take up much room. How about six or seven?"

With a sage nod—and traitorously shaky hands—he took the panties from the drawer.

"Uh...wait," she burst out. "You didn't take the fuchsia ones, did you? They're not really practical. They're cut too high, so they're uncomfortable with clothes of a rougher fabric, like jeans."

Brice thumbed through the pile of panties until he touched on the fuchsia ones. Removing them, he replaced them with a pale pink pair. He liked pale pink. It was feminine and sweet. Set under a robe that was red and hot, it was dynamite.

Blotting his damp upper lip with the back of his hand, he forced himself on. "And bras?"

In any other situation she would have blushed and said, "I'll take care of those." But she was rather enjoying his discomfort. So she asked, "What have I got there?"

For just a minute he lost his composure. "What do you mean—'what have I got there'? You've got *bras* here."

"How many?"

"How the hell do I know?"

"If you count them," she said sweetly, "I'll know how many to take. I think I have six in all, but I'm wearing one, and another one is probably in the laundry bag in the bathroom. I'd like to leave a clean one here so I'll have it when I get back."

Brice took a slow, calming breath, then one by one counted the bras in the drawer. "Five here."

"Five?" She frowned. "That would make seven in all. I didn't think I had seven…. Oh," she brightened, "I know, you must have counted the strapless one. Is there a strapless one there?"

Brice took a second slow, calming breath, then one by one sorted through the bras in the drawer. His control was being tried. There was something incendiary about dealing with bras that had at one point or another been filled with the breasts of the woman behind him. He didn't know whether it was better or worse that he'd never actually seen those breasts. He'd seen vague curves, but that didn't count. Once he'd come close to touching them—when he'd listened to her heart—but she'd been so sick then that the last thing on his mind had been her body. It wasn't the last thing on his mind now.

"Yes," he said in a voice that was beginning to fray at the edges, "there's a strapless one here."

"Well, I don't need it. I really only use it in the summer when I'm wearing a tank top or a halter dress, but I won't have use for anything like that in this weather. Put the strapless one aside. How many does that leave?"

"You know how many," he gritted under his breath.

"Hmm?"

"Four."

"Okay, take three and leave the other. That should do it." Feeling a certain amount of pleasure at the sight of this tall, oft-arrogant man doing her bidding, she watched his bowed head in the mirror as he replaced the strapless bra in the drawer. He was halfway between the dresser and the bed when she said, "Maybe I should leave the blue one here." He stopped. "I'm not sure I'd use it. The softer colors are more practical." He started back toward the dresser. "No...wait...bring it here for a minute."

As he returned, she took in the ruddiness of his complexion. She liked that added color. It made him look younger, more vulnerable. She liked to think of him as vulnerable because somehow that evened the tables a little. If he was uncomfortable handling her things, tough. He'd asked for it. He'd *insisted*. Any discomfort he felt was his due.

Dropping her gaze to the bra, she retrieved the blue panties from the bag, and held the two side by side. She slid the fabric between her fingers, comparing the color and the lace. "They do look nice together. Maybe I should take them as a set. What do you think?"

Brice was thinking that with the sensual swirl of silky stuff between her fingers, he'd reached his limit. Head still lowered toward the duffel, he raised his eyes to Karen's. "I think," he said in a deep, sandy rumble, "that this has gone on long enough."

Karen felt a moment's unsureness. He didn't look as awkward as she'd thought moments before. "What do you mean?"

"I mean," he said, "that the game is over. You've worn it out."

"What game?" she asked, thinking that while he didn't look exactly angry, he didn't look thrilled. He was somewhere in between, only she couldn't quite put her finger on the spot.

"I think you know," he said as he lowered his hands to the bed on either side of her hips. She leaned back to give him room, but he simply walked forward with his hands, crowding her, crowding her, until she'd leaned so far back that she lay on the bed. "You can't play with a man that way, Karen."

"I didn't mean—"

"Yes, you did. You meant to taunt me, only I'm not sure you knew the consequences of that." His hands were by her shoulders, thumbs sliding beneath.

"But you were the one who told me to sit and let you work," she argued meekly. She was beginning to identify the spot between angry and thrilled where Brice was. She was beginning to wonder if she'd indeed gone a little too far.

"I meant what I said," he claimed. "I wanted you to rest. So what did you do? You sat there like a little Hitler giving orders."

"Don't you like taking orders?" she asked with a spurt of indignance. "Think of how *I*'ve felt these past few days."

Brice's voice came to her on a low, husky wave. "I don't mind taking orders. I had no trouble when it came to your shoes and jeans and skirts and sweaters. When we got to the frills and lace, that was something else."

Belatedly, she felt a touch of remorse. "You should have told me you didn't want to do that part."

"I would have been fine doing that part if you hadn't made a major production of it." He threw his voice up an octave in imitation of hers. "How many panties do I have in the drawer, Brice? Count them, Brice. I don't *want* the fuchsia ones, Brice, they're cut too high. Maybe I should leave the blue bra here—oh, but it goes with the blue panties." His voice fell. "Do you think I'm totally insensitive?"

"Of course, not."

"I'm not made of stone."

"Sometimes you seem it," she bit off rashly.

He pressed his lower legs more firmly into the side of the bed, in the process forcing hers apart. "Well, I'm not. I'm flesh and blood. I have the same urges other men have. Have you forgotten last night so fast?"

That kiss. She'd tried not to think about it. She'd tried not to think about the powerful things it had stirred up inside her. But trying was one thing, doing another. No, she hadn't forgotten that kiss. And as for the things it had stirred up, she remembered them vividly. Remembered…and felt. Brice was very close, very large, very masculine.

"Did you think that was an aberration?" he asked. "Did you think I did it for kicks?"

"No."

"Didn't it occur to you that if I kissed you, it was because I found you attractive?"

"I…I didn't think about that."

"Why not?"

"I was sick. I didn't feel attractive. I'm not used to thinking of myself as attractive."

Brice supposed he could buy that. She said that she wasn't involved with a man and hadn't been for a long while. He knew that between school and work she was overextended. She barely had time to think of men, or sex, or attraction.

"Then why the underwear?" he asked.

She didn't know what he meant. "Don't most people wear it?"

"Not sexy stuff. Not stuff in colors like those. Not stuff that slips through your hand like a sigh. If you're on such a tight budget, how in the hell can you afford stuff like that?"

"I buy on sale," she murmured.

"But why things like that? They're out of step with the rest of your clothes. Looking at you when you're dressed, a person would never dream you had those underneath."

He was close, coming more so by fractions of an inch. She took a quick breath and whispered, "They're for me."

"They make you feel good?"

"Yes."

"Which means," he said in a husky voice, "that beneath the sedate facade of a hard-working college student is a siren."

Eyes fixed on his mouth, she gave a convulsive swallow. "No siren."

His answer was a heated visual exploration of her face.

"Brice…"

Lowering his head the few necessary inches, he took her mouth. She tried to turn her head away, but he framed her chin with his hand as he'd done the last time and whispered against her lips, "Shhhh." She twisted again. "Shhhh." He held her firmly. His tongue touched her lower lip in a single dab before he opened his mouth and gave her an ardent caress. He stroked her. He moved his mouth as though hers were a piece of clay that needed warmth, moisture and kneading to come alive.

In short seconds, Karen was back to the intense level of feeling that had frightened her the night before. "Um-um," she protested in a closed-mouth appeal and opened her hands against his arms to lever him away.

Brice eased up. He wanted to excite her, not frighten her. He wanted to turn her on and see if she felt what he did. He'd left their last kiss hungry, and the hunger had worsened each time he'd allowed himself to remember her taste. He wanted to taste her again, but even more than that, he wanted her to know the hunger.

So he slid his mouth over hers, back and forth, then from a new angle, creating a friction that was light and sensual. Giving her more space, he abandoned her mouth for her cheek, pressing slow, open pecks there that were deceptively lazy.

Karen was horrified. The more gentle he was, the more he stirred her. "Brice, please," she whispered. Her hands exerted pressure to keep his upper torso off her, but the weight of his hips pressed her into the bed. He felt good against her—too good. She squirmed to dislodge him, but his body grew more rigid.

"Don't," he commanded, raising his head for a minute. His voice was hoarse, his eyes dark, sensually alive as he looked down at her. He struggled to gentle his tone, but still it sounded sandy. "I won't hurt you."

Her eyes were wide. "I know…but I don't want this."

"Don't want what?"

Her cheeks grew pinker. "This."

"My kissing you? Am I that awful a kisser?"

"No."

"Was it so bad just now?"

"No, but—"

"But what?"

She sent him a pleading look that said, "You make me feel all hot and achy inside." For the life of her, though, she couldn't say the words aloud.

She didn't have to. Brice read them in her amber eyes. His own widened and went even darker. "It felt good?" he asked in a rasping whisper.

She nodded. "But it isn't right."

"Who says so?"

"Me."

"What about me?"

"You're a man. You want a body. Anyone would do."

Brice felt a spurt of anger. "Is that what you think?"

She hesitated. "Isn't it true?"

"No."

"Then why me? I'm not soft and curvy. And I'm not a siren."

"So says you."

Unable to buy his implication, she squeezed her eyes shut. But Brice only took that opportunity to kiss those eyes, first one, then the other in leisurely succession. His mouth moved to her forehead, then the bridge of her nose, then her chin. He discovered that each of those spots was as sweet-tasting as her mouth.

In the wake of his kisses, a heady warmth spread through Karen's veins. No longer squeezed shut, her eyes were no more than lightly closed. Her will to resist dwindled. She felt a little high.

When his mouth touched hers this time, she didn't fight. She didn't have time, because the touch was there, then gone, there, then gone. It moved over her face again, a magnificent monarch butterfly alighting and taking off in a pattern only it knew—a pattern, she decided after a minute or two, that was designed to drive her mad.

"Brice, don't," she breathed.

"Don't what?"

"Tease. It hurts."

Brice pulled himself out of a daze to look at her. Her eyes were half-lidded, her cheeks flushed, her lips parted. It was another minute before he realized what she meant. Then it was his body that responded first, by tightening reflexively. When his mind caught up, passion's kindling burst into flame.

Holding his weight on his forearms, he slid his fingers into her hair and captured her mouth in a kiss that was like none he'd given her before. This one was deep and thorough. It nudged her lips open and sent his tongue into the dark interior from which he'd previously been barred. The kiss was hot and wet—and it wasn't one-sided. Karen was kissing him back with a sweet, hungry need.

Moaning, he moved his body against hers. And she didn't complain. She needed the friction, too. Those hands that had once held him off were now clutching the dark wool of his topcoat. She didn't know if she was holding him to her or simply holding on, but it didn't matter. She felt positively drugged.

Releasing her lips, he whispered her name in a voice rough with need. The heat of his body penetrated her clothing. The smokiness of his eyes clouded hers.

"Let me touch," he whispered, and before she could think to demur he was pushing her coat aside, spanning her waist with a hand, moving upward. When he touched her breast, she made a soft, involuntary sound. She closed her eyes; her head drifted to the side. She felt his fingers spreading over her softness, moving from one side to the other and up and down as though to create a visual image from something as yet only tactile.

It felt divine. He molded his fingers to her breast, molded her breast to his fingers, and though his touch was firm, he didn't hurt her. Any pain she felt was from the gathering coil at the pit of her stomach. She was momentarily distracted from that when he scraped the tip of one finger over her tightly budded nipple. With a tiny cry, she opened her eyes.

"What?" he coaxed in a husky whisper. He continued to stroke her.

Covering his hand with her own, she stilled its movement. He waited for her to remove his hand, but she simply pressed it harder to her breast. As she did, she closed her eyes and arched her back.

Brice took one labored breath, then another. He had wanted to stay in control, had wanted to concentrate on arousing her, but she was already aroused, and seeing that, he couldn't hold back any longer. His mouth came down hard on hers, demanding an even deeper response than it had before. He received that response and more.

Abandoning his coat, Karen dug her fingers into his hair and held him close, while her tongue played with his. She had no idea what she was doing; it was all instinct and desire. But the results were so heavenly that she kept at it, and when she felt Brice's hand slip under the hem of her sweatshirt, climb again, then find her silk-covered breast, she felt a wave of relief.

Her skin was hot, and for a brief instant Brice wondered if the heat were from illness. Dragging his mouth from hers, he raised his head and captured her gaze. "Okay?" he whispered in an uneven breath.

She gave a tiny, quick nod. Her breathing was shallow, a little raspy, but her color was better than good. Her cheeks were a soft pink, her lips rouged. She ran her tongue along the lower one. She dropped her hands to his neck. She eyed him expectantly, waiting for him to move the hand that covered her bra.

For Brice, the anticipation was nearly as precious as what he finally found when he curled his fingers under the lace edging and peeled it back. He pictured it as he felt it, that small, hard nub popping free and straining toward his flesh. He touched it with the tip of his finger, then slid that same fingertip back and forth across the sensitive peak.

Karen gave a sharp cry and sucked in her breath— then broke into a harsh, hacking cough. Frightened, Brice forgot his own need. Withdrawing his hand, he pulled her to a seated position and rubbed her back until she'd caught her breath.

"Oh God," she whispered, trembling as she buried her face against his neck.

Not particularly steady himself, he folded her in his arms and he held her close. "Shhh."

"I'm sorry."

"It's okay." He paused for several short breaths. "Was it good?"

She nodded.

Feeling the movement, he closed his eyes and thought about how right she felt in his arms.

After a minute, her muffled voice came to him. "I didn't cough on purpose."

"I know."

"I'm not a tease."

"I know."

"Or a siren."

He said nothing to that, because though he was sure she didn't do it on purpose, she was seductive as hell. It wasn't a physical thing, though he thought she was beautiful. Her body was a dozen turn-ons—from her hair to her shoulders and breasts and hips. But the real seduction came from inside—from her innocence, from the quiet of her voice, her unpretentiousness. It also came from the fact that she had no intention of getting involved. That somehow made things different. She had no intention of getting involved, yet the sweet sounds that had come from her throat said she *was* involved, and that made him feel special. It made him feel as though he were the only man in the world who could please her, and that made him feel whole for the first time in his life.

Given the implications, he was deeply shaken.

CHAPTER EIGHT

FOR SEVERAL MINUTES longer, Brice continued to hold Karen, but not in passion. That had passed in part when she'd started to cough, in part when he'd realized that she had the potential for knocking him on his ear. He wasn't head over heels in love, but the seeds were there. He hadn't felt as touched by a woman since…no, he'd never felt it before.

His marriage had been a deliberately planned undertaking, lacking both spontaneity and passion. He'd thought himself in love because the timing was right. After the relationship had quietly folded, he'd decided that he didn't really know what love was.

Now he was beginning to get glimpses of something so rich and deep that, if it was love, it put all past impressions to shame. Those glimpses frightened him. He was frightened that they wouldn't prove to be real; then again, he was frightened that they would, and that he'd somehow blow it. He didn't have a good track record when it came to interpersonal relations. He'd never been comfortable with his peers and, aside from his marriage, had never dated any one woman for long. A relationship with Karen would be paving new ground. He suddenly felt that there was a whole lot at stake.

Gently, he released her. Quietly and a little humbly, he rose from the bed to resume packing. Without looking at her, he suggested that she see to her toiletries.

More than a little unsure, herself, Karen was grateful for an excuse to escape into the bathroom for a minute. Her insides still quivered—and not from coughing. If Brice's first kiss had been a nine on a scale from one to ten, this one had been a fourteen. No, she amended, it had entered a whole new range; it wasn't in the same category as that first kiss at all.

The first time around she hadn't participated. This time she had, and it had been wonderful—wonderful, but not nearly enough. She was in a state of suspended desire. She was frustrated. And that was a new experience for her.

One by one, she gathered toiletries in the crook of her arm, then returned to deposit them in the duffel bag. Brice was at the window with his back to her, all broad shoulders and straight, lean hips. She wondered what he was thinking, whether he was regretting the kiss, or whether he was wanting more. He was a healthy male. She knew that he'd been aroused; she'd felt the strength of him against her, had heard his rough breathing, had seen the heat in his eyes. Oh yes, he'd been aroused, but whether that pleased him was another story.

Crossing to the desk, she busied herself loading texts, papers and notebooks into a book bag. Only when she had everything she felt she'd need did she zip the bag and turn to Brice. He was waiting, wearing a thoroughly uncharacteristic look of confusion. After studying her for a minute, he blinked, and the expression vanished.

"All set?" he asked in a mellow tone.

She nodded.

Slinging the duffel bag strap over one shoulder and her book bag over the other, he motioned her to the door.

DISORIENTED MOST APTLY described how Brice felt through the rest of that day. He dropped Karen back at the house, went to the hospital, returned to the house and saw patients until late in the afternoon, so it wasn't a case of his having nothing to occupy his mind. He was for the most part on familiar turf. Only when he thought of Karen did he feel upended.

Karen, meanwhile, was diverting her own mind by visiting Rowena, who greeted her with a skewed smile and the longest stream of words Karen had ever heard from her.

"You're all…r-r-right! I was worried. Brice doesn't like me t-t-to worry…b-b-but I didn't know if I could believe him when he…s-s-said you were better. Y-y-you looked so sick last Friday."

"I was," Karen said with a wry smile. The smile warmed. "I'm better now."

Rowena's gaze homed in on that smile. "Tell me… w-w-what happened Friday."

Feeling somewhat cavalier with that part of it over, Karen told her about passing out in the snow and being scooped up by Brice. She told of how she'd been out of it when she'd first arrived at his house and how she'd slept through most of the weekend.

"How was…B-B-Brice?"

"He was fine."

"He isn't s-s-social."

"I wasn't looking for social. All I wanted was a warm place to lie down. He gave me that, plus medicine and hot tea."

Rowena's wrinkled mouth puckered even more. "I hate tea."

Karen nearly laughed at the older woman's expression of distaste. "Me, too. But it was hot, and it helped. Brice knew what he was doing when he brought it."

"Kind?"

"Was he?" Karen asked in clarification, then nodded.

"The t-t-truth," Rowena demanded, eyes chiding.

"He was very kind."

"Always?"

"Whenever I needed him, he was there for me."

"Karen…"

Karen took the old woman's gnarled hand and said softly but with force, "He really was good, Rowena. He has his moods. He can be curt, even rude. But he took care of me. You can be proud of him."

Rowena seemed only marginally satisfied with that. Wanting to please her, Karen added, "I'm going to be staying at his house for a while. He's convinced that the only way I'll get the rest I need is if he supervises my convalescence. I thought the idea was absurd at first, but he has it all worked out."

She told of the leaves of absence he'd arranged for her from her jobs. "He's even contacted a fellow to drive me to Syracuse and back when I have classes. Apparently the man is unemployed, his two sons are patients of Brice's and he can't pay the bills. That doesn't bother Brice, but it bothers this man. Brice thought that giving him something to do in exchange for his children's medical treatment would offer him a measure of dignity. I agree."

Rowena was looking more and more satisfied. "You… l-l-like him."

"Who? Brice?"

Rowena's eyes said, "Who else?" in a smug kind of way.

"I respect him," Karen said.

"Like him," Rowena insisted.

Karen didn't have to think about whether she did, just whether she should admit it. Whatever existed between Brice and her could disintegrate any day in a spate of angry words. It wouldn't do for Rowena to get her hopes up.

She went with a gentle version of the truth. "Yes, I like him. But that doesn't mean there's more. Brice has his life, I have mine. We're both loners. Neither of us is used to living with someone."

"You can…g-g-get used to it."

"Maybe, but Brice can be difficult. I don't know if I want to get used to that."

"He needs you."

"He may need a woman. I'm not at all sure he needs me. I remind him of unhappy things."

"Like the accident?"

Karen nodded. "He looks at me and remembers that it was my car that hit you."

"Maybe once. No…m-m-more."

"How do you know?"

"His…v-v-voice." When Karen shook her head in denial of that, Rowena asked, "Why did you agree to… s-s-stay with him?"

Karen gave a one-shouldered shrug. "I don't know. Maybe because I love the house."

Rowena's lips thinned.

"It's a beautiful house," Karen rushed on in an attempt to give merit to the argument. "It's large and warm. Brice keeps the living room fire going. I've never been as comfortable anywhere."

Rowena said a very quiet, "No," so Karen tried again.

"Meg is there. It's nice to know I'm not alone."

"Maybe."

"Maybe Brice is right. I need a rest. If I were at my own place, I'd spend all my time studying. He won't let me do that."

"Good."

A harried look crept to Karen's eyes. "I don't know about that. I'm already behind in my work."

"You'll g-g-get it done."

The harried look began to dissipate. "That's what Brice says. He says it's a matter of pacing, that since I won't be working I'll be able to get everything done without killing myself."

"He w-w-wants you there."

"He's taking the role of healer seriously."

"He *w-w-wants* you there."

"It's a big house. He can come and go without seeing me."

"He won't. He wants to…s-s-see you."

"But how can he want me there when he doesn't have you there?" Karen asked. Seconds after the words left her mouth, she regretted them, but they'd been hovering at the back of her mind for too long. They'd had to come out sooner or later.

Rowena didn't appear the least bit fazed. To the contrary, she seemed to straighten in her chair. "He doesn't have me there…b-b-because I won't *be* there."

Karen was taken aback. "You mean, he's asked?"

"Asked, demanded, ranted and raved…he wanted me to live with him b-b-before the accident. I refused then. I feel s-s-stronger about it now. If I were in… B-B-Brice's home, I'd be lonely. Here I have friends."

"But he's family," Karen argued and quickly felt the movement of Rowena's hand in hers.

"You feel that way because you have…n-n-no family. I do. Brice and now you."

Karen held her hand tighter.

"I have the…m-m-money for this place. I won't be a burden to anyone."

"You wouldn't be a burden."

"Sweetly said. But daily care is d-d-daily care. I have moods, too. The apple…d-d-doesn't fall far from the tree."

"I've never seen your moods."

"Brice has."

"Oh."

"B-b-besides, he needs to be lonely." When Karen frowned, Rowena took a breath and went on. "He has to know loneliness t-t-to know he doesn't want it. It's too easy for him to fall b-b-back on me. But I won't be around forever. And then where...w-w-will he be? He needs a wife and children. He loves children."

"So I guessed."

"So I know."

Karen couldn't help but grin at the quick reply. In turn Rowena couldn't help but comment on the grin. "You look...b-b-better. More relaxed. Happier."

Lowering her eyes to the hand that held Rowena's, Karen thought about that for a minute. "I do feel better," she admitted softly. "Not as oppressed." She raised her eyes to her friend's. "But it's wrong for me to be leaning on Brice like I am. Everything my life was before will start up again in less than a month. If I'm spoiled...."

"You won't be."

"I do wonder about it."

"Don't."

"But what happens if..."

Rowena's eyes pressed for completion of the sentence, but Karen couldn't finish. She'd been about to ask what would happen if she fell in love with Brice and he didn't return her love. But that wasn't Rowena's worry. It was Karen's...only Karen's.

KAREN DIDN'T ALLOW herself to think about it after she left Rowena. She returned to the house and spent an hour rereading the notes from which she planned to write her history paper. To her subsequent chagrin, she fell asleep on the living room sofa, before a blazing fire, with the papers in her lap.

When she woke up, she found Brice in the kitchen slicing the pot roast Meg had cooked. "What can I do?" she asked.

He darted her a glance. "Want to set the table?"

"Sure." Going to the same cabinets and drawers she'd seen him go to the night before, she took out what they'd need, set everything on the table, then sank quietly into one of the chairs. Minutes later, Brice filled both plates with hearty servings of meat, potatoes and carrots, poured two glasses of milk and joined her.

It was a most surprising meal for Karen because it was peaceful from start to finish. Brice wanted to know how Rowena was; Karen told him, then told him about the article she'd read her about boat-building in Nantucket. "Rowena said she owned a boat once."

"She did. It was a sloop. We used to sail it off the coast of Maine. She had a place up there for a while."

"Did you spend a lot of time there with her?"

"Vacations and summers. My parents couldn't get away from the city for more than a week at a stretch, so Rowena made a point of being there for me. She thought it was important." His eyes had strayed toward the floor at the last but quickly returned to find Karen's. "She hasn't had the boat for years. She sold it along with the house when she decided that she'd rather spend her vacations traveling than going to the same place over and over."

"You were grown then?"

He nodded. "And too busy to spend more than a few vacation days at a time anywhere."

"Are you still?"

"I can be as busy as I want, but too busy is no good. I make time for vacations, now."

Karen ate a little. Then, making innocent conversation, she said, "Rowena's thinking of taking a cruise."

As soon as she heard the words, she cringed inwardly and prepared herself for an outraged protest from Brice. It never came.

"She could do it," he stated calmly.

After a breath, Karen asked, "Really?"

"With a companion, sure. Her condition isn't at or near any kind of crisis. She's making steady improvement. The best thing for her is to live. She'd probably love a cruise. She's the type."

"Are you?"

Brice denied it at first. He claimed that he needed more action than a cruise had to offer. Then Karen started regurgitating some of the facts she'd picked up about cruises in the course of her reading, and Brice reconsidered. The kinds of cruises she described were a far cry from the stereotype. He didn't have to ask if she would like to go on one of those offbeat types of cruises. Enthusiasm sparkled in her eyes, her voice, the animation of her face. And it was contagious. He found himself asking more and more, as though she were a travel agent and he a potential client. They were reveling in dream material, and it was lovely.

Three hours— and much food, drink and conversation—had passed when Karen yawned. She couldn't remember the last time she'd carried on such a prolonged discussion with a single person. Brice, too, seemed surprised when he looked at his watch.

Excusing herself when he wouldn't let her help with the dishes, she retrieved her papers from the living room and went up to bed. Once again, she fell asleep with the papers on her lap. When she awoke the next morning, they were neatly piled on the dresser along with a note, which read, "If you'd like to use a desk, help yourself to the one in my den. The typewriter and word processor are in the records room next door to that. Don't overdo it. I thought we'd go out for dinner tonight."

Karen's heart did a little two-step as she reread the note. The prospect of going out to dinner with Brice excited her. He'd been fun to be with the night before.

With something to look forward to, she had an easier time than she might have otherwise had applying herself to the writing of her paper. Having completed the research, she set right to work. She paused for a break at noon to have lunch with Meg, and even allowing for a nap at midafternoon, she completed the five-page piece and was in the process of typing it when Brice stopped by.

He stood over her shoulder, reading the few lines of the page she'd just typed. "Sounds interesting."

"Not really. Well, maybe it is, a little. There isn't too much leeway in freshman courses. I really wanted to address a different historical issue, but that one wasn't on the list of choices."

"The professor wouldn't make an exception for you?"

"Why should he?"

"Because you're older than the rest of the students and obviously taking this more seriously. Professors are skeptical of students who ask for substitute assignments in hopes of getting something easier. You wouldn't do that."

Gratified by his vote of confidence, Karen went back to her typing. But Brice remained at her shoulder. She was acutely aware of him, of the size of his body and its heat. And something else. With her sense of smell slowly returning, she was catching wisps of a most subtle scent. It came and went. She wasn't sure whether it was cologne, soap or simply clean male, but it intrigued her.

When she found herself superimposing Brice's image on the words she was to type, she lowered her hands to her lap and said softly, "I can't do this with you watching."

"Why not?"

"You make me nervous."

"Am I crowding you?"

"No. But you're *there*."

"And you were never a Kelly Girl."

Karen's lips twitched at the corners. "Not quite."

"Why don't I have one of the girls type that? You've got everything written clear as day in longhand. Any one of them could do it up in no time."

"You're not paying them to type my papers."

"No, but my receptionist spends a lot of time with a paperback novel in her lap. Am I paying her to read?"

"No."

"So she can type."

Karen looked up—way up—to meet his gaze. Once again that scent came to her. She felt a weird sensation in her knees and was grateful she was sitting. "Let me see how much I can get done on my own. It took me less time to write the paper than I'd expected, so I'm really ahead."

"But I want to go out to dinner."

He sounded so petulant that she couldn't hold back a smile. "Real hungry?"

"Yeah," Brice said in the hoarse voice her smile had given him. "The place I have in mind has great filet mignon. I can never get it to taste that way here."

Karen began to salivate. "Is this restaurant dressy? I didn't bring anything dressy."

"Your gray skirt and sweater would be just about right."

"Are you sure?"

"I'm sure."

They were perfect, she found. There were people at

the restaurant wearing everything from silk cocktail dresses to denim jumpsuits. What Brice had suggested put her right in the middle. Not only that, but he co-ordinated himself with her outfit by wearing a pair of gray slacks and a tweed blazer. She had to admit that with a crisp white shirt offsetting the healthy coloring of his skin and a paisley tie knotted neatly at his neck, he looked dashing. She was proud to be with him.

Brice was experiencing similar feelings. It wasn't often that he took women places in Ithaca. Most often in the past, when he'd felt need of female companionship, he'd spent the weekend in Manhattan, where he was less likely to run into people he knew. He studiously avoided an Ithaca social life.

But he'd wanted to take Karen out. He'd wanted to see her dressed up, with her hair brushed out and flowing. He'd wanted to treat her to something she probably hadn't had much of before. It hadn't occurred to him that he'd reap a side benefit even as he walked with her to their table. He felt proud that she was with him, rather than with one of the other men in the room.

On the tails of those auspicious beginnings, dinner was as amicable an affair as it had been the evening before. Brice had his tongue under control. The only sharp word he offered was a pithy one, spoken early on and under his breath, directed at a couple whose son he had treated for various injuries not long before.

"That is probably the most frustrating part of my practice," he explained to Karen after he'd taken a healthy drink of his wine. "It's heartbreaking when a child comes in suffering from a serious illness. In the past year I've had kids with newly diagnosed cases of muscular dystrophy and cystic fibrosis. No one plans to get diseases like those; they just come. But when I see a child who's been battered—cruelly, unnecessarily, repeatedly—it's infuriating."

Karen noted the hard set of his mouth and was grateful that this time around she hadn't caused it. "Do you report the parents?"

"Sure. For whatever good it does. When the family has money and a reputation to protect, they'll do anything to keep child abuse from coming to light." He looked off in the direction of the pair in question. "That particular family is one of the more prominent in the area. Well liked and professionally respected. They've been active at the university for years. Shortly after I reported a series of injuries with suspicious causes, I received a visit from their lawyer stating that if I dared breathe the slightest scandalous word again, I'd be slapped with a multimillion-dollar libel suit."

"You didn't stop, did you?"

The determined expression he wore when he looked back at her added strength to his already rugged face. "Are you kidding? I told the guy that if he wanted to talk blackmail, we could trot down to the local prosecutor's office, which was where—I told him—I intended to go anyway."

"Did you?"

"Sure did."

"What happened?"

Brice flipped his spoon over and back. Then he slowly raised his eyes to Karen's. "Last I heard, the case was dropped for lack of evidence. It'll be back in court, but only after that child suffers more."

Karen felt his frustration. "Will you see the child again?"

"I'd gladly see him again, but you can be sure the parents won't let me."

He grew quiet. His dark head was slightly bowed, eyes

focused on the spoon as he turned it from side to side. She was watching him, thinking about dedication and frustration and how closely entwined they were, when the waiter arrived with their food.

It was an instant diversion. Karen, who had had a hint of things to come when the maître d' had spread her linen napkin on her lap, was delighted with the elegant presentation of the meal. Brice, who was more accustomed to fine restaurants than she, took pleasure in her pleasure—and when he took pleasure in something, he relaxed—and when he relaxed, he let down the defenses that kept him aloof.

He wanted to know about the courses she was taking. Helpless to resist, when she was being wined and dined so finely, she listed them, gave brief descriptions, answered his questions about requirements and electives. Then, when she'd finally stopped for a bite of her steak and a forkful of lyonnaise potatoes, he asked, "Did you originally plan to go to college in Syracuse, or did you choose it because of Rowena?"

The potatoes went down Karen's throat in a lump. She was surprised—not so much because he had asked, since she was used to his bluntness, but because he had asked in as innocent a manner. She studied his face, searched for signs of disdain and found none. What she did find were eyes that were warm and had less of a crease between them than usual, a nose that was straight but relaxed, a mouth that was very, very male. The tiny flick of a muscle at his jaw only added to the virile image.

Swallowing again, ostensibly to make sure the potatoes were down, she composed herself. "Up until five years ago, I lived with my family in Connecticut. After my mother died, I moved to New York to work, but living there wasn't as much fun as I'd imagined it would be.

When it came to choosing a school, I thought I might like to try the South."

"Why the South?" Brice asked in a voice that was smooth and low.

"Because I'd never been there. I like going places I've never been, and I knew that it would only have to be for four years." She took a breath and went on as confidently as she could. "I'd been accepted at Emory, in Atlanta. After the accident, I decided to stay up here."

Brice echoed his earlier question. "Was it because of Rowena?" He meant no criticism. He was simply curious.

"Yes."

"Then why not Cornell? That's right here in town."

"I didn't get into Cornell. Syracuse gave me a scholarship."

Quietly finishing his steak, Brice thought about the disappointments she'd suffered in life. Everyone experienced disappointments; nobody made it through without some. But it seemed she'd had more than her share.

Cornell had no right to reject her, he decided. Next time they called *him* to address a child psych class, he'd think twice.

Oblivious to his thoughts, when her own were, strangely, on his hands as they manipulated his utensils, Karen ate, too. When she'd had as much as she could, she put down her fork, let out a breath and said, "Between Meg's cooking and meals like this, I think I've gained five pounds."

Brice hoped so. He examined her face with a tactile gaze. "They become you."

"But if I keep on at this rate, I'll be a blimp."

"No."

"I'm used to getting exercise. Back in Syracuse, I was

on the go all the time. Waitressing is like a full night of aerobics."

"I'd rather you didn't do anything until you're better."

"I am better."

A muscle moved in his jaw, and he took a long, slow drink of water before he spoke. "I'll amend that, then. I'd rather you didn't do anything until you've taken the last of the penicillin. You've done a job on your body. It needs time to heal." Again he paused, this time wondering if he'd blown it with the comment about the job she'd done on her body. But she didn't seem upset. Maybe she was getting used to his manner. In a gruffer voice, he said, "When it's healed, you could run with me."

Karen's eyes lit up. "Run? You run? When?"

He caught his breath. Momentarily forgetting the serious issue of her health, he broke into a grin that was both amused and wry, "That's classic Rowena."

"What is?"

"What you just did—asking three questions in one breath. When something interested her, she wanted to know everything about it at once."

"Running fascinates me. How often do you go?"

"Every morning."

"From the house?"

He nodded.

"What time?"

"Early—six, sometimes five."

"That's why you were wearing a running suit when you woke me yesterday morning."

He nodded. "Do you run?"

She shrugged and gave a small, sheepish smile. "Nah."

"Why not?"

She thought about that for a minute. "I suppose I could say that I wouldn't feel safe running alone, but the truth is that I don't have the energy. I'm too tired in the morning and too tired at night, and I don't have the time during the day."

Again, a muscle moved in Brice's jaw. Karen realized that happened whenever he was holding in a retort. She rushed on.

"I know. You feel I'm doing too much, and maybe I am. But that's beside the point. Tell me about your running."

Wanting to avoid unpleasantness every bit as much as she did, Brice was glad to comply. Over cups of cappuccino, he told Karen about being a health nut as a teenager, then an exercise nut as he'd matured. Over a split order of English trifle, he told her of running six miles a day, of entering 10K races, of finding himself that much more energetic after his morning runs. Over refills of the coffee, he told her that she was built for the sport and that she'd enjoy it. And when she was sitting back, utterly replete and feeling like a stuffed pig, he outlined a sample program for getting her started.

She grinned broadly at that, and when Brice grew suddenly serious, when his eyes darkened and focused for a prolonged moment on her mouth, she acknowledged something about their dinner. It had been a delight—peaceful and interesting. It had also been stimulating in ways totally aside from the intellectual. Her body was humming with awareness. She knew that Brice turned her on, but she hadn't expected to feel the heat so strongly in such a public place. He hadn't touched her other than to place a light hand at her back as they'd walked to their table. But she felt him. She felt his height, his strength. She felt the difference between his body and hers. And she felt his eyes, dark gray and alight, sending a message she couldn't ignore.

No man's eyes had lured her like this before. A flush rose in her cheeks, and she might have made a fool of herself by starting to stammer about something totally irrelevant had not Brice regained his own control first and said, "Shall we go?"

She nodded. He rose, came to her chair and drew it out as she stood, then took her hand in his and led her to the door.

For as short and quiet as the drive home was, the atmosphere in the car was charged. Karen didn't dare look at Brice lest her eyes reveal her desire. He kept his gaze rigidly on the road.

Not a word was spoken until they were back in the house, and then good manners overrode her fears. "Thank you," she said, looking up at him. "That was delightful."

Hanging his coat in the closet, he turned to take hers, but one look at her brought back his need in a rush. Only now it was magnified. He hadn't remembered ever enjoying an evening as much. Karen was lovely to look at, lovely to be with. She was bright and even-tempered, personable and responsive. And she'd had eyes only for him. In the midst of a full restaurant, she'd made him feel like the only man there. That was the corker. He needed her like a flame needed fuel.

Before he could deny himself, he lowered his head and captured her mouth. He kissed her softly, then with greater force when the answering movement of her mouth demanded it. But just before he reached that next step of crushing her body to his, he pulled back.

"No," he said roughly, to himself as much as to her. "I didn't take you to dinner for this." He snatched her coat from her boneless hands and said in a voice reminiscent of his earliest commands, "Go to bed, Karen."

For a minute she didn't move. She had an intense need to hold him, to feel him, to be held and felt. The fact that

she'd never been a toucher was irrelevant. Her empty
palms ached to be filled.

But that wasn't all that ached to be filled, and when
Karen realized what the hollowness deep down in her
belly was, she found the strength to move. Too much
had happened too soon. She needed space to think. With
a shaky breath and on legs that were little better, she
turned and climbed the stairs to bed.

CHAPTER NINE

KAREN SPENT A GOOD DEAL of time lying awake in bed that night wondering what would have happened had not Brice ended their kiss when he had. The more she wondered, the more frustrated she grew until sheer tiredness conquered even that. She slept late the next morning. When she awoke, she busied herself with work in an effort to escape the dilemma.

To some extent she succeeded. When she was doing reading assignments or talking with Meg, she wasn't as apt to think of needing Brice. She was apprehensive about being with him that evening, but her fears proved groundless. He said nothing about what had happened the night before, instead engaging her in discussions on various topics that seemed to crop up, one after the other, in easy succession. He was much like his grandmother in that sense, Karen discovered. He was curious. He enjoyed broadening his mind. Since she was the same, the conversation never lagged. And by the time she went to bed, leaving him before the living room fire, she was tired enough not to think about sex.

Friday she worked, then visited Rowena. Friday night Brice took her to see a play that was being staged at the university. Neither of them liked the production, but over sundaes at a local ice-cream shop afterward, they had a good time criticizing playwright and cast.

Saturday morning, telling her that he had to do research, Brice took her to McDonald's for breakfast.

"What kind of research is this?" she asked in bemusement after he'd plopped an Egg McMuffin in front of her.

"I have to keep up on these things for the sake of my kids."

"I think you're just lazy," she teased. "Meg's off for the weekend. It was either this or do it yourself."

"No way. There are restaurants that serve fancier breakfasts. We had a choice." He paused and said more quietly, "I had a choice." He paused again, his eyes deep and questing. "Would you rather I'd made a different one?"

"No way," she echoed him and meant it. Breakfast at McDonald's was a fun thing to do. She hadn't had the luxury of doing many things just for fun in her life. She was enjoying herself. "But I have to get home to work after this."

"You do not."

"Sure, I do. I didn't make it to any classes this week, so I want to get ahead in the syllabus. Next week I'll have to borrow the class notes I missed and copy them. That could take a lot of time on top of regular assignments."

"You're not actually planning to do them by hand, are you?" he asked in a critical tone.

She tipped up her chin. "Do you have a better idea?"

"Xerox them."

"Uh-huh. Thirty-plus pages, plus a dozen in handouts for each of four classes, at ten cents a shot—"

"Use my machine."

She took a quick breath. "You have one?"

He nodded.

Sitting back, Karen mused at how easy he was making her life. His machine could save her hours of work. "On one condition."

"You can't pay me."

"Then let me cook dinner tonight."

He shook his head.

"Why not?" she asked.

"Because I want us to go to an inn that I've been hearing about lately."

Karen studied his eyes. In the shadow of the yellow arches, they were varying shades of gray. She saw an odd mixture of determination and unsureness in their depths, plus something else. She sensed that he was discovering the same hunger for human companionship that she was. Loners they might have been, but something happened when they got together. Brice could have gone to McDonald's a million other times before. But who wanted to go to McDonald's alone?

So they went to the inn for dinner that night, but that was after a full day of running errands. Brice decided that the freezer was low, so they went to the supermarket. Then they went antiquing, searching for an early-American bench for Brice's front porch. Then they went to the camera store to buy film and darkroom supplies, which sparked an entirely new discussion when Karen learned why a camera had been lying around in the den.

She was fascinated by his being a photographer, albeit a closet one. No one ever saw his pictures. But she wanted to, and she wore him down enough so that after a late lunch at a local mall, he gave in. When they returned to the house, he dropped a box in her lap and left her to examine its contents while he busied himself elsewhere.

Karen was in awe. Working entirely in black and white, he'd photographed houses, churches, trees, horses, fences—all from unusual angles and with the eye for light that Karen read praised so often in her books. He'd photographed places he'd visited—Alaska, New Zealand, the Aran Isles, Madagascar. But mostly, he'd photographed his kids. Apparently there was an outdoor waiting room, a play area in the yard during spring, summer and fall. There he'd taken some of the most touching pictures she'd ever seen.

When she said so, he got defensive. "I wasn't looking for praise."

"I know, but I'm offering it anyway."

"Well, don't. It's a hobby. That's all."

"But you're good at it."

"So?"

"So maybe you'll teach me. I'm an art history major, I've been reading about light and shadow and shape and form for years, but I can't draw. Maybe I can do this."

Apparently she'd said the right thing, because Brice warmed back up, which was not to say that he had her in the darkroom the next day. He had other things in mind—such as taking her to a chamber music concert Sunday afternoon, then a movie that night.

When Monday arrived, she was no more ahead on her work than she'd been when she'd set it aside on Friday. Oddly, that didn't bother her as it once might have. She'd had a wonderful weekend. She was feeling stronger and more rested.

And she was in love.

That was why she never quite got into the article on the Newars of the Kathmandu Valley when she visited Rowena on Tuesday. There were more urgent things she wanted to discuss.

With little preamble, she said in a soft voice, "Tell me about Brice."

Rowena didn't even blink in surprise. "He's my grandson. He's a doctor. He's thirty-nine and s-s-single."

"What was he like as a little boy?"

"Ask him."

"He doesn't like to talk about himself. He'll beat around the bush or change the subject."

"W-w-why do you think that is?"

"Because he's hiding something," Karen said. While she wasn't ready to admit to Rowena that she was in love with the man, she had nothing to lose by being honest about her thoughts and observations. "Something happened earlier today. John Parker, Brice's friend, drove me back to Syracuse for two classes. I got back in time for a late lunch, but Meg was out and I didn't feel like eating alone. So I went looking for Brice. He was with a patient."

"You knew he would be," Rowena remarked.

"Yes. I guess…I guess I just wanted to tell him I was back." She'd wanted to see him, it was as simple as that, but when she'd arrived at the office, she hadn't had time for regrets. "He was in one of the examining rooms, but the door was open. There was Brice, a little girl who couldn't have been more than three and her mother. Brice was holding the child, talking to her."

She paused for a minute, recalling the scene. It had touched her deeply. "He was wonderful—his voice, expression, arms all gentle. I mean, he wasn't gooing and gaaing. He wasn't playing with the child, but he was so… *sweet* with her. Then her mother asked a question and the softness disappeared. His entire manner changed. He became shuttered." She took a breath. "He doesn't relate well with adults. I've noticed it a lot."

"He relates with you."

"Now, but only because he knows me. He didn't at first. And he bluntly acknowledges that he dislikes adults. There has to be a reason. He relates to the wounded, but it's like he has a chip on his shoulder when it comes to the strong ones."

Rowena sat quietly for a minute. "You are very p-p-perceptive."

But not perceptive enough, Karen rued. "Why does he do it?"

"Because he *is* the wounded."

"He's as hale and hardy as you and I would ever want to be!"

"He wasn't always."

That hadn't occurred to Karen. "He was sick as a child?"

Rowena made a tiny, almost imperceptible movement of her head that, magnified, would have been a nod.

"What did he have?"

"Nothing d-d-deadly. Obviously. He had asthma and...j-j-juvenile rheumatoid arthritis."

"My God."

"All outgrown. He's fine now."

"But that he should have had one of those, let alone both..." Her heart ached for the sickly child he'd been.

"Other children weren't always k-k-kind to him. He was small for his age. And s-s-spindly. He couldn't play sports. They made fun of him. S-s-so he turned his back on them."

Karen was beginning to understand. "He read and studied. He did well in school, went to college, then medical school. Somewhere along the line he got physically stronger and larger."

"His senior year in h-h-high school. He was a handsome boy, then. But not happy. He wanted r-r-revenge."

"Did he get it?" Karen asked warily.

"Mmm."

"How?"

"He stole pretty girls from other boys, then dropped them. He wrote s-s-scathing editorials in the school newspaper. He ran away w-w-with achievement awards others wanted."

"But if he got his revenge, why hasn't he put all that behind him?"

"It's...p-p-part of his personality. Has been since he was three. All the formative years. He is cynical."

Karen began to see it. The chip had taken root on his shoulder when he was too young to understand, and by the time he was old enough, he just didn't care. He had his life, his career. He made sure that he wasn't beholden to anyone.

"Didn't his parents see what was happening?" Karen asked. It seemed there should be someone to blame. "Didn't they get him into counseling?"

"They married late. His father—m-m-my son—was in business. His mother was a social b-b-butterfly. They were busy. They saw what they wanted to see."

"Brice told me about the summers and vacations he spent with you."

"I did what I could. It wasn't enough."

Gazing off toward the window, Karen considered that. Brice did have a productive life. He had far more than many people dreamed of having. But his personal life was stunted.

She knew that he enjoyed himself with her, that he'd enjoyed all the things they'd done together. "I could help him," she murmured. "I know I could."

"Yes," Rowena said.

Karen looked at her. "But I can't help if he won't let me, and I won't help if I'm going to end up hurt. I want a little happiness out of this, too." She glanced away. "If only we'd met under other circumstances."

"You didn't."

"I know."

"Trust him, Karen."

"I want to."

"Y-y-you can."

Karen eyed her sadly then. "Can you guarantee that he won't look at me once or twice a week and remember what I did to you?"

"You weren't at fault," the old woman said with the conviction that only she and Karen could share.

"But does he believe that?"

"Ask him."

"I can't. I can't."

"Why not?"

Why not? Karen conjured up images of the Brice she'd first seen, the man whose hateful stare had haunted her during her trial. She heard echoes of harshness, of sarcasm and pointedness in his voice—echoes from those early days at his house. Why couldn't she ask him whether, deep down inside, he still held a grudge?

"Because," she murmured despairingly, "because I'm afraid I won't like his answer."

IT WAS A MATTER OF TRUST, she decided. That was what it boiled down to. Karen trusted Brice with her care. She trusted that he'd never physically do her harm. She trusted that he had the ability to make her happy. But she didn't know whether he would *choose* to do so, and that was where her trust lagged.

Her discussion with Rowena had helped. Knowing what Brice had been through as a child enabled her to better understand what made him the man he was. It also made her see how far he'd come with her. She was, theoretically, no longer one of the wounded, still he wanted her with him. He spent all his free time with her. And he desired her.

Oh yes, he desired her. He hadn't kissed her in days, but he wanted to. She could tell by the way his eyes would go dark when he looked at her—not dark, as in angry, but dark, as in hungry and hot. Whenever it happened, he looked quickly away, but not quickly enough to spare her the frustration. Because, whether he was looking at her or not, whether she was looking at him or not, she was never far from a state of arousal where Brice was concerned.

She had studied him long and hard. She had stolen glances while they'd been walking down streets, while they'd been waiting in lines, while they'd been moving around each other in the house. She had, often and with hidden pleasure, imagined every inch of him naked. She no longer needed to look. He was engraved on her mind. She wanted him.

That knowledge was never far from her during that second week at his house. Each morning she returned to Syracuse, either for classes or to work in the library. Each afternoon, except for the two when she visited Rowena, she studied. And her evenings were spent with Brice.

She was in love. She was in need, and though the fear of making a one-sided commitment remained, the ache grew deeper and deeper. It was no wonder, then, that when Brice suggested they bring in pizza for an early dinner on Friday and spend the evening in the darkroom, Karen had serious doubts about the plan. A darkroom was asking for trouble; temptation would be magnified in such a close environment, and she wasn't sure she could handle it. But he seemed so eager, in his own understated way, that she couldn't refuse.

The darkroom was in the basement of the house and fortunately, wasn't as small as Karen had feared it would be. Nor was it as dark. At the start, when Brice was mixing chemicals, filling trays, organizing the negatives he wanted to print and gathering miscellaneous small tools, bare bulbs lit the room. When those bulbs went off, her eyes easily adjusted to the dim glow cast by the two red safelights that were strung above the long worktable.

Brice wasn't a talkative teacher, clearly more of the show than tell school. Without a word, he put the first negative in the carrier, slipped it into the enlarger, adjusted the image to his satisfaction, put photographic paper in the easel and made a test exposure. Still without a word, he slipped the paper into the developer solution and began to rock the tray.

Though Karen had never been in a darkroom before, she was aware of what was going to happen, so she wasn't totally surprised when a form began to appear on the paper. What surprised her was the incredible beauty of the image.

Catching her breath as Brice transferred the paper into the stop bath, she stared at it through its minutes-long immersion in the fixer. The child she saw was very young, very small, very dirty and, if its ragged clothes were any indication, very poor.

"A patient?" she asked in a whisper.

Hooking a forefinger under the corner of the tray, Brice rocked it just lightly enough to ensure that the solution worked evenly over the surface of the print. "Former patient. His family left the area three months ago looking to live where they wouldn't have to worry about heat. Both parents were unskilled and unemployed. It didn't matter much where they went."

Karen said nothing more, because the photograph said it all. Brice had captured despair in a child who was probably too young to understand what it meant.

When the print was fixed, he turned on a white light and studied it. "Needs more contrast, I think." He pointed to a corner of the print that was lighter than the rest. "And a little more time here." He dropped the print in a tub of clear water, turned off the light and repeated the printing procedure, making the changes he wanted. When that print had been fixed and examined, he decided that he wanted it cropped more tightly. So, after adjusting the height of the enlarger head, he made a third print. When all three lay in the holding tub, he took a different negative and made a trial print.

This one was a world away from the first. It was the typical small-child-with-cone-in-hand-and-ice-cream-on-face shot, but there was nothing typical about the child—as devilish-looking a one as Karen had ever seen—or the technical perfection of the photograph.

On the heels of that came a silhouette of three children of different heights peering through a chain-link playground fence, then one of a pair of identical twin toddlers studying each other through the rungs of a ladder.

By this time, Brice had Karen doing the work. Quietly and succinctly, he explained the purpose of each step and advised her about exposure and development times. When the small cordless phone that he kept in the corner of the room rang, she was perfectly capable of carrying on for the few minutes until he returned.

"Problem?" she asked. She dropped the last print she'd done into clear water and looked up at him. He didn't look pleased.

"Yeah. I'm going to have to run over to the hospital in a few minutes."

"What's wrong?"

"Car accident. One of my patients—a boy—was tossed around a little."

Karen felt her pulse beating faster. "How old?"

"Five."

"Go," she urged.

"Not yet. He'll be in X-ray a while longer, and the orthopedic specialist will take him from there. The parents called me mainly for reassurance that they'd done everything they should have."

"Was one of them driving?"

"No. The boy was in the car with his grandmother. He was the only one injured—has a broken arm, possibly some ribs. He'll be fine, but they'll want to keep him at the hospital overnight, and his mother says he's terrified. If I'm there when they finally get him into a room, I may be able to help settle him down."

"I think that's nice," Karen said with an admiring smile.

Brice frowned and said gruffly, "I don't. I really wanted to work longer here. Come on. Let's see what we can get done in another twenty or thirty minutes. Then I'll go."

"Are you sure you wouldn't rather leave now? I'll be—"

"I'm not leaving you alone with my negatives."

She studied his face through the dim red light. He looked serious. "I won't steal them."

"You might scratch them. One scratch, and the negative's no good."

"Have I scratched one yet?"

"You've only *handled* one."

"And did I scratch it?" she asked indignantly. She didn't like being talked down to, particularly when she'd done nothing to warrant it.

"No."

"So I'm not a lost cause. And now that you've warned me, I can be careful."

"I warned you at the very start to be careful."

"About fingerprints. Not scratches."

"Jeez, you don't give up, do you?"

"Do you?"

Silence stretched between them for what seemed

an eternity before Karen finally turned back to the enlarger, very carefully removed the negative, very carefully returned it to its sleeve and said, "What's next?"

Brice reached for another sleeve, but his thoughts were on what he'd just said. *Jeez, you don't give up, do you?* She didn't, and that was one of the things that drew him to her again and again. She wasn't intimidated. She wasn't driven away when he was raunchy. For all her fragile looks, she was a strong woman.

Changing his mind about what print to make, he replaced the strip of negatives he'd just taken with another. Karen wasn't prepared to see her own face appear on the enlarger easel.

"When did you take this?" she cried.

He leaned in over her shoulder. "At the mall."

"I thought you were photographing the fountain."

"I was. You got in the way."

Karen studied the projection. "I look awful."

"You look like you're enjoying yourself."

"I look like a fat cat."

"Not fat."

"Then content. And lazy."

"You look very relaxed."

With his warmth close behind her and the image on the easel bringing back lovely memories, she felt more tranquil than she had moments before. "I was listening to the fountain. It reminded me of a bubbling brook, and I was thinking how nice it would be to be out in the woods by the water's edge and…just sit. It was nice sitting right there in the middle of a mall. Just sitting. Not working. Not thinking about working. Not running around or thinking about running around. Just sitting." She felt his body touch hers and relaxed against it. It felt so right. "A tiny voice in the back of my mind kept telling me that I should have been feeling guilty, but I wasn't."

"In hindsight, do you?"

"This is the wrong time to ask. Ask when I'm opening my books to do all the work I should have done last week."

He slipped his arms around her waist. "I'm asking you now."

Closing her eyes, she said, "No. I don't feel guilty now." She didn't think she could possibly feel anything but good just then.

"Do you feel guilty about staying at my house?"

"Sometimes."

"Why?"

"I'm not a freeloader."

"But do you enjoy staying here?"

She hesitated, distracted by the feel of his breath against her cheek. She moved her head the tiniest bit to feel the roughness of his jaw on her skin. "Yes," she breathed. "I enjoy staying here." When his mouth dropped to her neck, she tipped her head to give him better access. "I do enjoy it here," she whispered. "I shouldn't. It's habit-forming. And I'll have to leave soon." Unable to resist, she covered his hands with hers, then followed their movement when his fingers began a gentle massage of her tummy. They left wonderful circles of heat. She sighed in pleasure.

Buoyed by that tiny sound, Brice dragged his mouth back and forth against her neck. He loved the smell of her, loved the softness of her skin. He'd tried to stay away, but he needed to touch her now. "You can stay here."

She made a small, breathless sound. "Not forever. My life is back in Syracuse."

One of his hands moved higher, steadily massaging until it brushed the undersides of her breasts. "It doesn't have to be."

"Sure, it does," she said, but her voice was strained. Her breasts were waiting, needing, swelling. "My apartment is there, my jobs, my classes."

"You've been handling everything fine from here."

"No…" She caught in a breath when he covered her breast, then whispered his name in such a way that other words weren't necessary.

"It's okay," he said softly. "Just relax."

Her voice came out several notes higher. "You shouldn't be doing this. You have to leave."

"Shhhh." He moved his hand slowly over her fullness. The fleece of her pullover sweat suit top was a soft conduit for the sensual flame of his touch.

"Brice…"

His other hand rose to mirror the motion of its mate, fingers circling, palms pressing, kneading her to awareness. His voice was as husky as her insides were beginning to feel when he said, "I like having you here."

She turned her head against his chest. "But I can't stay forever."

"You promised me until vacation was done."

"I know."

"There's nothing for you back in Syracuse."

"Not right now."

She gasped. He had slipped his hands under her sweatshirt and was touching her breasts more intimately.

"Easy…easy," he whispered when she seemed to have trouble catching her breath. Her hands had fallen and were curved tightly around the backs of his thighs.

He took her earlobe into his mouth and sucked on it to the rhythm of his thumbs. "I like touching you."

"You have to leave," she said, aching at the thought.

"Not yet." He nipped at her ear, then while she was recovering from that, released the front catch of her bra and took her turgid flesh in his hands.

She moaned.

But his fingers were magic, and the flow of his deep voice gentled her. "Ahhh, Karen, so soft…like silk… womanly warm." With deliberate care, he rolled the pad of his thumbs over her nipples. Already engorged, they grew painfully tight.

But that sweet pain wasn't only in her breasts. It was deep down in her belly, and it was spreading. Her breath came more shallowly, catching every so often in her throat. Somewhere in the back of her mind, she knew Brice had to stop, though for the life of her she couldn't hasten the moment. What he was doing to her felt too good. Besides, the fact that he had to leave was the safety valve she needed. Nothing of true consequence could possibly happen.

Then one of his hands left a breast and slid downward, and she stiffened. "Brice?" she cried in a tremulous voice. "What are you doing, Brice?"

His hand reached its goal. She made a convulsive move to escape it, but that only drove her into the masculine heat raging behind.

"Shhhh," he murmured hoarsely. "I want to give you pleasure…."

She gripped his thighs tightly and gasped, "You are." Then she turned her cheek sharply to his chest and bit her lip when small whimpers threatened to reveal just how pleased she was.

His hands were relentless. While one continued to taunt her nipple, the other slid under the band of her sweatpants, breached the barrier of her panties and found her darkest, most moist heart.

Hit by a sudden stroke of fire, she did cry out then. She begged him to stop, but he didn't listen, and there was nothing her traitorous body would do to free her from the onslaught. His fingers were parting her, caressing her, delving ever deeper into her hidden warmth. She wanted to fight—it was too much, too strong—but the wave of sensation was even stronger, and before she'd been able to whimper more than a few cries of protest, she was sucking in her breath, closing her fists on the corduroy of his jeans and arching her back into a powerful release.

Her body was still trembling and her breathing ragged when she covered her face with her hands and made soft, mortified sounds.

"Don't," Brice commanded in a low and shaky voice.

"I'm sorry," came her muffled cry. "That shouldn't have happened."

"Don't say that," he replied even more gruffly.

"I'm embarrassed."

"Because you're a woman who feels passion to the fullest?" He turned her to face him with perhaps more force than was necessary, but he wasn't going to let her besmirch the pleasure she'd felt. Taking her face in his hands, he tipped it up. His voice was deep and rough. "That happened because it should have. It's been coming for days."

She tried to shake her head, but he allowed little movement. Still she could talk. "No. What's been coming for days is our making love. But what happened just now was one-sided. I should have been able to stop."

"I didn't let you."

"Then it's your fault, too."

"My fault for *what?* What's so bad about what happened?"

"You got nothing out of it!"

That caught him for a minute. "Are you serious?"

She tried to break away, but he simply enfolded her in his arms and held her close.

"See?" she said. "You're not satisfied. I can feel you… feel you there…."

She was looking so pink-cheeked, even under the safe lights, that Brice had a sudden urge to laugh. "I'm still hard," he admitted. "I've been hard for the better part of a week. And if it weren't for the fact that I'm expected at the hospital, I'd carry you upstairs and make love to you well." He set her back. "We will make love, Karen. At least, we will if you stay here another night. So maybe it's just as well that I have to leave now. You'll have some time to think about whether you want what I do." He took a step away.

"You're going?" she asked dumbly. She was still shaky. And he was still aroused.

"Yes."

"You can't leave just…just like that."

"Why not?"

Her gaze fell to his fly.

"I'll live," he said.

"But what about—" She turned and looked at the enlarger head, still projecting a picture of her face.

"Leave it. I'll clean up when I get back."

With that said—and not trusting himself to say anything more—he was gone.

CHAPTER TEN

KAREN BARELY SLEPT that night. She was lying in bed when Brice returned from the hospital at one o'clock in the morning. By two, he still hadn't come to her, and by three she realized that he didn't plan to.

She was disappointed, frustrated and hurt.

By the time dawn rolled around, she was heartsick. Hoping that a glass of warm milk might soothe her, she crept softly through the still-dark halls to the kitchen. On its threshold, she stopped, frozen in place by the sight before her.

Brice was standing with his back to her. His arms were straight, hands flat on the tiled countertop. His head was bowed. But it wasn't his pose that held her breathless. It was the fact that he'd carelessly kicked his running shoes aside, just as carelessly scattered his wool hat and mittens, running suit and turtleneck jersey on the table and chairs—which left him wearing nothing but a thin pair of nylon running shorts and a sheen of sweat.

Her pulse began to race. She'd imagined so often how he'd look beneath his clothes, but her imaginings paled before the real thing. He was all man. His shoulders were made broad by twists of muscle that tapered gently down his arms and torso. She'd known to expect that tapering, but she hadn't expected such symmetry, muscles flanking his spine from shoulder to hip. Nor had she expected such smooth skin. Or such tight buttocks. Or such long, well-formed legs.

She'd found him attractive before, but she'd never experienced such a sudden flood of desire. And then, slowly, he turned and she was lost. His chest was sculpted, an artistic creation of bone, muscle and flesh. He wasn't hairy; only a thin sprinkling of dark hair dotted his upper chest, condensing into an even thinner line that arrowed downward. His legs were more hairy, but his legs weren't what drew Karen's attention. It was his sex, blatantly heavy as it was cradled by the soft nylon fabric.

Aware that everything inside her was swelling and moist, she dragged her eyes up. His were dark and vulnerable, sensual and questioning. In answer, knowing that the love she felt had no more appropriate outlet than this, she silently crossed the floor to stand before him. Lifting one trembling hand, she touched his skin.

It was hot and damp and vibrant. She slid her hand over it, opening her palm on the more textured spots, splaying her fingers to better delineate virile swells of muscle. Her touch was light, feathery. His sweat was a lubricant, easing the flow of her hand, and when her skin stuttered against his, it was in pure awe.

From one shoulder to the other and down, she explored him in wonder. Touching both hands to his upper arms, she whispered an open trail over corded lines to his wrists, then rose on an upward route from his waist.

His nipples were small, tight dots. She moved her thumbs over them simply to know their feel. When Brice inhaled suddenly, she looked up.

His hair was a riot of darkness, rendered that way by his wool cap and sweat. His face was rough with a day's growth of beard. His lips were tense with need. His nostrils flared slightly with each breath. And his eyes burned for her.

She touched his cheek. She touched his hair, allowing only her fingertips burial in the vibrant thatch. She touched his lips with her thumb. She touched his jaw, then his ear with the back of her hand. Then she touched him as she desperately wanted to, lip to lip.

The kiss was slow, tentative and exploratory at first, more sure as Brice joined in, then more thorough. It was the intermingling of breath, the glide of one tongue against another, the scrape of teeth against lips and chin. It was openmouthed and erotic, and if there had been any doubt about a mutual desire, this kiss put it to rest.

Hands framing her face, Brice paused. He would never get enough of looking at her when she was hot with needing him. And she was. He could feel, hear, taste her arousal as clearly as he could see it.

That minute's exchanged glance was all they needed. Their open mouths met again, but now their hands were busy. Hers lowered his shorts to free his sex, while his drew up her nightshirt. Then, while their tongues delved deeply into each other's mouths, Brice lifted her and thrust into her warmth.

Karen cried out at the sudden fullness, but a rare beauty overpowered the slight pain she felt. Arms coiled around his neck, she panted, whispered fragmented words of love.

Brice squeezed his eyes shut. He held himself still inside her partly to let her adjust to his size, partly to control his own blazing need for release. She was a hot, tight glove around him; after years of abstinence, she was nearly a virgin. But he tried not to think of that, because it set his blood to rushing even harder.

Forehead to forehead they stood, their breathing fast and ragged. Brice turned until she was braced against the

counter, then with trembling hands stroked the length of
her legs as they wound around his hips. When he felt her
insides flex, he took her mouth again and began to move
his hips. What followed then was a passion that snow-
balled with such speed that neither of them quite knew
what had seized them until it was over.

It was a while before their gasps faded into the dawn
air, a while after that before either of them could move.
Brice leaned against Karen, who leaned against the counter. His head was bowed low over her shoulder, hair
damp, skin damp, arms limp, hands locked behind her.
Her own circled his neck as she buried her face in his
shoulder. Her hair hung wild and loose. Her legs clung
to him with stubborn strength.

She made a small sound of protest when he separated
himself from her. "Just for a minute," he whispered.
Kicking his shorts aside, he swept her into his arms and
carried her up the stairs to his bedroom. There, he drew
off her nightshirt and laid her on the bed, then proceeded
to love her with the kind of gentle finesse that neither
of them had been able to abide earlier. Not until he'd
touched and tasted every inch of her body did he enter
her, and then he led her to a peak of pleasure that left her
dazed.

That was why she wasn't sure she heard right when
he said he loved her.

She eyed him blankly. "You what?"

"Love you."

Snaking an arm across his chest, she pressed her face
to his damp skin. Then she inched up until she could
reach his mouth, and kissed him softly. One part of her
wanted to jump for joy; the other part was frightened.
"Do you?"

"Yes."

"Why?"

"What do you mean, 'Why'?"

"What do you find to love in me?"

Brice tucked in his chin and looked down at her. He couldn't believe what she was asking, but she seemed entirely serious. "I think you're bright and interesting. You're a hard worker. You're curious and compassionate."

"You're saying that you respect me."

"Isn't respect the basis of love?"

"You can respect a woman without being in love with her."

He was silent.

"So what is it?" she prodded softly. "What do you feel, deep down inside?"

"I feel like I want you here with me forever," he said in a voice that was rough but not begrudging. "I've never felt that way before."

"You must have when you got married."

"No. I was thinking that I should be married, and I was envisioning the immediate future. That's all. I wasn't thinking forever."

She searched his eyes. "Are you now?"

Very slowly he nodded.

Karen tightened her arms around him in an attempt to get even closer to him than she already was. It was an impossibility, but still she tried because the closer she was, the more he filled her senses, and the more he did that, the less she thought about the one thing that could ruin it all.

After a minute, her arms began to tremble. After another minute, her shoulders did, too. That was when Brice got worried.

"Karen?"

She didn't answer.

"Karen?" Sliding his hands under her arms, he raised

her. The sight of tears in her eyes brought a lump of fear to his chest. Easing her down to the bed, he lifted himself over her and said in a voice that shook, "What's wrong?"

She didn't answer at first, simply looked up into his face. His expression was as tender as any she'd ever seen there, which choked her up all the more. Only after several sniffles and a swallow did she manage to say, "I love you, too." Then she threw her arms around his neck and silently bid him hold her for as long as he could...or would.

BRICE WOULD HAVE BEEN the happiest man alive if he hadn't been as attuned to the fine points of emotions. Just because he was a loner didn't mean he didn't see things. Just because he chose not to play social games didn't mean he didn't understand why others did. His specialty demanded a certain insight into the nonphysical side of life. He had that insight, to some extent.

He believed that Karen loved him. He believed that she wanted the same forever he did. But something bothered her, and he didn't know what it was.

Not once were they apart on Saturday. Nor were they sleepy, though neither had slept the night before. Running on adrenaline, they spent most of the morning making love, most of the afternoon driving to the western part of the state, most of the evening making love in the small room they'd taken for the night in a quaint bed-and-breakfast place.

Karen smiled, and smiled often, and Brice appreciated that for the victory it was. But she didn't smile as broadly as he wanted. She didn't smile with the kind of carefree indulgence that she deserved.

So he began to attack her possible worries one by one.

He wondered if she thought he'd want her to quit school. While they were driving back to Ithaca on

Sunday afternoon, he said in no uncertain terms that he thought she should finish, that he was sure she could transfer to Cornell at the end of the year if she wanted to, and, if not, she could continue to commute to Syracuse.

He wondered if she thought he'd want her to quit her jobs. He did, so he broached that one more gently. They were on their way home from visiting Rowena on Sunday evening—their first joint visit, noted well by Rowena, whose eyes were filled with pleasure and speculation—when he asked what Karen thought about work.

"That depends," she said quietly. Her eyes were on the road. "I want to do something with my degree once I get it, but I want to have kids. I'm not sure I can do both and do either well."

Unprepared for that particular answer, Brice took a minute to catch his breath. He would have hugged her had it not been for the BMW's bucket seats. As second best, he took her hand and held it tightly in his. "If anyone can, it's you," he said and cleared his throat. "But that's something we have time to discuss. I was thinking more about now. You don't have to work. You won't need the money—" he rushed on "—but if you want to work, I'll understand. The only problem is that your hours at the Pepper Mill aren't great. If you stay on there, we won't have much time to spend together, so I was thinking that you could keep on with McGuire if you want—"

"I'd rather be here," she said softly.

He took his eyes from the road long enough to shoot her a glance. "You would?"

"Do you mind?"

"Hell, no!"

So that issue was settled, and by the time Monday rolled around, Karen was studying for midterms. Rather than broaching any others, he concentrated on pampering her and doing all he could to be supportive while she studied.

By the end of the week, though, when her exams were done, he faced it again. She was clearly relieved and looking forward to vacation. But still she held back. He felt it in the way she occasionally touched his arm, then pulled away. He heard it in the catch at the end of a laugh. He saw it in a flicker of worry that passed through her eyes so quickly that he probably would have missed it if he didn't care so much. But he did care. He cared more than he'd ever have thought possible. He wanted Karen to be happy. He was determined to make her happy. It was quickly becoming an obsession.

Failing to pinpoint the source of her worry, he decided that he had to be more blunt—which was a laugh, he mused, since he was notorious for his bluntness. But he was different with Karen. Less abrasive…less defensive…less blunt. She hadn't wanted to live in a war zone, so he'd declared peace. Now, though, a little prodding was in order.

So, Friday night, after he'd wined her and dined her to celebrate the start of her vacation, after he'd made love to her before the living room fire—with a tenderness he hadn't thought himself capable of—he turned on his side and faced her.

"Something's bothering you," he said quietly. "What is it?"

"Nothing's bothering me," she answered with a smile—that smile that was bright enough to fool anyone but him.

"Something is."

She shook her head and reached up to trace the line of his mouth. Then, grabbing his ear, she pulled him close for a kiss, and when the kiss was done, she asked whether he liked apple pancakes, which she wanted to make for breakfast. When he said that he loved them, but only with real maple syrup, that started a discussion about the sugaring season, which effectively changed the subject.

Brice let it go. But again on Sunday, when he caught her staring pensively out the window, he asked what was bothering her. Again she denied that anything was.

On Monday night, when she couldn't concentrate on the book she was reading, he repeated the question. She smiled, said she was a little tired and fell asleep soon after with her head in his lap.

On Wednesday, he asked again, this time when she was unable to make a decision on what kind of engagement ring she wanted. She simply wound her arm tightly through his, pressed her cheek to his shoulder and begged for a little more time.

On Thursday, he didn't ask, but he spent much of the evening watching her pretend involvement in a movie. He felt stymied. He was beginning to imagine that, deep down inside, she didn't want to get married. When he couldn't come up with any viable reasons why that should be so, he began to come up with bizarre ones.

By Friday, he was feeling insecure. Karen meant the world to him. In the short time they'd been together, she'd changed his life. She'd given it vibrancy and flux. She'd made it exciting. When he was with her, he felt complete, satisfied, richer than he had. He'd stopped fighting ghosts. He was more pleasantly disposed toward the rest of mankind because of the happiness she brought him.

The thought that for some mysterious reason he might lose her unsettled him, and when he was unsettled, he withdrew into himself and frowned a lot. That was precisely how he was when, finishing up early with his patients on Friday afternoon, he went with Karen to visit Rowena.

Karen wasn't oblivious to his mood. "Bad day?" she asked as he drove stony-faced toward the home.

"It was okay."

"Any problem cases?"

"Nope."

She was quiet then, but two minutes later he was still frowning. So she said, "Do you still want to drive to Vermont tomorrow?"

"Yes."

"You're sure there's snow?"

"There's snow on Killington Peak until the Fourth of July."

"Won't I slow you down?" She'd never skied before, but he had insisted that she try it.

"You won't slow me down," he said, sounding as though he meant it—and as though her slowing him down was the last of his concerns. She wondered what the first of them was.

So, when they'd turned into the drive of the nursing home, she abandoned beating around the bush and asked, "Is something wrong?"

"Nope."

"You don't look thrilled to be here."

"I'm not. I'd rather be visiting my grandmother anywhere but here."

Karen didn't say another word. Wishing she'd left well enough alone, she climbed from the car and accompanied him inside.

Rowena was waiting for them. She was filled with questions, wanting to know how Karen was feeling, what she was doing with her time, whether she was enjoying the rest. She asked Brice about his work, inquired about the progress of a patient he'd mentioned before, expressed pleasure when he told her that the recent article he'd written on psychosomatic illness in children had been accepted for publication.

She asked whether they'd made a decision on the engagement ring, and Karen said no. She asked whether Karen had moved the last of her things from her apartment, and Karen said no. She mentioned that one of the other women in the home had gone out that afternoon to pick out a dress for her granddaughter's wedding, and Karen didn't say a thing.

Rowena fell silent. Karen smiled at her. Brice did the same. They were sharing a large winged chair, Brice on the seat, Karen propped on the arm. Rowena's eyes shifted slowly from one face to the other, then she said as clearly as if she'd never had a stroke, "This is a mistake."

Brice frowned. "What is?"

"You two."

"What do you mean?" Karen asked.

But Rowena's eyes were on Brice. "Y-y-you shouldn't be together. You won't forget what happened."

Karen's heart began to hammer against her ribs. She'd thought that Rowena was all for a union between Brice and her. Confused, she looked at Brice, but he was scowling at his grandmother.

"I think you'd better explain yourself," he said in a controlled voice.

Rowena didn't hesitate. "Karen was driving the car that hit me."

"She wasn't at fault."

"But she w-w-was driving."

"She was tried and found not guilty."

"What do juries know?"

"Rowena…" he warned softly.

But Rowena wasn't to be stopped. "Karen hit me. A j-j-jury found her not guilty. The legal…c-c-case is closed, but you still believe she was at fault. How can you think of s-s-spending the rest of your life with her?"

Brice leaned forward and put his elbows on his knees. His fists didn't quite hang. "I don't believe she was at fault."

"You did."

"Maybe once. Not now."

Rowena sat and stared silently at him, daring him to defend his switch. He had no problem with that.

"I needed someone to blame for what had happened to you. I couldn't very well vent my anger on the moon that wasn't out that night or the narrowness of the road or that excuse of a bicycle you were riding. Karen was there. She was it. But I've gotten to know her since. There isn't a negligent, a reckless or unkind bone in her body."

Rowena let that declaration settle for a minute before she said, "You're in love. That m-m-makes you blind."

Brice's shoulders were growing more tense by the minute. "I don't think," he said in a low, sharp voice, "that there is any point to this discussion."

Rowena disagreed. "There is. You offered…h-h-her your services when she was s-s-sick because you knew she'd…been…visiting me. But she's fine now. Isn't talk of marriage carrying hospitality too far?"

"I don't believe I'm hearing this," he muttered and glanced at Karen. "What's the matter with her?"

Karen couldn't answer. She was too busy studying Rowena's face, trying to figure things out herself.

The older woman's mouth puckered. "It's a betrayal."

"That's bullshit."

"Don't use that l-l-language with me, Brice Carlin."

He drew himself straight. "I'll use whatever language I want." His features were tight. "And there's no other word that better describes what you're saying. I don't understand you. You were the one who had Karen coming here first. I thought you liked her."

"I'm not the one planning to marry her."

"Damn right you're not," he said, coming to his feet with a slow grace that was downright intimidating. Karen had shifted her stare from Rowena to him, but he barely noticed. He was too intent on setting the record straight. "I'm the one in love with her, I'm the one who'll marry her, I'm the one planning to spend the rest of my life with her, and I won't stand for a repeat of the kind of things you've just said.

"Karen was no more at fault for that accident than you were. I freely admit that I thought it once, but I was wrong, and I refuse to make the same mistake twice. The accident happened. It's over. Done. I won't have Karen feeing guilty, and I won't let you make *me* feel guilty."

"Don't you…c-c-care about me?" Rowena asked with an odd meekness. An odd meekness. It brought Karen's wide eyes back to her face.

Brice's, meanwhile, was ruddy with tension and frustration. "I love you, damn it. You mean more to me than my own parents did. I'd do nearly anything to make you happy. But I won't let you sabotage the one thing that means more to me and more to my future than anything else in the world. If it's sabotage you have in mind, Rowena, you can kiss Karen and me goodbye, because, so help me, I swear—"

Karen caught his arm. "Don't, Brice," she whispered.

He turned on her with eyes full of fury. "I won't have her saying that we don't belong together."

"She's not—"

"She is! She's saying that the accident will always be between us, but she's wrong. I haven't thought about the accident in days."

"Yes, you have," Karen argued softly. "You mentioned it when we were driving over here."

"I did?"

"You were in a lousy mood, and when I asked about it, you said that you'd rather be visiting Rowena anywhere but here."

"And I meant it," he said, looking confused, "but that had nothing to do with the accident. It had to do with Rowena's condition—today—right now. I wasn't thinking of how and why she came to be here, and I *certainly* wasn't thinking about the fact that your car hit her. That was an *accident,* Karen." He tossed a hand her way. "It wasn't your fault." He gestured toward Rowena. "It wasn't her fault. It just happened. But it's over. My God, I'm *tired* of thinking about it. Isn't it time we moved on?"

Karen's eyes began to fill with tears.

Immediately, he cupped her face and whispered, "What is it, babe?"

Clutching his wrists, she closed her eyes for a minute. When she opened them, she dragged his hands to her mouth, kissed both open palms, lowered them to her heart and broke into the kind of smile he'd staked his future on.

He stared at that smile, then widened his gaze to include her whole face. Her eyes were bright with tears, brilliant with love. And the smile remained full and unfettered.

Taking a step closer, he whispered, "That was it. That was it, wasn't it? That was what bothered you. You thought I wouldn't be able to put the accident behind—" His voice broke, and seconds later he'd pulled her from the chair and was holding her close. "I put it behind days ago. When I look at you, I see the woman I love. The accident is something that brought us together," he drew back to meet her gaze, "and I don't care what Rowena says—" His voice broke again, but this time on a note of dawning. He stared at Karen for a minute, then slowly turned toward Rowena.

She was looking as smug as you please.

"Why...you...witch," he said, but fondness underscored each word. "Betrayal—baloney! You made all that up. You did that on purpose—" Eyes widening, his gaze flew back to Karen.

She shook her head. "I didn't know what she was up to until three quarters of the way through her act. I believed her, at first. It hurt," she confessed in a very quiet voice.

His voice, too, grew quiet. Intimate. "Why didn't you ask me? If you were worried about it, you should have asked."

"I didn't want to lose you."

"You wouldn't have."

"But I didn't know that. I've never come so close to having something I wanted so much."

Wrapping his arms around her, he rocked her from side to side. "You have me if you want me."

"I want you." She was on tiptoe with her arms around his neck. Pressing a kiss to his ear, she said, "I also want the pear-shaped diamond, and a small wedding soon and a honeymoon somewhere warm. You choose."

He put a hand in her hair and held her close. "St. Kitts."

"Fine."

"For a week?"

"Great."

"But you're on vacation now. The next time you can get away will be after finals. When's that?"

"May."

"Too hot for St. Kitts. How about London?"

"Is it rainy there then?"

"I think it's rainy there anytime. How about Rio?"

"Not bad."

"Or Yugoslavia—the Dalmation Coast."

When he drew her head back, she smiled up at him. "Interesting."

The smile, ah, the smile. It held promise for such happy tomorrows that he had to force himself to think. "Or Australia. Which will it be?"

"You choose."

"Which will it be?"

"I don't know."

"Which will it be?"

"I can't make a decision like this on the spur of the moment."

"Karen…"

"The Dalmation Coast. I want to stay in a huge stone villa overlooking the sea, and I don't want to do anything but lie in the sun, eat, sleep and make love—"

"I think," came Rowena's voice from out of the blue, "that there are s-s-some things my tender ears shouldn't hear. Run along, children. You have p-p-plans to make."

Brice released Karen, who immediately bent over Rowena and gave her a hug. "Thank you," she whispered. Her eyes were moist again, but she couldn't stop smiling.

Rowena's eyes beamed.

Brice leaned in and gave the older woman a peck on the cheek. "You haven't heard the end of this," he warned, and as he straightened he saw the beginnings of a grin on her face. For a minute, he stood and enjoyed it. Then, turning, he took Karen's hand, and they headed home.

* * * * *

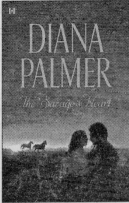

REQUEST YOUR FREE BOOKS!

2 FREE NOVELS
FROM THE ROMANCE COLLECTION
PLUS 2 FREE GIFTS!

YES! Please send me 2 FREE novels from the Romance Collection and my 2 FREE gifts (gifts are worth about $10). After receiving them, if I don't wish to receive any more books, I can return the shipping statement marked "cancel." If I don't cancel, I will receive 4 brand-new novels every month and be billed just $5.99 per book in the U.S. or $6.49 per book in Canada. That's a saving of at least 25% off the cover price. It's quite a bargain! Shipping and handling is just 50¢ per book in the U.S. and 75¢ per book in Canada.* I understand that accepting the 2 free books and gifts places me under no obligation to buy anything. I can always return a shipment and cancel at any time. Even if I never buy another book, the two free books and gifts are mine to keep forever.

194/394 MDN FELQ

Name	(PLEASE PRINT)

Address	Apt. #

City	State/Prov.	Zip/Postal Code

Signature (if under 18, a parent or guardian must sign)

Mail to the Reader Service:
IN U.S.A.: P.O. Box 1867, Buffalo, NY 14240-1867
IN CANADA: P.O. Box 609, Fort Erie, Ontario L2A 5X3

Not valid for current subscribers to the Romance Collection
or the Romance/Suspense Collection.

Want to try two free books from another line?
Call 1-800-873-8635 or visit www.ReaderService.com.

* Terms and prices subject to change without notice. Prices do not include applicable taxes. Sales tax applicable in N.Y. Canadian residents will be charged applicable taxes. Offer not valid in Quebec. This offer is limited to one order per household. All orders subject to credit approval. Credit or debit balances in a customer's account(s) may be offset by any other outstanding balance owed by or to the customer. Please allow 4 to 6 weeks for delivery. Offer available while quantities last.

Your Privacy—The Reader Service is committed to protecting your privacy. Our Privacy Policy is available online at www.ReaderService.com or upon request from the Reader Service.

We make a portion of our mailing list available to reputable third parties that offer products we believe may interest you. If you prefer that we not exchange your name with third parties, or if you wish to clarify or modify your communication preferences, please visit us at www.ReaderService.com/consumerchoice or write to us at Reader Service Preference Service, P.O. Box 9062, Buffalo, NY 14269. Include your complete name and address.

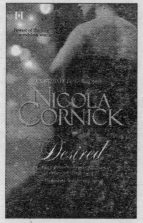

BARBARA DELINSKY

77494	FRIENDS & LOVERS	___ $7.99 U.S.	___ $9.99 CAN.
77425	DREAM MAN	___ $7.99 U.S.	___ $8.99 CAN.
77345	TRUST	___ $7.99 U.S.	___ $7.99 CAN.

(limited quantities available)

TOTAL AMOUNT	$ _____
POSTAGE & HANDLING	$ _____
($1.00 FOR 1 BOOK, 50¢ for each additional)	
APPLICABLE TAXES*	$ _____
TOTAL PAYABLE	$ _____

(check or money order—please do not send cash)

To order, complete this form and send it, along with a check or money order for the total above, payable to HQN Books, to: **In the U.S.:** 3010 Walden Avenue, P.O. Box 9077, Buffalo, NY 14269-9077; **In Canada:** P.O. Box 636, Fort Erie, Ontario, L2A 5X3.

Name: _____
Address: _____ City: _____
State/Prov.: _____ Zip/Postal Code: _____
Account Number (if applicable): _____

075 CSAS

*New York residents remit applicable sales taxes.
*Canadian residents remit applicable GST and provincial taxes.

HQN™ | **HARLEQUIN®**
www.Harlequin.com

PHBD1211BL